'Damn you, damn you,' I was chanting under my breath. My head was spinning and my arms were suddenly as heavy as if they were sausage skins filled with sand. I had been cut somewhere on the head, for I could feel something warm trickling down my neck and back, but I did not remember the blow. The king and his companions were out of sight. 'Oh, God,' I moaned. I had to follow Louis. I had nowhere else to go. It was a terrible thought, but at that moment a sheet of flame sprang up in front of me as a whole thicket of reeds caught fire. The wounded Saracen screamed and his horse jumped through the fire. My own horse, terrified by the flames, gave a piercing whinny and flung herself after it. For an instant I was engulfed in searing red and orange, cupped in a fire-giant's hand, the fingers closing around me. Then I was out in the night once more, hurtling down the narrow path, the river on my left, darkness on my right. And then my horse stumbled.

I felt myself flying through the air at an unearthly speed, faster than anything I had known before. The ground suddenly appeared. I remember seeing one broken reed stalk in perfect detail. And then nothing.

Pip Vaughan-Hughes is the author of three previous Petroc adventures: *Relics*, *The Vault of Bones* and *Painted in Blood*. He lives on Dartmoor with his family.

By Pip Vaughan-Hughes

Relics
The Vault of Bones
Painted in Blood
The Fools' Crusade

The FOOLS' CRUSADE

PIP VAUGHAN-HUGHES

An Orion paperback

First published in Great Britain in 2010
by Orion
This paperback edition published in 2011
by Orion Books Ltd,
Orion House, 5 Upper St Martin's Lane,
London WC2H 9EA

An Hachette UK company

1 3 5 7 9 10 8 6 4 2

A CIP catalogue record for this book
is available from the British Library.

ISBN 978-0-7528-8312-0

Typeset at The Spartan Press Ltd,
Lymington, Hants

Printed and bound in Great Britain by Clays Ltd,
St Ives plc

The Orion Publishing Group's policy is to use papers that
are natural, renewable and recyclable products and
made from wood grown in sustainable forests. The logging
and manufacturing processes are expected to conform to
the environmental regulations of the country of origin.

www.orionbooks.co.uk

For Poppy and Ringo,

with love

Acknowledgements

My heartfelt thanks to Christopher Little and Emma Schlesinger for their hard work and friendship; to Jon Wood, for his constant encouragement and deft editing, and to Genevieve Pegg and Jade Chandler at Orion for keeping me on track; and as always to my long suffering family and particularly to Tara, who knows me better than I know myself.

Historical Note

In the middle of the thirteenth century, the Italian Peninsula had begun to divide deeply and bitterly along a political, ideological and spiritual fault-line. From Sicily to the Alps, Italy was split into many small dukedoms, princedoms and the newly emerging city states like Florence. But over this patchwork lay the presence of two great powers: the Holy Roman Empire and the Papacy. Church and State had existed for centuries side by side, an uneasy balancing act, but in the 1200s this became fatally disturbed. The Holy Roman Emperor, Frederick II von Hohenstaufen, believed that the pope was overstepping his authority and trying to establish the Church as the main earthly as well as spiritual power-broker in Italy. The conflict that followed became open warfare that pitched Imperial armies against papal ones. In the towns and cities, the division became political. Supporters of pope and emperor split into factions: the Ghibbelines were for the emperor; the Guelphs were the pope's faction. Street fighting, assassinations and mob rule destabilised almost every city. In Florence, as in other places, the balance of power often switched from one to the other and back again. These were not wars of religion, although both sides attacked each other's orthodoxy in surprisingly modern propaganda campaigns, but territorial struggles about money and land. Italy itself took many centuries to recover. Outside the peninsula, the other Christian kings watched keenly. It was not in their best interests for the Church to claim kingly authority, but they did not want to be excommunicated. So, behind the scenes, tense rounds of diplomacy and whispered back-stabbing added to the tension. And despite all this confusion – and partly because of it – a new power began to arise: the banks.

Prologue

The Nile Delta, April 1250

The outline of the door was a dazzling line of white light on a slab of darkness, and the dark itself was thick and dusty and full of the reek of sheep and chickens. I sat with legs drawn up tight against my chest, eyes streaming from the fetor that rose from the damp straw beneath me. My guts were clenching and unclenching as if a giant's hand were milking them, but I had nothing left to give. My breeches were iron-stiff with my own filth. I had drunk nothing for a day and a night, and no food had passed my lips for more than two days, and now thirst had become my whole world. The hut was crawling with insects. They had got inside my clothes and my groin, and the backs of my knees were already welted and smarting as they gorged on my thin, sickly blood. 'May it poison you,' I muttered.

'What did you say?' The quavering voice of Matthieu d'Allaines came from somewhere on my left. Another man groaned softly in the blackness. There had been five of us yesterday. I had heard two lives gurgle to their ends in the night. Soon they would add their stink to the terrible air.

'I was praying for the lice that are eating me alive,' I said. 'Their god must hate them, to have sent them a meal like me.'

'You blaspheme,' croaked Matthieu. 'This is . . .'

'Not the time? Are you sure?'

There was a rustling and suddenly Matthieu's fingers were clawing at my neck.

'*Give it me . . .*' he whispered suddenly. '*Give it to me . . . I will destroy it. And then I will shrive your soul.*' I shoved him away and he rolled into the man lying further off in the black stink.

'Hell-mouth is yawning for you! I can see it . . .'

'You are mad, priest,' I muttered.

'Use your breath for repentance. Death is very near,' he croaked.

I could have told him that we had both been as good as dead since Shrove Tuesday, two months ago. We had been part of an army of walking corpses, our flesh rotting even as it clung to our bones, the stink of the living no different from that of the heaps of dead. I wondered if Jean had escaped, or the king, but I thought mostly of my wife, and of a little stream that ran beside the house in which I had been born, its cold, clear water dancing over golden rocks, nimble barred trout swimming and drinking, drinking, drinking . . .

There was a sudden clashing of sound and the door burst open, drowning us in unbearable daylight. Loud, angry voices hacked at the vile air, and the chink and slither of drawn weapons. Great black shadows appeared in the doorway. The straw beside me churned as the sick man, whoever he was, tried to burrow out of sight. A leg, clad in mail and blue leather boots, stamped down next to me. He bent and shouted into my face.

'Are you ill?' It was a strange question, given that I was a living skeleton sprawled in my own shit, but I knew that he was not expecting an answer, for he had used his own tongue. The spear tip was already pointing at my sternum when I replied in Arabic.

'I am as strong as you, my lord!' The soldier squatted down before me, his nose wrinkling in surprise, or disgust. He was my age, with grey beginning to pattern his trimmed beard. The white of his turban was almost blinding me.

2

'No, Frankish jackal, you are not.' He had dropped the spear, and somehow a long, curved knife had appeared in his hand. The men behind him were all talking at once. I guessed they were demanding to know what I had said, what it was that had taken their captain by surprise. They were pushing into the hut, shoving against the man so that his knife wavered and jabbed at the air just in front of my breastbone.

'I can stand, lord,' I was telling him. And indeed, like a dying crane-fly at the end of summer, I was struggling upright, the jagged stones of the wall scoring my back. The Saracen watched me, whether in amusement or revulsion I could not tell. As soon as I was roughly standing he grabbed my ankle and pulled me down and the stones flayed my back once more.

'Keep still, you revolting cur! You are a priest! Say it! You are an infidel priest!' The other voices were snarling now, egging the man on. The whites of his eyes were showing. And the knife, cool and silver as a fish in a Devon stream, was at my throat. He could slice me now, and let the coolness in. Then I would drink for ever.

'Lord, I am not,' I told him. The soldiers were gripping their captain's shoulders now, and I could see the rage growing in him. I had seen it many times, and I had felt it myself. I understood, somehow, that this Saracen was not a bad man, just a tired, overworked soldier with men who needed to have some fun. Matthieu was praying. I heard the fear in his voice, and the anger, the self-righteous anger. To bring his god into this place . . . What kind of man would invoke the god of love in a charnel house, with rage in his voice? My head was swimming. This *was* Hell-mouth, then.

'Why are you not praying, priest?' the Saracen was barking at me like a dog.

'Because I am not a priest, lord.'

'Do Franks not pray when death comes for them? Why is your friend praying, then?'

'Him? Not my friend, lord. He thinks this is hell, and that you are *Shaitan* come for my soul.' I giggled, and tasted blood in my throat.

'Does he? Does he, the dog? The worm?' The Saracen leaped to his feet and grabbed Matthieu by the tunic. The rag tied round Matthieu's head fell off and revealed his stubbly tonsured scalp, scabbed with ringworm. The soldiers in the doorway all cried out at once: *Priest! Priest!* There was a confusion, a rush, and many hands clawed at Matthieu and dragged him out. I glimpsed his heels jouncing over the dried dung, and then I was seized as well.

The sunlight was white-hot needles thrusting into my eyeballs. I cringed, and the men laughed and shook me until my teeth rattled. Through bloody tears a world took shape: a dusty courtyard – no, a threshing floor between low, whitewashed buildings thatched with reeds. Spears were stacked against walls and a green standard had been thrust into the thatch of one hut. A lop-eared goat chewed on something as it watched us with its lizard eyes. Men – soldiers in dusty chain mail and white robes, with helmets or white turbans on their heads – leaned against walls or squatted in the narrow strips of shade. They were hooting and cursing at Matthieu, who was being hauled into the middle of the threshing floor. The Saracens pulled him up until he was kneeling, face towards the sun. His eyes were squeezed shut but his lips were still moving in prayer. He fumbled inside his ragged clothes and brought out a silver cross, which he clasped tightly. The Saracens were all jeering now, and their captain was strutting to and fro, stiff with rage. He bent and said something to Matthieu, and in answer, the friar raised his clasped hands as high as the chain of his cross would allow. He called out in a cracked, trembling voice:

'*Pater, in manus tuas commendo spiritum meum . . .*' And the Saracen drew his long, curved sword, raised it backhanded across his body and with a hissing slash brought it down upon

4

the friar's neck. A lovely stroke it was, the wrist loose, one finger curved over the hilt, the left hand extended delicately to one side. The flesh of Matthieu's neck cleaved and I saw the neat white ring of bone flash before the blood, one thick gout of it, sprayed out. There was a hollow crack as his head struck the packed clay of the threshing floor. The soldiers hooted as their captain bent and wiped his blade on Matthieu's back. Then he swung, loose as a dancer, pivoting on his heel, to face me. His face was set, indifferent. He gestured with the point of his blade and my guards jerked me forward. The goat was running to the end of its rope again and again, panicked by the yells and the smell of blood. But the circle of the threshing floor was empty save for the Saracen and the corpse of Matthieu. The soldiers shoved me onto the hard clay and stepped back. I stood, swaying. The sky was deep blue, the threshing floor pale as butter, the huts blazing white. The Saracen captain was ordering me to do something, but I could not make out the words, just the sounds of his language, and into my mind drifted the face of a man I had known when we had sailed together, and the songs he had sung. There was a good one, about dying. 'The One You Kill, Lord . . .' And then the hand of memory, fickle servant that he is, had found me the very song. I shuffled forward, smiled reassuringly at the Saracen, and began to sing.

> *The one You kill,*
> *Lord,*
> *Does not smell of blood,*
> *And the one You burn*
> *Does not reek of smoke.*
> *He You burn laughs as he burns*
> *And the one You kill,*
> *As You kill him,*
> *Cries out in ecstasy.*

I had learned it in Arabic, so I sung it in that tongue as my feet faltered towards the black stain spreading around the friar. A hand caught me under the arm and I knelt obediently. The man's sharp face appeared before mine, very close. I smiled: I knew he would do a good job. I felt nothing now, and that was wonderful. The Saracen was speaking urgently to me, and so I stopped singing and cocked my head drunkenly to catch his words.

'What are you doing? How do you know those words? Frankish man, why do you sing the words of Sheikh al-Ansari?'

'I'm sorry . . . I will stop. Please do your work, lord.' My head was growing intolerably heavy, so I let my chin drop to my chest. The sun was flooding me, even as I closed my eyes it seeped in until my skull was filled with it, breaking into fragments like stars, like bees, buzzing, buzzing . . . Then the buzzing became, for a moment, the voices of men, and hands reached for me as I pitched forward into the tumult.

Chapter One

Florence, two years earlier

Enough. I had had enough of this. I pushed back the vast ledger, heavy as a grave marker, and stood up carefully. Three years as a banker had put a bend in my spine, and I felt I must be creaking like an unoiled hinge as I stretched wearily towards the painted beams of the ceiling. Wincing, for one of my legs had gone to sleep into the bargain, I limped out of the reading room and called for my cloak. A young clerk, new to us — I had forgotten his name already, if anyone had even bothered to tell me what it was — brought it, holding it out to me gingerly, as if I were some large and unpredictable dog: might bite, might not. I did not bite, not often, but I was rarely in a good temper these days, especially here. I made an effort to smile and thank him, but he just stood there. He would have had the same look on his face if a stone statue in his church had wished him good day. Once I would have paused and taken a little time to draw him out. I could still recognise that look in his eyes, a young man's terrified fascination with the world that is engulfing him. I could have told him how I had once been young, a monk from the country, and that the world has many rows of sharp teeth and may take you in its jaws, but if you are clever and lucky it may not chew you up and gulp you down.

But I did not. And I didn't stop to bid goodnight to my old friend Isaac of Toledo, head of the Florence branch of the Banco di Corvo Marino. I would see him tomorrow, and though I loved him, he would want to discuss the Uberti loan and some papers that had arrived from Lyon, and I only wished for some food, a drink of wine and bed.

It was not as late as I had thought, however, for I stepped out into dazzling sunlight. The reading room was like a tomb, windowless and airless, the atmosphere a thick, nose-worrying mist of dust, mouldering vellum, tangy ink and candle-grease. I leaned on one of the pillars that stood on either side of the door, letting my eyes get used to the glare. Jesus, I was becoming a bat, a leathery old bat with ink blots on its wings. Should I go back to my toil? No, I hadn't simply left, I had escaped. The ledgers would have me again tomorrow. I took a deep breath and stepped out into the Via dei Tavolini. With nowhere to be, no one needing me, I felt almost dizzy with the freedom of it all. What to do?

Perhaps some shoes. I had heard of a bootmaker near Santa Maria who, his customers said, would surely go straight to heaven when he died, to make shoes for the angels. Try as I might I could not imagine why angels would need them, but Iselda, waiting patiently for me at home in Venice, would like a pair of Florentine shoes, and perhaps he could measure me as well.

I was so deep in these soothing thoughts that I did not notice the man who had fallen in step with me until he skipped ahead, turned and bowed, very politely forcing me to stop. Polite or not, my hand went to the green stone of my knife hilt, for this was a city where people had fallen into the habit of slicing each other up over the most trivial slights. But this fellow was smiling and bowing again, and I decided he was probably not an assassin.

'What do you want?' I demanded crossly. An escape is an escape, and I was not going to let myself be troubled by duty, at least not for the rest of the day.

'Sir Petrus Zennorius?' I nodded, curtly. 'My master would be vastly gratified if you would indulge him with a scant . . .' He waved his arms gently, like seaweed in a rock pool. 'A mere nibble, a morsel of your time.' I sighed in exasperation and looked him up and down. Tall, dressed in sober colours – although the cloth was expensive – he held himself loosely, as if every sinew of his body were waiting for the command that would make him most appealing to whoever stood before him. But I was not in the mood for foppish interruptions.

'And who is your master?' I growled.

'Cardinal John of San Lorenzo in Lucina,' announced the man, with a sort of breathless triumph. He might have been announcing the end of the world, and my imminent acceptance into the bosom of the Lord – shoeless, at this rate. At least the angels would not be jealous. But wait. Cardinal John – John of Toledo, as I thought of him – what was he doing in Florence? A very powerful man indeed, far too powerful to have a fop like this wretch run errands for him. But perhaps he was not such a fop after all. He had a pale, indoor face, nondescript save for a slight wall-eye, and his hair was covered by a black coif tied tight. There was something steely beneath his apparent limpness. Perhaps that was why I still had a finger on the hilt of my knife.

'Why would your exalted master require even a morsel of my day?' I wondered aloud. But of course I knew the answer: a loan, a deposit – even, perhaps, a relic, though I was asked for those less and less these days. I would have to follow this nitwit, then. I had escaped the bank's masonry, but not its responsibility. God's liver! Iselda's shoes would have to wait for an hour. 'Very well, lead me,' I said. 'But I cannot stay long.'

'No, no, of course not,' simpered the messenger, and bowing again, he set off up the street.

I followed, admitting to myself as I did so that it was curiosity more than anything else that was steering me off course. For in those years the city of Florence was very much in the hands of families like the Amidei and Donati, who were loyal to the Holy Roman Emperor, Frederick von Hohenstaufen. And Cardinal John – an Englishman, in fact, a Cistercian abbot who had ended up in Spain before receiving the call of His Holiness – was the pope's man through and through. It would be hard to imagine a more staunch supporter of Pope Innocent, and such a fellow would not expect to be made welcome in Florence. No indeed: he would have to feel quite certain of his safety. And it was partly for that reason that I had begun to doubt that this simpering personage clicking along in front of me was as ineffectual as he seemed.

I had been heading towards Santa Trinità, and I was being led in that direction, but we passed the church and dived into the alleys between it and the river. The buildings ended and there was the Arno, sluggish and disreputable, its waters low, streaked with grease and dye from the tanneries and butchers upstream on the Ponte Vecchio. My guide turned to make sure I was following, and beckoned me onto the old wood of the Ponte alla Carraia. Why in the name of Saint Lawrence's sizzling hide were we going to Oltrarno? He turned right into the Borgo San Frediano and after a minute halted beside the nondescript brick front of a church. San Frediano – I knew it only because, years ago, some workers repairing the floor had dug up a jumble of old bones and the ambitious deacon had tried to sell them to Captain de Montalhac as priceless relics of an ancient martyr. But now I caught on. San Frediano was also a Cistercian cloister, and where else would John of Toledo feel safe in this dangerous city?

The church was empty except for a man wrapped in a dark cloak, sitting in a pew in front of the altar. The messenger signalled for me to wait halfway down the aisle. He tapped across the tiles, bent and whispered something in the shrouded figure's ear. Cardinal John of San Lorenzo in Lucina stood up and his messenger nodded to me. I squared my shoulders and marched towards them. I was in no mood to be intimidated. If they wanted something from me, they could ask. And there was nothing I wanted from them. I had seen the cardinal once before from a distance in the Lateran, but I recognised the triangular face, the hollow cheeks and the large eyes that seemed out of place in their owner's austere visage. He held out his hand and, like the professional courtier I had come to be, I kissed his ring of office.

'Thank you for coming to see me, my son,' he said. He spoke in English, though his speech had been warmed by the southern lands in which he had spent his life. In this he sounded, I supposed, somewhat like myself.

'Any opportunity to serve Mother Church,' I replied, icily polite.

'Of course. I knew you could be relied upon. Now, if you can bear another short walk, shall we allow Remigius to lead us?' Without waiting for my reply, he inclined his head meaningfully towards the messenger, who all of a sudden seemed to have found a new tightness in his joints. He strode out of the church with us close behind.

'You are not married, are you, my son?'

'No, Your Eminence.'

'Iselda de Rozers – is that her name? Charming, by all accounts. You are such a fortunate man, Sir Petrus. But the godly, my son, the godly seek the sanctity of the vow of marriage.'

'Might I enquire where we are going, Your Eminence?' I asked.

'Certainly. We are going to visit an alchemist.'

I blinked. I had obviously not heard properly. 'An alchemist? That is . . . unexpected.'

'So much is, my son, especially in these times. Don't you agree?'

Did this require a diplomatic answer or a casual one? I had been trying, quite successfully, to remove unexpectedness from my life these past three years. As a banker I dealt in stability and safety. As a banker . . . A thought struck me and I stole a glance at the cardinal. He did not look like a charlatan, nor did he seem particularly gullible. But alchemists and bankers both concerned themselves with gold. I sighed. I did not have the time for fool's errands, and if my suspicions were correct I was, at this moment, being taken for a mooncalf. Surely the Church had not come to believe in the transmutation of base metals? How ridiculous. But then I caught something in John of Toledo's expression. There was a jest here. Was I being made the butt of some juvenile sort of ecclesiastical japery? A cardinal and that ridiculous Remigius, trying to set up one of the richest bankers in Christendom for . . . for what, exactly? And then an even less palatable thought struck me. What if I were not being set up for a joke, but for something entirely different? Iselda and I had been more than scrupulous about appearing to the world as perfect Christians – obsessively so, given our business and our clients. But this short walk . . . By 'alchemist', did the cardinal, by any chance, mean Inquisitor, someone who brought truth from the vile matter of heresy, as an alchemist brought forth gold from dross? Very carefully I laid my forefinger back onto the hilt of my knife.

At that moment, thrumming through the air and the walls of the houses, came a low, muffled but powerful *BOOM*.

'What the devil . . .' Cardinal John glanced at Remigius, and for a moment the two men looked quite stricken. Then Remigius gathered himself.

'If Your Eminence will forgive me?' he muttered, and all his floppy exquisiteness transformed itself suddenly into hard, purposeful angles. He sprinted off and vanished round a nearby corner.

'Follow me,' snapped the cardinal, and set off briskly after him.

My tumbling thoughts had not yet ordered themselves in my skull by the time we had negotiated a brief tangle of mean, smelly passageways and climbed the gentle slope of the Monte San Giorgio. In a few minutes we had found Remigius had stopped in front of a nondescript doorway in a low building of wood and brick that was slowly leaning across the alley as if it meant, one day, to kiss the house opposite. He was hammering on the door, listening, and then hammering again. As we trotted up, the handle shook and the door creaked open. I had expected to see some wild-eyed creature in the robes of a magus, but instead a very young Cistercian novice appeared, his face as white as his robes, where those were not spattered with drying blood and streaked with soot.

'Ah. Ivo. What in Christ's name is going on?' said the cardinal. The young man looked at us with red-rimmed eyes and slumped against the door, dragging it wider. Now I saw thin lines of blood running from his ears. Remigius draped himself against the jamb and bowed elegantly as John of Toledo stepped past him.

No Inquisitors, just a large, cluttered room, walls dark, stained with smoke, lined with shelves groaning under the weight of jars, boxes, stacks of parchment, the skulls of men and beasts, skins, lumps of stone. The one window was filthy and let in a thin beam of whey-coloured light that struggled through thick ropes of smoke that coiled slowly midway between floor and ceiling. I stood, blinking, breathing in the heavy air. Flies were humming, a single deep note.

'Up there,' said Cardinal John.

The alchemist's head was staring down at us from the ceiling. At least, I assumed that was who I was looking at. Like a small, shaggy ape it squatted, wedged between a rafter and a beam, leering. The rest of him sat in a high-backed chair before a workbench cluttered with papers, vials, alembics and bits of stone and metal, in the midst of which spread a dark flower of charred wood and blackened shards. The body was leaning forward slightly, propped on its arms, which were burned and blistered. There was a strong smell of roast meat in the air which masked something else, something . . .

'Brimstone?' I asked Ivo. The young novice was at my side, looking as if he was about to puke down the front of his robes.

'WHAT?'

'Brimstone . . . damn. BRIMSTONE?'

'IF YOU SAY SO,' he bellowed, his voice rich with rising bile.

'What happened here?' the cardinal leaned over and shouted in the poor boy's wounded ear.

'There was nothing I could do!' The lad was trembling, his voice raised over a sound only he could hear. 'I . . . I came at first light, as instructed, with the letter and the gold—'

'All here,' said Remigius, holding up a charred purse.

Ivo threw him a terrified glance. 'And he was very excited, as you said he would be, Eminence. He said he was going to put on a demonstration for you, and he ran around like a madman – he *was* a madman – sticking foul powders under my nose and grinding, mixing, cooking up devilment . . . I didn't know what was going on, did I? He was bending over his pestle and mortar, trying to light an oil lamp with a taper, there was a flash . . .' Ivo dragged his hands down his face, his red eyes staring. 'I didn't hear anything then, but now I do! Now I do!'

'God's breechclout! Get outside, you idiot!' The cardinal grabbed the novice's shoulder and shoved him towards the door. The lad took a last wild look around the room and vanished into the light outside. Meanwhile, Cardinal John was squinting up through the swirling dust motes at the head. 'Get that broom,' he said to me, more politely. I saw it, leaning against the wall. As soon as I handed it to him he passed it to Remigius with a nod. The messenger made a face, raised the broom handle first, and began to jab at the head.

'Stuck fast,' he hissed. 'Ah. There it goes.' He gave a last prod, and in a sudden flurry of wet hair and pallid skin it fell off its perch and landed with a hollow thud at our feet. Remigius stooped and, grabbing it by a forelock, picked it up and held it dangling before him. The head swung like a lazy pendulum, spinning slowly, and a blue eye, dull and dead, seemed to regard us one by one. The other eye was lost in a churned welter of charred flesh.

'Give me that,' said the cardinal. He took a handful of hair and held the thing up in front of him.

'You bloody fool,' he muttered malevolently into the ruined face.

'Who was he?' I asked the cardinal.

'Called himself Meister Nibelungus. German – of course, with a name like that – from Franconia. An odd sort of fellow, but then again: alchemists . . .' To my relief he stopped twirling the head and set it down on the workbench, so that it gazed up with its one good eye at the stump of the neck where it had so recently made its home. I leaned over and closed the eyelid: that gleam of dulling blue was beginning to play on my nerves.

'Your Eminence, why exactly did you bring me here? This is not, I take it, what you intended me to see,' I said. Cardinal John turned from examining a row of misshapen skulls and shook his head.

'Alchemists. Heretics and devil-worshippers, in my opinion. Judging by this mess, our friend Nibelungus did not stumble upon the Philosopher's Stone . . . or there again, perhaps he did, eh?' He chuckled.

'A little extreme, as epiphanies go,' I agreed, to be polite.

'I had intended you to meet him,' he said, ruefully. 'Meanwhile, it seems that his labours are at an end. What a shame.' He winced as he examined the bloody stump of the man's neck. 'Careless. Now then, you are as courtly as they say, my son. You have not demanded to know why you are here.'

'I was about to, never fear,' I said. I should have been angry – angry, at the very least – but the carnage in this room seemed to have drained all the outrage from me.

'The answer is before you,' he said, tapping gently at the centre of the charred circle on the workbench. Remigius, whose long fingers were tinkling through the litter of broken glass at its far edge, looked up and narrowed his eyes.

'Alchemy? My dear cardinal, you surely . . . I mean, I have gold enough, and this is far from the business of Mother Church, is it not?'

'Ha ha.' Cardinal John laughed perfunctorily. 'Nibelungus was not searching for gold or the Philosopher's Stone when this happened.'

'What, then?'

'The *Drug*.'

He said it under his breath, though it was an ordinary enough word.

'Medicine? *Medicine* did this to him? What, in the name of . . . of . . .' My voice was rising, and John of Toledo was eyeing me sharply. 'Your Eminence, I certainly know nothing, not one thing, about medicine.' Then light, such as it was, dawned. 'Ah. Some ingredient was required? Some esoteric tincture? Dried mummy powder? Really, Your Eminence: you of all people should reject this superstition.' I fell into a whisper. 'I suppose Your Eminence has some malady, and . . .'

'Not I,' said Cardinal John.

'The Holy Father, then.' I looked at him, frowning.

'No, not Innocent. His opposite.' John of Toledo was

studying me so intently that he might have been counting the pores on my nose.

'Wait – we are speaking of the emperor? Frederick is ill?' I said, surprised out of my anger. 'And what affliction was this drug supposed to cure?'

'Ah, well. Not *cure*.'

'Oh.' Suddenly I hardly dared draw breath. 'So this was poison.'

The cardinal chuckled, but his teeth were clenched. 'Oh, indeed. A poison for the whole world.'

'What are you conjuring here, Your Eminence?' I asked him quietly but urgently. 'I will have no part of it: you may be sure of that.'

'This was not a plot, Sir Petrus – your conscience may rest easy.' The cardinal seemed to be making a jest, but his voice was smooth and cold. 'I wanted to show you a glimpse of what is to come – it seems I was too ambitious, however.'

'To come? Poison is as old as the mountains,' I said. 'If you mean to poison Frederick, I would rather not know about it.'

'As a businessman?'

'You need only ask me where my loyalties lie, Your Eminence,' I told him, icily. 'Indeed yes, I am a businessman, and so my loyalty stands with my clients. Amongst whom I count the most pious King of France, various of your own esteemed colleagues, and indeed the Holy Father himself. I'm guessing that you already know I have also dealt with several of the emperor's more important allies – Ezzelino da Romano for one. But, again as a businessman, I have found that Frederick's warring in Lombardy has disturbed the flow of trade, and that does not help my bank.'

Cardinal John leaned over and picked up the head once more. He began to swing it lazily between us like a censer. 'Let me put it bluntly, my son. Are you Guelph or Ghibbeline? We are in Florence, after all, and you have certainly had to answer that question before.'

'Your Eminence, I am, like you, an Englishman, and my liege lord is Richard, Earl of Cornwall. By that token alone I am Guelph: England is for the Holy Father.' It was not hard to inject just the right note of self-righteousness into my voice, and I could tell from the cardinal's face that he was convinced. Of course he was: I claimed as many allegiances as I had customers, and could make my honour bristle for each of them. But in truth my only loyalty was to the few people I loved, and the rest, to me, was nothing but gaudy show, cheap and flashy as the stuff hung out on Venetian holidays. Still, cheap as I held it, my skill had kept me alive thus far: alive and rich.

'Nicely put, Sir Petroc,' said the cardinal. 'I did not bring you here to question your loyalty, but to strengthen it.'

'I still have no idea what you mean,' I insisted. The cardinal seemed to have relaxed: he was smiling again.

'Unlike you, the wretched Nibelungus was neither scrupulous nor a good businessman – and apparently not the great alchemist his reputation promised.' He set the head down again and wiped his hands on his robe.

'Apparently.' We stood there listening to the alchemist's blood drip, drip, drip onto the scorched wood.

'We heard he was brewing something the emperor intended to use against the Holy See,' the cardinal said at last.

'Oh. And you were going to turn it against him, I suppose? I cannot imagine how this concerns me, but . . . what is it, this *Drug*?' I should not have asked, but by the flash of amusement that darted across his face it was plain that he had known I would.

'I confess that I understand too little of such things,' said the cardinal. He laid his hand thoughtfully upon the matted locks of Herr Nibelungus, turned the alchemist's head and thumbed the eyelid open, so that the eye, dull now and quite filmed with dust and dried tears, stared wearily at the centre of my chest. 'Frederick von Hohenstaufen, though – the creature makes every sort of devilry and maleficence his affair. It is not to be wondered that he set his heart on this . . . this trumpery.'

'Is it poison?' I tried again, grudgingly. The cardinal did not answer, but tapped again at the circle of devastation on the workbench.

'Well, it isn't subtle,' I muttered. 'The emperor . . . you put some in his wine, he drinks it and his head springs off? Messy, but spectacular. On the other hand, arsenic does the same job with less fuss, and I do know where to find that.'

'No. This is, I believe, what it does when it is not disciplined.'

'Discipline? This is alchemists' talk, Your Eminence.' I wiped my forehead. It was close in here, and I was beginning to sweat.

'But no, Sir Petrus. This was not alchemy, and he was not concocting some fabulous poison. The Drug is apparently a weapon, nothing more nor less.'

'Apparently. You've said that before, Cardinal John. Apparent to whom, exactly?'

The cardinal spread his hands, as if disclaiming any responsibility, but there was a lupine gleam in his eyes that gave him away.

I regarded the earthly remains of Herr Nibelungus. 'And if this is a weapon,' I countered, not bothering to keep the scepticism from my voice, 'how do you know? It is either imaginary, like most things alchemical, or useless. Why not simply train men to cut off their own heads with the swords they already own? 'Twould be simpler.'

'We have been assured that it is neither imaginary nor useless. Hohenstaufen has spent a great deal of money on concocting it. The substance is known in the East, but its secret has reached us here through the Mussulmen, and only in tiny drops: an ingredient here, a ratio there . . .'

'But *what does it do?*' I insisted.

'It blows heads off. Isn't that enough? And the Mussulmen say it hurls lances and stones, sprays fire, knocks down walls.'

'I haven't heard of any such weapon. Besides, that sounds like witchcraft, Your Eminence.'

'Do you believe in witchcraft, Sir Petrus? If so, you surprise me.'

I did not believe in witchcraft, any more than I believed in the Church's magic that turned wine into blood and back again, but that was none of the cardinal's business.

'If it isn't conjuring, what is it?' I demanded.

'*Chemistry* it is, my son, chemistry. And while we in Christendom have been lucky enough to remain in ignorance of the Drug, it has been a scourge in the lands of Cathay for a thousand years.'

'And now you have decided that the time is right to bring the scourge here? It is not for me to question the Holy See, but . . .' A huge black fly whirred out of the sun glare, brushed my ear with its tiny bristles and landed with a faint plop in the tarry pool of drying blood on the alchemist's neck. 'Do we really require this? Are we not killing each other fast enough?'

'The question is, my son, who judges? Come. You have seen enough of this.'

We stepped out into the street. The sunshine was so bright that it pierced my eyeballs and set my blood throbbing deep in the bony warren of my temples. I pressed my fingers hard against my closed lids and watched purple light bloom inside my head and burst into a hundred tiny golden bees, buzzing bees. I opened my eyes. The buzzing was coming from beneath my feet, where a legion of flies were lapping at the dark river of gore that had run out of the door towards the gutter. Ivo the novice was watching it with pallid fascination. He started

20

guiltily when he heard us. Remigius slipped from the shadows and stood, alert, hand on a hidden weapon at his waist.

'We are leaving!' John said to the novice. 'Get some men from the cloister. Have this cleared up, my son, and send every scrap, every crumb in this room over to my lodgings.'

'What about him?' stammered Ivo, plainly terrified.

'Have him burned. Do not leave one speck of ash. And don't forget his head.'

'So the emperor wants the Drug simply to use against the Holy Father?' I asked the cardinal. We were walking back through the alleys towards the river, Remigius padding a few discreet paces behind.

'He wants it, we understand, because – listening to fools like Nibelungus, no doubt – he has come to believe that sooner or later it will be known all across these lands, and no one will be able to stand before the ruler who has the most of it, and who knows how best to make and use it. A notion he has picked up from his Mussulman friends.'

'And the Curia thought that, if such a thing existed, the ruler who controlled that power must be the Church.'

'Of course.'

'God be praised,' I said, dutifully – convincingly, I hoped.

'But I think Herr Nibelungus has satisfactorily proved that the emperor has been wasting time and money on a . . . Perhaps you are right, Sir Petrus. On witchcraft.'

'Well, it has been an interesting diversion, if nothing else,' I said, suddenly keen to get as far from Cardinal John as might be possible within the walls of Florence. 'But I'm still curious. What was to have been my part in this?'

'You are, my son, one of the richest men in Christendom.'

'You are too kind. The bank, in which I am a partner, has been blessed with some success.'

'And that has made you, as I said, one of the richest fellows in this or any other land – well, will you allow, this side of India?' It was a casual jest, but I was meant to be flattered.

'If you insist, Your Eminence,' I said with exaggerated good grace.

'You saw, back there, what the world is coming to,' said the cardinal. 'No longer a battle between believer and infidel, or true believer and heretic. No. This is a war between the godly and the godless.' He stopped, to make sure I understood what he had just told me. 'The Holy Father's crusade shall succeed, with or without the so-called Drug – and I would suppose without, judging by what we saw today. Make no mistake: the godly, and the godless. My concern today is merely to ensure that you have chosen the right side. For the godless, my son, the godless shall not stand.'

'Are you telling me, Your Eminence, not to make loans to Ghibbelines?'

'I am telling you, as a friend, a fellow Englishman, that the Holy See would wish for such a rich and powerful banker to take the side of God.'

'Or? There is an "or" implied in your words, Cardinal.'

'Of course there is, my son.' John of Toledo smiled and held out his hand. The gold ring of office gleamed.

I had had enough of this strange dance. My clothes still reeked of the Drug and of Herr Nibelungus's roasted flesh. I had no doubt missed the bootmaker. And now this cardinal . . . I blinked. The ledgers I had been toiling through were full of the proof that I could buy and sell a man like John of Toledo eight times over, and yet here he was, stealing my time and threatening me into the bargain. If Pope Innocent wanted a loan, let him knock on my door himself and show me his collateral. So far I had seen nothing but a room full of smoke and a dead man.

'I have business to attend to,' I said, 'and my time is considered an expensive commodity by those who wish to buy it.' I stepped back, away from the ring and the frozen smile of its owner. 'Good day, Your Eminence. I wish you a safe return to Rome.' The incurious folk of the city were flowing around us like water in a flooded ditch. Cardinal John opened his mouth to speak, but I had already given him a stiff bow and walked off into the crowd.

Chapter Two

The next morning, spurred by my lingering guilt over abandoning my duties the day before, I rose early and went to the bank before business had begun. I let myself in, thinking to be alone, as I was still puzzled by yesterday's odd events and thought the ledger room would be a good place to turn my thoughts over. But Isaac was already there, sipping a cup of hot water and herbs. I almost told him about John of Toledo and the dead alchemist, but decided not to burden him. Isaac was no longer young, and though he professed to love running the Florence office, I had noticed, this visit, that his shoulders were beginning to stoop a little. Surely, I thought now, we could find some younger man to do this work? Isaac was a partner – the captain had seen to that – but he deserved some rest, and besides, I missed him in Venice, a city he far preferred to Florence. I would dine with him tonight, I decided, and see what he had to say on the matter.

'How goes this young day?' I asked him.

'Delightfully!' he replied. 'A party in Montpellier, whom I thought was about to default, has settled his account in full. Pisa is making overtures about a loan.'

'Delightful indeed,' I agreed. 'Isaac . . .'

'Yes, Patch?' Isaac was making his way absent-mindedly towards the counting room, and I followed him. It was a damp stone room at the heart of the palazzo that Captain de Montalhac had chosen for his bank, but someone had lit a small fire in the hearth, and there were a couple of finely carved chairs with Saracen cushions upon them. I waited until we had settled ourselves.

'Isaac, do you think I should get married?'

'Married? Patch, dear boy, by the look on your face I thought at the very least that King Louis had declared himself a bankrupt! Married? To whom, dare I ask?'

'To Iselda, of course!'

'Ah, of course you meant the lady Iselda. But forgive an old man, Patch: aren't you already married to her, in most of the important ways?' I nodded. 'I take it you mean a church wedding, a . . . a *Christian* wedding? Why?'

'That's exactly what I mean, Isaac. As to why . . .' I did not think my friend needed to hear of my afternoon with Cardinal John, not until I had worked out exactly what it signified. 'I've begun to think that my lack of respectability, and Iselda's, might be hurting business. It's apparently no secret any more that we, well . . .'

'Quite. And you are right: it is no secret, if it ever was. You do not seem, the two of you, to have tried very hard to keep it hidden – not that I think you should, not for a moment. What you do is your affair and yours alone, and I might even presume to say that Michel de Montalhac, peace be upon him, would have said exactly the same thing. In fact I am certain of it.'

'You're right, of course. Michel didn't believe in marriage.'

'I don't think I ever heard him talk about it.'

'Nor I, until . . . Well, when Iselda and I came back from France after he died, and you learned that she was Michel's daughter, we didn't go into much detail, did we?' Isaac shook his head, intrigued. 'Before he died, he told Iselda, and then me, how it had come to pass. The Cathars do not believe in marriage. They believe that the Church sanctifies it for the purpose of procreation, which to them is evil, as it prolongs the sufferings of mankind here in Satan's prison.'

'Satan's prison? Perhaps I remember less than I thought.'

'The world. Created by the Evil One to ensnare the light of God that dwells in all our souls. Anyway, this is not the time for Cathar theologics, but as to marriage, they reject it, but don't see any harm in letting the flesh do what flesh does, as their sacrament, their *Consolamentum*, washes away all such sin and lets the soul go free.'

'As simple as that,' said Isaac, an eyebrow cocked in amusement.

'Hmm. And so Iselda came into being. Michel thought of her mother as his wife in everything but name. Iselda and I think of ourselves the same way.'

'But you are not Cathars,' Isaac pointed out. 'Or are you? You know I don't mind one way or the other.'

'No, we aren't Cathars,' I laughed. 'We are not, well, we aren't anything, really. Don't tell our clients, though!'

'I won't. They have difficulties enough dealing with a Jew.'

'So do you think it would matter if we wed or not? Don't you think the Church might be more inclined to use us if Iselda and I weren't smearing the whole enterprise with fornication?'

'I rather like the sound of that,' said Isaac, leaning back and sipping his tisane. 'Why do you ask, Patch?' He shot me a look that was so gimlet-like, so shrewd, that I dared not dodge the question. So I didn't, not exactly.

'A cardinal of my acquaintance has been extolling the virtues of marriage in a rather pointed way,' I told him.

'So?'

'This cardinal is quite close to the Holy Father. Very close, in fact.'

'John of Toledo?'

'Christ, Isaac! Can I hide nothing from you?'

'Well, you weren't trying very hard, dear boy. "Very close to the pope." That made me think of your fellow countryman – that, and the fact that he is in Florence.'

'How did you know that?' I said, amazed.

'He's hiding in San Frediano, in mortal terror of the Amidei.'

'But—'

'One of the good brothers of San Frediano is carrying on with the sister of our clerk Pero's cousin. This is Florence, Patch. Secrecy is relative.'

'Well, you are right. I had a brief audience with him.' How much should I tell Isaac? I wasn't sure if any of this would matter to him, or even what it meant. 'A friendly chat. He might be thinking of borrowing money. Hence my thoughts on marriage. Perhaps the Holy See will become a proper client if I'm not roiling in sin.'

'Well then, as a businessman, I exhort you to get married as soon as possible,' Isaac said, grimacing. 'As your old friend, I say you have money enough to build a golden island in the middle of the ocean, so it doesn't really matter. Do as you will. What, though, would Iselda make of all this?'

'She won't marry willingly.'

'You've asked her?'

'Not like that! We've talked about it a bit. She believes even more strongly than I do that it's nobody else's business what we get up to in the bedroom.' Isaac chuckled. I thought of him as an old man but he had lived no more than fifty years, and I knew he kept a mistress, a very tall, black-haired woman, the daughter of a rabbi. 'Don't worry,' I added. 'I won't make you wed Signorina Maymona.'

'God be praised,' said Isaac. 'I don't think, however, that anyone would care what an old Jew like me does. There:

27

perhaps you should convert. I'll have a word with the rabbi, shall I?'

'Why not?' I sighed. 'No, you are right. Our difficulty is that we have to feign piety when we have no faith. We might as well be true heretics. The godly against the godless. Jews are godly, Isaac . . .'

'At the moment, yes, we are permitted so to be,' he pointed out.

'So do you think it would be good for business or not? Getting married, I mean – I don't think I would care to be circumcised at my age.'

'What did you mean, godly against godless?'

'Something I have heard – how the pope is styling his fight with Frederick.'

'Aha. So this is about taking sides.'

'Apparently so. Ridiculous, isn't it? That they should presume to govern love.'

'But they do. So am I to understand that this marriage question is bound up with the contretemps between Frederick and Innocent?'

'I think it is,' I said. 'I'm not sure why I care, but something . . . I feel something in my bones, Isaac. I can hear Michel telling me to *pay attention.*'

'Indeed. Well, we can ignore the living, but never the dead.' He got up – rather stiffly, I noticed – and prodded a smouldering log with the toe of his shoe. 'Do you think the bank has earned the pope's displeasure?'

'Not yet. I think we'd know if it had. Tell me, though: how would you say our business leans – more to Guelph or more towards Ghibbeline?'

'Well, it is an interesting question,' he said, scratching thoughtfully under his skullcap. 'We are strictly neutral, as Michel wanted it, but of course . . . hmm. And it is interesting that you should ask now. Money is very active at the moment, as you *might* be aware.' He peered at me from under his eyebrows, mock-stern. Isaac knew I did not relish this world, but he also knew that I did my best, in memory of Michel de Montalhac.

'I know I sneaked off yesterday, Isaac!' I said, 'I . . . had to buy some shoes for Iselda. Besides, you all do so much better without me.' We both laughed, and Isaac settled back in his chair. 'Now then, even I haven't failed to notice that the King of France is raising money for his crusade,' I said. 'That's keeping things flowing. But go on.'

'King Louis is, of course, a good customer. An *extremely* good customer. It doesn't hurt to have the friendship of kings, does it, Petroc?' I snorted. Louis Capet had made our fortune, after I had brought him the Crown of Thorns of Our Lord from Constantinople. He had paid half the coin in the treasury of France for the thing, and the Company of the *Cormaran*, as we called ourselves then, had taken a commission so staggering that our lives had changed for ever. And Louis had kept on paying until the last relic had left Constantinople. Now he was kind enough to borrow back the money he had paid us whenever he needed it, and as he was about to go on crusade, he needed it quite badly. Fortune – plain luck, really – was on our side, for ordinarily a pious king in search of coin might have turned first to the Knights of the Temple, but Louis had not forgotten me, his Procurer of Holy Relics. The Templars were no doubt furious; but banking, as I had been discovering, is even less fair than the general run of life. 'Business, Patch, just business,' as Michel de Montalhac would have said.

'Yes, Louis is our most generous client,' Isaac went on. 'But beyond that, I am pleased to say that the Banco di Corvo Marino has finally joined the ranks of the most respectable Venetian banks, for we are now, it appears, loaning out money to both sides of Pope Innocent's crusade against Frederick von Hohenstaufen. Yesterday afternoon – after you had gone shoe-shopping, Patch – a fellow arrived with papers from Frederick himself, requesting a very decent sum. Just last week we agreed a loan to the city of Viterbo, which I take to be a back-door approach from the Holy See. There are others – you will find them eventually.' He slapped my knee to show he was joking. 'Nothing better than funding both sides of a war, eh, my boy?'

'Ach, I'm not sure I have the stomach for that aspect of it,' I said ruefully.

'I agree. It is ridiculous – hilarious, really, if men did not die as a result. Alas, our trade is now money, and money does not seem to be spent on peace in these times.'

'Really, I should like to give it all up,' I sighed. 'And Iselda – God, she loathes all of this.'

'Why, then, do you go on with it?'

'We made our promises to Michel,' I said.

'Really? You promised him that you would be bankers?'

'Not exactly, but . . .' That was true. I had promised my dying friend and mentor that I would make Iselda happy, and see that the affairs of the *Cormaran* prospered. But – and I had pondered this a thousand times since the captain's eyes had trembled shut for the last time – what had that meant? Captain de Montalhac had already turned his own back on the Banco di Corvo Marino. He had chosen faith over money. I had no faith, and neither did Iselda – leastways, none that could be explained to a priest or even a heretic – but that did not make the cultivation of money our only choice. And yet what would happen if we walked away from this life? We had obligations. When we had taken it over, the bank already had agents in two dozen cities and towns, thousands of livres on loan, many thousands more in reserve. Now we were financing trading fleets, armies, weavers, a cathedral . . . And the Templars already had their hackles up. It had taken us a year just to find our feet, another to learn what we were about, and by then . . . *By then, our spirits were crushed.* I could imagine Iselda saying that, though she hadn't, not yet. But it was true, if spirits can be crushed by fine living. For if we often imagined ourselves in a cell with golden bars upon the window, it was a very comfortable cell indeed.

'Patch?' Isaac was studying me, amused.

'Your pardon,' I said, a little flustered. 'I was trying to remember. You know, I don't think we did promise him anything of the sort. And yet here I am, a banker. It is . . .'

'Better than sailing a boat to Greenland?'

'I was going to say better than sleeping in ditches, but that'll do. Don't you miss dining on smoked puffin for two months without relief, though?'

'I'm sure we could procure some for you, dear boy. Do we have any ships bound for the Faroes? But no, this is not the life you chose, nor I for that matter. I am a physician, and I have not so much as lanced a boil since Istvan died. And I miss Michel, and the old days of the *Cormaran*, of course I do. But I am not young, Patch. I don't mind the work, the numbers – I will confess it intrigues me more than a little. I enjoy Florence. I have the lady Maymona. I will never have to eat another puffin so long as I live.'

'It really is just you and I from the old days, Isaac.'

'And Dimitri,' he pointed out. The quartermaster lived nearby in Venice, and I saw him every now and again, though the old Bulgar with half an ear had been keeping himself to himself since his dear friend Istvan had died. 'Who would have believed it?' Isaac sighed and stared into the fire. I knew he was crossing old shipmates off the rolls of the living: Istvan the Croat; Horst von Taltow; Zianni Corner; Roussel; Gilles de Peyrolles. All dead now. And the others, where had they vanished to? When the *Cormaran* had, by the grace of King Louis, found its fortune, the crew had filled their purses and scattered, off to buy back the lives they had escaped. How many of them were still living? For every prosperous tavern owner in Thuringia or Guyenne with a mysterious past, how many of our old shipmates had ended up dead of drink or a knife thrust? I did not blame them for going. After the captain had died, after the pyre at Montségur, I had roamed for a while, riding from dawn to dusk; and when I had found Iselda again we had ridden the dusty tracks of the Languedoc and the muddy roads of Lombardy with no plan save the day's food and shelter before forcing ourselves to come home at last to Venice. Not home, though, really, for either of us. But after so much wandering, stillness had its own seductions. Now we lived in the captain's old house, the Ca' Kanzir as he had called it, an ancient palace full of ghosts and shadows, and we loved it for its strangeness and for the captain's own shade that we sometimes felt brushing against us on a dark stairway. But the place had seen so many strangers come and go, born in one room only to die in another, that we knew we were nothing more than lodgers. I often wondered how many of the old *Cormaran* crew had found a home for themselves, and some peace. I hoped it was all of them, however much I doubted it could be so.

It was time to get to work, and so I kissed Isaac on each cheek and went off to the waiting ledgers. I spent that day and the next dutifully checking over the bank's affairs, reading until my eyes had started to fog and my neck felt as if it were growing a hump. When I was not reading and calculating, I was dictating letters to Arrigus or Pero, the two young clerks, or exploring the lush terrain of profit and loss with Isaac and Blasius. Having determined to lead by example – I had not forgotten the look Arrigus had given me when I had left on my ill-fated quest for shoes – I arrived early at the bank and went back to my apartments late, taking my dinner of bread and cold meats alone. The nights were warm, and I would lean on the window sill, watching the bats chase their own dinner through the towers of the Guelphs and Ghibbelines until my tired eyes commanded me to my bed.

I woke up feeling cobwebby. There had been a full moon the night before, rising huge and golden-orange above the eastern mountains, and I had stayed up later than I should have, sipping some heavy wine the same golden colour as the moon, thinking of Iselda and wondering if she was watching the same moonrise. So it was a little later than usual when I turned into the Via dei Tavolini. The street was full of people, for it was a market day, but even so I saw a figure detach itself from the doorway of the Banco di Corvo Marino and run towards me. I stopped and dropped my hand to the hilt of my knife, but it was only Pero. So I went towards him with a smile, until I saw that his own face was ashen and his eyes were red.

'What is it, boy?' I said. He stopped in front of me, shaking his head. He had been weeping. I took him gently by the shoulders. 'What is the matter?'

'Signor Isaac,' he mumbled.

'What about him?' I gripped his shoulder a little harder.

'Oh, master . . . He is dead!'

'I don't believe you,' I said, calmly. 'I saw him last night. He was as well as you or I.'

'No, no!' Pero blurted. 'He didn't *die* . . .' He looked at me, eyes panicked, blood-rimmed. 'He . . . Someone killed him!'

Chapter Three

'No. No!' I let go of Pero. 'Follow me,' I barked, and set off towards the bank, forcing myself not to run. Pero hesitated and then dashed after me.

'He's not there, master,' he said, plucking at my sleeve. I spun round and caught his wrist, gripping it until he winced.

'Listen, Pero,' I said, teeth clenched. 'Tell me what has happened. Take a breath, and tell me exactly what is going on.'

'Oh, Master Petroc! Dear God, dear God . . . Master Isaac was not there when I got to work this morning. He is always the first to arrive, always, and so I thought he must be sick. I sent Barta the serving boy to his house, to see what the matter might be, but very soon he came back, looking sickened. He . . . I had to calm him down too, master! He told me that he'd come upon a crowd in Via de' Lamberti, blocking the whole street, and when he pushed through he found Master Isaac . . .' Pero stopped, and turned from ivory to the colour of lichen.

'It's all right, Pero,' I said. 'Take another breath. Go on.'

'He found Master Isaac, sir, with his throat . . . He was lying in the street with blood all over him, all over the stones. The watch grabbed him, but he saw that Master Isaac's throat was cut.'

'Christ. Who's at the bank?'

'Barta and Arrigus, sir. They've locked the doors. I sent Ugo to fetch the armed company.'

'Good man.' I stood in the middle of the street, baskets of chickens, carcases of bloody beef passing on either side. The bank maintained a small company of mercenaries to guard the premises and any shipments of valuables that might pass in and out. Ugo was their leader, a grey-stubbled veteran of the emperor's wars in Umbria and the Marches. I thought that I trusted him – we paid him enough. But . . . My mind spun, sickeningly, as if I had suddenly looked over the edge of a very high cliff. Why murder Isaac? To rob him. Everyone knew him for a wealthy man, but he did not carry a big purse. If it had happened at his house . . . I looked down the street. Two men with buckler shields, their hands on their swords, stood one on either side of the bank's door. To rob the bank, one might kill the owners and take control. I drew Thorn, my Saracen knife, and tucked her blade up into my sleeve, keeping two fingers curled round the hilt, taking care not to alarm Pero.

'We'd better see what's happening at the bank,' I said.

'But Master Isaac—'

'Is dead. Pero, are you armed? No, of course you aren't. Then keep behind me, and if you see drawn steel, run. Get the watch. Do you understand?' He swallowed. It sounded as if he were gulping down a hot chestnut, but he nodded gamely.

My feet felt like stone ballast as I pushed through the crowd to the bank. The men at the door were wry-faced, narrow-eyed. Neither had shaved and one looked hung-over and bleary under his rust-flecked mail coif. But they did not, to my relief, look like thieves, for they looked far too annoyed to have anything bank-related on their consciences. When they saw me they came to attention, which was another good sign.

'Is Sergeant Ugo inside?' I demanded. They nodded. 'One of you fetch him. I will wait here.' The hung-over one ducked through the door and returned in less than a minute with Ugo, a thin, slightly bow-legged man with a small pot belly and very blue eyes. I studied him carefully but saw only relief, the relief of a job made very slightly easier. Another good sign.

'Do you know anything?' I asked. Just to be safe I stayed in the flow of passers-by, and Pero, if he but knew it, was shielding my back. Ugo shook his head and scratched the side of his face.

'Nothing, your lordship. Master Isaac is dead, right enough. A fellow from the watch is inside, waiting . . . for you, I suppose, sir. The other lads are in there too.'

'Who did it?'

'No one seems to know. And tongues are already wagging, you can be assured of that. The watchman thinks it was the Guelphs, being that all Jews are for the emperor.'

'Was he robbed?'

'He was not. The watchman told me – left the purse where it was, he claims.' He spat. Ugo's men thought of the Florentine watch the way that ferrets think of rats.

'What do you think, Ugo?'

'Haven't a clue, to be honest, sir. Master Isaac was a nice enough old fellow, for a Jew.'

I let that pass, though ordinarily I would not have. 'Ugo, get me a sword,' I said. He raised his eyebrows, and turned to his men. One carried a falchion, the other a short sword, and at a word from his sergeant the man undid his belt and handed it over. I buckled it on. 'Let's go and see the body,' I said. 'Ugo, come with me. Pero, go inside. Keep the door locked.'

'What about the watchman?' said Ugo. 'He wants to speak with you.'

'Fuck the watch,' I said. Ugo grinned, surprised. Another good sign. 'Right. Come on, and don't let anyone get too close.'

The crowd was still thick in Via de' Lamberti – peasants

36

here for the market and now getting an eyeful of the horrors of town; servants; two vagabonds. Isaac had come about halfway between his house in Via de' Vecchietti and the bank. He was lying across the cobbles, face up, his heels in the gutter. His eyes were wide open, already filming over, still reflecting the pigeons that wheeled above the street. His lips were drawn back and his tongue, thick and liver-coloured, stuck out, clenched between his blood-streaked teeth. Beneath his chin, just where his beard ended, there was a glimpse of pale skin; then blood had swallowed everything.

A watchman stepped forward, staff in hand, but Ugo warned him off with a livid string of oaths. I pushed through the crowd and knelt beside my friend. Ugo stood over me, hand on sword, glaring at the men of the watch, who did not quite know what to do but strutted to and fro like gulls on a beach, daring each other to attack some dying creature coughed up by the sea.

I touched Isaac's still-warm cheek. He looked much older. All the blood had drained from his face and the hollows of his eyes were turning blue. I made myself look at the wound in his neck. The killer had known what he was about, and how to sharpen a knife. A deep cut ran from Isaac's windpipe under his left ear. Wincing, I moved his head to the left, and the wound gaped to the neck-bone. Death had been quick, then. This wasn't a common thief's work. And I doubted it had been some Guelph bravo. I looked down: I was squatting in a great fan of sprayed blood. A kind of frozen emptiness was growing inside, as if I had swallowed poppy juice, and I was thankful, because it let me stand here in the blood of my dearest friend and think, like a man without a soul, about who had killed him.

So I thought, and I saw: a trained killer had done this. Isaac had been strolling along. He might have noticed a man coming up on his left side. I guessed the murderer had been left-handed or skilled with either hand, for the wound was deepest next to the spine. Right hand over Isaac's mouth, left hand round the neck. All the blood had sprayed away from the killer. A steamed-up Guelph would have come from the front, no doubt to speak his hatred into his victim's face as he stabbed. A thief . . . well, a thief would have thieved. I slipped my hand inside Isaac's wet robe and found his purse, weighty with coin. Pulling it out, I slipped it into my own tunic. It dropped down to my waist, leaving a slug-trail of cold blood against my skin. Leaning close, I looked into Isaac's eyes. A few specks of dust had settled on the filmy surface of one. The pupils were wide. I saw myself, very far away, but no other face, no murderer. Isaac would not have believed that super-stition anyway. I kissed my finger-ends and gently closed his eyes.

'Did any of you see what happened?' I rose to my feet and faced the crowd. There was a muttering. Heads were shaken and feet scuffled. 'Who knew this man?'

'The Jew from Via de' Vecchietti,' someone shouted out: a boy, leaning in a doorway. There was a murmur of assent.

'I saw him fall over,' said an older woman holding a trug of celery. 'I thought somebody had bumped into him and he'd tripped.'

'Did you see who it was that . . . that tripped him?'

'No, signor. Just someone walking fast . . . in dark clothes. I don't know, signor. Just a passer-by.'

No one else had seen anything, or cared to say if they had. I beckoned the watchmen and they slunk over, hungrily. There was going to be a good tip for them, they knew. But as I was about to give them their instructions, there was a tug at my sleeve. A young man, almost a boy, stood there. He blinked at me nervously.

'What?' I said rudely. He flinched, but gamely signed for me to lean closer. I sensed Ugo half-draw his sword behind me, but I bent to let the boy whisper in my ear.

'I have sent for the elders,' he said. 'The *Chevra Kaddisha* are coming to fetch Signor Isaac.'

'Who?' I said, confused.

'Those who take care of the dead,' he said patiently. 'And the rabbi too – he has been told.'

'Oh.' I suddenly felt very tired, and put my hand on the boy's shoulder. 'Thank you. Forgive me. He was the last friend I had left from . . . from another time.'

'It's all right,' said the boy. 'Look, they're here.'

Six nondescript men in sombre clothes that had seen too many seasons had slipped quietly through the ring of on-lookers. Two of them carried a wicker hurdle between them. Behind them a man I recognised: Isaac's rabbi, who lived over behind the market. The watchmen were scowling at the new-comers, so I snapped my fingers under the leader's nose and made him look at me.

'These worthy men have come to take care of their friend – our friend,' I said. 'You will give them the help they need, won't you? Here's for your trouble.' I held out a palm full of small coins – enough, though, to make his lips purse with satisfaction.

'Right, signor,' he said.

The rabbi was hanging back at the edge of the crowd. He saw me and hurried over.

'What happened here?' he demanded.

'He was killed,' I told him blandly. 'It was cleverly done. Who would wish to do such a thing? Isaac was well liked, wasn't he?'

'Well liked can mean many things when applied to my people, but rarely does it mean for us what it means for you,' he said curtly. 'I do not think Signor Isaac had any particular enemies, if that is what you mean. But if your question is, who in this city would wish a rich Jew dead, I might reply, who would not?'

'That is harsh. Is it true?'

The rabbi sighed. 'True, and not true. Really, I don't think Gentiles care if we live or die, when they think of us at all. If we are lucky, they forget we are Jews and so we go about unnoticed. For a man like Isaac, a rich man who dealt in money, it . . .'

'Might be different? I don't know. He did not mention anything particular to me.'

'Would he have?' the rabbi asked, sceptically.

'Isaac and I spent many years together, on a not very big ship, sailing the sea,' I told him. 'He nursed me when I was sick, and I did his chores for him when his hands were raw with cold. I do think he would have told me, yes.' The rabbi's eyes were still narrowed. 'He also told me, many times,' I added, lowering my voice, 'that he did not care for religion very much – his own, or that of others. I understand all too well that to us Gentiles a Jew is a Jew whether or not he is pious. But it might also be said that to a Jew, the same is true about Gentiles. So I tell you now, as a friend of my friend, that Isaac and I thought the same way about faith. I am perhaps not what you think of as a Gentile. And having trusted you with that, would you please tell me if anyone – anyone at all – might have wished our friend dead?'

The *Chevra Kaddisha* had lifted Isaac onto the hurdle, taking care to stop his head lolling. I wanted to help, but the tenderness with which they were handling the corpse, the way they seemed to have somehow recreated the substance of Isaac from the awkward jumble of bloody rags and flesh that I had found in the street, made me hang back. These folk loved him. No, I would not interfere.

'Messer Zennorius,' said the rabbi quietly. 'I do not know of any man or woman who would cause Isaac to be killed like this. But I will ask. There are not so many of us in Florence, but we hear much, and perhaps . . . Perhaps.' He risked a small smile. 'They are ready. Signor, we will bury him tomorrow morning at nine bells. Come to his house. It is against our custom, but if you wish, you may help carry him to the grave.'

'I will be there,' I said, and bowed. He returned my bow solemnly. The six men of the *Chevra Kaddisha* lifted the hurdle onto their shoulders, and at a nod from the rabbi they moved off. The crowd parted nervously, as if avoiding contagion. I watched them go, the still form of my friend swaying gently above the slowly pacing men, the rabbi walking ahead. Many in the crowd were crossing themselves or flashing devil's horns at the Jews' backs. I stood, staring at the pool of blood, already beginning to blacken and clot. Flies were paddling happily. Someone said they would fetch a pail of water and a broom. Ugo cleared his throat. I took a deep breath and pushed through the crowd. I had no idea what I was going to do next, but we were needed at the bank. As I walked on stiff legs back to the Via dei Tavolini, the numbness inside began to burn, and I bit my lip, understanding that I had been taught well, and that the last of those teachers had been Isaac. So I went to work, drowning myself in the scrawled figures of debt and redemption, because it was the only way I could find to honour my dead friend.

The rest of that day, and very deep into the night, I toiled in the Banco di Corvo Marino, of which Iselda and I were now the sole owners. The armed company was set inside and outside the door. I sent Iselda the news by the fastest courier I could buy, just the plain facts and nothing else, because as I sat there in Isaac's reading room I had nothing else to say. Only very slowly did a plan of any sort begin to form in my mind, for I was constantly interrupted by worried clients who had learned of Isaac's death, by annoying clients who did not know or care, and by Isaac's friends and acquaintances, of which there seemed to be many, and that at least made things not so terribly bleak. But when the door was shut and I was left in the dusty quiet, I pondered feverishly. Who would take over the Florence branch? Was there any point in even keeping it open? Was there, indeed, any point in keeping the bank open at all?

Isaac's murder was the excuse I needed to bring the whole enterprise to an end. Sell it. Take the money and go away somewhere with Iselda. We didn't even need the money. Could we not just vanish? Why not?

But then the same old answers came back out of the silence: this is yours. This is a responsibility that was given to you. And the worst: a man does not run away. Trying to listen to my heart but hearing nothing except the muttering of dead men, I paced across the tiles in front of the hearth. The captain would not have given up. He would . . . I squatted down and poked at the cold heap of cinders in the hearth. He would be trying to find those who had killed Isaac, first of all.

What else, indeed, was there to do?

I stood up and opened the door.

'Blasius!' I called. The young man appeared from the counting room, looking alarmed. I beckoned him to join me. We sat together as Isaac and I had sat three days ago, talking of marriage and promises.

'Young man,' I said. 'How old are you?'

'Twenty-seven, Messer Zennorius,' said Blasius, sounding a little choked.

'Good. Young enough, but not . . . Never mind. How close did Isaac bring you to the meat of our business?'

'He treated – God rest his kindly soul, he treated me as a younger partner,' stammered Blasius. 'I have been his shadow for two years now. Indeed, Isaac allowed me to deal with the French envoy, last time he was here.'

'And the books?'

'I am diligent, sir . . .' The fellow looked like Marsyas, about to be flayed.

'Good,' I said. 'Then you are in charge. I appoint you head of the Banco di Corvo Marino in Florence. You may start immediately. Does that suit you?'

Blasius left his chair so fast it fell back against the wall. He rushed to the window, knocking a sheaf of vellum off the table, leaned out and was copiously and noisily sick. When he was done he turned back into the room, shaking, ashen. He wiped his mouth tremulously, and then gave a cautious smile.

'I should be very, very honoured, sir,' he rasped.

'Good. Blasius, are you married?'

'Sir?'

'Are you married? Yes or no, man.'

'Well, yes.'

'Huzzah. And you are a Christian?'

'Of course!' And he crossed himself with vomit-spattered fingers.

'There's no "of course" about it. Was Isaac a Christian? Did you care that he was not?'

'No, sir! Signor Isaac was the kindest man I ever met . . .'

'That's no doubt true. Well, you are a married Christian. Very good. You will do, Blasius. You fit. You will be acceptable.'

'I'm so glad to hear it, sir,' he said faintly. For a moment I thought he was, in fact, about to faint, but instead he stooped and picked up the spilled documents.

'The Mascherati loan,' he said, glancing at it. 'Pope Innocent won't like this one.' He had calmed down, it seemed, the moment he had touched the vellum. Now he was composed. He looked at me, eyebrows raised sardonically.

'Won't he?' I asked.

'A Fieschi, wanting the Mascherati to prosper? Ghibbelines in a Guelph city? I hardly think so,' he chuckled.

'Well then: should we make the loan?'

'Of course.'

All the agitation and fear had gone from him like mist struck by the sun. I examined his face, realising as I did so that I had not paid very much attention to him until now. As Isaac's second in command, Blasius was quiet and efficient enough to be left to his own devices. I had trusted him, and that was good. He was a handsome young man, or would have been if he had spent more time out of doors. He had foxy hair and there were still freckles on his pale face, but his eyes were wide and piercing, and he held his head up. He had been trying to grow a beard but I was pleased to see that he had given up and shaved off the sparse foliage on his chin. He was missing one of his upper front teeth, though the rest seemed sound – a fight? And there was a small scar in the corner of one eyebrow. How interesting. He was not, in fact, the pallid bookworm I had taken him for.

'Blasius, what about you? Guelph or Ghibbeline?'

He surprised me once again by laughing aloud. I might have been mistaken, but there seemed to be a twinkle in his eyes. 'As the pupil of Signor Isaac I am, very scrupulously, neither one,' he said. 'Outside these walls, though I do not make a show of it, I am a Ghibbeline.' He had drawn himself up as though to meet, or to make, a challenge, but he had reassured me. By owning up to his loyalties he had shown that he understood me.

'Excellent. I am neither, Signor Blasius – do not think the worse of me for it. No – I will tell you the truth, which is that I am not a Guelph. Make of that what you will. But like you, as head of this bank I am friend to both camps and to none. Now then, sir. I have a great deal of work to do, and so do you. I shall be leaving Florence in two days at the latest. Can you

44

have the reins firmly in your hands by then?' He nodded, wordlessly. 'Good. Send word to your wife, Blasius. You will spend the night here, until we are sure that no one is planning to rob us. Now, do you really have no idea who murdered our friend?'

'I don't,' said Blasius. He came and sat down next to me again, and leaned towards the dead fire as though the cinders could warm him. 'Isaac was very careful, and, you know, very capable. He wasn't just an old financier, was he?'

'Not just that. He came to this life quite late. Capable? He was that.'

'He was a . . . a sailor, once?'

'As was I. You can say "corsair" if you want, Blasius, though it wouldn't quite explain what we did when the *Cormaran* was a ship and not a bank. Did he ever tell you about his past?'

'A little. I found it hard to believe, to tell you the truth, and actually I think he preferred to talk of his studies at Toledo and the scholars and philosophers he'd known.'

'That sounds like Isaac. But it was all true, no doubt. Let's call for some wine, and I will tell you a little more about him, and about this bank. On the understanding, mind you, that you don't change your mind about my offer.'

So we sat and talked, and Pero brought us wine and honey bread, and lit the fire. I tried to bring Isaac back to life, to bring some warmth back to his shade, to feed his bewildered ghost on the warm blood of memory. And to warm my own frozen soul. Away on the other side of the marketplace, past the stinking debris of business done and forgotten, Isaac's corpse was being prayed over, candles at his head and feet, his friends struggling to keep away dangerous spirits, heathen spirits like mine.

Chapter Four

Isaac was buried in a tiny graveyard that lay, completely overhung by the backs of old houses, at the end of a little alleyway to the north-west of the marketplace. Nothing more than a square of almost bare earth, tufted here and there with yellowing grass, and a family of snakes sunning themselves in the one patch of sunlight. The still air smelled of snake: spoiled garlic and baby piss. There were only ten mourners, for no Christian man would come to the funeral of a Jew, even though that man had been his friend and colleague. The rabbi was there; the six men of the *Chevra Kaddisha*; Signorina Maymona, swathed in black from head to toe like a Saracen woman; a very old Jewish man whom I did not recognise; and myself, for though I was no Jew, I was no Christian either, and no priest or rabbi could have kept me from Isaac's farewell. The service was long and as I did not understand Hebrew, I stood and watched the pigeons go about their business in the eaves above us, tears pouring down my face and into my tunic, listening to the strange and beautiful words drift down onto the plain wooden box that held the husk of Isaac, physician of al-Andalus.

The rabbi was waiting for me outside the gate. He was sorry, but he had discovered nothing. I had not expected anything from him. Isaac had not been murdered by one of

Florence's Jews, I was sure, and the rabbi no doubt moved very little outside the tight circle of his community. The other mourners, even the lady Maymona, left without speaking, to me or to each other. So I thanked the rabbi and waited until he was out of sight. Then I went back into the burial ground and knelt by the fresh grave. The earth was mean and full of sharp white pebbles. I gathered up a fistful and let the stones dig into my skin before letting them trickle out again. But no answer came to me, no message from the dead, no inspiration. I dusted off my hands and went back to the bank.

Blasius had already found his feet, it seemed, and he greeted me with that tinge of condescension that talented underlings reserve for their less able masters. All well and good. I asked him to see that Isaac's estate be made over to the lady Maymona, and that she would receive all that she was due as the widow of a partner in the bank. And then I left him to his new powers and made my way to the Via de' Lamberti. Ugo had offered to come with me, but I waved him off. I knew something of paid murderers – not that Captain de Montalhac had used them, but there had been a couple of erstwhile killers on the *Cormaran* at any given time – and I was fairly sure that, if I had been singled out along with Isaac, they would have tried to take me yesterday. Today, the murderer was far away, or had gone to ground. Which made me wonder all the more: why Isaac, and not me? I was the prize: if someone wanted my business, I was the one to put out of the way.

The street where Isaac had died was quieter today. A few old folk were sitting in doorways and an exhausted-looking woman was scrubbing the steps of a modest palazzo. I thought I remembered her from yesterday, and went to speak to her. She looked up in surprise at my greeting: damp, stringy hair plastered across a florid forehead, pale eyes that had surrendered to drudgery. She licked her lips cagily when I produced a silver coin, and stood up, still suspicious.

'Signora, did you see what happened here yesterday?' I asked gently. She folded heavy arms across a heavy bosom. 'I'm not the watch,' I added. 'He worked for me, the man who was killed. And he was my friend.'

'The Jew?' She examined me, curious now. Her eyes, I noticed, were quick, oddly birdlike in her defeated face.

'Yes, the Jew. His name was Isaac.'

'Well, I'd seen him before, of course. He walked past here every morning, same time.'

'And yesterday?'

'I don't remember. Yesterday was the same as every other day, if you take my meaning.'

I did, and showed my understanding with another piece of silver. She palmed it with chapped fingers and sucked her teeth speculatively.

'I work for Signor Bartholomeo, who lives here.' She jerked her chin at the half-scrubbed steps. 'On my way to market, I was, yesterday morning. I'd just shut the door behind me when I saw the Jew come walking along—'

'Why did you notice him?'

'Only because he's so regular – *was* so regular in his ways, and I used to, if you like, tell the time by him. So I saw him, and I knew I'd be in good time for the man who sells me *cotechino*, because the best ones go early and it would never do to bring back mouldy ones . . .'

'Quite.'

'So then, just as he walks by, another fellow who's walking behind him catches up and then down goes your friend. I thought he'd tripped, and that the other fellow, who I thought was catching him up, you know, to speak to him, I thought the fellow would pick him up and dust him off. But he didn't. He was already running, down that way.' She pointed in the direction of Santa Trinità.

'Didn't anyone try to stop him?'

48

'What for? It wasn't for a moment that I saw the blood. He was lying there, and his legs were moving, and then they stopped. And then the blood – it had sprayed out all over, on some ladies, and they started to scream and yell. That's when everyone knew.'

'What did he look like, the other fellow?'

'Tall, tall and skinny. Long legs – that's what I noticed. Sort of clumsy, like a lad that's grown too quickly. But when he ran, he was quite different.'

'What do you mean?'

'Well, like all his strings had been tightened.' She sniffed, thinking. Then she held out a red hand, wiggled her fingers, and made a sudden fist. 'Like that.'

'Did you see his face?'

'No . . . well, it was pale, I think, but he was wearing a black coif – that's what I really noticed. Very tight, like a priest – no, not like a priest, but not fashionable.'

I thanked her with another coin, and she smiled properly for the first time. 'So he was a friend of yours, the Jew?' she asked, and I saw that I had begun a train of gossip that might well rattle around this street for years. 'And yourself, you aren't from Florence, are you?'

'No, I'm not,' I said, not unkindly.

'Not even from these parts – not Sienese, are you? Or a Jew yourself, begging your pardon?'

'No, my good lady. I'm from much further away than Siena.' Let her think what she would. She had told me enough, more than enough. Leaving her with a bow, I ducked into the crowd heading south towards the river.

The church of San Frediano was empty, and needed sweeping. There was a faint sweet-rotten smell of dead wasps, and a few crunched underfoot as I walked up to the altar. The door to the cloister was not locked, and I walked through it into a small covered walkway surrounding a little patch of well-tended grass. Pigeons spoke to each other from the roof tiles, but there was no other sound. It took me a while to find anyone, an old monk gently sweeping up in the refectory who looked up in toothless amazement when I called to him. No, Cardinal John had left two days ago. His servant? The old man's wrinkled brow contracted into even deeper furrows until he found the right memory. The ridiculous young man! No, gone as well, yesterday. Where? North, to Lyon. He folded his hands in a warm spasm of happy piety. To see the Holy Father! What a joy, what a joy . . .

Oltrarno crept sluggishly around me in its mid-morning daze. I wandered, overpowered by the need to get out of Florence, and my feet took me ever uphill, until I was in the olive groves that lie like green skirts around the church of San Miniato al Monte. There was an ancient path, scuffed-out earth and old steps of stone dished and polished by generations of toiling feet. Mange-ridden cats basked in the brown drifts of last year's leaves, and wasps circled the green pendants of unripe grapes, expectantly. So much patience here, away from the city.

Remigius, the cardinal's dangerous fop, had killed Isaac. It had taken not even a morning's work and I already had my answer. So I was intended to find out. John of Toledo had caused my friend to be murdered, and wanted me to know it. A big ginger and dirty white tomcat appeared on the path above me. He planted himself in a patch of sunlight and began to lick his balls. I stopped and let him get on with it. A flock of small brown birds was swarming from tree to tree above us. The tomcat paused and ran a yellow eye over the scene. He glanced at me, gave his cods a parting lick, and with a twitch of his manky tail jumped onto the wall that ran alongside the path and disappeared behind it. I began to climb again.

When I finally reached the ancient church, surrounded by the spreading flat-topped pine trees of the Florentine hills, it seemed as patient as everything else, enduring the heat behind its patterned shield of black and white stone. I went inside to escape the bludgeoning sunlight, and strolled for a while between the columns, cooling off. But I could not escape the thought that was circling me like one of Saint Anthony's tempters, which was if I found a good horse I could catch Remigius on the north road by tomorrow afternoon. One ill turn deserves another, and I would see that lanky body tumbled in a ditch, after he had told me why he had killed Isaac.

But he would not tell me, would he? Anyway, I already knew. I went and sat down in one of the side chapels. There were a few people in the church, mostly pious sightseers, pilgrims on their way to Rome, and the sound of northern voices echoed softly. John of Toledo, English cardinal, friend of Pope Innocent, had wanted me to understand something. He had taken me to see a headless alchemist, but apparently that hadn't been enough. The plan had been to show me an apocalyptic weapon, but instead I'd witnessed a grotesque embarrassment. So Isaac, a disposable person, a Jew, had to die as well, to get my attention. I understood well enough: do not cross the line between godly and godless. Do not consort with Jews or heretics. Marry. All this, to prove I served the pope and not Frederick von Hohenstaufen. I took a candle from the box where it lay awaiting a supplicant, and rolled it between my fingers. What childishness it all was, teaching me a lesson with murder as a child is taught to count with acorns. One here, one here. Put them together. Do you see? Yes, I saw.

I dug my thumbnail into the white tallow, shaving off a little curl, and another. Soon my lap was full of them. So I was being invited to defy the Church, was I? Fuck them, all of them. Isaac hadn't been disposable to me. I would accept their invitation.

I stood up and a shower of white, waxy curls drifted to the floor. I lit the candle, whittled as it was to a knobbled twig, and stuck it in the tray of sand before the altar. I did not check to see what saint I was honouring – already, in my mind, I was on the north road, my sword knocking eagerly against my thigh – but turned to leave. More pilgrims had come in out of the heat, and I passed by them unnoticed, just another foreigner. I felt brimful of rage, and it was tinged with bright, furious joy. To be doing *something* again. To be doing real business at last: blood for blood. The door was open, and I screwed up my eyes against the light that was about to ambush me.

'Now, now. You lit a candle and didn't put your coin in the box,' said a voice I knew from somewhere. 'That will never do, my dear Petroc.' It was soft, this voice, tinged with the soft lilt of a northern country. A friend's voice, surely, and yet it made the fine hairs prickle on the nape of my neck. And who in Florence, besides Isaac, knew my true name? I turned quickly. There, just beyond the door, stood a spare-framed shadow, a man-shaped black void in the afternoon dazzle that poured in from outside. Then he stepped inside and I saw that he was not black but grey – grey robe, grey hood, grey wisps of hair framing an elegantly chiselled face. And grey eyes, the colour of a winter sea. I had never forgotten those eyes.

'Doctor Scotus?' I breathed. 'Michael Scotus?'

He pushed back his hood. I had not seen Michael Scotus for many years, and I had guessed, in fact assumed, that he was dead, for most of the world had thought him dead ten or more years before we had first met. And yet here he was, and nothing seemed to have changed. Time had long ago scoured all softness from his face, leaving it both aged and ageless. Between us, on the border between glare and shadow, the air seemed to swim like heat haze, as if Michael Scotus were regarding me from another place, just beyond the real. Then I blinked, and he was nothing but an old, straight-backed man in priest's robes, holding out his hand, a smile on his gaunt lips.

'You've had a fright,' he said, with just a hint of rueful merriment.

'No, no! But I thought . . . that is, I had heard . . .'

'Such rumours seem to follow me, as birds follow the plough,' he said. 'And yet I plough on.'

I stepped out onto the hot flagstones. Michael was no spirit. I took his hard-palmed, cool hand and shook it.

'What are you doing in Florence?' I said. 'Following me? This isn't a chance meeting, my dear old friend.'

'I came here on another matter,' said Michael. 'At first. But yes, I've been following you. Shall we go down? It will be cooler amongst the olives.'

We set off down the hill, into the groves, the patient kingdom of brown birds and thin cats. 'What are you doing here, Michael?' I asked again after we had walked for a while. 'I am intended to ask that, aren't I?'

'Of course. So that I might tell you I came here to meet a German alchemist.'

'Nibelungus?' I stopped, and he turned and looked up at me from a lower step. The world had become even stiller than it had been. 'Why, Doctor Scotus?'

'He was manufacturing something for me.'

'Jesus Christ. The Drug – that bloody Drug? Then you are with Cardinal John?'

I stared into his face, but saw nothing. He could make of that face a mask as hard and cold as diamond: that I knew from our past friendship. I had seen him mourn, though; and laugh, and despair. But that was rare. The face Michael Scotus wore most often was the ethereal, impenetrable one that shifted like sunlight on mercury. 'Do you think I have brought you here to kill you, like poor Isaac? What a squalid end for such a noble man. All those ideas. All that knowledge seeping out into a Tuscan gutter. No, take your hand off your knife, Petroc. I am not with Cardinal John in any sense. But what did the good cardinal want with you?' he asked.

'To show me your supposedly terrible *Drug* – which, by the way, is about as useful as a blind man with a poleaxe – and to warn me about choosing sides. I thought he wanted me to procure some ridiculous magical ingredient for him. And Michael, if that is what you want with me, once I was indeed someone who went off hunting for strange and wonderful things. But I don't do that any more, so if you think I'm going to go and find you dragon's sweat or some such nonsense, you are mistaken. The needs of the alchemist are more strange and more self-deluding even than those of priests.'

'Now, now. I am a priest. And I am an alchemist. Strange that you did not know that. Nibelungus was my student, once upon a time, until he put too much faith in a bad recipe. He was my pupil, but he outshone me like the sun does the moon. And he'd used the best *sal nitrum foliatum*, from Aleppo, which I bought for him. But it turned out to be fortunate, in the end. It would have been quite a disaster if his talents had fallen into the hands of the great enemy.'

'So on the subject of choosing sides, you have chosen yours at last, then? There was a time when you could not decide.'

Michael took my arm and we walked slowly and, to a casual watcher, companionably down the path. The groves were ending, and we were coming to the gardens that lay outside the walls. And here was the gate, guards half-asleep in the shade. 'Didn't Michel de Montalhac, God rest his soul – if that is the right thing to say about a Cathar – teach you anything about appearances?' he said when we were through the arch and back inside the city. 'Nothing is as it seems. Which is demonstrated rather aptly by this pope who has called himself Innocent. I have chosen nothing. But I have ended up here, now, because—'

'But you did have to choose, Michael,' I cut in. 'Cardinal or necromancer? That was your title once, so I heard. Necromancer to the Emperor. Truthfully, I can picture that more readily than you in a cardinal's biretta.'

'I counted old Gregory as a friend,' he said patiently. I remembered my own meeting with the late pope, and how his ancient eyes had bored into me like awls. 'But our new pope is . . . is a lesser being entirely. Despite the endless tempest of lies blown out by Rome, Frederick von Hohenstaufen is not a bloodthirsty man.'

'Really? And yet, if I'm understanding you, you're trying to make him a weapon that will blast the world to pieces.'

'If he is seeking to master the Drug, it is only because, if it falls into the pope's hands first, he and all his family will be destroyed as if they were rats in a hayrick. You will ask whether the same would be true were Frederick to have it first. I do not believe so. Frederick is the wisest . . . no, not wisest, *cleverest* man I have met in my long life. I have known many who were wiser by far, but none so adept at drawing knowledge into himself and using it as a tool to master the world of men. He knows he cannot defeat the pope, for to do that he would have to defeat the Church, and with it faith itself. And he is not a Mussulman or a devil-worshipper, no matter what the priests say. In fact he is an unimpeachably orthodox Christian, save where the power of Rome is concerned, and . . . well, no matter.'

I remembered long hours spent on a boat slowly beating home through winter seas, watching Michael Scotus swing in an agony of the mind between his two great loyalties; that for his friend Pope Gregory, who had almost made him Archbishop of Canterbury, and for Frederick von Hohenstaufen, who had made him his necromancer and astrologer and allowed him to wrap himself in the shadows where he felt most at home. But Gregory was dead, and Innocent – Innocent! A fine name

55

for the man who had burned the Cathars of Montségur and set the Inquisition tearing like maddened beasts at the bodies and spirits of faithful and heretic alike – had resolved to destroy the emperor for good.

'Titles never impressed you,' I said.

'Ach, well, I would have made a decent archbishop,' he replied wistfully. 'But no, I went over to the emperor in the end. And do you know why? I find him a more godly man than Saint Peter's current successor.'

We had come back almost to the Ponte Vecchio, and the stench from its butchers and tanneries was eye-watering, even from afar.

'Well, Lord Necromancer,' I said, waving away a cluster of bluebottles, for we had reached the outskirts of the verminous swarm that hung about the bridge. 'I have been wooed by the Holy Father. But since we are old friends, I will tell you plainly: you find me about to leave Florence. I am going hunting for Cardinal John of Toledo and his servant – one Remigius, a boneless abomination. Remigius killed Isaac, and I shall kill him. I have to tell you, too, that at this moment I see no reason why the cardinal should be left alive. I looked into his eyes just two days ago, and I can recall nothing that might suggest he deserves mercy.'

'Really, Patch? Murder? I cannot blame you, of course. The world is already a duller place now that he is gone. I was planning to go and speak to him, in fact: he shared with the emperor a fascination for the inner workings of this human form. Isaac would have enjoyed the Hohenstaufen court, you know: his own people, and many fine Arab doctors, learned discourse, a fresh cadaver whenever he required one—'

'I have nothing left of my past,' I interrupted. 'Isaac was all that remained. The captain, Gilles – and all those nights on the *Cormaran*, planning and scheming. All their stories, all that they'd seen. All dead. I'm still here, but I feel . . . I feel like a murderer, actually. The men around that table would have avenged him, and as I'm the only one left, it's my job.'

'And your pleasure?'

'Why not? The world is full of murderers, and the more they kill, the more easily they escape punishment. For instance, what temptations does the emperor bring me? I assume that's why you are here, Michael. Cardinal John put it quite plainly: I should take care to be on the side of the godly, not the godless. The Drug doesn't look like it's going to work, so what other slaughter am I being asked to fund, eh? Why should I throw in my lot with godlessness? If I'm to use my gold to buy the death of many, why shouldn't I take a life or two with my own hands? Who, in this vile fucking world, would dare object to *that*?'

My voice had risen and I saw an old man at the edge of the street looking at me with his toothless gob open in surprise.

'An excellent question,' said Michael, calmly. 'Jesus Christ would dare object, but alas, he is not much in fashion these days. Another reason I turned my back on Rome. But to answer your more simple question, I haven't come to tempt you, Patch!' he said, and laughed in his hollow fashion. 'No,' he went on, striding unperturbed into the reek that roiled, invisibly, from the bridge. 'Nibelungus was my only reason for being here. But when I discovered you were in the city, and after I heard of Isaac's murder, I decided to warn you.' We were on the bridge now, walking on trampled chicken guts, bloody sawdust, feathers, the fumes of boiling piss and spoiled blood all around us.

'About what?' I wheezed. God, I was becoming soft: time was when a city's foulness would not have made me so much as blink.

'Cardinal John . . .'

'You'd do better to warn him about me, Michael. I have the measure of that piece of—'

'The cardinal is but one scale of the basilisk,' said Michael. 'If you are thinking of revenge, I would advise against it. There, you have your answer. When I heard that Isaac was dead, I knew what would be in your mind. This you know: you are caught up in things, Petroc, very deeply caught. Do kings disappear? Do popes vanish into the air?'

'Of course not,' I snapped.

'Well, you are a king, Petroc. You rule over a vast kingdom of money. You cannot disappear while you still wear your crown.'

'Then I'll throw it in the privy and be done with it.'

'Kings abdicate when they are allowed to. You are far, far too important to the schemes of Christendom. You may take Iselda and sail to Skraelingland, and they will bring you back, so that you may sign their loans.'

'Michael, you have always made these grand predictions. Not so long ago you thought the Crown of Thorns would make peace between pope and emperor,' I reminded him. 'That was what you believed – that an apocalypse was coming. It hasn't, though, has it?'

'You should know, Petroc.'

'Meaning?'

'What were you doing five years ago, when you were still unimportant enough to disappear? No, don't worry. You have nothing to fear from me, or from the Hohenstaufen. But you vanished for a while, you and Michel, and Gilles too. I heard you were at Montségur. Tell me: were you waiting for Emperor Frederick to send reinforcements? Did you curse the pope as your friends died? I will not ask how you survived, but wouldn't you call what happened to the poor Cathars an apocalypse? It is all about power – always has been.'

'Don't lecture me about power, Doctor,' I said, bitterly. 'I deal in it every day – cut it up and dole it out like bread. So you know that Isaac was fascinated by blood, and how it travels around our bodies? He showed me once. Cut a man open and laid it all bare, like a great, wet map. But Michel de Montalhac showed me how power moves. That was his life's work, I've realised: mapping out the secret roads and streams on which power travels about the world. Everything is connected, nothing is chance. "Pay attention" was what he used to tell me. Well, I've been paying attention, and now I am so filled up with what I've learned that I'm beginning to sicken with it. Do you know what I talked to Isaac about, the last words we had? Whether I should end all this – the bank. Just walk away. I don't care, Doctor. About any of it. Let the emperor and the pope claw each other to bits.'

'With your money paying for the show,' said Michael, gently.

'Listen. I will gather all the money in the bank, pile it in the middle of a field in Lombardy, and let Guelphs and Ghibbelines tear themselves to pieces over it. Isaac was all that was left of the *Cormaran*, Doctor. Now he's gone, there's no point to any of this.'

'Ah, but you won't.'

'Will I not?' I demanded.

'You cannot. You are caught, my poor friend, at least for a while. And that is what I came to warn you about. The pope is going to use you to force Louis's hand against Frederick. And you might say, then let them kill me, like they killed Isaac. But they won't. They will torment you, Petroc. Even if you kill John of Toledo, they will let you live, so that they can make your life a living hell.'

'They would not catch me. And why? Why do you predict all this horror for me?'

'Listen to me. Even if the pope himself caught you with Cardinal John's guts in your hands, he would let you go. As you've understood yourself, you are worth a thousand Cardinal Johns. If the Curia arrested you and convicted you of murder –

or heresy, or whatever else – and confiscated your estates, would they get all that you are worth?'

'Of course not,' I scoffed. 'I'm a banker, Michael. I have more secrets than the Sphinx, now.'

'Precisely. They will keep you alive so that they can find out your secrets and punish you for them, one by one. Who do you love? They will find out, and destroy them. They will leave you standing in the midst of a burned wasteland, and only then will they start on you. Innocent intends to do that to the emperor – the emperor, Petroc! You are just one common banker, with many, many things that would interest the Inquisition on your conscience, many crimes, of body and of spirit. I do not judge you, but they will, they certainly will.'

'What exactly would you have me do?' I cried, helplessly. He was right, curse him. I stood in the middle of the street, fingernails digging into my palms, hopelessness settling upon me like the snows of Greenland. 'Choose your side? Pay for you to make that Drug of yours? Buy you the end of the world?'

'If only it were that simple,' said Michael. 'Forget the Drug. The Mussulmen know of it, and have used it in their wars, but it is still a weak thing, a flash and a bang to scare the peasants. Frederick was excited by it – one of his fly-by-night passions – and Nibelungus was trying to make it more powerful, but . . .' He sighed. 'There was no more skilled alchemist,' he went on. 'Even he could not control the thing, and I am too old to try. Frederick will abandon this scheme on my advice. Let the cardinal and his spies fiddle with the recipe if they wish – nothing will come of it. However, they will terrify themselves, believing that we have some terrible secret. No, I'm afraid the emperor's true strategy is something of a let-down compared to the Drug. He simply intends to let Innocent make such a fool of himself that the other princes of Christendom abandon him or even knock him off his throne.'

'Really, Michael? That doesn't seem very likely. The Church never gives up, as you've just been assuring me.'

'We shall see. Innocent has already run off to Lyon. But now I must run off as well.' He reached out and took my hand, turning it over as if he would read my palm. 'It has been lovely to see you, Petroc. I believe I told you we should meet again.'

'Yes, you did: in Venice. Christ, that would be ten years past,' I said. 'But . . .' I peered under his cowl. Grey eyes gazed back at me. The hairs on the nape of my neck pricked: the man looked no older, I would have sworn it. And I realised that I had not been very surprised to see him, up on the hill, as if we were friends who strolled together all the time. 'Time behaves strangely around you, Doctor Scotus,' I muttered, stepping back, though he still held on to my hand. 'Ten years . . . I have changed, haven't I? The years have been gnawing at me like rats. And you, you're no older, though surely . . .'

Michael laughed softly. 'And no younger, my friend, no younger. Now I am going to advise you, and advice from the necromancer . . .' He smiled, and again my neck-hairs stood up.

'My warning you've heard. My advice: go home. Mourn Isaac. Your time is coming, Petroc. You have grown very great – a tall, tall tree in this thicket of fools. When the storm comes, you will feel it, never fear, no matter if you have chosen one side, or the other, or none. Prepare yourself, my old friend. Make sure your roots go deep. Wrap them round ancient stone, or better still, anchor them on love. And trust. Hold these things close, if you have them, and if you do not, find them quickly. You do not have much time.'

He released me, and turning, slipped into the crowd that, naptime over, had surged out into the yellowing light of a waning day. He was gone in a moment: his grey cowl, which I thought to see bobbing away above the river of heads, for

Doctor Scotus was unbowed, however many years were upon his shoulders, was nowhere to be seen.

I breathed in the rich air of creation and decay that is a summer city: food, rubbish, shit. And looking round, saw that I was just across the street from the shoemaker I had set out to find so many days ago, though I had thought we were in quite another quarter of the city. I saw a sheet of leather the colour of ragged-robin flowers, and found myself wondering if Iselda would like it.

Chapter Five

I took Michael Scotus's advice. As if the old man had drawn the rage from my body, I found myself too sad, too tired for revenge. It could wait. Let John of Toledo be comfortable. I could kill him if I chose, with nothing more than quill and ink. That day I went back to Isaac's grave, the next day I bought shoes for Iselda, and the day after that I left Florence for home.

I left young Blasius in charge of the bank, though I had not had any time to teach him the finer points of the business. He, on the other hand, was eager to see me gone, for he had changed from the whey-faced cleric I had known to a hard-eyed, tight-lipped man with a certain bounce in his step that should have annoyed me but instead I rather liked. Ambitious, stubborn, certainly devious, as his eventual solution to the Genoese loan showed – yes indeed, I did like him. So rather to my surprise, when I set out from Florence on the Bologna road, I was easy in my mind so far as what I left behind me was concerned.

No, it was that which lay ahead, beyond the high ridge of the Apennines, beyond the miles and miles of bad, steep roads. I wanted nothing more, now, than to see Iselda again, but after that the future began to tremble and distort, to fade into the grotesqueries and repetition of a fever dream. As I climbed up towards the Futa Pass, where the land of the Tuscans meets that of the Emilians, I tried to keep my mind empty and serene, which I usually found easy in that high country of pines and ravens. But instead it kept returning, like a skulking, guilty dog, to the advice I had received, unasked, from an enemy: get married.

Marriage. What did Iselda and I care about marriage? We lived as man and wife quite openly in the Ca' Kanzir, and anyone who cared to pry into our affairs (and as we lived in Venice, where prying is the favourite pastime of rich and poor alike, there were plenty who did) had known this for years. How many of even the most respectable Venetians had been married by a priest? Not all of them, not even most of them. We were hardly different in our own arrangement. In as much as we believed in anything of heaven and hell, we believed what Iselda's father had taught us: that God is not interested in our fleshly exploits one way or the other. Neither blessed nor damned, we did what pleased us. And we were happy.

So why should the pope care? What business was it of Frederick von Hohenstaufen? I was a banker, and that meant I was hardly respectable in any case. One step up from a Jew, as Isaac was fond of reminding me. Well, that suited me. Having lived from hand to mouth for so long, and travelled so far with no home at all, I found it a small miracle that the same faces greeted me every day at the Ca' Kanzir. Not very ambitious for a man of my stature, but now that I could have whatever I desired I found I did not want much more than that.

I did not care to be wed – fine. But as my horse trudged up the rough road, as chestnut trees gave way to pines around me, I began to wonder about Iselda, and then I started to become uneasy. Had I ever asked her what she wanted? Had she perhaps told me and I hadn't heard, hadn't paid attention? Christ, it was possible.

It had been the captain's dying wish, laid out in letters and legal devices, that Iselda, his natural daughter, and I, his adopted son, should inherit all of his possessions, his wealth and his business interests. And when we sat down at last in his chamber in the Ca' Kanzir and took stock of our inheritance, we found that we were rich as kings. Exactly that – indeed we were far richer than many. Iselda was my business partner, as the captain had intended. At first there had still been some relics to sell and to buy – or *translate*, as we said, so that the Church could not arrest us for simony – and Iselda seemed to enjoy that as much as I did myself. It was devious and under-handed and fun, selling fakes to rich cardinals, and every time we took their money and set them to worshipping some old bit of withered monkey leg or leper's skull we felt a tiny pinch of satisfaction, as the captain would have done, for shooting one more little poisoned dart into the corrupt flesh of Mother Church. But as time went on, it was the bank that brought in our money and took up our time, and as for the captain's old trade, it seemed that I was finished with the relic business.

It was Iselda's misfortune to have a quick and ordered mind, and to her horror she discovered a hidden talent for keeping accounts and divining the ebb and flow of trade in the endless lines of ink that ran through our ledgers and our lives. She was beautiful and charming, of course, and that did no harm, but the truth was that she found it easy to keep clearly in her head the great tangle of trades and accountings, incomings and outgoings and all the other abstractions to which the Company of the *Cormaran* had been reduced. I suspected it was because of long years spent memorising songs and poems that she could store up all these dry, disjointed facts and figures and bring them forth exactly as needed; a skill it had taken me half a lifetime to master, and then badly.

That was why I travelled alone these days. Every year I would make at least two journeys to Florence to check on the bank, and sometimes I would be called to Rome or even to

Lyon. Iselda craved the freedom of travel, but now when I travelled she stayed in Venice, dealing with the business there. As I always did, before I had set off on this journey I had begged her to come with me.

'You know I can't,' she had said. I had found her in one of the storerooms, checking an inventory. 'One of us has to stay here.'

'All right, why don't you go instead of me?'

'Don't be ridiculous, my love.' With a flick of her wrist, she had cut open a hemp sack and thrust her hand inside, drawing out a handful of long pepper spikes. 'Look at this.' She held it up for me to smell. It was dusty, tarry, and then the scent opened up as her hand warmed the fruit. 'So beautiful. It comes from Kodungallur. Do you know where that is?'

I shook my head. 'India,' I said. 'But where in India, I don't know.'

'India is vast – that's what the traders say.' Iselda breathed in the pepper and let it trickle back into its sack. 'If you were going to Kodungallur, I would come with you, dearest. But Lyon? I've been there. Go soon and come back quickly.'

Apart from the exotic consolations of spice and silks, she hated the business as much as I did, but the customers and clients adored her, and it was Iselda who they wished to deal with, while I was forced to journey alone. And without her for company, I found that, more and more, my travels up and down the lands of Italy did not delight me as they might have done before. When I was away from Iselda I longed only for the day when we would be together again.

Meanwhile, the more Iselda learned, the more she grew trapped, for it was our misfortune that the captain had created, whether he had meant to or not, a business that had grown into a great organisation spread over twenty or more realms and domains, all held together with gold and with ink, until we were caught like weak spiders in their own web. We could

66

not escape. We didn't dare to. And that was it: when I caught sight of myself in the silver mirrors of our palace I saw a man who was ageing well, though much scarred by life, but in his eyes something I did not like to name, for I was afraid that it was cowardice.

I reached the Furta Pass and began the long descent towards the plains of Emilia and Lombardy, lost beneath a golden haze of fog in the mornings and dust at the day's end. I was travelling alone, which was my habit. I was not carrying any gold, and the important papers had been sent by courier ahead of me. I had long since stopped worrying about bandits, and in those years the trouble between Rome and the emperor had put many soldiers on the roads, and the robbers had either joined them or slunk off into the chestnut forests. I reached Bologna in good time, stayed for an indulgent dinner and set out the next morning with my liver chiding me for all that I had subjected it to. But one cannot pass through Bologna without testing one's digestion, so I calmed it with one of the vile herbal tinctures they make in those parts and worried, for a while, that I was getting old.

My habit, and as I had made this journey many times in the past few years it was a habit indeed, was to ride north from Bologna to Ferrara, from there to Rovigo and then head east to Chioggia, where I would take a boat across the Lagoon to Venice. But when I reached Ferrara I heard that there was trouble in the flat country south of the Lagoon, and so I decided, reluctantly, to make for Padua and come to Venice by way of Mestre. It was late September by then, and the weather was fair and golden, so this did not seem like much of a hardship. Padua was a stronghold of the emperor, but that was of no concern to me. I had clients there and all over Lombardy, and I had always come and gone as I pleased. So when I rode into Padua I went straight to my usual lodgings, a welcoming tavern near the river with good food and linen that was almost always free of vermin. The innkeeper, a somewhat cadaverous man with thinning black hair and large, jutting ears, gave me the best room in the place and called, loudly, for the best goose to be killed in my honour.

It was late afternoon. I knew of a respectable bathhouse nearby where I would not be bothered by whores or ganymedes, and there I passed a drowsy hour, scrubbing days of road dust and horse-sweat from my body. I could afford to have a tub to myself, and I basked in the deep, hot water, idly stretching out the stiffness from my limbs. I noticed, with a twinge of something I could not put a name to, that my waist was growing thicker, and the familiar terrain of muscle had, without my realising it, been swallowed up by a smug layer of fat. My chest, too: there was a drooping, not much but still a surprise. And, God! How white I was! But what had I expected to see? The lad who had slept on the deck of the *Cormaran* in all weathers? The man who had criss-crossed the mountains again and again, homeless as a petrel, carrying gold and promises between Constantinople and Paris; or the wretch who had endured the endless winter of Montségur's death? I saw none of them. I was getting old, that was all.

Not very old, I told myself, ducking my head underwater and scratching out the nits who had jumped aboard my scalp in a drab way-station at Monselice. By my reckoning I had lived through thirty-two years, many of them better forgotten, and if I had let the good life add a bit of ballast to my belly, hadn't I earned it? But I didn't feel entirely settled within myself as I dried off and put on my clean clothes. What was I going to be fed tonight? Goose? With gruel, cheese and endless porky confections, no doubt. At least I still had some of the repulsive tonic I had bought in Bologna.

I strolled back to the tavern through the gathering dusk, the light turning amber and the cats beginning to stretch themselves on walls and window sills. Inside, I nodded to the innkeeper, not really noticing him, and wandered towards the big room where dinner was no doubt waiting. But as I reached the doorway there was a wild outburst of throat-clearing behind me and I turned, expecting to see the innkeeper choking on a fishbone.

But instead I found myself looking at four big men in the red and white livery of the city guards. They wore leather hauberks under their surcoats and their hands were on their sword hilts. They were not smiling, and neither was the innkeeper, who had gone as pale as an eel's belly and was pulling on his fingers as if they were a goat's udders.

'Petrus Zennorius?' The shortest man, who was taller than me, stubble-headed and beady-eyed, spat my name. Someone or something appeared to have been chewing on his ears, and they throbbed, redly. I looked him up and down and, though I didn't like what I saw, nodded with reluctant politeness.

'Come with us, please.'

'What for?' I had no reason to expect trouble, and I could not for the life of me imagine why I was being taken by the guards. But I was not very worried, for no doubt a coin or two would smooth this ripple in a rather comfortable day. I reached for my purse absently, and at once two of the men lunged at me and grabbed my arms hard just above the elbows, while the stubble-headed one relieved me of my knife.

'As I said, come with us.' No please this time. Hard fingers were digging into my arm muscles, and I could feel my shoulder sockets beginning to protest.

'I am coming,' I said, with all the haughty indignation I could dredge up. 'And you'd better have other ways to earn your living, my lads, for I'll see you slung out of the guards.' The fingers dug deeper, but the leader narrowed his eyes, pursed his cracked and wine-stained lips and gave a grudging nod. His mates let go and I shook the blood back into my arms. 'Did you cook my dinner yet?' I asked the innkeeper. He shook his head, looking as if he badly needed to go to the privy. 'Then keep it for me.' I handed him a couple of silver pieces. 'And take care of my horse.'

So I retraced my steps through the narrow streets, darker now, a wall of cloud bearing down from the mountains to the north, more people about, slinking out of our path and spitting behind us as we passed. The city guards, then, were not the favourite sons of Padua. Guards are never loved, but in Padua there was good reason to keep out of their way, for these walking sides of meat in their red and white surcoats that made them look like misplaced crusaders served a man called Ezzelino da Romano, and even in those days mothers were scaring their children with that name. Eat your supper, or Ezzelino will get you. Well, apparently he had got me.

Ezzelino da Romano, *podestà* of Padua, was Frederick von Hohenstaufen's most powerful lieutenant in his endless wars on the plains of Lombardy. Ten years ago I had seen the smoke rising across the Venetian Lagoon when Ezzelino's army had ravaged the country between Treviso and Chioggia, and heard the stories of atrocity and shame wailed in the wine shops and marketplaces. The man was a byword for torture and massacre – if you were of the Guelph persuasion, that is. Ghibbelines liked to call him a liberator and a paragon of justice. Being neither, but having learned long ago that paragons are usually monsters anyway, I felt less and less happy the closer we got to the palace.

I had expected to at least be given a chance to pay my bribes, but instead I was taken up a narrow stone staircase, up and up, the big men starting to pant and sweat malodorously, to a small landing under the beams of the roof, and shoved through an open door into a small room. The door slammed behind me and a key was turned impatiently in the lock, and when I turned I saw nothing but old oak and rusty iron bands.

Sounding very far away, the guards were swearing their way back downstairs. I looked around the cell. It had a low-beamed ceiling, a tiled floor and bare stone walls. There was a small window covered with a crude lattice of ironwork. A pallet of straw lay against one wall, and there was a three-legged stool such as you might find in a barn, and a bucket. 'Where's the cow?' I said aloud, but the stone made my voice sound hollow and tinny. I jiggled the door handle. Locked tight. Feeling as though the walls were watching me, I sat down reluctantly upon the milking stool, but it was too low and I stood up again. There was a sudden soft noise from outside. It had begun to rain.

A fat, pallid moth hung above the narrow window of the *podestà*'s dungeon, pumping its flaccid grey-pink body as it waited for the night to come. Outside, Padua seemed to crouch under a cold drizzle that had swept down like a winding sheet from the mountains. The insect was a hawk moth. He had hatched too late, and tonight he would either freeze to death or end up in a bat's stomach. I watched him as the light failed, and after a while I decided that he already knew his fate and was making the most of these idle hours, enjoying his blood as it coursed through his brand-new body while he had the chance. I closed my eyes and listened to the knocking of my own heart and wondered what fate intended for me.

I would never have let the emperor kidnap me had I not been softened up by good fortune. Like tough meat in a bath of wine, the river of gold that had carried me along through the winter and into spring had marinated me in its warm luxury until I was as tender as a milk-fed calf. And like a calf I had trotted smiling into unlooked-for disaster.

The auguries were not good. No one wanted to become one of the involuntary guests of Ezzelino da Romano. As Frederick's pet monster, all sorts of whispered rumours attended him, a recent one being that he donated his prisoners for the experiments of the emperor, who, everybody knew, liked to look inside living men to find out how their innards worked. I didn't want to know how my innards worked. I'd seen enough of other people's, spilled, reeking, rotting. I'd seen a lot of death. As the rain dripped from the window frame and the night came on in bruised gloom, I told myself that I wasn't going to die, not in Padua, anyway. But I could have been in a cheerful room, eating goose and drinking wine, and instead I would have to piss in a bucket and sleep on damp straw.

The air was dead here in my dungeon. So much for escaping my responsibilities. Tired of watching the moth throb and flex its soft, crumpled wings, I closed my eyes and conjured Iselda's face from the darkness. Her pale skin, which the sun turned nut brown, she kept shaded with the thick tresses of her black hair – except that it was not black, but in the light was shot with colours I never saw twice: garnets, old honey, the glimmerings of the peacock butterfly's eye. Her lips were full and dark – wine-stained, I would tease her – and she had a strong chin, a little of her father showing there, and in her nose. But it was her eyes that I tried to find now. Green, they were, like moss seen through the golden water of a Dartmoor brook, and deep.

But to see their depths you had to be lucky – or loved. Iselda had spent her life wandering, and very early, so she had told me, she had learned to hide within herself, to make her face and body nothing more than an accessory to her voice, so that the men for whom she sang could forget she was a woman on her own, forget everything but her words. And if that failed? 'I was clever, and it did not fail,' she might have said. 'And besides, I had a knife.' She never had to use it, so far as I knew, for her audience had been noble, the tattered remains of Languedoc's gilded days of peace and fortune, and because she sang the songs of a dying time in a way that brought it back, however briefly, into the light of a dangerous, suspicious age, the nobles treated her as one of their own.

I had fallen in love with Iselda's voice before I had ever seen her face. Cold and yet beautiful, as lovely as notes from a golden harp yet drenched in its own sense of implacable loss, it had caught me one icy morning in the keep of Montségur. She had been singing for herself and for the dawn, an old song of mourning for love that cannot reveal itself to the light of day. But I had been a soldier then, and more than a year passed, of endless days filled with death and dragging, fearful misery, before we spoke again. And then I had lost her once more. Perhaps I had changed after that – nay, I know I had. The two people I had loved most in the world were dead, the men who could have been my father and my brother. The woman I had once thought I'd marry had wed another man. So I went looking for Iselda, because Captain de Montalhac, just before he died, had asked me to find his daughter; and because, out of all the ruin and horror of Montségur, of all the memories I had struggled to evict from my mind, I had preserved the memory of her voice. I found her in the autumn, and she had smiled at last, and let me glimpse what lay behind her eyes. And then she had sung for me, only for me.

I slipped uneasily into a shallow kind of sleep that I was shaken out of several times in the night by noises outside: a door slamming, a bell being rung, a dog barking so insistently that the noise wormed its way inside my head. Once I got up and went to the window. Still raining softly, and the moth had gone. I wrapped myself in the rough blanket and dozed unpleasantly until dawn.

The sun came in and warmed the miserable little cell, which in truth was not really so miserable. Men are thrown into far worse places. Dear God, I even had a stool of my very own. I told myself to act grateful as I sat down to wait. And wait I did, while more bells rang and other dogs pleaded or threatened at the tops of their lungs. Six bells, seven. Nine.

It was a little before the tenth hour of the day that muffled steps sounded outside my door and the key thrust into the lock so hard that a little cloud of rust drifted out into the cell. The door swung open to reveal the crop-haired fellow from yesterday. His ears looked a little more chewed, and perhaps invisible imps were nibbling them as he stood there, as he look pained, indignant and furious at the same time. So it was an unexpected surprise when he produced Thorn and held her out to me, hilt first. I rose cautiously from my ridiculous stool and took the knife.

'If Messer Zennorius would like to accompany me,' he rasped, and gave a painful little bow.

'To where?' I asked, tucking Thorn away in my belt and brushing the straw off my clothes.

'I am to take you to the audience chamber,' he said. Then he simpered, an unpleasant sight, but now was not the time to ignore convention and so I dug in my purse and gave him a good piece of silver. Then I followed him back down the stone stairs, across a small courtyard and into the palace itself.

As I followed the guard I was guessing what would happen next. An audience? They had given me back my weapon, so presumably I had not offended anyone too deeply, or unwittingly broken any Paduan laws. I supposed that I was about to meet Ezzelino's chamberlain or some other high functionary, who I would have to bribe, most likely. Or perhaps there was some favour that the city needed doing, and the chance arrival of one of Venice's richer businessmen – Padua and Venice were then at each other's throats, at least in theory, but it did not ordinarily affect trade – had given Ezzelino the chance to annoy his rival.

We had passed under a pointed doorway and into a long hallway hung with richly sombre weavings – surprisingly tasteful, I noted professionally, for the furnishings of a famous monster – and then through another archway. There the guard halted and looked me up and down, eyes narrowed worryingly.

'I should straighten your clothes if I was you, sir. You're going to see the emperor.'

Chapter Six

My mouth lost every drop of moisture, as if I had just breathed in the burning air of the African desert. Frederick von Hohenstaufen. Since I was a child, his name had flickered through my life like fire through fields of stubble, strange and terrible images coming and going through the smoke of ignorance. Even in Devon the monks of my monastery had picked up threads and tatters, which they had woven into grotesque tapestries of fable. In the cloisters they would pronounce, ominously, on that great lord who ruled lands they would never see, nor even find on a map. Depending on what peddler or cleric brought the news, the emperor became a bold crusader, a godless tyrant or the Antichrist himself. Over the years he blossomed in my own mind until he resembled nothing less than the many-armed, many-headed idol from the spice kingdom of Tamilakam that Captain de Montalhac had bought from a spice trader in Jaffa and which now stood on my writing desk.

I was not ready to meet such a creature of fantasy, not without breakfast, not without a goodly swallow of wine. But no such thing was forthcoming as the guard swept me along in his lumbering, angry wake, through the halls of Ezzelino's palace, past glowering courtiers and cringing guards, and into the *podestà*'s own chambers, a suite of rooms on the first floor lit by high, pointed windows in the style of Venice. There was a magnificent Cairo rug on the floor on which a huge dog lay, half-hidden in a pile of large Saracen cushions. And there, lounging in a chair, fondling the ears of a brindled wolfhound, I first saw the Wonder of the World, *stupor mundi*, Frederick II von Hohenstaufen. He looked up in mild surprise, and rose to his feet.

He was tall: that struck me first. Tall and elegant. He had straight fair hair fading to grey – cut to the very needlepoint of fashion in a way that disguised the fact that it was quite thin – that framed his beardless face. It was not a young face, but still handsome, and my first thought was that I had seen it before. Frederick looked like nothing less than an ancient statue of the Romans, of the kind one can see lying tumbled in the weeds of the Campo Vaccino. He had piercing blue eyes, a high, lined brow and red, somewhat bony cheeks. His nose was straight and his chin jutted, and his mouth was thin but curved like a Saracen's bow. I saw age there, and wisdom, and a lifetime spent in the burning sun of Italy. But not cruelty. The blue eyes alighted on me, unblinking, alarmingly birdlike for a moment, and I swallowed in sudden fear. Then he did blink, and I realised that I had been regarded, not with malign intent, but with a ferocious intelligence, an almost inhuman keenness. And yet the emperor had stepped across the room and was smiling, half approving, half amused, at the most extravagant and courtly bow I was making before him.

'No need for that,' he told me, and indicated that I should rise. His voice was that of an Italian, but there again was a keenness, a northern tension behind the southern warmth. 'And no time. We understand we are keeping you from your beloved.'

'I was on my way home, yes, Your Majesty,' I replied. 'But I have lost no time at all. A lame horse would have caused me more delay.'

Thankfully, the emperor laughed. 'And your lodgings?'

'I have spent perhaps the greater part of my life in less comfort than that which your *podestà* has so far shown me. A roof and a dry bed is the greatest blessing a traveller may wish for.'

'Ha. Spoken like an Englishman. How do you like Venice, Master Petroc?'

I was startled, but hid it with an extravagantly airy, indeed Venetian, gesture. To the world I was Petrus Zennorius, for I had laid Petroc of Auneford to rest many years ago, along with the price on his head. In truth I wondered if anyone cared any longer about a murder done so many years ago, and I had fortune enough now to buy off judge, jury and hangman. But to hear my true name on the lips of the Wonder of the World gave me a shock. And the question itself . . .

'The Serenissima is the whole world boiled down to a seething tar and poured onto a clutch of tiny islands,' I said. 'To a man of my profession such a place is a gift beyond words. And yet I grow tired of it very easily. I would say that I love the open road more than I love Venice.'

I had told the truth, and thankfully it seemed to please the emperor. Venice was less of a thorn than a viper's fangs in the embattled flesh of the empire. She had aligned herself with Rome out of self-interest, and though Frederick had trounced the republic in battle, she never ceased to plot and connive against him.

'A man such as yourself. What manner of man would that be?' The emperor's blue eyes narrowed. It was plain to see why his emblem was the falcon. I felt myself observed as if from a great height. The gaze that tirelessly swept the lands of Italy had momentarily alighted upon me, and I felt no more comfortable than a field mouse on a new-ploughed field.

'I am a businessman,' I told him. 'No more, no less. Your Majesty knew my late mentor, Jean de Sol, I think?' He nodded, sharp eyes hooded for now. 'He taught me his trade and gave me his knowledge, though I fear I am too small a vessel to hold all that he tried to pour into me.'

'I heard that Master Jean had left this earth,' said the emperor. 'It is a loss, a true loss. He died at Marseille – a sickness, I heard.'

'It shocked us all,' I agreed. 'He was a strong man, and yet he was carried off—'

'He had vanished, however, before that,' Fredrick continued, cutting me off. What did he know? I could read nothing in his face, nothing that showed he knew that Captain Michel de Montalhac had died from a wound he had taken at Montségur. Yet somehow I guessed that he did know. Frederick had made vague promises of help to the Cathars, but no help had ever come, and I had long supposed it had been the captain who had asked him for aid. Was this a challenge, now, or some strange, adamantine sympathy?

'Jean de Sol only made a part, a very small part of himself visible to the world, Your Majesty. A man whose true self is invisible cannot vanish. I loved him as a son loves his father, and I can tell you that he left this life as one who leaves an old friend to seek for new companions.'

'Did he pass on his secrets?' said the emperor, and I saw something dart across his face, a tremor of something . . . greed, perhaps. Then I understood the man. Necromancers, alchemists, Baghdadi astrologers: his lust was for the hidden, for the secrets beyond secrecy. I had heard all the stories: how he fed men, had them killed and then rummaged through their guts to see what became of the food; how he placed infidels above good Christian men; how he had men like Michael Scotus in his employ. I had never doubted any of these slanders. Would it not be a good idea to know what process transmutes wholesome food to shit? It is our very own alchemy, but our insides are as mysterious to us as the centre of the earth.

I knew many infidels who were the better of most Christians. And of course I liked Michael Scotus, who I supposed was his companion in these explorations. But I knew that look, and the lust it betrayed. Knowledge is where true power lies, and those who understand this can be the most dangerous creatures in all of creation. This was no ordinary prince of the kind I had come to know well, men fashioned from a coarse mix of greed, honour and piety. I would have to tread very lightly around Frederick von Hohenstaufen.

Meanwhile, I answered his question. 'No,' I said, blandly. 'Save for one, and she is no secret any more – indeed, I believe I shall have to marry her.' To my relief, Frederick gave a well-bred laugh. So he knew all about Iselda. Well, of course he did. Michael Scotus would have told him everything about us.

Frederick clapped his hands and called for food and wine. The servant who had been standing silent as a log in the corner of the room vanished through the door. Frederick stalked across the floor to his chair, and indicated with a graceful sweep of his arm that we should sit on the cushions that lay scattered on the carpet. He sat with practised ease, and I sank down gingerly, taking care not to plant myself too close to the snoring hound. But soon I found myself relaxing into the cushions and feeling calmer than I had since my supper had been denied me last night. The emperor did not question or probe. Instead he set about putting me at my ease with cultured expertise. We talked a little about Venice, not just politics and gossip, but things that apparently interested us both – the mosaics in the basilica of Saint Mark, new buildings along the Grand Canal. He had been there only once, fifteen years ago, but he remembered much. The Venetian blend of Italian and Greek reminded him, he told me, of his city of Palermo, and that led us to Constantinople and my memories of that wrecked giant. Frederick enquired after his impecunious cousin Baldwin, Emperor of Constantinople, and shook his head at my news of the tribulations and miseries of the Latin Empire. That brought us to Michael Scotus, and we discussed that strange creature with a certain shared affection, though of our recent meeting I said nothing. We talked of seafaring, of Moorish poets and of the foods of different lands – our own food arrived just in time, for the rumblings of my stomach had caused the hound to open a large, yellow eye – and then of my homeland, which he regretted he had never seen. I told him a little of Dartmoor, in which he showed polite interest, and more of London, which engaged him a good deal more. He told me some rather scurrilous gossip about King Henry, and I let slip something I had heard about a well-known cardinal, which made him chuckle delightedly. And so the conversation described a gentle, companionable arc through matters arcane and trivial until I realised we were discussing Louis Capet's relationship with Pope Innocent.

'Dear Louis puts us all to shame with the depth of his faith,' the emperor was saying. I wondered if I was included in that 'us', or if he simply meant the cosy little family of those who ruled over Christendom. I agreed, though, and told him a couple of small anecdotes about the French king and his collection of relics. But Frederick steered us deftly back onto course.

'I find it astounding – a marvel, really, in these times – that Louis has decided he will not bow to Innocent. Extraordinary. Do you know, His Holiness tried to suggest that Louis make his crusade, not against the Holy Places, but against me?'

I did know, and made a small diplomat's contortion to show that I did, and that I was strictly neutral. Frederick was quick to put me at my ease again, and we both shook our heads over the strangeness of the world.

'Messer Zennorius, I understand you are a soldier of some renown. The field of Saintes did not cast a very flattering light on most, but one hears that you met the Sieur de Bourbon face to face and slew him. Have you been on crusade?' I said that I had not. 'Every Christian man should, you know,' he went on.

'Of course, but some of us are fated, alas, to reap the rewards of others' bravery,' I said modestly. 'I'm a reluctant warrior, Your Majesty. Having said that, I have been in enough fights to last any sensible man more than one lifetime, but . . . if you'll allow me, though, I must say I have always greatly admired your own crusading feats. To win back the Holy Places through diplomacy was, well, extremely Christian, I've always thought.'

'How very nice of you. What a shame that your sentiments aren't shared by those who consider themselves the arbiters of what passes for Christian zeal, however.'

He pursed his lips, as if something bitter had seeped into his mouth. He had every right to bitterness, I thought. The late Pope Gregory, the wizened spider who had manipulated the goings-on of Christendom for many years and had set himself against this man when he was young and full of promise, had hounded Frederick to fulfil his crusading vows, even excommunicated him, and when the emperor had gone off to Jerusalem at last, had waged war against his lands. And now the present arse warming the throne of Saint Peter had declared another crusade against him, claiming the emperor was a heathen while all the time it was as plain as day that the pope fancied himself an emperor in his own right and coveted the lands of the Hohenstaufens. Really, the more I thought about it, and the more time I spent with this mild, grave-faced man, the more I felt a rising indignation, a sense that I was, and had been all along, a Ghibbeline.

Someone came into the room with a plate of Turkish sweet-meats, and the hound raised its shaggy head and woofed, approvingly. 'Now, you are a friend of Louis Capet, I think?' said Frederick, passing me a tray of small almond cakes dusted with powdered Arab sugar. I demurred.

'I am a commoner, Your Majesty, whose fortune it has been to help a good and pious ruler bring some very holy things into his kingdom, to enrich it. Louis is, I believe, a friend to every good man, but I wouldn't presume to claim that friendship for myself.'

'Well, that was nicely put, but really, you are not without influence, are you? The Sainte Chapelle – one has not seen it, alas, but it is by all accounts one of the wonders of our age – could not have been built without your efforts. It is a reliquary, and you provided the relics.'

'Your Majesty flatters me, but really, I was simply fulfilling my vocation. Translating relics was my humble labour. But now that I own a bank . . .'

'You handle Louis's finances. I know, dear man, I know. But tell me: is Louis going on crusade? He is taking his time about it, though perhaps I should not scold him for that.' Frederick smiled ruefully, as if to admit that it had taken him eighteen years to fulfil his crusading vow, and Louis was hurtling onwards by comparison.

'He is, yes. I believe the army is already gathering at Marseille,' I said.

'So he is going to fight the Turk, not me,' said Frederick lightly. 'That is a relief.'

'Your Majesty, King Louis has always been very forthright with the pope – or so I hear – that it is wrong and unjust for the ruler of the Church to meddle in temporal matters,' I assured him, and immediately saw that I had given myself away. But Frederick pretended not to notice.

'And we thank him for it,' he sighed. 'My good man, I have taken up far too much of your time. You are on your way home. But, Messer Petroc, if you should have a change of heart and take the vow of a crusader – there's a chance for grace and glory, and an army of God about to sail, after all – it would not go unnoticed if you kept my cousin Louis's gaze away from me. Or perhaps you, as someone with great knowledge of the wants and needs – one might almost say *lusts* – of Mother Church, might even be able to turn his mind to the notion of a more deserving arse upon Saint Peter's throne? Pope Innocent makes alliances but not friends, and one day soon the balance of friend to enemy is going to tip, and not to his advantage. Meanwhile he is a wily man and not to be denied, and I fear he sees the great army that Louis has raised and would like it ravening through Christian lands, not infidel ones.' He rose to his feet, a little stiff in the knees, and the wolfhound unfolded itself and rose too. I stood and bowed, deeply. My audience was clearly at an end, and I felt that, hawk-like, the emperor's mind had turned to something else and I was almost forgotten, far, far below. But as I was turning to leave, his eyes focused upon me again.

'Might I give you some advice?' he asked. I nodded, disappointed, steeling myself for the request that was surely coming: lower interest rates for Imperial loans, or no interest at all . . .

'Marry your lady.'

'I beg your pardon, Majesty?' I stammered.

'Get married. It will do you no harm.'

'But—'

'But why do I give you this advice? Tell me: has Pope Innocent been sniffing around your affairs? Unwanted attentions, strange requests? One hears that a Jew was murdered in Florence. Your functionary . . .'

'My partner. My friend.'

'Quite so.' He raised a long and elegant finger to his face. The nail scratched once, twice, at the skin between his eyes. 'Are you a heretic, Messer Petroc?'

I almost jumped where I stood, so great was the nervous shock that thrummed through my limbs. But nothing showed, not one blink, no twitch to alert the wolfhound, who was watching me as intently as his master. Instead I forced my backbone to straighten, stiff as a pikestaff, and raised my chin a fraction – not defiant, of course not, but just a touch of injured piety.

'I am a Christian man, Your Majesty,' I uttered, my voice as stiff as my spine.

'A good Christian?' Something glittered in the depths of his eyes, but then it was gone. Perhaps I had imagined it. 'Nay, I know, I know,' said the emperor, chuckling good-humouredly. 'Of course you are. So am I, but yet the pope calls me heretic, devil, Mussulman, conjurer . . . It is his way, his wise and holy way. Good Lord, he has called a crusade against me, so I must be a heretic. You understand me, of course. Remove yourself from suspicion. Heretics do not get married in church, so one hears.' He cocked an eyebrow, as if daring me ask, *From whom does one hear it?* 'So find a bishop – nay, an archbishop – to marry you. Make a lot of noise about it. That, my good man, is how I should advise you.'

'Thank you, Your Majesty.' I bowed, feeling the strain hiding in the back of my knees.

'I detect a certain resignation,' said the emperor with a half-smile. 'Have you heard this from others – your lady, perhaps?' I laughed ruefully.

'Perhaps . . . from my own conscience,' I said lightly. 'It shall be done, Your Majesty – if the lady will have me, that is!'

We shared a polite little chuckle over that, and then I was backing through the door, a free man. I caught a final glimpse of Frederick von Hohenstaufen, fondling the ears of his hound, the sunlight shining through his thinning hair. Then a guard was politely ushering me away, and I followed, gratefully.

I was making my way back to the inn, where I intended to take a flagon of wine to bed with me and sleep the rest of the day away, when a long shadow detached itself from the gloom of an archway. Thinking to find another of Ezzelino's guards, I cursed and turned, arms up, already protesting. But instead, I found myself looking at Michael Scotus.

'Hello, Petroc,' he said.

'Doctor Scotus.' I folded my arms, feeling exhausted and peevish. 'Was this your doing?'

'Your interview with Frederick? Not at all. I told him to leave you alone, but the emperor, while fond of advisors, is not much given to heeding their advice. My guilt is in praising you, perhaps too much. Still, it wasn't so unpleasant, was it?'

'No. The emperor's condemned cells are sumptuous,' I said bitterly.

'A misunderstanding between the emperor's chamberlain and Ezzelino's captain of the guard,' said Michael, looking as stricken as his bony face would allow. 'I was in the countryside, otherwise it would never have happened. I'm truly sorry.'

I softened, reluctantly. 'What do you want, Michael?' I asked.

'You are worn out. I will not keep you,' he said. 'I wanted . . . I want to give you something. A gift, if you like. If you will have it.'

'This life makes us brutes, my friend,' I said. 'It is I who am sorry. Come with me to my lodgings. We will sit and talk.'

'Alas! No time. For you, for me. I must tell you something – words before the gift. You are not free, Petroc. It is the thing that eats at you, more hungrily than the years,' he said. I winced at his words, and a ripple of gooseflesh ran up my body, in spite of the heat. 'Now Innocent seeks to bind you yet further, but to use you, or to ruin you? That is for you to discover. But when I look into your eyes I see a snail inching its way along the edge of a newly sharpened sword. You are caught, by obligation to a dead man, to a living lord, to gold itself.'

'The snail can leave the edge and find the flat blade,' I said, queasily.

'But slowly, slowly, for the edge is already pressed deep into the flesh, though it has not yet cut.'

'What, in God's name, are you telling me?' I tried to laugh, but it sounded hollow.

The grey eyes searched my face, perhaps seeing where the years had clawed it. 'You have grown, Petroc. You have become very strong. We can all see the past – I can read it on your skin, and in everything around us. The present . . .' He held up a long finger, and blew upon it gently. 'The present is here. But the future. Soft flesh and hard steel: the snail crawls and its own motion kills it, cleaving in two as it inches onward, onward. The blade is the present: we all crawl along its edge. Those whose touch is light move further and live a little longer. But life presses us down onto the edge, buffets us from side to side. We balance – that is what you are learning. I see your flesh pressing upon the cruel edge, Petroc. Soon you will be bleeding, and then—'

'In God's name, Michael!' I cried. 'What is it that you want with me?'

'To tell you something, as a friend,' said Michael Scotus. 'Keep your balance. It will be hard for you. The world is out of kilter, and, my poor Petroc, you and your riches are one of the pivots upon which it teeters. It is the spirit of the age.'

'So it comes back to spirits after all. Do you remember, in Rome, what you showed me?'

'Something that was in your head.'

'Something more than that. You brought me to where the hidden things of the world converge.' Even in the light of a Paduan afternoon I shuddered at the memory: the Coliseum at night, the great bowl of stone, a fire burning at its centre, and in the flames . . . The emperor had chosen his necro-mancer well, for Michael Scotus had shown me the spirit of one I had loved, and she had spoken to me out of the flames, out of the spinning void of loss.

Now I felt it again: the stone beneath my feet becoming something insubstantial, until I was standing on the cobwebby weft that fences off the dead from the living, the strands of time itself. I felt myself teetering, searching for poise, my sense of what was up and what was down fading. Doctor Scotus's eyes were staring into mine, and with an effort I turned away and looked down. There were the worn flagstones of Padua, with their scabs of horse dung and dried spit. I took a deep breath.

'Did you feel it?' He smiled, tight-lipped. 'Ah. You did. There is a long way to fall, isn't there, if we do not keep our balance? And that is my counsel to you: this world is becoming a place of black and white. A man must be this, or else he is that. You, Patch, must be neither: use all your arts, all your artifice, to keep yourself from taking any side but your own. Be loyal to no one but yourself, and you might win through. I have managed it, though it has cost me somewhat.' He held up a hand and smiled at it wanly, and for a moment I thought I was looking through his flesh and bones as though he were a creature formed out of mist. 'We are not unlike one another, you and I. So I offer you my paltry advice. Somewhere between godly and godless, I should say, but lovingly meant.'

'It isn't in your interest to help me, Michael,' I said, gently.

'You are right. But that is my affair.'

'Thank you, though, for your . . . for your words. I'll be home soon. What should I do?'

'Whatever you can, to keep the steel from the snail's flesh. We have not spoken of this, you and I. Others will come to ask, but you can send them away. Tell them you've turned Guelph.' He chuckled grimly.

'And when the emperor has won, and Innocent is ridiculed

– if that ever comes to pass – what then? I'll be a Guelph in a Ghibbeline world.'

'I do not think so, Petroc. Perhaps you will be nothing.' He held up his hand again, fingers pursed like a flower bud, then opened it to reveal the emptiness within. But I thought I saw something on his palm: specks of light, thistledown-fine, vanishing up into the air. And yet . . . No, there was nothing there at all.

'What was it that Michel always told you? "Pay attention." Be careful,' he said softly. 'Be a shadow. Keep your feet, even if it means contorting yourself like a madman. We are all madmen, my lad.' I reached for his conjuror's hand and grasped it. The flesh was surprisingly, comfortingly warm, and I pulled the old man to me and embraced him.

'Goodbye, Michael Scotus,' I said. 'Will I see you again?'

'You may,' he said softly. 'You may.' And then he brightened. 'Ah, Petroc!' he exclaimed. 'There is something you can do. And you should, as soon as possible.'

'And what is that?'

'Get married,' he said.

Chapter Seven

The courtyard of the Ca' Kanzir smelled of hot tiles and young figs, a clean and optimistic scent under which lay the ancient, patient rot of Venice. I had come in by the canal door, a little shaky in the legs from the choppy Lagoon, across which I had just been sailed from Chioggia. The boatman had grunted my baggage up the slippery steps and dumped them in the doorway, against which he leaned, waiting for his tip. When he was gone I kicked the door closed behind me with my foot and greeted the serving man who was already busy with the bags. He looked as pleased to see me as any Venetian servant ever does, but as I had forgotten his name I reckoned that made us even. Telling him to take the bags up to my quarters, I went and leaned for a moment against the marble well-head that stood in the centre of the courtyard, the stone worn smooth and almost translucent by countless years, countless hands.

A shutter scraped and banged above me. I squinted into the midday sun.

'Patch! Come up!' Iselda's face was framed against the dark window opening, her hair loose and hanging against the pale grey stones. An ancient ivy clung to the wall, a great, straining sinew of knotted wood, and I fancied, for a moment, that I would clamber up it to my love, like some eager swain from one of her songs, but instead I waved and found myself running across the flagstones. The familiar mustiness of the Ca' Kanzir's ground floor enveloped me. Bales of silk were stacked against the walls, and a faint tang of pepper hung in the air, a shipment only just sold on, no doubt. I launched myself up the stairs, and found myself panting when I reached the long hall that ran the width of the palace. The year before, we had had the great open windows framed in delicate stone tracery, the very height of fashion – not so much to be creatures of that fashion, but because the stone had all but rotted away – and now, against the thin columns that curved up into little pointed arches all fretted as if bitten by giants' teeth, Iselda stood, the faint breeze from the canal stirring her black tresses. Another moment, and she was in my arms.

'My God, I've missed you so much,' I finally said into her hair. 'I can't—'

'Then don't. Now you're home,' she said gently. 'Come. Eat. Tell me stories.'

She led me to the dining hall, where Marta, the thick-limbed fisherman's widow who was our housekeeper, chamberlain and steward and ruled the old palazzo with a sensitivity at odds with her salty tongue, was laying out platters of food and pitchers of wine, ale and buttermilk. As I took my usual place in the big oak chair with its high back and carved arms, the chair in which Captain de Montalhac had once sat, I had that odd sensation that travellers sometimes feel when returning home after a long absence: that everything familiar was rushing into me, filling me up faster than I could think. I settled back and let the place welcome me.

But although I was happy for all the sounds and smells of home, for Iselda loading my trencher and Marta clucking over my travel-stained tunic, my mind was still on the road between Padua and Chioggia. I had ridden through curtains of rain that had trailed across the countryside like vast billowing lines of wet laundry, wave upon wave of them with blue skies in between, and all the while I had pondered, head down and rain dripping from my eyebrows, what Michael Scotus had advised me. Marry. Hide within the safe conventions of Mother Church. Emperor Frederick had said it too, and Cardinal John. As a particularly heavy shower had lifted I had kicked my horse into a trot and splashed through the puddles that mottled my way, all shining now as if the road were paved with mirrors. As I trotted I asked myself two questions: why, and why not?

I had decided, even before Padua, that the cardinal's advice had been floated before me in order that I might refuse or ignore it, thus giving the Holy See a hold over me and my business. *Petrus Zennorius consorts with Jews and keeps the household of a heretic – no smoke without fire, remember . . .* Indeed, in temporal matters the Church is as crude as it is subtle in matters theological, and for years now it had been bombarding Christendom with the vilest, wildest slanders and insinuations about the Holy Roman Emperor himself. Lies as much as force had hurt the empire, and if such a mighty edifice could be wounded, what hope was there for a commoner like me, no matter how wealthy I had become? If the pope wanted my money, he would get it, one way or another. And if Iselda and I were to marry, would that get Innocent off our backs? Not likely. But it might buy us some time.

As my skin started to chafe from the wet folds of my clothing, a gust of wind blew a veil of raindrops into my face, blinding me for a moment and blotting out everything: the dripping landscape and the ragged clouds, and my tumbling thoughts. Into that shocked, blank space came the words of Doctor Scotus: put down roots, anchor them on love. Three people had given me the same advice, but two of them cared only about my money. But Michael Scotus, I realised, cared not one hair for gold. He was telling me how to save my soul.

'Iselda, do you love me?' I said, without thinking.

Without thinking? But I was thinking: about Montségur. Four years ago we had stood at the edge of the burning place where the grass still stood up from the ground, though it was black and crunched to cinders beneath our feet. The wind had risen, and ash was rising in little whorls, thin columns that swayed and danced through the lengthening shadows.

I had picked up the sack, feeling the captain's bones slide and settle into the ash from the pyre. Just now, Iselda and I had scooped up two handfuls each, and let the almost weightless ash trickle through our fingers: two hundred lives, two hundred names, a faith burned to fine, grey dust. Now I offered my dusty hand to Iselda and she took it, so that together we stepped from the dead place into the living grass, tall and heavy with seeds: rich hay that no one had lived to harvest.

We rode back through the abandoned village, walking our horses slowly, as if we had silently agreed that clattering hooves might anger the unseen, who were everywhere, calling to us in the buzz of the flies, in the scolding of the jackdaws, in the trickle of water from the village spring. Even the smoke from their pyre had become a ghost, vast and heavy, blanketing everything in an invisible fog of desolation. As soon as we had passed the last empty hut we broke into a canter, and did not stop until we were down alongside the river, heads to the north, the *pog* of Montségur beginning to lose itself among the higher peaks that surrounded it.

It was late afternoon. We rounded a bend in the road, which had bent itself round an outcrop of rock, and saw our way ahead, straight and clear to the end of a wide valley.

'Look,' said Iselda suddenly, reining in. I shielded my eyes. In the far distance there seemed to be a smudge on the road. I squinted and blinked.

'Horsemen,' said Iselda. 'A troop of them.'

'Your eyes are better than mine,' I answered ruefully. 'Who are they?'

'I'm not an eagle, my friend,' she told me. 'But I think they are soldiers. I don't want to meet them. Do you?'

'No. Not here.'

'Right.' She wheeled her horse and led me back around the crag. Then she patted her horse and steered him off the road and down a steep bank. She seemed to be following a sheep track, and with some misgivings I urged my own horse after her. The bank led down to a little stream, and beyond that the ground sloped steeply up. Iselda was already climbing the stony hillside, bare save for patches of sage and rock roses.

'Do you know where you're going?' I called.

'Yes. There is a shepherd's hut up here, and then a track into the next valley. I found it last year.' She spurred her horse on and up, and I followed, my mare's hooves slipping on the pebbles. It was a long climb, but there was the hut at last, three rough stone walls and a stack of old furze for the roof. Iselda swung out of her saddle and threw the reins over a stone post that jutted out next to the empty doorway.

'We should eat,' she said. 'It is a long ride to the next shelter, and there is rain coming.'

I followed her gaze, and sure enough, the high peaks behind us were wearing caps of heavy grey cloud. I unhooked my saddlebag and joined Iselda where she sat, leaning against a bundle of old kindling. What a strange creature, I was thinking to myself: so beautiful, and she has sung for great lords and ladies, and yet she is quite at home out here – as much as I am myself. We were lovers by then, but in the way that people who have weathered some awful calamity often are: thrown together by need and by the bad dreams they share.

'Here,' she said, and held out a heel of bread. At that

moment the rain began to fall. A fat drop, an outrider of the squall that was about to swallow us, hit her on the forehead and ran down her nose. I reached out and brushed it off, and our eyes met. She smiled, for the first time that grim day, still holding out the bread. And I felt it inside me: inside my chest. Everything fell away: the grief, the appalling devastation, the dead we carried in our hands and in our heads.

'Iselda, I love you,' I said, taking her hand, feeling the bread crackle under our fingers. 'I love you – do you mind?'

'Oh God, Patch!' she said, and I thought I had spoiled everything, but instead she wrapped her other arm around me and pulled us together, as the storm hissed towards us, filling the air with the smell of wet stone. We fell back into the shelter and fed each other pieces of crushed bread as the world dissolved into seething grey, and when the sun came out again I could still feel her smile inside my chest, cupped like a gentle hand around my heart.

'Iselda,' I said now, 'if the pope himself ordered us to be married . . .'

'To each other?'

'Yes, to each other! Would you . . . ?' I took her hand, and she looked at me, surprised, unsuspecting. 'Would you marry me anyway? Because the pope wants to prove we are heretics, and heretics don't wed. And the emperor wants us free, so we can lend him money. And fuck 'em, every one.' Still holding her hand, and hoping as I'd never hoped before that the singular expression on Iselda's face was not horror, I slid off my chair and went down on my knees at her feet. 'But the thing is, my love, I want to. More than anything. If it had been the other way around, if the pope was going to cut off my head if I married you, I would still be asking: Iselda, will you be my wife?'

'I've been waiting,' she said, sinking down beside me. 'You

can look at me, Patch: it's yes. I'm saying yes. I would have waited for ever, you impossible man. To hell with the pope, and to hell with the emperor. I'll be your wife.'

Chapter Eight

A bird was trapped high in the arching void above the altar, fluttering panicked wings across the gold mosaic, the bearded saints with their pale, blandly offended faces. Dust drifted down in slow, shimmering cascades onto the mitre of the archbishop and the tonsured scalp of the deacon. It found its way up the nose of an altar boy, who was trying to stifle a sneeze. It speckled the Tyrian purple velvet of Iselda's sleeve and she brushed it away distractedly with the back of her hand. And as she did, the gold ring on her third finger caught a spark of light from a candle. The slow, dry rain fell past rising columns of incense and through the words of 'Gloria in Excelsis Deo'. A single shaft of the flat glare of Venice angled down and picked out the shoulder of Saint Clement.

I stole a sideways look at my wife. She was staring up and a little to the left, no expression on her face, her chin lifted ever so slightly. I followed her gaze but it led to nothing except the tracery of the rood screen. Behind us in the body of the basilica, people were shuffling their feet and clearing their throats apologetically. The archbishop was telling us about the wedding at Cana. I rubbed the sole of my shoe softly against the smooth marble of the floor, and a shard of stone embedded in the leather scraped, scraped. Time seeped past us. But we were married.

I had slipped the ring onto Iselda's hand less than an hour earlier, on the steps of Saint Mark's Basilica, before a crowd of cheering people we barely knew. Pigeons, annoyed by the fuss, wheeled through the gilded spikes of the cathedral. We had thought to get married, Iselda de Rozers and I, somewhere quiet and private, with only a priest – for even the godless require a priest to wed, such is the jesting nature of the world – but peace and quiet was not, from the beginning, to be our fate. And fate sent us, not a priest, but an archbishop and a personal message from Pope Innocent himself, delivered by a genuine Roman cardinal. But after all, we were two of the wealthiest folk in Venice and perhaps in all the lands that paid tithes to Rome, and privacy is hard to come by for people such as we had become. Waiting for us at home were gifts from a king, several princes, a whole conclave of cardinals and merchants too numerous to count. The Doge himself was waiting for us inside the basilica. As we stood there in our finery, enclosed in a fog of scent from the flowers that surrounded us, our only consolation was that we had spent our lives gnawing at the foundations of the very authority which was, at that moment, pronouncing us man and wife.

'Well, I don't feel any different,' said Iselda much later that day, when we were finally alone in our chamber. 'Do you?'

'Ach, it's worse than I thought it would be,' I laughed, picking at the gilding on a goblet, the gift of a Bavarian prelate. The gold was thick and genuine, more genuine than the apostle's head that Iselda's father had sold him. 'Not our being married,' I added quickly, 'but' – I threw the goblet onto the bed and picked up a candlestick – 'the rest of it.'

'Michel would . . .' Iselda paused. She was struggling with the lacing of her sleeves, picking at a stubborn knot with her nails. 'What *would* my father have made of it all?' she said, thoughtfully.

'Michel de Montalhac would have loathed it silently; Jean de Sol would have played the part to the very hilts and beyond,' I said. 'What, by the by, do you think the archbishop would have said if we'd told him we were brother and sister?'

'You vile thing!' laughed my wife.

'Well, it's true,' I insisted. 'I *am* your brother – ask a lawyer! But . . . wait, come here.' I pulled her to me and started to pick apart another troublesome knot while she perched on my knee. 'He would be delighted. He made me promise something, at the end. I have wondered what exactly it was that I promised for a long time, but, my love, I think I've fulfilled it at last.' I kissed her. Then I raised her left hand and kissed the new gold of her wedding band. She took a gentle handful of my hair and rested her forehead against mine.

'After such a traditional day,' she sighed, 'isn't there one more tradition we need to . . .'

'To observe? I believe there is, at that.'

Alas, a few laces were torn from sleeves, necks and hose, but suddenly we were in a hurry to discover if things felt different now that we were man and wife. 'We should get married more often,' I murmured, drawing the gown from her shoulders. The prelate's goblet was digging into my bum and I shoved it onto the floor.

'Is that rabble downstairs expecting to see a sheet with blood on it?' wondered Iselda, throwing a damp leg across my thighs. The Ca' Kanzir was still full, by the sound of it, with wedding guests draining our wine butts dry. The ancient place had not had so many people inside it since the First Crusade. But few if any of the well-heeled folk peering into our dusty corners were friends. Dimitri, last of the captain's old crew was there, no doubt terrifying the other guests. But the throng, whose babble was ringing in the stairwell outside our door like a cage full of geese, meant as much to us as had the endless marriage service we had lately endured. Business associates mainly – traders and merchants, bankers, more than a few higher functionaries from the Doge's Palace, a papal envoy and the French ambassador, who had brought gifts and a personal message of congratulations from the King of France himself.

'Here. This is my gift to you,' I said, remembering something. I padded over to the chest in the corner of the room and brought back a little twist of soft red leather. 'I wanted to give it to you earlier.'

She took it from me and shook the leather until it unravelled and dropped a slender golden shape onto the bed.

'Oh! It's beautiful,' she murmured, picking it up and letting it hang between us.

I had found it among her father's things when we had first come back to the Ca' Kanzir. It was a little stag wrought of pure, pale gold. The creature had antlers that spread along its back like the branches of an oak tree, and it reared up, one front leg tucked beneath it, its body twisting and flowing like water or flame. It had come from a tomb in the land of the Kumans, beyond the Black Sea, or so I guessed, for I had seen other things like it, from some journey the captain had made long before I had known him. I had hung it on a silken cord, and now I took it and slipped it over her head. The stag seemed to lie back against her skin, at rest.

Taking her in my arms again, I turned my face into the crook of Iselda's neck and inhaled the heat rising from her skin. 'And I'm glad we did it,' I breathed. Indeed, what was there to regret? Iselda was mine, I was hers, and now we did not have to pretend otherwise. I let myself sink into the soft bed, into gentle calm. Was this ours, now? Would our lives be spent cupped in this gentle safety?

'Now we're married,' said Iselda, slowly undoing her long, heavy tresses, 'does that mean . . . ?' She slid a bare foot under my bum and wiggled her toes.

'Mean what?'

'That it isn't a sin any more.'

I turned to her. She had shaken out the last cord of plaited hair, and dark wisps were clinging to her face and lips. I smoothed them away.

'You know the way we don't ever do it? The boring way?'

'Me counting the cracks in the ceiling, you mean?'

'Um hmm. Well, that's the only way that isn't a sin, even now. Even though we're man and wife.'

'No. Really?'

'Really. I used to be a monk, don't forget. I know all about it.'

'Then you'd better show me.'

Downstairs, the party was livening up. The good wine would be all gone by now, and our guests would be guzzling the bad vintage from Treviso. Iselda wrapped a leg around my waist and pulled me down onto the bed.

'Isn't it nice,' she said, before I quieted her mouth with my own, 'that this is still a sin, even though we've gone respectable?'

Chapter Nine

Nothing changed. After all the soul-searching and all the unasked-for pageantry of our wedding, everything was the same between Iselda and I. We did not love each other more, so far as we could tell. We certainly did not love each other less. At first I was surprised. 'Men are children': I have heard that more than once in my life, usually from women I was trying to impress. But like a child I found that I had been expecting magic. Everyone knows the story of Tristram and Iseult, how they drink the love potion meant for King Mark, and how their magically engendered love ends up destroying them both. Apparently I had expected something of the same from the archbishop's incantations, the choir, all that money . . .

But then again, perhaps something had changed. Down in Florence, Blasius was so capable that we found we could leave him to his own devices. All the things I had seen in him – efficiency, forward-thinking and a sort of veiled bloody-mindedness – were having an excellent effect on business, so much so that I diverted some of the less important Venetian clients to Florence. That left us with time to spend on matters that interested us, though they were not as lucrative as the bank: we had a small fleet of trading ships that went back and forth from the Levant and Alexandria, bringing cargoes of silk, pepper, ginger and cloves; and though we were not in the relics trade any more, if some puffed-up cardinal wanted something special, who was I to refuse? It was dabbling, really, but for the first time in years, Iselda and I were beginning to enjoy ourselves. The apocalypse that Michael Scotus had predicted seemed to be less threatening. Frederick von Hohenstaufen did not bother us, and neither did the Church. I knew what was happening in the world of polity, that there was a truce of sorts between pope and emperor, and I found it all too easy to see the dangers of the past year fading into memory. I had not forgotten Isaac. But I had learned, from my adopted father, that revenge can wait, if need be, for a long time.

And now that we were respectable, Venice wanted us. Invitations to parties and palaces came almost every day, and most we refused, not caring for the artificial world of fawning and being fawned upon. That seemed to make us more desirable, and so we ate with Dandolos, Zenos and Zorzis; and even Doge Tiepolo, who had nearly had me executed a long while ago, requested our presence at the great palace on the Molo.

But it couldn't last, and in June a letter arrived from our agent in Lyon. It told me that King Louis was due to be there, passing through on his way to the coast, for he was finally ready to go on his great crusade, and as the Banco di Corvo Marino was loaning him perhaps the greater part of the money for it, he wanted to settle some matters before he left. Could I meet with the king in person? It seemed reasonable. After all, there was a perfectly good chance that he might not come back from the Holy Land, and I wanted to know who was going to settle the bills if he didn't. Iselda sighed and said I must go, and then avoided me for the rest of that day.

'You could come too,' I said, after I had cornered her in the kitchens, examining some over-hung pheasants with the cook. To my astonishment, she dropped the smelly bird she had been prodding and shrugged her shoulders.

'All right,' she said. I almost fell over with surprise, and she laughed. 'The look on your face!' she went on, and led me downstairs to the storerooms.

'I've been thinking,' she continued, leaning against a fragrant sack of ginger. 'I hate this life, Patch. Let's be done with it.'

'With life?' I reached out and held her gently at arm's length, examining her face.

'No, no. But with this bloody . . . this bloody bank. And figures, and watery-blooded clerks with dewdrops hanging off their noses, and ledgers . . .' I pulled her to me again and held her as tightly as I dared, feeling the fineness of her bones within my own crude strength. She seemed as light as dandelion fluff, and yet in her arms, as always, I felt like a half-drowned sailor who, in the midst of storm and darkness, has miraculously laid hold of solid ground.

'If we're going to give it all up, why not start now? We'll go to Lyon, just the two of us. And then . . .' She smiled mysteriously. 'We'll go somewhere else. You can show me England – take me to that *Devon* you're always talking about.'

'I'm thunderstruck,' I said.

'So I see. Good! Now listen. I wish we could just take to the roads. I know this is supposed to be one of the centres of the world, but that just makes it stifling. I want to be out there!' She pointed towards the window, which faced east. 'And so do you. You are always muttering about the *Cormaran*, and all the things that happened to you in the mountains or in Constantinople.'

'I'm too old!' I protested, smiling as if I didn't mean it, but the truth was that I did, a little. Iselda was right: I wished for nothing more than to be out on the roads with her, in summer, riding across the hills above Spoleto or through the water meadows of France. Or over the high moors of my home, to where the land flattened into a soft plain of brown and blue, up past Aune Steps and Ryder's Hill, with only the sheep and the ravens for company. But what would Iselda make of Dartmoor? I had taken Letice Londeneyse there, and she had loathed it. And how could I tell this woman, whom I adored so deeply, that in order to truly please me she must love a great, empty, damp upland and make her life upon its slopes?

'I think you'd like the Moor if you saw it,' I said feebly. 'And all that land! It would be income enough for us to live as well as ever we wished, for the rest of our lives. It's true, though. We'll become a pair of mushrooms if we stay here.'

'Or moss,' she said, one eyebrow raised, exploring the idea. 'But be honest: Devon? From what you have told me – and you never really shut up about it, actually – it rains all the time there. At least we have summer here.'

'But you hate Venice!'

'Hate . . . Maybe. I don't care about the gondolas, and the chairmen, and the dances, and . . . any of it, really. This house was my father's, so I love it for that, but it is not *my* home. And for God's sake, it is the oldest building in Venice, or nearly so! Truly, I meant what I said about moss – I swear I feel it growing on me as I sleep.' She came over to me and drew me down to sit next to her on one of the heavy, ugly Venetian settles that lined the walls of the room. 'I love this city – all the streets, and the water, but it's true: I hate it as well. It's like living inside someone's guts, and not just the smell. And I loathe the constant talk of money, money, money . . . So no, we do not *need* any of it. But are you ready to go back to sleeping under trees? I do quite like our bed, I will admit.'

'Me too,' I said warmly, and she gave me a shove. But then she snaked an arm around me and kissed me gently on the mouth.

'Let's see if we can just fade away,' she murmured. 'If we can, if no one comes after us, we'll quietly dissolve the bank and disappear. If there's a fuss, we'll have to come back and do it more officially.'

'God.' I took a deep breath of the warm, spiced air. The dire warnings of Doctor Scotus stirred in my mind like spidery things moving beneath a stone. But was there any need to turn that stone over? We seemed to be fading away of our own accord. The storm had not come. We could put down our roots, bury them deep, somewhere else.

'Yes. Yes! All right. It can't possibly be that easy, but . . .'

'We'll say we're going on a pilgrimage. To Jerusalem. No one can say anything against that.'

'Then let's go! Just to ride with you again, like we used to. I don't really want anything else.'

We left the next day, before dawn, the first tendrils of mist curling up onto the worn steps that descended into the canal. As the boatman waited to take us across to Mestre, I pulled Iselda to me and we held each other tight as I felt the warmth of her body seep into mine.

The going was easy across the flat, fenny plain of Lombardy, for a shaky truce was holding between the Guelphs and Ghibbelines, the emperor was down south, and Ezzelino was keeping to himself in Padua. We picked up the Via Francigena at Piacenza and slid into its river of noisy pilgrims from the north: Germans and Swedes hoping to get to Rome and back before the weather turned nasty, smug Frisians and Scots on their way home. We rode into Lyon at midday on the first Tuesday in August, and went straight to the Two Foxes, where I always stayed whenever I was in the city. It was run by a surly bastard, but he was discreet, the food was excellent and the beds did not smell, a rarity in a city as busy as Lyon.

The landlord, a thin, hairy fellow with a brewer's nose, welcomed me with his accustomed sneer.

'Here for the crusade, sir? You're a bit late.'

'What do you mean?' I asked, pulling off my cloak and tipping the stable-boy who was hovering at my side. I wasn't really listening to the landlord, but I caught the word 'crusade'. 'Do I look like a crusader, man?'

'It was a pleasantry,' he told me, stiffly. 'But the crusade's been and gone, regardless. A good month ago. He'll be on the sea by now.'

Now I was listening. 'Wait. The king is not in Lyon? He's already been here?'

'What I said, sir,' said the landlord, humouring me with difficulty.

'All this way for a jest? I will eat their livers!' I seethed.

'Ach, my love, they've done us a favour. Come and sit down.' Iselda looked more exasperated than anything else. But I was furious.

'If any man thinks he can make merry at our expense and take our silver into the bargain . . .'

'Wait, Patch – at least until after lunch. I'm starved!' She was regarding me with tired amusement. I shook my head, too angry to say anything more, and stormed out of the door. It was a short walk to the offices of the Banco di Corvo Marino, and by the time I got there I was seething. The agent, Marc, a gentle, middle-aged man with a Paris education and a large family, was in the counting house. He stood up in evident surprise when I burst in unannounced.

'Messer Petrus! To what do we owe this unexpected—'

'Unexpected? I am surprised you care to jest with me, sirrah! What is the meaning of this?'

'Meaning of what, sir? I don't understand.' Marc was regarding me with utter confusion.

'You sent a letter to me in Venice, telling me the king was expecting to meet me here at the beginning of August. I am here, against my will, and the king is not. I ask again: what, in the name of Mary's womb, is the meaning of this?'

'I sent you no such letter!' stammered Marc, wringing his thumb with a clenched fist. 'I do not know what has happened, but . . . but King Louis *was* here, and left perfectly adequate provision for his debts, and even asked me to convey to you his warm regards whenever I should happen to write next. The last letter I sent to you was three weeks ago, regarding the Bruges cargo . . .'

'Which plainly I have not received,' I snarled.

'And . . . and before that, at the end of April, in the matter of sundry loans to the Crown and a shipment of wool that foundered off the Nore.'

'Of course I got that,' I snapped. 'But a letter sits on my writing table, in Venice, with your seal and signature, summoning me here to meet with Louis Capet. Who is not here. Who has not been here for a month or more.'

Marc bit his lip. He was sweating, though the stone-walled room was not warm. 'I do not know how that could be,' he muttered. 'I – you must believe me, sir – sent no such letter.'

'Someone did. With your signature.'

'It is possible that I signed a letter, in haste, to which I had not given my full attention. One does that, from time to time, if the thing is a petty matter.'

'Does *one*? I do not,' I said. That was a lie, of course, but I did not intend Marc to know that. 'How many letters go out from here, with your signature and seal, that you have not read?'

'Not many, and I remember all of them. This year, exactly two. One near the Epiphany, a reply to some solicitation. The other . . . let me see.' He squinted. Marc had an all but flawless memory, which was why the captain had hired him, years ago. Well, it seemed to be failing him. 'No, I have it. In April. There was an invitation to the wedding of a local merchant's daughter. We do not go to such things. Eudes brought me the letter politely declining the invitation, and I signed it.'

'Did you read it?'

'Sir, I did not. That day the king's chancellor himself was here, asking for a summary of all loans outstanding, and I was very, very busy. But there was no need. Eudes was trustworthy.'

'*Was?* Where is this Eudes now?'

'He left us, about a week later. Left town, in fact. Which was strange, as he was a good lad: very bright, but steady. Not at all the sort to get himself into trouble, but then it is so hard to tell with the young people these days . . .'

Marc was spared my own thoughts on the matter, for at that moment a clerk stuck his head around the door and coughed loudly.

'There's a gentleman to see you, master,' he said.

'Not now, Hugo, for pity's sake,' moaned the agent.

'Begging your pardon, but it's Messer Petrus he wants to see,' said the clerk.

'Don't be stupid. I've just arrived. Nobody knows I'm here.'

'Nevertheless, sir, I think he means to see you. The gentleman is an Englishman, and a knight.'

'Oh, for God's sake,' I said. The day was getting stranger and more infuriating with every minute that passed. Leaving Marc to fret, I stormed out of the counting house.

'He's in the antechamber,' called Hugo the clerk, behind me. And indeed, there near the door stood a man dressed in the style of the English court. His hair was close-cropped and sandy, and when he turned, hearing my footsteps, I found I was looking at Gervais Bolam.

I had not seen Gervais Bolam – Sir Gervais de Bolam, to do him all courtesy – since the battle of Saintes, and that was six years past. He had been a boy then, but the intervening years had thickened him and he held himself with a discreet swagger. There had not been much to do for an English knight these last few years save drinking and brawling, and there was ample evidence of both in his face.

'Sir Petrus Blakke Dogge! You are here at last!' he cried, grinning and sticking out his hand. I was so surprised to see him that I took it and let him crush my fingers warmly.

'At last? Gervais de Bolam, if it really is you, what are you talking about?'

'We have been waiting this past week.'

'Sir, I have been dragged, unwillingly, from my home and across the fucking Alps on what turns out to have been a fool's errand, and I am the fool. Forgive me if I do not feel like indulging you. How did you know I was in Lyon?'

'Oh, we brought you here!' he said breezily. 'It was a bit of a challenge – your people are loyal to you, sir, and tediously hard to corrupt. It took an indecent amount of money before I convinced young Jean to get that letter signed and sealed. A promising boy, by the way: destined for great things, I shouldn't wager.'

'We? Who is *we*? Riddle me no riddles, Gervais. I tell you, by Saint Lawrence's crackling rind, that I am not in the mood.'

'Earl Richard, of course,' said Gervais. 'Who else? Oh, but of course you would not know: I am the earl's equerry.'

'Richard of Cornwall is here in Lyon? But, for Christ's sake, why didn't he just send word himself?'

'Would you have come, Black Dog? No, you would not. Loyalty is a treasure, or so says the earl, and he did not wish to put yours to the trial. The lesser of two evils? The greater of two goods? I am no philosopher, Black Dog, and Earl Richard is waiting. Shall we go?'

I went back to the counting house to apologise to Marc, who appeared not to have taken a breath since I left him. And then I followed Gervais through the thronging streets to a small nobleman's palace near the church of Saint Justus. He left me with a bow and a comradely wink, and an old, bald serving man showed me into the solar.

Richard of Cornwall had grown a little plumper since I had seen him last; a little ruddier, too. His reddish-blond beard, with its prettily styled curls, gave him the air of a well-fed dog-fox. I greeted him with a bend of the knee and he made a show of waving away any formality.

'Let us sit,' he said, and beckoned me over to the table, already laid with a trencher of cold roasted larks, sweetmeats and a silver ewer of wine.

'I must thank my lord for our magnificent wedding—' I began, but Richard laughed.

'A lord must be generous,' he said. And with that he took the ewer and poured me a cup of dark red wine. He handed it to me, and his eyes narrowed ever so slightly as I took it. You are not free. I grasped his meaning as plainly as if he had bellowed the words into my face. Still, I raised the cup to my lips and took a careful sip. I knew the poison he had offered me, and it was called vassalage. Like an obedient vassal I drank what was given to me.

I decided not to give him the satisfaction of idle conversation about his wife, his brother the king, the travails of the English court. This little resistance was meaningless – I was painfully aware of the fact that, though I was not Richard's inferior by very much if it came to wealth, I was bound to him by something more powerful even than money. Instead I decided to get the unpleasant moment over with.

'My lord, how may I serve you?' I enquired, trying not to grind my teeth as I said it.

The earl looked taken aback for an instant, though he hid it well. Then he beamed. I was behaving myself, doubtless far better than he had expected me to. But then again, a man like the Earl of Cornwall did not expect challenges from vassals.

'It is not a small thing, Sir Petrus. It is . . . it is what one might call statecraft. You are a man for whom that should not be onerous work.' We leaned back in our respective seats and eyed each other. I sipped my wine, waiting for him to go on.

'Have you met the pope?' Richard asked. He might be enquiring if I had made the acquaintance of a new cook or major domo. I nodded.

'The present incumbent?' I replied. 'I have. Once, and briefly. My lord the King of France was good enough to recommend me to the Holy See. I had an audience in Lyon, when last I returned from Paris.'

'How many popes *have* you met, Black Dog?' Richard was interested despite the lazy game of indifference he was playing.

'Two only, my lord. The late Monsieur de Sol introduced me to Pope Gregory.' I shuddered inwardly, remembering the half-mummified basilisk who, despite the withering of age, had filled the throne of Saint Peter with his malevolent energy. I had been little more than a boy then, but I had never forgotten the sharpness of his gaze, dissecting me like a surgeon-barber in search of a hidden canker. 'It is a memory I shall carry with me always. Your Lordship knows Pope Innocent, I believe.'

'Indeed. I enjoyed the friendship of Sinibaldo Fieschi, as he was; and now His Holiness is good enough to keep me in his thoughts. So. You know something of our pope. What do you know of the emperor?'

'Fortunately I have been able to keep out of the way of all this . . . this trouble between the parties of Church and Empire,' I said. 'I live in Venice, which is staunchly for His Holiness; and my bank has its home in Florence, where there is much squabbling, but the Florentines being what they are, everyone takes care not to disturb business.'

'And you, Black Dog? What of you?' Richard had put down his cup and steepled his fingers. We were getting near the matter at hand.

'My lord, the business . . . you know I have only one profession now: with my partners I own a bank which by the grace of God is so far flourishing, though as to relics, from time to time . . .' I shrugged. Did he want me to find him a relic? It was possible. Well, that would be easy, if dull. 'In my old business of translating relics I served the Lord. In my present occupation, if I did not serve Him, I would be putting my immortal soul in jeopardy. I am a banker, not a usurer, but there are temptations, and if one is not firm of spirit . . .' I tapped on the silver foot of my cup. 'The Church supports one business and allows the other to proceed. I believe you might divine my loyalties from that.'

'Good man.' Richard was far too controlled a man to breathe a sigh of relief, but he had doubted my loyalty. That was interesting. 'And one further question: have you been to Sicily?'

'Yes, I have,' I said, surprised. 'As a sailor I put into Messina and Palermo many times, and last year I brought a minor relic from Constantinople to Palermo, for the cathedral.'

'I mean the kingdom – not just the island. Apulia and the rest of it.'

'Again, yes. Why does my lord ask?'

'Hmm.' Richard scratched his beard, then reached for the purse at his belt and brought out three coins: two English silver pennies and a gold ducat, which I saw was stamped with the head of Roger, King of Sicily – an old coin, a century old or more. Richard laid them out in a row, penny, ducat, penny. Then he took his wine cup and placed it next to the ducat.

'This is His Holiness,' he said, touching his fingertip to the cup. 'This is the Emperor Frederick, and this is myself.' He touched first one penny, then the other. Then he moved the ducat a fraction to one side. 'And this, as you may have guessed, is Sicily.'

'Sicily is the heart of the Hohenstaufen empire,' I said. 'And

Pope Innocent has been trying to cut it out – not very success-fully. As I have heard, he has been wooing the churchmen there, but they are loyal to Frederick. I have spent some time with Berardo – he is one of the emperor's best friends, is he not?'

'The bishop of Palermo? That's so,' said Richard. 'You know about this – of course you do. That is why we are talking.'

'And the rebellion three years ago – Frederick had no trouble with that. I spoke to someone who watched Guglielmo di Sanseverino hanged alive over a slow fire – after they cut off his manhood and some other parts. Frederick brooks no nonsense in his kingdom. You know that, of course, my lord.' I sat back, watching Richard move the coins tiny steps across the table, nudging them with a manicured fingernail. What did he have in his mind? The pope had been making clumsy efforts to get rid of Frederick von Hohenstaufen from the hour of his coronation, and it had been bad for business. I looked at the coins, and the cup. It was empty. I reached for the ewer and filled it. A few drops of red wine scattered around the silver and gold.

'Innocent wants you to take Sicily,' I said, filling my own cup again.

Richard looked up sharply, then grinned.

'No, he wants me to buy it!' He threw back his head and laughed. Then he fell silent and picked up the ducat. 'Should I, Petrus?'

'What does he want for it . . . he means the kingdom itself, I presume? You would be King of Sicily.'

'Innocent is not a fool, and he is . . . hmm.' His hand went once more to his beard. 'The pope has made it his mission, as God's representative, to sweep Frederick von Hohenstaufen from this world. Since prayer is not working, he must needs accomplish this by temporal means, and that – I can see you are following me – will require a very great deal of money. I am surprised you have not been asked for a . . . a donation.'

I shrugged. 'I try to give before I am asked,' I said, blandly. 'It really is not my business, of course.'

'No. Nor mine. But Sicily . . .'

'Is tempting, my lord? It is a rich and beautiful land. Not more beautiful than Devon, of course.' I permitted myself a courtly chuckle. 'But you are meant to buy the crown. Might one ask for how much?'

'An insane sum. Ludicrous!' Richard spun the ducat so that for a moment it became a golden orb. Then it careened off course and struck the cup with a dull ping.

'But . . . ?' I felt myself beginning to wince. Was this my next duty as vassal, to buy Sicily for the man who thought he was my master? But Richard was chasing the ducat across the table and did not notice.

'It might be possible,' he said at last. 'But I am not convinced it would be worth the money.'

'Well, it is a rich land, but fractious – though perhaps given your lordship's present folderol with the English barons, it might seem restful. It is a long way from England. What does King Henry think?'

'I have not told my brother,' said Richard. 'Not that he would mind, if it was the will of the Holy Father. No, I have been thinking about something else. Black Dog, we have come to the meat of the matter, and my words shall not leave this room, do you understand?' I nodded silently. 'Good. Well then. What, sir, are your loyalties to Venice?'

'None, my lord.' This time I could not hide my surprise.

'None?'

'I am not a subject of the Republic. I live there – when I do live there – because I inherited a . . .' I was going to say house, but modesty was not to my advantage in this company. 'A palace. Most of my business these days is in Florence, with some in Paris and more, lately, in Lyon. Why do you ask?'

'Spices. You do not deal in spices, do you, Black Dog?'

'A little. You know that the Republic is the entrepôt for most of the pepper and other goods coming from the East. Pisa takes a large bite, Genoa is hopeful but not a threat – so far, that is. I have an interest in a few cargoes a year – likewise with silks. But I speculate, nothing more. I have no wish to buy a warehouse or ships. Too much worry, my lord: floods, storms . . . rats.'

'But it is lucrative, this trade.' Richard knew all this. I could not for the life of me tell what he was getting at.

'Of course.'

'And it comes from where?' He had set down the ducat and folded his hands in front of him.

'Egypt,' I said patiently. 'The Mongols have pinched off the overland routes through Anatolia, so the trade comes from India and China across the Arabian Sea, up the coast of Africa to ports in Nubia and then up the Nile to Cairo.'

'Exactly. What will happen when my cousin Louis lands in Egypt?'

'He will control the flow of goods – if he is wise, that is. The Nubians are Mussulmen, and might take their trade elsewhere. I doubt Louis has plans to conquer Nubia.'

'What do you know of Louis's plans?' said Richard, sharply. It took me a moment to understand that this was a question and not a rebuke.

'I know what the world knows,' I answered, frowning.

'I don't believe that. You are deep in Louis's counsels.'

'No again, my lord. The king . . . The king owes me money. We speak about matters of gold and silver, nothing else. Not even relics, now that he has found crusading to be his new passion.'

'So you do not think that Louis intends to conquer Egypt for France?'

'It is easy to guess his hope: that if he captures Damietta, the sultan will offer him Jerusalem in exchange. But who knows if that will change once he is there? He has a good chance of taking Damietta, and if Damietta falls, then Cairo . . . I do not know what your cousin intends, my lord, but if he takes enough land and the sultan does not give up Jerusalem, why should Louis not sct up a Frankish Kingdom of Egypt? It is a rich country even without spices. Corn, for instance. You would have corn in Sicily too, of course.'

'What if I could have both?'

'Your meaning, my lord?'

'Leaving my cousin aside for a moment, could the flow of spices be diverted to another entrepôt?'

'Ah.' Everything fell into place. 'Such as Syracuse, or Messina, or Palermo, perhaps?'

'How quick you are. And?'

'You would need very powerful financiers,' I said, wearily, feeling the trap closing around me. I had known there was a trap waiting for me, but not one this grandiose, this over-blown. 'You would also need a strong fleet, because you would be fighting Venice from the very moment you showed your hand, and Venice . . . Do you know how fast they can build a war galley, my lord? It is quite a spectacle.'

'So I have heard. But ships can be bought, and sailors as well. If they were—'

'If, my lord, if! If you succeeded in fighting off the Repub-lic, and Pisa – and doubtless upstart Genoa as well – you would fill your warehouses. Then you would need to find buyers, many of whom would be loyal customers of Venice. All of those would be feeling the full heat of the Republic's charm, so to speak, and you would find your spices rotting in their sacks. But no. You have fought off Venetian and Pisan navies. You have out-bribed the Serene Republic and won back the buyers. You have orders to fill. How are you going to satisfy your clients? The roads of Italy are watched by Venice, courtesy of her greatest friend, the Holy Father. The seas, likewise – a battle for every cargo ship crossing from Palermo to Marseille or Barcelona. Restive Mamluks in Egypt, requiring bribes, bribes, bribes. You will be throwing out silver as a man throws out grain to geese. And to outbid Venice, silver will not do. You will need gold.' I picked up the ducat and held it between us, a dull little sun.

'Christ, I have gold! But perhaps I have something else.' He raised his cup and chinked it against the coin. 'The blessing of Pope Innocent? What say you to that?'

'Innocent will take the trade in spices from Venice and give it to you? Why?' I was incredulous.

'The Holy Father wants to destroy the Hohenstaufens completely. His rage is not aimed simply at Frederick: Innocent will not be stopped until the entire family is wiped out and their name forgotten in Italy. To do that, yes, he would risk the good will of Venice. It is a good plan, though, don't you agree? Our pope thinks like an emperor himself: carving up the world according to his whim. And he is waving this particularly succulent morsel under my nose. It is hard to know what to do.'

'With the greatest respect, my lord, might I guess that you have a notion, though, and that is why we are talking? I cannot believe you require my advice, lord, though I am immensely flattered . . .'

'Not your advice, Black Dog. Your assistance.'

'Again, I am flattered, but in what way—'

'I am giving you a job,' snapped Richard.

'That is your right, my lord,' I sniffed.

'Curb yourself. And listen: I said just now that his terms were exorbitant, but Innocent will sell me the crown of Sicily for terms I can well afford, and make Venice behave, *if* I do something for him in return.'

'Something? That would be a very big thing,' I said. 'He would risk war with Venice. What would be worth it?'

'Of course: a big something. Enormous. I agreed. This is the business of kings. And – you ought to be flattered – I have volunteered your services.'

'For what?' I asked. My heart gave a small knock. The air in the room seemed, suddenly, to be crackling with power, and it wasn't mine.

'I fancy a man like yourself, a warrior who has also beheld the holiest things in this world, would like to go on crusade. Happily you have the opportunity. Cousin Louis is waiting in Cyprus for the weather to change so that he can attack Egypt. My brother would like to have been with him, but, alas, too many wayward subjects have kept him at home. We sent a party of knights, though, two hundred of them under William Longspée. Do you know him? The Earl of Salisbury's bastard. A lovely man. It is not too late for one more English knight to join the holy cause, is it? Think of your immortal soul, man.'

'I do. Frequently,' I lied, bitterly. 'And if I should be blessed enough to reach Egypt, what then?'

'You will slip away up the Nile to Cairo, and deliver this to Sultan Ayub.' He reached down and opened a small chest that lay under the table. When he straightened, he held a roll of creamy new vellum.

'Deliver a letter?' I asked, incredulous. 'You *are* jesting, my lord. I have no intention of going on crusade. And I would never deign to be your errand boy – with the greatest of respect,' I added, icily.

'I expected you to insult me,' said Richard, grinning nastily. 'But your pope? Have a care, sir.' He laid the letter on the table and rolled it back and forth with a jewelled forefinger.

'The pope and I are not . . .' I looked Richard in the eyes.

'As a banker I must be above the fray,' I went on. 'That means treading a middle way between Innocent and Frederick. It is a knife's edge, to be frank. One slip either way and a man in my position is finished. If I do the pope's business, Frederick will destroy me. No need to say what would happen if I were caught carrying Frederick's letters.'

'I understand,' said Richard. 'The supple reed, and all that. To be supple, to be adaptable, is to conquer. I have always followed that course myself.'

'Exactly, my lord,' I said, somewhat relieved. 'I was at Taillebourg when you went and spoke to King Louis . . .'

'Nevertheless, what is desirable in the master is detestable in the servant. Do as you are bid, or Innocent will crush you, and your wife, everyone and everything you have touched. The orders are written already. If you doubt me, then I have plainly misjudged you.'

'Then this is treason?'

'The Church does not – *cannot* – commit treason. Heresy, Petroc?'

'Are you calling me a heretic? So far *you* have mentioned treason and heresy, my lord, and yet you call me names?'

'It does not matter what *I* call you. Refuse me, and the dogs will be fighting over your corpse outside the Lateran. And Innocent has, of course, agreed to hand me a goodly portion of your estates – as is my right as your earthly lord.'

'May I at least read the letter?' I said, hoping to buy some time for myself. Richard had finally got me off balance and I felt, as if Michael Scotus were there to conjure it for me, the razor on which I teetered.

Richard grinned, a rictus of triumph. He leaned over and passed the letter to me. I drew in my breath silently through clenched teeth, took the roll of vellum, and opened it. Innocent's scribe had impeccable handwriting. The words fairly yelled off the page. Christ, even an illiterate would be able to read this!

'Could they not even have managed Arabic?' I enquired icily. Richard just gazed at me, a big tomcat with cream all over its whiskers. 'Or code?'

'You're a clever fellow, Black Dog: just make sure it stays with you. You'll be amongst soldiers, man: the written word *is* code.'

True enough. I bit off my words and dropped my eyes to the page.

The honorifics and diplomatic verbiage were as dense as might be expected, considering the parties involved. The bitterest enemies, both in the realms of earth and spirit, must needs woo each other with a continent of lily-scented nonsense. Or perhaps the florid words were to mask the stench of a ripe corpse. I let my eye rove over the page like a circling carrion bird.

Let it be known and understood that,

Whereas Our son in Christ, Louis Capet, King of France, has chosen to mount a Crusade against your lands and person, said Crusade pleases the Holy See of Saint Peter only so far as it removes the person and might of the French king from the soil of Christendom, where through ill-counsel or threat it could be induced to form an alliance with Our great opposer, Frederick von Hohenstaufen

And whereas the said Frederick von Hohenstaufen is a mighty apostate and betrayer

And whereas it has come to Our knowledge that the aforesaid Louis Capet is intending to make an attempt on Your Majesty's kingdom of Egypt

Therefore, be it understood between us as two most powerful rulers of men upon this earth, that it is Our wish and desire that Louis Capet be allowed to land his armies in Egypt, and that Your Majesty's own armies be not swift to engage him,

but lead him into such circumstances that he might be delayed
in Egypt for an indefinite length of time

In this matter, Let His Majesty know that he shall have
every support and succour that is within the remit of the Holy
See to supply. Also Our undying friendship, and that of Our
allies in His Majesty's undertakings in those lands and
territories deemed by tradition and usage to be his by right is
hereby promised and affirmed. Further, that in matters of
trade and free passage of goods and persons in the lower
portions of Our common sea, the Holy See and Our allies shall
give way to Your Majesty's interests. Likewise in the matter
of the Holy Places, the Holy See and Our allies shall render
such assistance as We are able in the event of attack from the
Mongol Emperor in the east . . .

There were sums of money, quite ridiculous in size, and
further demands and promises. Reading it, it was easy to
imagine that this was a letter from one friendly Christian
ruler to another, and not two men bitterly divided both by
religion and territory. I was, I confess, shocked – not by the
calumny of man, for that I knew very well indeed, but by the
brazenness of the thing. I dropped the letter onto the table as
if it were a pus-soaked bandage.

'So the pope is betraying the most pious man in all of
Christendom.' I sighed, and drained my wine cup. Richard
filled it again, smiling his tomcat's smile. 'So that Louis won't
be able to take Frederick's side if . . . when Innocent moves
against the emperor. So Innocent hates Antichrist more than
he loves Christ. Or so it seems to me, a mere errand boy.'

'No joking matter, Petroc.'

'And this is not some trick? Some elaborate scheme to part
me from my money?'

'Neither jest nor trick. It is exactly as it seems. Signed and
sealed by His Holiness. Now all it requires is delivery.'

The temptation to sink my head into my hands was overwhelming, but with a huge effort I resisted. Meanwhile, my fingernail had gouged a pale groove into the table.

'So if I refuse . . .'

'You won't. You have read the letter. You are a party to this folderol, like it or not. Innocent knows of this meeting. How long do you think he'll let you live, my dear man, if you give the wrong answer?'

'If I refuse,' I went on, doggedly, 'I condemn my wife to death. And myself, of course. What, just out of interest, do I get if I play along with you and your friends in Rome?'

'The rewards for this adventure would be choice, and I would not be grudging. Well – your life, of course. And that of your wife – Iselda, isn't it? But if that isn't enough . . . Do you love banking, man? Are you one of those pale and pinched creatures with heads empty of anything save numbers? I do not think so. How would you like to be Lord Chancellor of Sicily? Or Constable, eh? Something befitting your unique talents. I could make you a prince. Royal blood in perpetuity: not bad for a Cornish merchant's son – that is what you said you were, isn't it?'

I had Thorn hanging from my belt. It would be simplicity itself to stick her into Richard's complacent belly. And perhaps I'd get away, and reach Iselda before . . . No, I wouldn't, and then the pope would unleash his wolves on the one thing I loved in this world.

'My lord . . .' I stood up, for my stomach had turned sour with the effort of listening quietly to the terms of my entrapment, and paced out a step, two steps, until the length of the table was between us. 'My lord, I should like to be free.'

'Free?'

'It isn't a blasphemy, Earl Richard. I am talking about the oath you made me swear in Saintes. I'm not a greedy man: I have more of everything than I could possibly need, including power. More, in fact, than I ever wanted. A chancellor's chain of office? I already wear a chain, and though I do not feel it often, when I do, it is as if I were shackled to the living rock of this world. I'm richer than most kings, and it means nothing. I feel my servitude now, and so I ask you: if I try to do this thing, will you set me free?'

'Is it so onerous, your service to me? When have I called upon you . . .'

I ignored his stupendous nerve. 'You asked me to bring you Sanchia of Provence to be your wife, even though she was promised to the Count of Toulouse. And you seem happy with the outcome.'

'True, you brought me my wife. But I could have made you pay homage to me at my whim. There is a great deal you could have been doing for me, my man. And why should I release you? This is not business! This is not some banker's game! It is how the world is held together!'

'Of course it is. But that is my condition – my only condition.'

'Foolishness. I will not.'

'Very well, then.' I began to walk towards the door. 'I regret, my lord, that I cannot be of service to you this time.'

'Sit down, my man, and do not bluster so much. I do not want you dead. And I have found you out. There *is* something that you lack, and which I can give you.'

'And what is that?' I snapped, not bothering to hide my impatience. But Richard, it seemed, had understood that I was serious. He did not wish me dead: he wanted me alive, and at his service.

'A home.'

'Thank you! But I have one of those, in Venice.'

'Your Ca' Kanzir.' He shot me a look, and caught my surprise. He had been investigating me, then. 'Your damp old palace, in Venice to which you have no loyalty. About to become the property of the Church, if you leave this room. No, no, that is not what I am talking about. You are an interesting man, Petrus Zennorius. I have had some time in which to find out about you. You are no merchant's son from Cornwall. No, you appear to have sprung, fully formed, into the company of Jean de Sol. And your name is Petroc, not Petrus or Peter. A fine Cornish name, true – or a Devon one, maybe?' He had become positively merry, and it was not pleasant.

'Very well, my lord. I am found out. Zennor is in Devon, in your Dartmoor. Petroc is my name. Petrocus does not sound very pleasing in Latin, so I shortened it.' Close enough to the truth, as are all good lies.

'And are there merchants in Zennor?' He knew very well that there were not.

'Zennor, my lord, is a moorland hamlet of sheep farmers and peat cutters.' I was concocting my lie even as I told it. 'My father might have been either – I was an orphan, lucky enough to be taken in by the brothers of Tavistock Abbey. They taught me my letters, and when I was old enough I was apprenticed as a clerk to a Plymouth merchant. He owed a sum of money to Jean de Sol and I ended up being given to his company in part-payment. Not very salubrious, any of it. You can perhaps see why I have chosen to smooth over some of the less attractive details.'

'And from there comes your love of Dartmoor,' said Richard. 'I remember our first conversation. Do you? At Lydford. We talked about my Moor. Now, you and I share one thing in common: we both love that . . . that rather unlovable place. I understood it then, and I have not forgotten. So you are not so great a mystery as I had thought – there are some intriguing rumours in the stories *I* have heard. But' – he squinted appraisingly at me down his nose – 'it will serve.'

'Men of lowly birth must tell stories if they are to claw themselves out of the muck,' I said coldly. 'Captain de Sol cared only for a man's thoughts and his deeds, my lord, and I have never needed to give my pedigree to any man. I am not ashamed of my birth, though you scorn it. And I came by what I have with nothing but this head and these hands.'

'Dear me, calm yourself! I saw you on the field of Saintes – you do not need to prove your worth to me.'

'How kind of you, my lord,' I muttered, thinly.

'You are a wanderer, Sir Petrus – Sir *Petroc*, I might say. And yet you have never forgotten your home.'

'Well, you are right. I have not. What of it?'

'There is a manor on the southern edge, near Cornwood. Three knights' fees it has, fifteen hides of wood and ploughland. It is a good living. A river, two mills, a village. A fishpond as well. The house is no Venetian palace, I'm afraid, but a good Saxon pile with a decent roof and a new tower.'

This, I thought, was why Richard was the richest man in England. He could anatomise men like a surgeon – or an Inquisitor. And he had found his mark. Even as I searched for the words of appropriate disdain with which to disappoint him, my mind was searching through scraps of memory for a manor near Cornwood. And fifteen hides – that was almost two thousand acres. A river? That would be the Erme, running off the Moor under the stone teeth of Stall Down. Dear God, that was beautiful country. For a moment I thought I had the deep brown scent of a north wind off the moors in my nose. And then I found I had padded back to my chair. I blinked, trying to clear this foolishness from my head.

'You could give me the whole Moor, from Okehampton to Ashburton, but if it came without my freedom, I would . . .' I snapped my fingers.

'Sir Petrus Blakke Dogge, you are an English knight, an Englishman, despite your Italian ways. If you were to take a manor in England and hold it, you would be declaring yourself a subject of our English king. Is that too great a thraldom for you? If you would deign to serve my brother in that way, I would relinquish my claim on your service. Now, is that fair enough?'

Richard had found me out. A man like me had no business with a heart. And worse, one with a heart's desire. The earl could have offered me his brother's throne and I would not have taken it. But a hillside in Devon?

'My lord, the fact remains that this is a difficult task. Perhaps you think too highly of me. What if I accept your commission, but come back having failed to carry it out, as I surely will? What then?'

'Then you will still be bound to me, save that then I will question your loyalty. You will find that a disloyal vassal who has something his lord covets is as secure as a field mouse come reaping time. And there will be Innocent, who does not love you. Spit in the street, and he will have you burned. Perhaps, Petroc, if you do not succeed, it might be best to seek a glorious death – a crusader's death. Because I can assure you there will be nothing glorious for you in my displeasure.'

'You forget my partner – my wife, Lord Richard.'

'Do not threaten me with a woman. There are ways to deal with a scold, Petroc. For her sake as well, I advise you to succeed. She is here in Lyon – how nice. You married for love, like me. I appreciate that. Understand it. But do you remember Cardinal John of Toledo?'

'He murdered my oldest friend – so indeed, I do remember him.'

'Dear me. I had heard. The man's methods . . . The point is, Petroc, that he gets the job done. As I say, I understand love. But I cannot protect your wife, for example, from Cardinal John and his very capable lieutenant – Rodolpho, is he called?'

'Remigius,' I said through clenched teeth. 'Cannot, or will not?'

'Oh, you decide!' laughed Richard. But there was something in his eyes as he did so, and I wondered, for a moment, if he was warning, not threatening.

'Then I have no choice.'

'I am glad you see it that way.'

'But why must I go with the crusade? Surely it would be simpler just to sail across to Egypt straight away? I know the way to Cairo, my lord.'

'Spies, Black Dog. There are spies everywhere. The pope spies on the emperor, as well he might; and the emperor watches everything that Innocent does. Frederick has eyes in Egypt, and many between here and there. This way, you'll be covered by the confusion of war.'

'So be it.' Gritting my teeth, I rolled up the pope's letter and hid it away in my tunic.

'Excellent,' said Richard, and leaned back, cool and easy in his chair. 'Between a lord's wishes and a subject's actions there are no choices to be made. I am delighted to find your loyalty so strong, Black Dog. Now you had better be gone. The king will be halfway to Egypt by now. The fun will be over by the time you join him.'

Chapter Ten

Iselda was not at the inn when I got back, and I passed an hour clenched with foreboding, until she breezed into our chambers carrying some packages from the market. When she saw my face she dropped them onto the rushes and took my outstretched hands. I hugged her until her bones creaked.

'Ow, Patch! That hurts! Whatever is the matter?'

It poured from me, angrily, from tight jaws, and the colour drained out of her face as she listened.

'So what did you say?' she whispered, when I had told her Richard's offer.

'I said yes.'

'Ah.' Iselda's mouth had formed the O of a thought about to be made word, but no word came.

'I could only say yes. Christ's bloody hands!'

'Oh, Patch – now what?'

'The problem is that I think I actually meant it.'

'Meant it how? You call Louis Capet your friend. And for God's sake, we almost got away! We almost escaped . . .' She sank down among the rushes and covered her face with her hands. I sat down next to her.

'I was a drowning man, and a little shard of wood drifted past. I thought, listening to that smug bastard, *What if . . .* What if this will really get us away? Away from this. Away from us, who we've become.' I put my arms around her. 'Louis is not my friend: the friends of kings are other kings. He's my generous patron, and he owes us a vast amount of money. For that reason alone I would have refused Richard. But only if I had had a choice, and I didn't. No, I meant it because if I can keep my head, perhaps we can really be gone.'

'Only if you come back alive.'

'Right.' I sighed. 'This had to happen sooner or later. You cannot paddle in the marsh and expect that the leeches won't find their way into your flesh. I've got what I deserve.'

'There isn't much point in feeling sorry for yourself,' Iselda said gently.

'No. But I have to betray a man I like – not to mention an entire bloody crusade, thousands of men with wives and little ones – at the bidding of a creature I loathe. I've spent a lifetime fighting Rome, and now I'm the pope's spy. His serpent.'

'So what will you do?'

'I'll go. To Egypt, at least – join Louis and the army. And then . . . But that's not the point. I'll be stained. *We'll* be stained. Even if no one knows except Richard and Innocent, we're ruined. They'll have their fangs so deep into our flesh that we'll be helpless slaves until they bleed us dry and throw us to the Inquisition. And that's only if Innocent succeeds in getting rid of Frederick von Hohenstaufen, which is a long shot. If he doesn't, we'll have the emperor trying to kill us into the bargain.'

'A nice bargain,' muttered Iselda. 'I say we should slip away now, right this minute.'

'We can't. Richard's got men watching the house.'

'Well, this is grim,' Iselda said, lightly. But there was a tremor in her voice. 'They won't go away, will they?'

'I doubt it,' I sighed. 'I'm not scared of Richard. He isn't an evil man. He's a businessman, really. Like me – greedier than me. But this is Rome's doing, and I think that along with all the bluster, Richard was trying to warn me. Innocent has declared himself against us. We'd have to slip away to . . . to join the Mongols.'

'What makes you think the Mongols would take us?' said Iselda. 'But I've an idea: we could go now, to Egypt, both of us.'

'And deliver Innocent's letter?' I stared at her, puzzled.

'Sod the letter. We escape. They understand banking and suchlike. We could start again. And we'd be nearer the spice entrepôts.'

'No one likes an apostate, my love. We'd have to convert, and still no one would trust us. We'd be grubbing for a living, still putting on a mummery for priests—'

'Oh, fuck everything! We nearly did it, Patch!' Iselda got up and threw herself onto the bed. 'We almost got away.'

'No, we didn't,' I said gently. 'It was an illusion. We were just sitting in Innocent's cupped hand the whole time.'

'Meaning what? That it's impossible?'

'No. But when a wolf is caught in a trap, he gnaws off his own leg to get away. That's what it's come to. Going on crusade, betraying Louis – I have to set my teeth against my own flesh.'

'If you deliver the letter, Louis might win anyway – it's war, isn't it? Louis will be safe whatever happens. He's King of France, for Christ's sake. His hands are bloody, no matter how pious he claims to be.'

'I'll probably be killed before I manage it – perhaps that's the point. I don't know what's going to happen, Iselda. War . . . we both know what war is like. I can hide in the confusion until I can work out what needs to be done. You'll be safe in the meantime.'

'What makes you think that?'

'Because you will be the Banco di Corvo Marino. This letter nonsense is . . .' I sat down next to her and lay back, looking up at the dark beams. 'It's a distraction. It has to be. Innocent wants our money, because he's a greedy swine, and because he thinks that if he doesn't get it, the emperor will. Innocent knows that I understand what he's after.'

'So he thinks that you'll do whatever he says, because otherwise he'll just loot the bank? Can't he just do that anyway?'

'Not quite. There are still rules. Louis would protect me. So he's set me up to betray my protector. It's exquisite, really. So while I'm off doing that, it's in Rome's best interests to keep us earning.'

'I can look after myself anyway,' said Iselda, grimly.

'*I* know that,' I said, pulling her down next to me. We lay like brass plates in a church floor, gazing up blandly at the ceiling. 'But no one else does. You're a woman, remember?'

'I do occasionally remember.'

'Well, that's all we have. They think I'm scared, and you're weak.'

'I'm weak *and* scared.'

'Me too. But we've made it this far.'

'Maybe it's a dead end.'

'Maybe. But the wolf doesn't think that when it starts chewing its leg. It can't. Unless you want to jump into the Rhône with me and have done with it, there's only one choice.'

'Either way, I don't think I'll ever see you again.'

'But you might, if I chew hard enough.'

'Then sharpen your teeth, my love.'

I had to leave in a hurry, for there would still be boats leaving Marseille for Cyprus, and if I made good time down the river I might catch one. Three days I spent alone with Iselda, defying Richard – alone, save for the distant watchers who lingered, almost respectfully, on the edge of our sight. We walked for hours on the banks of the Rhône, and sat on the strand, looking southwards down the low, sluggish river. It was hot, and thunderstorms were rising like vast yeasty loaves out of the mountains, but they never broke, just sat upon us with their heat and leaden weight. Summer was coming to an end reluctantly, petulantly, and if ever a man should have longed to be out at sea it ought by rights to have been me. But I could not bear to leave Iselda.

This was not one of my trips down to Florence. This time I was leaving on a longer journey. And I was going to war. We made light of it all as we wandered about, waiting for the storms that never came, skipping stones across the water. It was there, though, as heavy as the air above. I might not come back. I might well end up dead in Egypt. Only as the sun set on the day before I was to leave did Iselda take my arm as we walked through a narrow passage near Saint-Martin-d'Ainay, and force me gently against the wall. Placing her palms against my chest she leaned against me, pinning me. I could feel her heart beating through her hands.

'Don't be brave,' she said. 'Don't.'

'I will not,' I said, trying to smile, but seeing the flicker of dread in her eyes. 'I'm not brave at all.'

'Ah, but you are. Do not be clever, either. Don't do anything. Just . . . let the others fight.'

'I will be careful, Iselda. You know me.'

'Swear it! Here.' She grabbed my hand and thrust it under her tunic to where her heart pumped between her breasts. 'Swear on my heart and yours that you will not die.'

'I swear.'

'And take this.' She slipped the cord that held her little golden stag over her head and hung it round my neck. 'Now I am with you.'

People were shoving past us on their way to supper or prayers, but Iselda did not blink. If I could see fear in her eyes, I wondered what she could see in mine. At that moment

I would have given the company away with a wave of my hand if it meant we could stay here for ever, with strangers' footsteps scuffling past, and pigeons snapping their wings in the eaves above us. But we could not, and let the growing crowd gather us in and carry us off into the hot, clamorous Lyonnais night.

We slipped out of the inn early the next day. A foetid mist hung over the rivers, where fishermen and farmers were guiding their boats silently to market, and crows and gulls were probing the water's edge for anything dead and rotten. I had found passage on a flat-bottomed sailing barge, and the master had promised me a quick descent to Arles, where I would pick up a faster ship to Marseille. I had sent my chest and my armour ahead the day before, and now I held nothing but my old satchel. A salt-stained cape hid my fine clothes, for Iselda had laid out a costume she liked for me, brown silks striped with red and ferny green. We strode briskly through the drowsy streets. Our footsteps echoed and were lost. And there was the river. A few masts swayed, and hulls scraped gently together. My heart lurched, heavy as a stone.

Men were beginning to shout, and ropes were rattling through rings. There was a clatter of wood upon wood. A soldier strode past me, whistling. I shook the heaviness from me. I could almost hear Iselda's heart beating beside me. What does a man say at such times? *See you soon. I will come back safe and sound.* Were such words ever true? My heart told me they were not. I took her hand and kissed it. There on her finger glowed the simple gold wedding band. I held up my own left hand. A thought passed between us, and without speaking we slipped off our rings. I slid mine onto Iselda's finger, but it was far too big.

'Here,' she said, laughing, and put it on her thumb. Her ring fitted loosely on my little finger. I kissed it, and the tiny white line on her hand where it had rested for a few short weeks.

'I do love you,' I whispered. Then I stepped down into the boat.

And as the men cast off and the barge began to gather speed in the current and the breeze, I turned the little band of gold against my skin, seeing it catch the light as the sun rose over the vine-covered hills, long after Iselda had dwindled into the mist and we had passed around a long bend in the river. The distance between us was growing, inexorably, but in the smooth, warm metal there was a connection. Perhaps I had been wrong. Perhaps there was some magic after all.

Chapter Eleven

Cyprus, January 1249

It was the day after Epiphany when I rode through the gates of Nicosia under a dull sky and a fine drizzle. The flat plain stretched away to the mountains in the far distance, dark save for their snow-covered peaks. I had landed at Limassol on Christmas Day, but it had taken me more than a week to get here on muddy tracks that often became mires that could swallow a horse up to its chest, or disappeared entirely under rushing streams. It was a dreary time to be on Cyprus. As I had been there in the spring I knew it could be lovely, painted with new oak leaves and carpeted with wild lilies. But as I toiled up forlorn valleys with nothing but flocks of hooded crows for company, who by their mournful croaking seemed as depressed as me, I took the weather as an ill omen, and wished, yet again, that I was back in the familiar damp of Venice, sitting before the great fireplace in the hall of the Ca' Kanzir with Iselda's head upon my shoulder.

The main body of English knights were billeted in an old Greek palace near the cathedral of Saint Sophia, and I was shown to a small room in the servants' quarters, which I was to share with a young man from Hereford. Symon was his name, but as it would turn out I saw him rarely, for he spent his nights out whoring, and I had the room to myself. William Longspée, the English commander, was puzzled at first by my arrival. But I told him I had made an oath to the Earl of Cornwall to free the Holy Land from the tyranny of the Mussulmen and was here with his blessing, and at that he made me welcome. He had heard of the Black Dog Knight, for I had made something of a name for myself on King Henry's ridiculous attack on Poitou, but if he was surprised to find a sunburned man with an Italian lilt in his voice and clad in Venetian silk claiming to be a knight of England, he had the manners not to show it.

The palace was full of noise and laughter. More than half of the English company were living there with their servants. It was strange being back among English voices, and it reminded me, not altogether happily, of my time with the army of King Henry in Poitou. Indeed, there were three veterans of that time here in the palace, and in a long wine-sodden night we brought it all back for ourselves: the boredom, the women, the march and the battle. Out of the blood-spattered muddle of Saintes we had managed to weave a few strange tales before one by one we sank, still muttering, into the rushes on the floor, to wake the next morning with heads pounding and mouths as dry as the plains that stretched beneath the city walls. I recalled, hazily, that we had not even decided if it had been a victory or a defeat, but each of us could name a dozen men who had not come home to England, but were buried there beneath the vines.

These were the men whom Richard of Cornwall expected me to betray. I carried the letter like a vial of poison, sealed into a thin tube of lead that I hid inside my boot. Though, as I had assured Iselda back in Lyon, I had no intention of delivering it, the fact of its existence weighed on me dolefully. I had not, even now, worked out what I was going to do – about the letter, about Richard and the pope – so it clung to me like a secret canker, like hidden leprosy, nagging at me, pointing insistently at a future into which I was charging at full speed, but in which nothing was clear except an overwhelming promise of danger.

My first duty in Nicosia was to seek an audience with King Louis. Henry de Lusignan, King of Cyprus, had given his cousin part of the royal palace. Nicosia is a mass of narrow, overhung alleys that reminded me, somewhat, of Constantinople, though it was a glimpse of that great city before the calamity of the Franks had turned it into a phantom place. I was wending my way through a crowded market, my head throbbing with last night's wine, when someone knocked into me, hard, twisting my shoulder around and making me lurch into a slumbering donkey. I turned, my hand instinctively on my knife and hard words on my lips, and found myself looking into the face of Remigius. He stood, long arms loose at his sides, leering into my face. When he saw I had recognised him he grinned.

'You are taking your time, aren't you, Friend of Jews,' he said softly.

Then he rolled his eyes like a mountebank and took off into the crowd. I found myself understanding what the old woman in Florence had meant when she described him: like a loose hand suddenly made into a fist. I took off after him, knocking over a basket of oranges. The donkey burst into enraged song behind me. I saw a black corner of his cloak vanish round a corner and dived after it, only to find myself stumbling down a flight of stone stairs. I kept my feet by a miracle, but when I reached the bottom and looked wildly about me, there was no Remigius to be seen. I ran down the street, guessing which direction he might have gone, but soon I was at the city walls. I doubled back, circling the market, but there was no sign. I wondered if I had imagined him, but the bruise darkening on my shoulder told me I had not. He could have killed me. He had killed Isaac in exactly that way: bumping him in a crowded street. I should have been dead beneath the hooves of that donkey. So I had been warned. John of Toledo – and behind him, Innocent himself – had thought it worth sending their assassin to check up on me. Well, I was doing what I was told. Here I was with the damned crusade.

I searched in vain for another hour, my blood boiling, Thorn loose in her sheath. Perhaps it was rage and vanity that told me I would kill him, because he was a murderer by trade and I had become a fat banker, but the truth was that I knew in my heart that Remigius was already long gone, well on his way back to Lyon to tell his masters that their tame serpent Petrus Zennorius was doing as they had bid. By the time I reached the palace I was quivering with frustration. I had not avenged Isaac. I had been too slow. I was furious that I was still being toyed with. I even felt vaguely affronted, if truth be told, that Innocent doubted my word. But perhaps there was some good to be gleaned: if Remigius reported me at Nicosia, with the crusade, would they now be assuming I would carry out the rest of my mission? That would be fortunate indeed.

I found Louis seated on a throne in a stateroom that overlooked the walls. He was delighted to see me, or seemed to be. We had not met since the year Montségur fell. I had been almost a courtier once, Louis's Purveyor of Relics, and over the years I had spent months at the king's palace of Vincennes, walking with him through the oak forests, far from the frantic bustle of Paris. But since fate had made me turn my attention to the stifling operations of the bank, I had not been back to Vincennes. Louis had not changed a great deal: his face was still unlined and strangely boyish, and indeed he seemed so excited to be on the brink of his great adventure that he might have been fifteen years old. He embraced me – no kingly airs with Louis – and led me straight to a table on which a jumble of maps was spread. To my surprise I saw that the queen was sitting by the window, reading a missal. I had rarely seen her at Vincennes. Louis did not seem to pay much attention to her, although all the gossip had it that they were greatly in love, and she had not been very interested in Louis's relics or the Sainte Chapelle. Marguerite of Provence was, I suppose, twenty-eight or twenty-nine then, and I had forgotten how lovely she was. Her black hair hung in waves from under a fine white scarf, and her eyes were large and wide. She looked up to see who had come in, and I bowed.

'Your Majesty,' I said, 'I am speechless. I would not have come wearing these dirty soldier's clothes had I known you were here.'

'Dear sir, I expect we shall all be very used to dirty soldiers' clothes before too long,' she murmured, and with a smile she turned back to her missal.

The king ignored her, and took my arm. 'You are a knight now, eh, Petrus? An English knight, forsooth! I should have knighted you myself while I had the chance!' Louis knew I had fought against him at Saintes, for by sheer chance I had killed one of his highest nobles, the Sire de Bourbon, on the field. But that had been war, and Louis had not begrudged me my loyalty to my own king and country. Besides, I had taken the red of Bourbon's shield as my own colours in honour of the man – since I had spatchcocked him like a capon, it seemed the least I could do – and Louis had appreciated that, even thanked me for it in a letter. Strange, for what I had thought would be taken, at the very least, for a betrayal of his trust, seemed to have increased my standing at his court. I would never understand this business of knighthood, I knew that well enough. Still, here I was known as Sir Petrus Blakke Dogge, and I had to stop myself looking over my shoulder every time someone called my name, for it hardly seemed to belong to me.

'We shall capture Damietta,' Louis said, tapping a tiny painted castle hovering between blue sea and the spreading branches of the Nile. 'And from there we shall march upriver to Cairo. The sultan of the Egyptians is a weak man, given to bluster but without true substance. Once we have Cairo, we will turn east and enter the Holy Land through the Sinai.' He chopped the side of his hand across the map. 'And so we shall take back Jerusalem.' He looked up with a vast grin on his young face.

'Well, it sounds simple enough, Your Majesty,' I said, laughing. 'When do we sail for Egypt?'

'I have been waiting for the rest of our host to sail from France,' he said. 'Ah, here's one of the newcomers!' he added, as a young man put his head around the door. Louis beckoned, and the young man bowed, and came over to where we were standing. He was about twenty-five, with a carefully groomed beard, slate-coloured eyes and a thick head of yellow curls. He looked familiar, but from where, and when, I could not recall.

'My dear Jean,' said the king. 'You must remember Sir Petrus?'

'Oh, indeed!' said the young man, and bent his knee courteously. 'Jean de Joinville, sir. Delighted to see you again.'

Now I remembered. 'The Seneschal of Champagne! The honour is mine. It has been a few years since we met.' Indeed: the year before Montségur. He had been very young, chattering about heretics and crusades. The years had been kind to him.

'They are all here now, but the weather has turned against us and we have resigned ourselves to staying here the whole winter,' said Louis. His face fell, then brightened again. 'But no matter! Do you know, I have received a letter from the great King of the Tartars? One Eljigidei, ruler of Persia, no less. He proposes that as I attack Damietta, he will strike at Baghdad, and so we shall divide the Saracens.'

'And then, what of Jerusalem?' I asked. 'Your Majesty knows the Tartars are not usually inclined to stop their armies once they are in motion, or to give up land they have taken.'

'An excellent question, Petrus. Do you remember Andrew? Of Longjumeau?'

'Of course.' I had not forgotten the amiable friar who had rescued me from Constantinople long ago, and who had been hunting for the Cathar Crucifix as war closed in on Montségur.

'Well, I have dispatched him to meet this Tartar king, this Eljigidei. We shall see what comes of it. Meanwhile I shall not wait. Damietta . . .' He prodded at the little castle.

'I know Damietta, Your Majesty,' I said. 'I traded there in days gone by. It is a strong place, but you have a great army.'

'And faith, Petrus: and faith.'

'Amen!' cried Joinville. Looking down at the map, hovering above the painted world like God himself, I realised that the moment I had dreaded was upon me: I had joined the crusade.

'Amen,' I said.

William Longspée unfolded himself from the casemate window in which he was sitting. He was an angular fellow, not excessively tall but lean and long-limbed, and he had a careful way of moving that reminded me a little of a praying mantis: poised, slightly ridiculous and dangerous. But he was less mantis-like in character, for I found him to be a jovial man, full of jests and quick to laugh. His gangling body was graced with a handsome face, a very English face: strong jaw, full lips, a somewhat thick nose, wide blue eyes and a high brow under cropped blond hair that would have curled if it were longer. He wore his beard cropped short as well, save for a gallant curl at the moustache-ends and chin. His voice was loud, which seemed to embarrass him a little, and that alone would have made me like him. But he had bid me welcome, and saw to it that I was settled and content among the English contingent, and though he was the Earl of Salisbury's son and I a mere knight of dubious issue, he went out of his way to treat me as an equal, which seemed to be his habit with all those who served under him.

'We are leaving tomorrow,' he said, reaching for the wine jug. 'And I for one could not have borne another day in this damned place.'

It was the beginning of March. The island was growing warm again, and the first spring flowers were starting to show as a pale wash of colour across the plain. Louis had given me a horse, a beautiful, tight-wound creature called Tredefeu – Tread Fire – and he had been grudgingly carrying me about the plain and into the hills. And with Tredefeu had come Warren of Eykenham, a freckled lad, second son of some Marcher lord, who would be my squire. I did not want to be responsible for the boy, but he knew the business of knighthood and its trappings far better than I and besides, Tredefeu tolerated him.

'Cyprus will turn into a raving beauty as soon as we leave,' I said.

'Quite the story of my life!' Longspée chuckled, and poured a cup of wine for each of us. 'Still, my oath has been weighing on me of late. As if God is impatient with me.'

I had taken no crusader's oath, though I had lied to everyone about that, and doubted it would have troubled me even if I had. But I shook my head.

'God requires us to do our work as soldiers,' I said. 'And that must mean picking the right time and place to attack the Mussulman. God might perhaps be impatient with the weather, but not with you, my lord, or with me. Monks wait out their lives patiently in their cells, and so we have been no worse than monks these last weeks. God is pleased with stillness as much as with action, if it is done to serve Him.'

'Christ almighty, Petrus! You sound more like a priest than the chaplain himself! D'you think the Lord is pleased with young Simon? He certainly hasn't been conducting himself like a monk.'

I might have told him that I had once been a monk myself, but I did not. Instead I grinned and shook my head. 'Agh! I do not know what came over me. Perhaps I am trying to start this holy enterprise with a clean conscience.' The truth was that I had grown so used to outdoing godly men at their own simpering, and had played the part for so many years while disguising the true nature of my godless heart, that I sometimes overdid it. And I had been spending too much time in the company of King Louis, for whom no pious platitude was too much.

'And what do you have on your conscience, Petrus?'

'Ah. If you see a confessor's hair turn white in one day, you will know I have paid him a visit,' I said.

'So bad?'

'Far, far worse . . .'

'Excellent. Then I will make sure you are beside me in battle. An unshriven soul tends to fight harder, in my experience! But tell me – why did you sign with the cross? No, don't fear. I don't mean to pry. But it's simply that so few Englishmen answered the call.'

I had been wondering how to answer this. 'My lord the Earl of Cornwall . . .' I began.

'Oh, dear suffering Christ! Do not conjure up Earl fucking Richard and ruin this pleasant afternoon!' cried Longspée. But he was laughing, and so I asked what he meant.

'Only that Earl Richard, wealthiest of the wealthy, richest man in the whole of bloody England, did *not* sign with the cross, but managed to convince His Holiness that he should be rewarded with a levy as if he were coming to Egypt himself, while I have had to beg the pope for the money to keep my brave knights fed and horsed! The nerve of the man!'

'Ah. Then perhaps I am Earl Richard's conscience,' I said wryly.

'Maybe, maybe,' said Longspée.

'But do not worry too much about money,' I said. 'I have plenty, and I will make sure the earl reimburses me for whatever I spend on our glorious English contingent!'

'Then drink up, Black Dog,' said Longspée, filling my goblet once more. 'For I think we are going to be friends.'

Much later, I was walking back to my quarters through the narrow streets when a man stepped into my path. He was a young knight, no different from the thousands crammed into Nicosia, and I nodded to him politely.

'Petrus Blakke Dogge?' he enquired. His French had a heavy tinge of German in it.

'Aye. Can I be of service?'

'Only to listen. Some words from Doctor Michael Scotus. He gave them to me, and I am passing them to you.' He paused, and ran his fingers absently through his short, pale hair. 'Something about a drug ... Ah, yes. They – you'll know who *they* are – have sent someone to do your business. Doctor Scotus bids you beware. He bids you to look for the God-fearing among the Mussulmen.'

'Wait. Doctor Scotus gave you this message? Michael Scotus?'

'Yes. I don't know what it means. Do your business . . .' He rolled his eyes good-naturedly.

'Do you know Doctor Scotus?'

'Of course not. I was paying my respects to the emperor – I am from Aachen, you see – on my way to take the cross. And this Doctor Scotus asked if I was bound for Cyprus.'

'Did he tell you anything else for me?'

'That . . . Oh, Lord. Terribly sorry. There was something else, but . . .' He winced, as though he were grating his memory like cheese. 'This person – he's doing something that you're doing, I think? Has something of yours?' He shook his head. 'I'm sorry, my comrade. I was vilely sick on the crossing – I've puked my skull clean. Ach . . . no, he said to be on your guard. But then, I suppose that might do for any of us, eh? Well, good luck, Sir Blakke Dogge,' he said, and slipped past me. Before I could ask him anything else, he was gone.

Chapter Twelve

The shores of Egypt were walled with gold, or so it seemed that morning in May. We had had a smooth crossing from Cyprus, three merry days of sunshine and fair winds, but as soon as the coast of Africa came into sight as a black line on the horizon, the mood aboard our ship changed. The men did not become less boisterous or boastful, but whereas before the boasts and jokes had been easy and relaxed, now they were egging each other on. It was time to go to work.

The golden haze on the strand before Damietta slowly came into focus as we drifted in towards the shore. The sultan's army awaited us in all its finery, sunlight blazing off helmets, swords and shields, silken banners snapping in the wind off the sea. And even from half a mile out we could hear the blare of trumpets and the frenzied drub of kettledrums. Men were galloping their horses up and down the beach, no bigger than gilded ants at this distance. From the king's ship came the order to keep sailing up the coast. There was a low hiss of disappointment and, I knew, disguised relief from the English knights around me. We were not going to fight today after all.

The king had decided to listen to his barons, who were telling him to wait for the rest of the fleet. For the rest of the day we watched white sails appear like gulls on the horizon, until by dusk my galley had been swallowed up in a great floating city of ships, and still more were arriving. I curled up against the rail at the prow and listened to the sailors calling and the ropes creaking, and the soldiers puking. Very late, as the Via Lactea streamed out across the sky like God's icy breath, I fell into an uneasy sleep and woke early in a wet mist, as rank and fishy as gull vomit. I went and found where the sailors were eating their breakfast, and passed an hour with them while the mist lifted and the day, bright and blue, was revealed overhead.

There was a sudden braying of horns from the king's ship. William Longspée appeared and hurried to the rail. Flags were summoning the leaders of our various companies for a council. William descended gingerly into a gig and went bobbing off across the cat's paws. He returned soon afterwards, and I gathered with the other knights to hear what our fate was to be.

We were going ashore right away. The king had ordered that Damietta was to be taken without delay. We all let out a great cheer, of course, two hundred English voices raised in murderous jollity, and myself joining in out of politeness. But there was a somewhat strained hush when Sir William announced that we would be attacking on foot, for our deep-draughted ship, like most others in the fleet, could not get close enough to the beach for our horses to be brought off. Longboats would take us in, and we would wade ashore, all for the greater glory of the Lord.

'Will the 'eathens give us a hand up out of the water?' called a Yorkshire voice. There was muffled laughter and the bark of a sergeant-at-arms. Not a bad question, though Sir William pretended not to have heard it. The Mussulmen were in plain sight, a huge army of them clustered under the walls of the town. There were several thousand men, on foot and in the saddle – even at this distance I could see their close-packed ranks and the dart of horsemen racing up and down the strand.

So this was a crusade, I thought to myself. No wonder they never succeeded.

Warren helped me into my suit of mail, silent, busy with straps and buckles, trying not to look me in the eye. Bad luck, was it, to meet the gaze of a doomed man? My armour had survived its journey well, but it reeked of the oil that had kept it supple. The hauberk settled on my shoulders, and I staggered for a moment, letting the weight sink into my muscles and joints. The hood went over my head and I slipped my surcoat over it, red cloth blazed with a black hound seated on its haunches, snarling, one paw raised. I went and leaned, fidgeting, on the rail, getting used to the drag of the mail on my limbs.

A minute passed, a quarter-hour. But all too soon I found myself clambering down a ladder into a longboat, shield slung across my back, helmet hanging from my neck by its strap. It felt a little as if I were being garrotted. The sea was calm, though a deep swell was riding in towards the shore and the boat rose and fell slowly against the side of the ship. All around me, other men were leaving other ships. The fleet was loud with confused sounds: the hollow thump of smaller boats jouncing against bigger ones; curses and cries of fear; shouted commands. Over us all rose voices raised in song: every priest and friar, it seemed, was chanting or singing a hymn to the Lord, but from every ship came a different song, and there was no sense to it, no order, nothing but a golden vibration that hung above the toiling men in their little boats. It was strangely beautiful, all those voices weaving in and out of harmony into discord, while a great flock of gulls, attracted by the commotion, added their own harsh counterpoint.

I got my balance in the pitching boat and made my way to the prow, picking up a lance from the pile that lay across the benches. My reasoning, so far as I had any, was that as we would doubtless be coming onto the beach into the teeth of an arrow storm, it would be better if I could get out quickly rather than get tangled up in panicked men or dead oarsmen. And it would be easier, I told myself, to escape if the boat capsized. The sea was calm but the swell was collapsing onto the beach in heavy plunges of spray. The lads at the oars were wide-eyed with fear, their faces the colour of fish bellies, and I doubted they had much skill. I rested the point of my shield against the wood of the prow and hunkered down behind it. Behind me, Guy Curtbac and John of Motcombe were jostling for position on the stern bench. Guy gave me a wink, and I gave back a mirthless smile. The boat was full now, and yet another knight was clambering gingerly down the ladder. One of the oarsmen called up anxiously, and someone cursed and swung his leg back over the rail. There was a splash nearby, and shouting: a man had missed his footing and fallen from the ship next to us. Everyone seemed to be yelling at the spreading ripples, but no head appeared. The poor bastard: weighed down with his mail coat and helmet, he would be heading for the bottom like a bar of lead.

Over the confusion a horn gave a blast, then more joined in the blare. It was the king's vessel giving the signal for the attack. My companions in the longboat tugged out their rosaries and kissed crosses or pressed them to brow or heart. For form's sake, next to Iselda's stag I was wearing an old golden Greek cross I had found in Constantinople years before, and I waved it before my face and moved my lips silently. No prayers for me, no magic armour, only Richard's letter, strapped against my arm with a length of silk. I rarely wished for the solace of the Christian faith, but at times such as this it seemed that the men winding strings of beads about their wrists or tucking little vials of holy water into their chain mail might have some small advantage over me. No, to hell with it: my shield was good English oak, and that would have to do. I thrust the cross back inside my armour as the lads bent their backs and the longboat pulled away.

Out from the shelter of the great ships came the crusaders, cautiously, little dark shapes on the bright water edging away from the fleet, which as I looked back at it seemed like a long, forested island. But as the oarsmen found their rhythm, our flotilla began to gather speed. Now we were in open water I saw with a surge of relief that I was in the midst of an army, for it had begun to seem as though I were attacking Egypt with only the eleven men in this boat. There were galleys as well as longboats, hurling themselves forward, pennants flying, men cheering. On the shore, the Saracens had begun to form up in the dunes behind the beach. It still seemed as if we were hopelessly outnumbered. I had a brief vision of myself running up the sand, waving my letter to the Sultan. *Hold on, you fellows! I'm supposed to be on your side!*

We were low in the water, weighed down with armour and weapons, and the rowers were sweating, bending and heaving, but with each stroke we surged towards the enemy. The lances that each man held were waving slightly in the wind. The sun was blazing down and I was already bathed in sweat myself. I could feel it running down my back and my legs. But my tongue was as dry as a sepulchre. The fear eating me was not that I would be wounded or killed, but that I would be hurt and the people tending to me would discover the letter. That would be the end of everything. I didn't care so much for myself – though as the beach drew nearer my flesh was cringing, as if the steel was already in it – but for Iselda.

I pushed back my damp hair and drew up the hood of my hauberk, fumbling with the laces that secured the flap across my mouth and jaw. My helmet was broad-brimmed and open-faced, a *chapel-de-fer* as the Franks call them, and when I had put it on and tightened the strap beneath my chin I felt oddly comforted. To keep my spirits up I rapped on the crown with my knuckles. Just then there was a sharp tap, sharper than skin on steel, and I looked to find an arrow hanging from the face of my shield. Arrows were sailing in all around, but the Saracen archers were far out of range and the barbed points could not do much damage. We were getting closer, and it seemed we were moving much faster now. The swell was lifting us and pushing us on. To our left, the long shape of a galley overtook us in a slapping and churning of oars.

There was cheering from the galley, but on our longboat every man was crouched in white-lipped concentration, save for the toiling rowers, who were grunting with exertion, veins standing out on their necks and temples. Every stroke took us a boat-length nearer. I caught Guy's eye. He nodded as if I had asked him a question. I shifted my wet-palmed grip on the shaft of my lance and fought off the urgent need to piss. An arrow sang past and buried itself in the scuppers. Every man had his shield up now, and the men behind me were holding theirs up to protect the rowers. There was a lurch and we were into the surf. The longboat pitched, the prow reared up wildly and fell, and I clung on, knees braced against the sides as there was another surge and the prow rose again, higher, higher, and as it dropped the yellow sand of the beach flashed past in a blur. A gout of spray struck me in the face and as I blinked it away, eyes stinging, the stern sank, there was a roar and a hiss, and the longboat ran aground.

'*Deus vult! Deus vult!*' God's will! Guy was yelling, John was yelling, I was bellowing something into the pad of chain mail that covered my mouth. Grabbing the rail, I stood up, planted the heel of my lance in the sand and jumped. I landed ballock-deep in cold water, and at once the undertow was sucking around me, almost jerking me off my feet. I must get onto the beach! Heaving against the undertow, I took a step, agonisingly slow as if in a nightmare. My helmet had tipped forward over my eyes and I shoved it back to find a patch of bare sand just ahead of me. I dragged another leg forward, the freezing water surging through the rings of mail, each footstep sinking into yielding sand. And then I was free, wading ankle-deep through foam, Guy Curtbac beside me.

'Where are they?' I yelled at him, and he turned to me, eyes ringed with white.

'Don't know!' he shouted back. From where we stood the enemy was nowhere to be seen, though arrows were falling on us, arcing up from behind the dunes which rose sixty or so paces ahead. To left and right the foam was filled with staggering figures. The galley had run aground further out and men were struggling chest-deep. And suddenly the first horses appeared on the crest of the dunes, over to the right, then the left. I looked up and there in front of me a dun-coloured horse was standing, and astride it sat a man in white, the sunlight shining from silver arm-guards and greaves, and from the high point of his helmet. He carried a spear from which fluttered a green pennant. There was a skirling of unseen trumpets, and in a few heartbeats, which were pounding in my ears like a ram against the gates of a besieged town, the dunes were crowded with horsemen. They stood poised for a moment and then like the waves collapsing behind us they began to drop down the face of the sand hills, shrieking as they came, sand flying up in tawny clouds all around them.

Up and down the line of the surf, men were calling to one another, shouting, and out of the confusion I found I had become part of a line of men standing shoulder to shoulder. The man next to me ran forward onto the dry sand and dropped, kneeling, behind his shield, shoving the heel of his lance into the sand behind him, point levelled at the dunes. The first line of Saracens had reached the foot of the dunes, checked their horses and charged. I dropped down next to him, and as I lowered my own lance a thousand others wavered and steadied. The ground was shaking beneath us from the beat of hooves. I braced myself for the shock, searching the blur of men rushing at me for a target. On they came. '*Deus vult! Deus vult!*' the men beside me were shouting. Everyone was shouting. My lips drew back in a mindless snarl.

And suddenly the Saracens turned. A spear's throw from our line, they reined in and wheeled, some to the left, some to the right, and began to ride across our front, shooting arrows at us and jeering at the tops of their lungs.

'Jesus Christ, why don't they come on?' said Guy. As he spoke another cry went up from the crusaders: '*Saint Denis! Saint Denis! Montjoie et Saint Denis!*'

'The king has landed!' croaked Guy. 'They fear him – the Turks fear our king!' And he joined in the clamour.

The Saracens were hesitating. They had turned again and were urging their horses back up the slope of the dunes, sand billowing, hooves slipping, beasts squealing in panic. Over on the right, the great white and gold standard of France was flapping, pointing towards the town like a weathervane. And there was Louis, kneeling on the sand, arms raised in prayer. A party of Saracens, five hundred or more horse, reared on the lip of the dune and raced down, and it seemed that the king, one man alone or so it looked to every drenched, sweating crusader crouched behind their shield, must be swept under their hooves into the sea. The king picked up his shield and couched his lance as if he meant to charge them alone. But again, as we all gave tongue and '*Saint Denis!*' burst from two thousand throats, the surging troop wheeled and retreated. In a long ripple the army rose to its feet and cheered. The Saracens were milling nervously above us, some riding along the crest, others appearing and disappearing as they rode down the reverse slope. Still we held, and still Louis Capet stood out in front of the shield wall, sword thrust into the sand before him, hands raised in prayer. And it must have seemed to most men that God had answered their king and delivered up the land of the Mussulmen to the army of Christ.

By the time the crossbowmen and foot soldiers had come ashore, the enemy had vanished. We formed up and charged the dunes, tearing up the gently collapsing slopes, feet slipping, shields and spears keeping us on the edge of balance, but somehow we knew the Saracens were not there and so our charge was little more than a sun-roasted dance, for what was our great army to do, all riled up and full of the anger of God? And indeed when we reached the clumps of grass at the top, we found nothing but horse-dung and flies, and the flat vastness of Egypt spread before us. At our backs, noble lords were already having their pavilions raised on the beach.

Louis sent a party towards the town to see what had happened, and before long a lone knight rode back, bareheaded, a foolish grin pasted across his face. The Saracens had gone, gone from Damietta. They were flying back towards Cairo. The town was ours. The priests were gathered there on the dunes and the army sang the '*Te Deum Laudamus*'.

Chapter Thirteen

Even now I shake my head when I remember that eight months passed from the day the crusaders rode into Damietta to when we set out again on our way to attack Cairo. Time, we are told, is immutable, but in Damietta it seemed to defy the laws imposed upon it by philosophers and trickle by as tediously as the brown waters of the Nile seeped past the city walls.

Saracen raiders were killing our soldiers every night, raiding the camps outside the walls and cutting off the heads of their victims because, it was said, the sultan was paying a bounty for every dead Christian. We found out later that the sultan had been poisoned as he campaigned in Palestine, and he had been too sick to give any orders to his army the morning we had landed. If he had been in Damietta that day, things might have been very different for us. The first charge of Saracen cavalry would doubtless have thrown us back into the sea and we would have been slaughtered. I could only bear to think about this after I had woken up the next day in a real bed. As I had knelt on the sand, as the Saracens in their silver helmets and silk robes had pranced and then charged, my head had been empty of thoughts save for the ones preparing my body for pain. So in the strange distortion of battle I had not felt relief but disappointment when the enemy had pulled back, for I had been ready to suffer. Instead, here I was, spared so that I might learn the tediums of life in a garrison town.

The king's first act was to order an encampment to be made outside the walls for the crusader army. The king himself took over the city's largest palace, and his brothers and their retinue joined him, but most of the lesser nobility pitched their tents in the camp. But I had never intended to live in a tent. Let them whose faith had brought them here wake up with scorpions and snakes in their beds: I would have four stone walls around me. The day we entered the town I had sent my lad Warren off to find me decent lodgings while I went with William Longspée to help the king set up a temporary court. The streets were teeming with frightened townsfolk, and the crusaders were bullying and insulting them and calling them infidel and Turkish dog, though all the Mussulmen had fled and the people who remained were Greek and Coptic Christians. But their dark skins, foreign garb and the fact that they smelled of rosewater and vetiver and not a year's worth of sweat meant that they were, along with everyone else in this country, not really human. I had been here before, though: the captain often stopped in Damietta to trade for the strange items that sometimes arrived here from the mysterious vastness of Africa. We had bought ancient cloths painted with unreadable script and symbols, wonderful jewellery and carvings in gold and ebony and blue stone, but most of all we had bargained for mumia.

Mumia: if ever there was a reason to avoid doctors and surgeon-barbers, it would be that dark, ominous-looking powder with the smell that stings the linings of one's nose. For the notion that drinking a solution of the ground-up corpses of long-dead, embalmed Egyptians might not kill one on the spot, let alone cure one's apoplexy or murrain or the hundred other maladies for which the doctors would have us believe that mumia is sovereign – that has long seemed utter madness to me. Granted, it had been my good fortune to have Isaac of Toledo as my physician, a man who had some real knowledge of the body and its hidden workings, and who regarded those who peddled bat-shit and mustard poultices, cat piss and the rest of it as little more than paid assassins – paid, moreover, by their willing victims. We did not need to buy the scraps and corpse-clinker that looked somewhat like sea-coal, for we were not in the business of medicine, though people paid a fortune for those sorry leavings when they had been pounded into mumia. Instead, we hunted for whole cadavers or recognisable limbs or appendages: fingers were always good, as were toes, and even a shrivelled pizzle or pap could sometimes be found. All so that a bishop in Denmark might buy himself a breast of Saint Catherine, and one of the many manhoods of Saint Christopher might end up in some newly built cathedral in Spain. An entire corpse was, of course, the biggest prize, but these came on the market rarely, though the captain had spoken once or twice of a fabled source of mumia somewhere beyond Cairo. We had been going to find it one day, the captain and I, when he retired from the sea and the relic trade. It was a jest of ours: we would gather an army of ancient corpses and send them out hither and yon over the face of the credulous world to do our bidding. Did we talk of it when we were besieged in Montségur? Perhaps, but we ourselves were the walking dead then, and soon enough death came for Captain de Montalhac.

Damietta was not a very pretty town: fifty years ago another crusade had taken it and the Franks, as they are wont to do, had knocked the place about. Since then there had been much rebuilding in the airy, elegant Saracen fashion, but the walls, and the people, knew all about infidel soldiers. I went and paid my respects to Louis, and then took myself off to the merchants' quarter to see if any of my old business acquaintances were still here. The first two doors I knocked upon seemed to belong to empty houses, and I was making my way to a third house, an old palace close to the walls where a Jewish dealer in silks and curios lived and worked, when I heard footsteps behind me. Ordinarily this would not have been a surprise, for these streets were usually teeming with people. But today the place was sepulchral, and all the noise was coming from beyond the walls, where the camp was being set up and the soldiery were toasting their victory. Louis had not let the army inside the walls, for I had heard that he intended to distribute the spoils in an orderly fashion, without the usual looting. So when I heard footfalls I turned quickly and loosened my sword, expecting to find an angry Damiettan looking to settle his score with one of the invaders.

A long shadow ducked up a side street. Keeping my hand on my sword, I doubled back and peered round the corner, but there was nobody in sight.

The curio merchant was not at home, or not answering his door, and I couldn't blame him for that. So I followed my nose to the souk, where some nervous traders had set up their stalls, though there were few customers. But a man was grilling spiced mutton on skewers; I bought a few and made sure to pay more than I owed, and to speak to him in his own language. He did not say a word to me, but did not spit on the meat, for which I was grateful. I wandered through the souk for a while, trying to find someone I knew, and making small-talk with the traders, doing my best to put them at their ease. King Louis was a just king, I said, even for a Christian, and they shouldn't worry about their safety. Not one of them was convinced, and why should they be? I went in search of Warren, feeling like what I was: a conqueror, a Frankish, barbarian conqueror. Men cross oceans and risk death in all its forms to have that feeling, but I would not have given the dirt from beneath one toenail. I made up my mind, somewhere between the souk and the governor's palace, to get out of Damietta as soon as possible, find the important men in the spice trade and work out some way to prove, beyond a shadow of a doubt, that Earl Richard's wishes would never be fulfilled. Strange to have such a task: to prove something impossible and not the other way around, but at that moment I felt so wretched, such an impostor, that I would have saddled a crocodile and ridden it all the way to Cairo just to be done with this crusader play-acting.

Warren – or the bag of gold I had entrusted to him – had procured me a fine house near the palace, with a long view over the shore and the great green plain of the Nile's mouths. The merchant who lived there had a wife and several daughters, and had seized this profitable opportunity to remove them to safety. I paid his servants – Abbi, the major domo, and his family – to stay with me, and when they realised I was not a boorish, dangerous Frank but someone who could speak their tongue and understood their ways, they served me well, even though they must have hated me. Money can buy respect and even a man's soul, but it can never buy his heart. It is a strange thing about Frankish conquerors: they destroy everything in their path, and then they expect their dispossessed, bloodied victims to fawn over them like besotted dogs. I did not want my throat cut while I slept and nor did I wish my new household to fear me, so I went about with kind words and a smile for all, and slept with my door locked.

That first night, I waited until the street door was locked and the servants had gone to bed. After closing the shutters tight I took Thorn and, squinting in the guttering light from one little oil lamp, cut the silk band that held Richard's letter, inside its leaden tube, against my upper arm.

In the dim light I took up a penknife and broke open the seal. The letter was unharmed, the vellum not even foxed. There was the confident, slashing hand of Richard's scribe, the ink still slickly, gleamingly black. The pope's seal was as solid and incriminating as it had been when I had hidden it away.

If any other man in Damietta found this thing, I was done for. The French are not kind to traitors, and to one who had planned to betray a king and God Himself . . . I would be tortured for days, with all sorts of refinements like burning sulphur poured into my wounds. Then I would be torn limb from limb by horses, and what was left of me – they would make sure I was still alive, in some hideous manner – would be burned. Then they would find Iselda and do the same to her. So I must hide it well. But it could only be hidden in plain sight.

In amongst my baggage was a small leather purse. Battered, unassuming, held shut with an old bronze buckle that was going green, it had once belonged to Gilles de Peyrolles, and held the distilled essence of the craft he had taught me: how to make a holy relic from whatever one might have to hand. There were a few delicate tools of the kind used by jewellers and a couple beloved of thieves; two little boxes with sliding lids that held, in glass-lined compartments, various powders; another box that held vials, some of glass, one of lead, of powerful liquors; and some odds and ends rattled around in the bottom of the purse, seemingly random. From these I selected a hard, shiny black cube. A Moorish amulet I had bought that morning lay nearby. I prised it open, shook out the concoction of coloured threads and scribbled-upon old parchment inside, and with a little effort managed to get Richard's letter to fit into the cavity. Then I closed it up and, holding the black cube in the lamp flame until it began to melt, caught a drop on the end of a silver pick, and let the black liquid seep into the join between the amulet's two halves. Two more drops, and the thing was sealed so tightly that it would need to be cut open. But just to be sure, I had already cut a thin strip from a piece of rawhide I'd bought and let it soak in a dish of water. Now I bound it three times round the silver, knotting it so that it looked like fellahin work. Then I hung the amulet round my neck and went to bed.

When I woke up the next day, the heat of my body had dried out the rawhide and bound it fast to the silver. Yawning, I brought out my forger's kit and, while the town came to life outside, set to work. By the time the servants had set my breakfast out in the little shaded courtyard below, my trinket looked like a piece of ancient sorcery, ominous enough to be treated with caution, but plain enough that no eyes would seek it out. Suddenly I felt much safer. Now I had only to slip out of Damietta, make my way to Cairo in one piece, convince the sultan – should I manage to get an audience – that although I was plainly a miserable traitor to my people and my religion, I was worth trusting, and finally, to convince the Defender of the Mussulman Faith that he should enter into an alliance with, of all people in this teeming world, the pope in Rome. The whole thing seemed so absurd that I burst out laughing, and sprayed yoghurt over the floor tiles. Then I calmed down. Was I really going to deliver the letter? In all honesty, I was not. The Saracens did not look as if they intended to put up much of a fight, which meant that something was wrong in Cairo. Promises from an infidel would not mean much if the sultan was not easy on his throne. But it occurred to me that I should be seen to at least try, for I could not be the only papal spy in Damietta, and the German crusader who had found me in Cyprus had more or less told me I was not. Perhaps I could vanish for a while and reappear . . . No matter. The opportunity would present itself. And the letter itself held a power of its own, although I was not yet sure how, or indeed if, that could be used to my advantage. Meanwhile I had kept myself alive so far: it seemed best to use my energies to make sure I stayed that way.

In those early days the king surprised us all by turning his back on tradition and keeping the goods we had captured in Damietta – large stores of corn and rice – for the Crown, and not giving up two-thirds to the army, as was the custom. There were rumblings in the camp over that, but by then the Saracens had begun their attacks, and there were other things to worry about. The army was itching to get moving – upstream, to lay siege to Cairo, or along the coast to Alexandria – for as far as they were concerned the Egyptians were no match for the cream of French knighthood and it would be an easy job to take their country. But Louis, who had two of his brothers with him – Robert, Count of Artois, and Charles of Anjou – was waiting for the third, Alphonse, the Count of Poitiers, who was bringing the rest of the French army across from Marseille. Jean de Joinville kept me abreast of things in the palace: some bickering between brothers, I gathered, and the king growing more and more anxious. On top of everything else, Queen Marguerite was with child. Joinville was proving to be a useful friend at court: he was clever and had a sharp eye, and seemed to have taken me under his wing, although all we had in common was a shared memory of Louis's court in a simpler time. I tried to teach him the language of the Saracens, and in return he made sure I dined often at the royal table. The king was always in good spirits, although his men were often ill-tempered, and the queen would sit apart, kept company by the few other noblewomen who had followed their husbands to Egypt. As time went on her belly began to grow, but still the king paid scant attention to her, at least in public, and I wondered, when I saw this, how such a kind and pious man could be so cold towards the wife he was supposed to love. It was a strange thing, and not pleasant to witness, but since we had left Cyprus, Louis seemed to have turned away from her. He reminded me of a little boy, lured away from the girl who has been his playmate by other boys who promise games full of noise and violence. Now the king dressed in chain mail and spent every minute between waking and sleep either with his priests or his commanders. If I saw the sad, confused glances that Queen Marguerite gave her husband when they were seated together at dinner, or when the court was assembled for some proclamation or decision, others did too, but there was nothing to be done. I wondered, all the same, if I was the only one who found it shameful that a man who put the love of God above all else should throw over the love of his wife for the doleful amusements of war.

Because I missed my own wife, I liked to sit in the courtyard of my lodgings writing letters to Iselda, and twice a supply ship brought me a letter in return. The letters spoke of little things: gossip in the market, the cook's nephew's new son, some bank news from Florence. The world seemed to be getting on quite well without me. But for the most part I spent my days exercising with the English knights and making enquiries amongst the remaining merchants, trying to get a sense of the trade routes and who controlled them. My Jewish friend Ya'qub bin Yazdad appeared after a few days, and some other Christian merchants too: they had been hiding in attics and cellars, expecting to be burned out at any moment, but when that didn't happen they began, so they told me, to wonder what profit might be made from the situation.

None, alas for them: the crusaders, denied their customary pillage, began to strangle the businesses that remained in Damietta by charging them outrageous rents for their own properties. Damietta had become a Christian city by then, the mosque was a cathedral, and the Frankish occupiers, as they had done in Constantinople, had begun to squeeze the juice from the conquered townsfolk. It was good to have Ya'qub to talk with: he was a sharp-eyed old rogue with a beard the colour of a wolf's mane, and though his stock-in-trade was silk, he sidelined in the sort of curios that the captain had found very profitable amongst the richer prelates, particularly

Roman cardinals. A Swedish bishop had bought the first one I had seen, two little ivory figures, a man and a woman, with broad, painted smiles and no clothes, who had fitted together in a charmingly lustful and intricate way. The captain had liked Ya'qub, and Ya'qub had fond memories of the captain, who had lined his pockets many times, he would tell me, patting his robes with a wolfish grin. I would drink wine with him in the evenings, and he would show me his wares: scrolls from Cathay showing a thousand ways a man might roger a woman; plump bronze dancers from Madurai; strange wooden pizzles from God knew where; exquisite ink and gold miniatures from Persia which were as beautiful as they were filthy; and even clay vessels of the ancient Greeks and Romans around which beasts went at it with languid girls, and men and boys did things that would get you burned at the stake in a heartbeat, though they went on in every monastery. He was quite crestfallen when he learned that I was in a different line of business now, but I promised to keep him in mind should the need arise, for after all, I did know a great many cardinals.

As soon as I had found my feet in Damietta I had decided to conduct an experiment. One morning I rose early, dressed in some nondescript Saracen clothes I had bought in the bazaar, and slipped out of the camp. The enemy patrols were easy to dodge, but I had gone no more than a quarter-mile when I realised that the flies were draining me of my blood as rapidly as if I had just opened a vein, and that the land was a maze of canals and irrigation ditches. I could not take the main causeway that led southwards, that was plain, and if I set off into this pest-ridden swamp on my own without a map, I would not last a day. So I slipped back into the town and made enquiries about finding a boat. That proved impossible as well: not that boats could not be found, for an exorbitant price, but Ya'qub assured me that the boatmen would slit my throat and leave me to the crocodiles. He knew them all, and none of them were to be trusted. Besides, the countryside was teeming with Saracens, and a lone Frank would not get very far. I could probably have passed myself off as a Greek, but they would be looking for spies and I did not fancy getting my throat cut for no real reason. My curiosity was satisfied. To make my way south towards Cairo would be an act of suicide. There was no point in leaving Damietta on my own.

Weeks passed. One night in Ya'qub's house I took myself off to the privy and as I stood there, watching the moon rise through the smoke of the camp beyond the walls, the baleful realisation that I was trapped here in this place, with this army, hit me in the pit of my stomach like the first pangs of the flux. Like it or not – and I did not, by God – I was a crusader, and whatever these Frankish buffoons decided to do next, I would have to go with them. The only way out of Damietta, if I still meant to reach Cairo, was with the army.

To fill my time I liked to wander in the bazaar, and as the traders came to know me they began to talk more freely. One day, four months or so after we had taken the city, I was admiring a rug that a Circassian merchant had spread out on his stall.

'Where has your shadow gone?' he asked, as we were bantering.

'Shadow?' I asked.

'Certainly. There was another Frank – though you are not so much like a Frank yourself,' he added politely. 'Everywhere you went in the bazaar, he would come after. Was he a friend of yours?'

'I don't know what you mean,' I said, puzzled. 'Who was he?'

'A Frank.' The man shrugged.

'And . . . ?'

'Well.' The man squinted, trying to atomise the differences

between one Frank and another, minute though they might be. 'Tall – he was taller than you, my friend. And he had a funny way of walking.' He started to squirm and flutter his hands.

'Dear God! Like a woman? Not much like me, I trust?'

'No, no!' The Circassian laughed indulgently. 'Not like a woman! More like a snake. And . . .' He thought some more, then brightened. 'Here!' He pointed to his eyes. 'This one looks straight, this one wanders.'

I felt a little breath of cold air on the back of my neck. Remigius, Isaac's murderer, in Damietta? But then I remembered what the German knight had told me: someone had been sent to learn about the Drug. Had Cardinal John really sent Remigius to Egypt? I spent the next day chewing this over, but decided, at last, that the merchant had been describing some Pisan or Genoese, sneaking about in search of a trading concession. Such people tended to attach themselves to anyone with a claim on the king's ear, and perhaps this snaky fellow had just been too timid to tap me on the shoulder.

It took six months for Count Alphonse to arrive with the rest of the army. Six months stuck in Damietta, listening to ludicrous court intrigues and, by the end, looking forward to the Saracen attacks, for then at least I could ride Tredefeu and breathe the open air. There was no danger, for the enemy would ride up, shoot off arrows and perhaps spear an unlucky soldier out foraging beyond the defences, and when the knights appeared, turn tail and run. It was calculated to exhaust and dispirit us, and it succeeded. So when the sails of the count's fleet appeared one Thursday morning at the end of October, the camp and the court went half mad with excitement. But it took another month of arguing in the governor's palace before the army set out, and besides, ships full of crusaders were still straggling into port. The barons wanted to attack Alexandria, a rich prize and not far along the coast. The king's brothers, especially the blustering Count Robert, argued for a direct assault on Cairo, as it was the sultan's capital and, as Joinville – who was of the king's party in this – told me, if one wishes to kill a serpent, one must crush its head. I hardly need to say that I was desperately hoping we would go against Alexandria, for no other reason than that it was nearby and would not take many leagues of toil through pestilential marshes to reach. And as an erstwhile sailor I knew that one can always escape by sea. But I was not a sailor any longer, I was a horseman, and when Jean de Joinville came to rouse me out of bed very early on the eve of Saint Nicholas's feast, I knew before he even opened his mouth that we were bound south for Cairo.

Later that day I was returning from the camp, where I had been part of a tourney – there having been no Saracen attack that day, we must needs attack one another. I was not in the best of moods, having been knocked off Tredefeu by an insolent young Breton, and was planning to cheer myself up with Ya'qub's company. I had gone to my quarters to get out of my armour, and as I was washing my face, one of the serving girls knocked on the door of my chamber.

'There's a Frankish priest to see you,' she said.

'Really?' I said. 'Please tell him I'll be with him directly.' And feeling a ripple of foreboding, I tucked my knife, Thorn, beneath my robe.

But it was not Remigius. Indeed, it would have been hard to conceive of anyone less like Cardinal John's knifeman. Waiting for me on the doorstep was a Latin priest in travel-stained black robes. I guessed he had come ashore that morning, on the French ship that had put in from Marseille bringing letters and the very last, the very tardiest crusaders. He was short, almost squat, with a rubicund, slightly pimpled face and a sharp nose with a white scar, that jutted from the roundness of his features as if someone had taken a ball of dough and pulled out a fleshy point from it. There had been no hardship in his immediate past, as he was as round as a dumpling and radiated self-satisfaction.

'Can I help you, Father?' I enquired.

'Assuredly.' He spoke with a jolly simper, but there was something underneath the merriment. 'I am Father Matthieu d'Allaines. Am I addressing Petrus Zennorius, lately of Venice?'

'That you are. What can I do for you?'

'Well, perhaps a draught of cool water? And then we will talk. I have come a long way to find you, my son!'

'Of course! Come inside, Father.' With a smile and a bow, and a sudden rush of foreboding, I ushered him into the shade of the courtyard, and shut the door. I showed Father Matthieu to the stone bench beneath the orange tree, and called to Abbi the major domo to bring cold sherbet.

'You've arrived from . . . ?' I enquired, delicately. The priest pursed his plump lips and smiled.

'Rome,' he said, his voice syrupy with self-approval.

'To see me? Surely not,' I protested.

'Surely not? That is an interesting way of putting it,' said the priest, inscrutably. Our drinks arrived, and Matthieu d'Allaines took his cup eagerly, but I noticed the look of disdain he cast at Abbi. 'Yes, interesting,' he went on, after he had taken a couple of greedy swallows. 'Because, you see, I came looking for you, expecting – hoping, indeed – that I would not find you.'

'And yet, here I am,' I said, puzzled. The man was beginning to annoy me with his riddles.

'Exactly. Here you are. Why?' He narrowed his eyes.

'If you had come tomorrow you would have found me gone,' I said, prickling. 'I am here with the army, and with the army I leave in the morning. For Cairo.'

'Most commendable. Most commendable – your duty lies with the army of the Lord. And with King Louis, yes?' He finished his sherbet and put the cup down with a dry clack. 'Such loyalty – but to whom?'

'You will have noticed I wear the cross of a crusader. I think that means we're both loyal to the same Lord, eh?' I was being glib, but the little man's face was souring quicker than puke on a hot doorstep.

'I have one Lord, but I serve one master, and one alone,' he snapped. 'And you: have you turned Frenchman? Your lord and master is Earl Richard of Cornwall . . .'

'That is common knowledge,' I scoffed, though it wasn't. And I knew, all at once, what was coming next.

'And is it common knowledge,' the priest's voice sank to a whisper, 'is it common knowledge that you have sworn an oath to Earl Richard, to deliver an item? And that the earl is doing *my* master's bidding? You, sirrah, have betrayed not only your lord, but mine – and in *that*, you have spat in the face of Jesus Christ himself!'

'You are far from home, priest,' I growled.

'But at least I have a home.'

'And what does that mean?'

'Why have you not delivered Earl Richard's letter?'

'For fuck's sake! Not so loud, you imbecile!' I looked about us, but apart from the rats in the date palm, we were alone. 'You have just got here, so you told me. It seems a Christian city: no dark faces, no muezzin wailing over the roofs. And that is right. Where, oh priest, do you think the good Mussulman people of Damietta have gone, eh? They wait outside the walls, to cut every Frankish throat that strays out of bowshot. Did you trouble to look about you? Have you been up on the walls? Between here and Cairo is one vast fen. A fen full to bursting with Saracens. Neither I nor my letter would be good for anything save the worms if I had set off like a blind calf to the shambles. My task . . .' My voice had risen, and I lowered it hastily. 'My task was to deliver the pope's letter to the sultan at Cairo. Tomorrow we march south to take the city. The army will spread confusion before it, and into that confusion I shall slip, deliver my letter—'

'You are a liar. And a bad one.' That hurt. If nothing else, I knew myself to be a flawless liar. And besides, I was telling the truth.

'No, I am not,' I hissed. 'I will carry out my side of the bargain. But listen to me! Do you suppose the sultan intends to let Louis conquer his lands? In what mad Lateran fantasy is this sultan expected to throw up his hands and surrender to the infidel host unless he receives a fucking *letter*?'

'You blaspheme . . .'

'I do not speak ill of Our Lord, priest, but merely of a gaggle of scribes and arse-lickers.'

'The words are those of Pope Innocent himself.' Father Matthieu's lips had gone as thin as cheese-wires.

'Listen, priest! It is not *blasphemy* to criticise a pope! Unwise, perhaps, but Innocent is not God. He serves God. As do we all.'

'I have been given cause to wonder about that,' said Father Matthieu, venomously.

'What do you mean?'

'You have not carried out your appointed task? Answer yes or no!'

'No, I have not.'

'Then' – the man stood up and marshalled his flesh into a pose that attempted dignity – 'Petrus Zennorius,' he intoned, 'I have come to bring you notice of excommunication *lata sententia* from Holy Mother Church!'

'Well, for fuck's sake!' I burst out. 'On what grounds?'

'For being an apostate, and for plotting harm to His Holiness Pope Innocent.'

'Ridiculous. Where is your authority?'

'Here.' He brandished a large roll of parchment at me. To

my amazement I saw that it did indeed carry a great leaden seal, the bull of Saint Peter. 'Do you see it? Tremble, you insect, before the Fisherman's justice. But in the midst of his righteous anger, the Holy Father has found it in his heart to offer you mercy.'

'What, in the name of Christ's foreskin, are you blathering about, priest?' I demanded. He smiled a codfish smile, infuriatingly smug.

'I shall burn this, and return to Rome tomorrow, if you swear the most solemn oath, on whatever holy relic might be available in this . . . this . . .' He looked about him at the Mussulman decoration that covered walls and ceiling. 'No matter – something will be found. Before witnesses and the holiest relics, you shall sign over the Banco di Corvo Marino to the Holy See.'

'*What?*' I found I had bent down, the better to look into the man's angry little eyes. I had known all along that somehow my promise to Richard would catch up with me, but now that it had, I felt nothing but a glorious, self-righteous fury.

Father Matthieu, perhaps blinded by his own self-righteousness, seemed to mistake my answer for interest. 'Not so loud, my son! His Holiness is all-merciful. He has no wish to punish a good son of the Church. Go to him, confess your sins and admit your failure. Your worldly goods are forfeit, of course, but your life . . . Have no fear. Innocent is the emblem of all that is good in this world. Does he not do battle with Antichrist? There will be mercy for you!'

'So my worldly goods will be forfeit, just like that?'

'It goes without saying that, when you leave here, you will proceed directly to Lyon and prostrate yourself before His Holiness, beg his forgiveness, and pledge your unwavering loyalty. Your worldly possessions and those of your . . . your *wife* . . .' He puckered his lips in plain distaste. 'Everything of yours, everything belonging to your wife and your retainers is of course forfeit. Failure to comply will cause your ex-communication to be pressed immediately – you, your wife, your dependents and employees will be investigated and put to the appropriate punishment.' He pursed his lips as if he were turning a sour cherry around in his mouth.

'So I hand over everything, as though I were a drover, or a knife-sharpener? An afterthought, eh? You have come a long way to make a bad joke, my friend. I don't think you're a businessman, but your master is, and he must know I'd expect a great deal more than mercy for that sort of outlay!' I laughed in the priest's face, and he winced as if I'd slapped him. 'The letter – I understand now. You never intended me to deliver it, did you? It was just a ploy to make me betray myself. Innocent never wanted anything but my money.'

'Why send a banker, a usurer, to do the business of princes?' spat the priest. 'Like any worm in the hands of the Fisherman' – he paused to make sure I had noted his wit – 'your destiny was always the hook.'

'Then why all this mummery? Did you expect me to die when we came ashore?'

'Why not? But no, it was to part you from your viper of a wife and the shelter of the bank. You are alone here. You may squirm, but it will only bring the barb deeper into your flesh.'

'Alone?' I burst out laughing. 'I am a crusader! Every man in God's army is my friend! I know Innocent wants my money. He's not the only one. I'll tell you what *is* funny, though, priest: I can see the pope's greed shining out of your eyes.' I had spent all day pretending to fight, and so my body was acting quicker than my mind, otherwise I might not have done what I did next, which was to reach out and snatch the parchment from the priest's fat little hand.

'The pope is threatening me? With this?' I said. Father Matthieu saw my face harden and he lunged for the bull as I wrenched at it and ripped a great tear down the middle of the roll. For a moment we both looked at each other in shocked surprise. I had certainly not meant to do that. Could you tear up a bull of excommunication? Probably not. But I did. As the priest danced around me shrieking imprecations and banishments I tore the parchment into ribbons and flung them up into the air. All I was left with was the disc of lead stamped with Saint Peter's keys. I hefted it in my hands.

'Follow me,' I barked at Father Matthieu. In the corner of my courtyard was a well. Ignoring the priest, who was now raving incoherently, I marched over to it and dropped the seal into its dark mouth. There was silence, and then far below, a hollow plop.

'There,' I said.

'You . . . In God's name!' sputtered Father Matthieu. And then he mastered himself. 'I am on the Holy Father's business. Apostate, I should thank you, because you have condemned yourself! Now, this very minute, I am going to King Louis—'

'And tell him you and the pope are working to doom his crusade? If you think your word will count for anything, remember that while I'm probably his chief financier for this campaign, I'm also the king's Purveyor of Relics. I have dedicated years of my life to helping him realise his dearest, most pious ambitions.'

'You are putting your head in the noose, you Ghibbeline filth! And after you were given fair warning! Cardinal John—'

'Cardinal John is a fool,' I snarled, 'and an ungodly schemer. If this is his doing, it is my pleasure to defy you.'

His eyes narrowed: he looked like a plump, pallid lizard stalking a big moth. 'But the letter . . .' he whispered, and I could have sworn I saw a blunt tongue-tip moisten his lips. 'You are still a traitor, Black Dog Knight – Black Heart, perhaps they'll call you, eh?'

'The letter bears Pope Innocent's seal, not mine. Please go ahead and tell the king about it, after you have presented yourself as the pope's emissary. And now, since I do not see you jumping into this well after your badge of office, I will tell you the truth.' I had him backed against the date palm. 'The letter has not been delivered. Nor will it be. I am loyal to no man through the swearing of oaths, or through piety or fear. But I am loyal to my friends, Father Matthieu, and to my debtors: and Louis Capet is both things. I am going to war tomorrow. And so is the king. Even if he had time for your spew, you have no proof, no proof at all! Well, do you? Where is your bull, and your precious scrawling? Where, come to that, is the letter, eh?'

'You think you have mastered Rome, but you have not, servant of Antichrist!' sputtered the priest. 'Do you really believe such a great enterprise would be entrusted to a creature like you alone? Are you so prideful to think that the Holy Father placed this responsibility in no other hands but yours? And that we cannot simply reach out and take what we wish?'

If I had listened to what Father Matthieu said to me next, I might have been spared what befell me in the months that followed, for I would not have stayed in Egypt, and I might have killed the vile little man on the spot. But because he started to rant about Iselda, and Venice, and because I did not want to be soiled by the kind of slanders a man like Matthieu would have slithering around in his mouth, instead I turned my back on him and went to fetch the watchmen of the house, who came running with their staves, and, with great relish, set to throwing the priest out into the street. I was furious, of course: seething with anger, because I knew as well as did Father Matthieu that an excommunication does not vanish if you flush it down a well. But, so I reasoned, the Church could do nothing to me here, and I had bought some time. The pope was testing my resolve, but I was out of his reach. I would go south with Louis, try to discover something that I could turn to my advantage – even, perhaps, something that would please

Richard of Cornwall, and then hurry back to Italy. Frederick von Hohenstaufen seemed to want my help, and wasn't he an excommunicate? It meant nothing. In fact, it was an honour, I told myself. Earl Richard was the pope's friend. He would sort this out for me. And ignoring the cries from the street as the watchmen saw off the pope's messenger, I went off to get myself ready for the march on Cairo.

We set off the next day. Father Matthieu d'Allaines had not shown his face again. The trumpets blew, the flags fluttered limply from the battlements of Damietta, and the queen stood forlornly, her hand on her swollen belly, surrounded by the old knights who would not be coming with us. As we rode off she waved, and Louis waved back, absent-mindedly. Then he galloped off to speak with his commanders. I wanted to wave to Queen Marguerite myself, and tell her not to worry, that we would be back before her child was due. But of course I could not, though I did turn once, when we had gone quite some way, and she was still standing there under the flags that had surrendered to the heavy air.

A great army it was, swaying and stamping its way south, thrusting itself towards Cairo like a vast, muscled arm, swollen with pride and faith. Many thousands strong, the column swayed and tramped, stirring up a long cloud of dust, a mile or more separating the mounted nobility and knights at the front from the toiling engineers who brought up the rear, cursing the oxen who dragged the timber – a forest's worth – that would become siege engines to destroy the walls of Cairo. This was God's army, so there was no straggling shadow-force of whores and camp-followers. And because this would be a quick campaign against a degenerate enemy, we had brought few supplies with us. Cairo was not far away, and we would live off this fertile land in the meantime. Whores we had shunned, and comfort we scoffed at, but we had nothing to fear, for a big, brash company of priests and their acolytes and servants marched just behind the knights, singing the Lord's songs as we thundered along in search of men to kill.

Almost at once we struck our first obstacle. The Nile was doing what the Nile does at that time of year: flooding the countless arms through which it reaches the sea with roiling, muddy water, though the floods were quickly receding. One of these arms was flung across our path, and we spent a day and a night damming it up so that we could cross over. This happened again and again, and then the Saracens attacked. There was a short and what one might call a neat battle, in which the Templars, who had been driven almost to the point of delirium by boredom in the camp outside Damietta, slaughtered every single Mussulman who had ridden against us, and there must have been five hundred of them, in less time than it takes to boil an egg. Thus refreshed, the army of God proceeded on its way.

South we went, on a muddy track that ran alongside the river. The mood of the army was downright jolly: it was as if we were all on some merry summer pilgrimage, the kind of pilgrimage in which beer and wenches play a solid part, save there were no wenches and not a drop of beer. But I was content to ride Tredefeu, who had accepted me over the months of jousting and charging after fleeing Saracens, and these days only bit Warren when the lad was careless with the hoof pick. Crocodiles slithered into the water as we passed, and strange birds teemed in the reeds, high as a house, that grew everywhere in spinneys and thickets. There were pink birds, and long-legged white ones with bald, black faces and long, curving beaks, and small brightly coloured ones that swarmed around the banks of the river, that were turning into little cliffs of mud now that the flood was going down in earnest. We saw the enemy rarely. They had pulled back all the way to Cairo, so we told each other, and that was because they already knew they were beaten.

One morning, as the mists were lifting off the marshes and the birds were vying with each other to bruise our eardrums with their cries, one of the pickets came into camp, leading a mud-spattered fellah. He was a Christian, come to sell news from Cairo for a few coins, and what news it proved to be. Sultan Ayub was dead. The poison he had been given before the battle of Damietta had finally done its work. There was a great uproar from the noble tents, loud enough to give the marsh birds some competition, for it seemed that the sultan's only son was far off, beyond Damascus, and Egypt had no ruler save the sultan's widow, whom Joinville called an Armenian whore. A woman on the throne? Cairo was defenceless!

Amid the rejoicing, and the bragging about victories not yet won, I slipped away to ponder my own troubles. Perhaps they had suddenly diminished. My task was to deliver a letter to Sultan Ayub. It was Ayub to whom Pope Innocent had made overtures. It was Ayub who controlled the armies of Egypt. Who, now, could I make my promises to? This Armenian widow – she would not, of course, be a whore – was called Shajar ad-Durr, and I knew a little about her from the Cairene traders I dealt with. She was wily and hard, so they said. She would be doing everything she could to make sure her son became sultan. But she would be fighting for her son and for her own life, and promises from an infidel would mean nothing. So I was free.

What now? I could ride back to Damietta, take the first ship back to Venice and whisk Iselda away before anyone was the wiser. But something held me back. I was playing a game, secret to those around me but quite public to a few powerful watchers back home. If the crusade was about to succeed, it would be best for me if I played the game to the end, so that there would be no doubts as to my loyalty. How could I slip away, when the Mussulman throne was already empty and the crusader army was moving so quickly towards victory? And then – I cursed myself, bitterly – there was something else. I could not leave the army now. Pride is the bane of man, and pride stopped me from turning tail. Pride . . . But something more. Because amongst this horde of blustering fools I had, to my alarm, made friends. What would Joinville think if I vanished one night? What would Longspée make of it? They would call me coward. My name would drip like spittle from one end of Christendom to the other if I went back to Italy now. And then the dogs would be unleashed. So I persuaded myself, so easily, to stay a little longer, to march into Cairo with the others and have my name put into the songs. I would return with some lustre to my name, and vanish with Iselda when no one expected it. That seemed the easiest thing to do, or so I convinced myself.

A few idle days passed, in which only four crossbowmen died, two of drowning, two of the flux, and then we came to a sudden halt. Across our path lay water. Not another of the countless ditches and culverts of that fenny region, but the Nile itself, or so it seemed. The barons, full of pride that they had already mapped out this conquered land, called it the Rosetta Branch. Alas for their pride it was not the Nile but the Ashmoun Canal, but Nile or not it was deep and wide, a long bowshot across to the other side, where a walled town stood. It was called Mansourah, and there, waiting for us, was the entire Saracen army.

Chapter Fourteen

'We shall dam the river,' the king said, one foot resting jauntily on the rotting, spongy trunk of a fallen palm, elbow on knee, a long-fingered, beringed hand inclined delicately towards the expanse of brown, muscled water that roiled, two bowshots wide, at the foot of the muddy bank.

'Of course, Your Majesty,' said Jocelin de Cornaut, and sniffed efficiently. He shaded his eyes and squinted across the Nile. Over there, between the walls of Mansourah and the water's edge, stood the Saracen camp, at this distance looking like nothing more sinister than the display of a Parisian sweet-maker. Peaked tents, domed tents, banners and awnings were lined up, gaudy as butterflies, their flags and pennants snaking in the faint breeze from the sea. Small detachments of horsemen galloped up and down the far bank. Further downstream, some of our men were yelling revolting words at them.

It was a week before Christmas. We should have been at the gates of Cairo by now – or inside them – according to the camp tongue-waggers, but instead we had fetched up here. I had been in the advance guard late in the evening two days ago, and when we had burst through the last thicket of reeds, tall as young trees, that grow everywhere in this low and dismal country, and saw the brown water ahead, I had cursed, shrugged, and guessed we would be turning south-east to find a ford or a narrower place where the army might cross. But when Louis had joined us, the circlet on his sweat-matted head wreathed with a whining halo of biting flies, I knew by the way he set his jaw and frowned at the water that he had decided on something else. By the next morning the enemy had made camp across from our own great straggle, and the king went into his tent with the great nobles and the Templar lords, and did not emerge again that day. The Saracens had rowed into midstream and shot arrows at us, killing two mules and blinding a pikeman, but the flies had been more of a nuisance, and by the second morning my skin was a red mass of welts. So when the king's herald found me I gave him no more than a tight-lipped nod, pulled on my hauberk and followed him, muttering imprecations to myself that were drowned by the low hum of flies from the towering acres of reeds all around us.

Jocelin de Cornaut was the king's engineer, a tall, bow-legged Flanders man with large ears and sandy hair. His eyebrows and beard were sandy too, and what with the sun and the flies he had begun to look somewhat flayed. But he was a nice enough soul, a soldier who had spent the last few years in the service of God, designing the cranes and winches that served the builders of the Sainte Chapelle in Paris. Now he was back in the field. I wondered what he preferred: raising the delicate, skeletal spires of King Louis's great shrine or the gross work he had now: siege engines, crude bridges and now this.

'How will you do it?' I asked him, offering him my flask of thin, vinegary wine. He took it and sipped, making a face, before handing it back with a grateful nod.

'Causeway,' he said bluntly. 'There's enough mud here-abouts . . .' He trailed off, measuring the ruffled waters with his eyes.

'Won't . . .' I paused and considered my next words. 'That

might be a lengthy undertaking,' I finally said. 'And you will be building your causeway straight at the infidel. Did the king not wish to search for a more auspicious crossing?'

Jocelin shrugged. 'Cairo lies yonder,' he said, chopping the side of his hand down as if dividing the Saracen camp in two. 'I think that the king does not want his army trailing about in these bloody fens. They are a maze – we have only just begun to advance, and already we have wasted days. Better to cut straight through. Besides, the infidel will have the crossings guarded.'

I decided not to point out the festeringly obvious: that the infidels were waiting for us directly across the river. 'I should have thought you liked fens,' I said lightly. 'Being Flemish and all.'

'Beer, my good Petroc,' said the engineer with a great sigh. 'My country has mud, reeds, quaking bogs, flies, same as here. But Flanders has beer. And Egypt does not.' He closed his mouth with a mournful snap and went back to studying the river banks. I left him there and went off in search of shade.

The camp set to work building two siege towers and a pair of movable, covered walkways, to protect the poor sods whose ill-luck it was to be chosen as causeway-workers. The men who laboured in these cat-houses, as they were known, had to put up with endless mud, leeches, flies and rotting feet, and the sporadic but accurate fire from the enemy's stone guns – great catapults, sixteen of them, all lined up on the far bank. The king ordered Jocelin to build eighteen of our own guns, and in a couple of days these were banging away, hurling stones across the dirty water, though more often than not our missiles splashed harmlessly into the river or the mud. But steadily, Louis's causeway had begun to creep out into the Nile.

The causeway was, in effect, a big dam cutting off this arm of the great river. It might even have worked had our enemy been an army of simpletons or idlers. They were neither, however, and as fast as Jocelin thrust the arm of his causeway out into the stream, the Saracens dug away the bank opposite, so that our men, despite their toil, never came any closer to the far shore. I had little to do, for along with the rest of the gentry I was not required to soil my hands. We fenced, and some men jousted. We gambled and quarrelled.

In the end it was the boredom of the camp which sealed my fate, for we all shared the routines and the rituals, the danger, such as it was; boredom bound me to the army. We were comrades in idle discomfort, and one does not abandon a comrade.

Advent came, and brought me a letter from Iselda. Old Doge Tiepolo had died, it told me, and there was a new doge: a spectacularly mediocre old priest called Marin Morosini. A mermaid had been sighted off Chioggia. The son of an acquaintance had run off with a courtesan. I wrote back, about sunsets across the Nile fens, biting flies and idleness.

I tried to wander off whenever I could, past the belt of trodden reeds and shit-piles that marked the boundary of the camp, to explore the little streams and deserted fields beyond. I fished, and brought back eels for my tent-mates. There were hoopoes and gaudy kingfishers to watch, and once I saw the scaly back of a young crocodile slipping into the water. I drew my sword, but the monster did not reappear. More dangerous were the snakes, as long as a man and with strange, flattened necks. If a man was bitten he died in an hour, and not a few of our soldiers perished that way, locked in frozen agony.

It was not hard for me to leave the camp. Apart from Joinville I hardly knew any of the French contingent, and while I was part of the little knot of English knights, I had resigned myself by now to the fact that they regarded me as an interesting oddity: a Cornish knight with a foreign lilt in his voice, with powerful allies at court, with a mysterious past.

I tried to steer clear of them when I could, for – typical Englishmen – they were a gaggle of sunburned complainers, most of them, save for Longspée himself who had kept his cheerfulness and had a certain grace about him. True, it was sometimes diverting to join them in their endless ritual of cursing everything under the Egyptian sun, but they were prone to work themselves into a dense and bitter gloom that usually turned to anger.

Twice a party of them set out to look for Egyptians to kill, and if they had found some bedraggled peasant and his family they would no doubt have slaughtered them, but both times they returned, shame-faced and fly-bitten, without the blood of innocents on their hands. And each time, Longspée scolded them and sent them slinking off to their tents. Once my page, Warren, had been among the malefactors, and I had added some stinging words of my own to Longspée's tirade. He had blinked at me, his eyes too blue for this land, freckles joining up across his face, and I knew that the poor lad was so far from Gloucestershire that nothing he saw or did made much sense to him. But he was a good soul, not very bright but agreeable, and I did not want him becoming a murderer. Besides, he was good with horses, and Tredefeu liked him.

I would sometimes go fishing with Longspée, who knew how to catch all sorts of fish and loved to share a jug of wine while we remembered the hills and woods of England. One thick, humid day we had managed to slip off after setting the English lads to complete a morning's much-needed sparring. We pushed through the forest of reeds until we found a wide, deep-looking stream where I had had some luck a few days before. We had encountered nothing more dangerous than a heron on the way, and the fens were quiet, so we trampled out a comfortable place for ourselves and set about baiting our hooks.

Longspée had found a nest of fat, pallid worms in the rotten crown of a reed clump, and was threading a writhing tangle of them onto his hook. He flicked the spidery mass across the stream with a practised nonchalance and settled back into the bank.

'I've never asked you,' he said. 'Black Dog. Strange name. How did you come by it?'

I scratched my head absently. There were a dozen answers I had concocted over the years, and I grabbed the first one that sailed past in my head.

'Aha. When I was born – and this was in Cornwall, mark you, where such things are given much credence – my wet nurse was wrapping me in my swaddling bands, and being caught by the sudden urge to piss, she set me down and went into the corner where the piss-pot was. My mother was in her chamber, still laid up from bearing me, and the menfolk had been driven out by the midwife, who, so my mother told it, was pitched forward and snoring into my mother's bedsheets. As the nurse squatted in the corner, there came a snuffling and a padding at the door, which gave out onto the open yard. And then, in padded a huge black hound. Black, so said my nurse, as the devil's lampblack, save for its eyes, which were as big as saucers and glowed like the setting sun through red stained glass.'

'Cry mercy!' chuckled Longspée, stretching, and giving his line a twitch.

'She did, sir. That woman had a tongue on her, I can assure you. But the great black hound took no notice of her, and padded over to me, helpless as a maggot in my bands, and not two hours old. It gave me a sniff, and then another, and touched its black snout to my brow. And then, before my nurse could heave the full piss-pot at the creature, it gave her a look which, she declared, set the blood in her veins as hard as granite, and slunk out. I needn't tell you that my father and the other menfolk, addressing a hogshead of scrumpy out in the yard, saw not one hair of the beast, but rushed in to find my wet nurse, her skirts tucked up around her waist . . .'

Longspée gave a soldier's laugh. 'A young thing, was she, this nurse?' he enquired, eyebrows cocked.

'Not a bit of it. Gnarled as a blackthorn tree that grows at the edge of a sea cliff.' I grinned. 'Now, as you know, in Cornwall and in Devon, the country folk believe in terrible black hounds. Some call them Yes Hounds, some Wish Hounds, and some give them the name Gurt Dog. They are ill-omened, no matter what they are named. Not a soul could agree what my visitor signified, save that it must portend either great good or great ill. And for most of my life I would have thought the former were true.'

'Until you fetched up in the marshes of Egypt,' finished Longspée. He brushed a platoon of flies from his face.

'Indeed.'

We fished on for a while. Longspée's worms were taken by a pike, who spat out the hook. I caught a brace of small, perch-like fish. My friend took a decent-sized catfish. I got tired of fishing and started to look for the crayfish traps I had put down the day before. I found one – there was quite a welter of beasts within it, snapping their claws.

'Gurt Dog . . . Gurt Dog? Somehow it seems I have heard *that* name before,' said Longspée. He was threading more worms on his hook, the end of his tongue touching his moustache as he concentrated. 'A song, perhaps? Not for a long time, though . . .'

'Salisbury is not far from Balecester. There was a song called "The Gurt Dog of Balecester". But I cannot remember what it was about.'

'Nor I. No, wait – foul murder in the cathedral. A man-beast who ate a bishop on his own altar?' Longspée flicked his hook distractedly into the water, brow furrowed. Then he brightened. 'I have it!' he cried. And to my horror, which I managed to conceal as I juggled a spiky ball of crayfish into my sack, he began to sing:

> *The Bishop he sits him down to dine*
> *Cold runs the river, o*
> *He cuts him some meat and he pours him some wine*
> *Cold and deep she runs, o*
> *When in comes a man with white face all a' quiver*
> *Cold runs the river, o*
> *And the wailing he makes sets the candles to shiver*
> *Cold and deep she runs, o*
> *'Lord Bishop, Lord Bishop,' the poor wretch he wept*
> *Cold runs the river, o*
> *'For to thy cathedral a black beast has crept.'*
> *Cold and deep she runs, o . . .*
> *. . . something, something, something . . .*

'D'you remember it now? You could hardly pass a wine-shop without hearing it, a few years back. "From the door of the minster a gout of black blood . . ." Good stuff!'

'Ah, yes. The monstrous black hound rips out the bishop's throat on his own altar,' I said, ruefully. 'And vanishes into the night. Do you know the Bishop of Balecester? The real one? He would scare the fur off any black dog, gurt or otherwise.'

I myself knew the bishop quite well. And I knew the song, word for word. And so I should, because it was about me. I was the Gurt Dog. It hadn't been the bishop's throat that had been slashed in Balecester Cathedral, but that of his deacon, and the murderer had been the bishop's bastard son, though I – Petroc of Auneford as I'd been then, novice monk and inattentive scholar – had been blamed and was chased across land and sea for my supposed crime. Still, I had revenged myself upon the bishop and, such is the play of fate, had saved the wretched man's life at the Battle of Saintes, though I had not intended to. By then the world knew me as Petrus Zennorius, of course, for I had long buried young Petroc under many layers of untruth and forgetting. Meanwhile, in the taverns of England, a hapless young monk had suffered an alchemical transmutation into a great hell-hound, several innocent men had been caught and hanged, and I had become a creature that mothers used to scare their little ones into obedience.

'Ha! Yes, I know Balecester, of course,' Longspée was saying. 'A creature ruled by his ambitions, but I will say that he keeps a damn fine table and cellar. He told me about you himself, as a matter of fact: how you dragged him through a vineyard after some Frenchmen had knocked him off his horse.'

I shrugged. 'The bishop has been . . . I was about to say *kind*, but as we both know the man . . .' Longspée laughed, and I joined in, glad that I had, once again, juggled the knives of my past life and remained unbloodied. But it was high time I changed the subject.

'Sir, I hope we know each other well enough for me to ask you this, but . . .' I shook a crayfish off my finger and tied up the sack. 'I fear I am always on the brink of giving offence, for some of your men call you Earl of Salisbury and some do not, yet you seem easy with both camps. If you will allow a commoner to ask, how can that be?'

It was Longspée's turn to look uncomfortable, and I felt a flicker of guilt, but not much, and besides, I did want to know the answer. He winced and I thought I had overstepped the mark, but after he had fiddled with his fishing pole for a moment or two, he shook his head and sighed.

'The great question of my life,' he said. 'I was born . . . That is, my father, when he died . . .' He set down the pole and laced his fingers, stretching them until the knuckles were white. 'The truth is, I am earl in deed but not in name, and as to why, only our good King Henry knows that. I inherited the name Longspée,' he said, 'and little else. Our ever-wise

188

Henry . . .' He flicked at his line. 'The king decided that my estate, and my earldom, had reverted to the Crown, and as I was only fourteen at the time, and my mother had locked herself away in an abbey, I could do nothing about it. Still I cannot blame the king. He—' There was a commotion in the water and Longspée jerked his line, but the hook flew out empty. He cursed good-naturedly, and baited it with some more worms. Seeing I was looking at him expectantly, he sighed and went on with his tale.

'My father, the third earl, was a loyal friend to Henry, and helped put him on his throne. Yet the story goes that he was poisoned by the king's favourite, old Hugh de Burgh. If that is true no man has proved it. And yet for no reason that I have been able to divine – and I have spent my life trying, do not doubt it – the earldom of Salisbury seems to have reverted to the Crown. I say *seems*, because the king has never flat-out admitted that he has stolen that which is my due . . . You know all this, though? Every man in England knows it.'

'I am a Venetian, sir. My affairs in England do not go beyond my dealings with the Earl of Cornwall. I'm sorry I asked, though. It obviously brings you much pain.'

'Nonsense. If a Christian man, and an English lord, cannot bear a little suffering, then he should call himself neither Christian nor Englishman.'

'Amen! So you are indeed both earl and not earl.'

'I am, or . . . Ha! I am not. Neither fish nor fowl. But still I am Henry's most loyal servant – out of all his unruly, quarrelsome, grasping, venal lords, I hold myself ever at his service, and thank him for every scrap he sends my way.'

'Why?'

'Because it is my fate.' He let out a deep sigh and leaned forward, his head drooping glumly towards the turbid water. 'Ach, not so. I'm beginning to sound like a Mussulman, eh? No – and this will remain between ourselves, eh? Can I trust you, Black Dog?' I nodded gravely. 'Of course,' he said. 'I have difficulty remembering, sometimes, that you are not "one of us", and that I can trust your friendship. Well, now you can be my confessor – you told me you were a cleric, once upon a time.'

'Never ordained – and I'm a long way from being a holy man these days, William.'

'Oh well, never mind that. Now, you have no children, Black Dog, but I have four – two daughters and two sons. Do you remember your father?'

'Yes, very well,' I said, startled. 'But he died when I was a boy.'

'So did mine, but I hardly have any recollection of him,' said Longspée. 'He was in exile, or fighting in France, or mired at court. He rebelled against King John, and so, even though no man would blame him for that nowadays, he was never trusted again, by the regent, or by Henry when he gained his majority. I knew him through rumours and stories, and the tales I heard weren't always kind. No, they were often of the whispered sort: *your father the traitor*. You can imagine, yes?'

'I can. And you wish your children to have better.'

'You are an excellent confessor, Black Dog! Indeed: I wish them to have a life free of whispers.'

'Will you tell me about them?'

'Go on with you! Nothing is duller than tales of other people's children!'

'Very true. But not quite: the fens of Egypt are duller.'

'Ha! True, my friend. So: Ida, Ela, William and Richard . . .' He heaved a sigh. 'Ida is twelve years old, and the rest are two years apart, save for Richard, who is two. Now, I am saying this to you as my friend and confessor, but I have come to believe that men are fools. When my Ida was born, my friends and companions all rallied around me to offer their condolences, because she was a girl. But do you know? I held her little form in my arms, and stroked her silky yellow hair, and I thought: the devil take you all, because she is perfect. And perhaps I was also thinking, *Why do I even need an heir? Heir to what – an earldom that doesn't exist?* In time I had my sons, and they were perfect too.'

'Really?' I asked, sceptically.

'Aha. You'll have to find out for yourself, when we sail away from here. I have missed three of their birthdays. And my wife . . .'

'My own wife's birthday was last week,' I muttered.

'Tell me about her,' Longspée insisted. I could see that thinking of his family was giving him pain, so I conjured Iselda up as best I could for him, and as I did I found my own spirits turning the dismal brown of the stream before us. My friend told me of his own wife, Idoine, though it was plain that he thought more of his children than of her – strange, but then not so strange. He had not married out of love – men of Longspée's station seldom do, and it is one of the many curses of nobility – but he spoke of her in a way that encompassed pride, kindness and even friendship, and although there was no passion, none of the heat I felt for my Iselda, I found I could not blame him for that, although once I would have. William Longspée was a good man, I had discovered – good by anyone's measure, not merely by the miserable standards of his fellow noblemen. He cared for his children, and for his wife. He felt the hopes and frustrations of the men who served under him. Though he felt God's presence keenly, he some-how managed not to be a pious bore.

Longspée had another bite. His cane quivered and bent into a trembling arc, and without ceremony he hauled on it and a large silver shape, dripping rainbows, sailed over his head and landed, thrashing, in the reeds behind us. It was one of the huge and vicious pike-like creatures that patrolled these muddy streamlets, big enough to take off a man's finger. As

Longspée jumped up to knock his catch on the head, the sadness, the heaviness that had settled on him as he thought of his children vanished. There was a brief struggle, and then my friend stood up, knife in one hand, the toothy head of the pike in the other. Fish and man were both grinning.

Just like that, action had swept away melancholy. Longspée was a soldier, and he had been one all his life. Someone would have put a little sword in his hand while he was trying to grab his nurse's teats. And the soldier finds refuge in action. Why sit and mope about your family when you can saw the head off something? It was a useful lesson, and many times I had wished, as my life had taken its unsettled course, that I had been able to take it to heart. But somehow I had left a part of me behind in the monastery library where I had passed my young days. I felt a flash of envy as Longspée waved his bloody trophy at me.

'Saracens with scales, these monsters, eh? Got you, you heathen bugger!' He squatted down next to me and began to gut the fish. 'I took Richard fishing for the first time just a few days before I left England,' he said, suddenly quiet. 'There's a stream near to the castle – runs clear over chalk. The boy caught his first fish – a rudd. Lovely golden thing. He wanted to throw it back, but . . .'

'Bad habit,' I agreed.

'I think so,' he said, 'but he was quite upset. Then I showed him the kingfishers, how they were spearing minnows. "God made the fish for us," I told him, and then he cheered up. I must have done the same thing, I expect, when I was his age.'

But not with your father, I thought. Longspée could have been catching rudd with his boy now, throwing maggots to tempt the little golden creatures flashing in the weeds like bezants. And then I understood his sadness: he knew he had sacrificed his life, and he had made his sacrifice in the name of doing the right thing. He had always acted out of a sense of what was right – not according to God, or to his own lights, but to what his fellow noblemen, and his soft-headed king thought was best. To be a good subject, and not an object of suspicion like his father; to be, in his turn, a good father to Ida, Ela, William and Richard, even if that meant leaving them to go off on crusade so that England could feel proud.

'Don't you wish for an heir, Black Dog?' Longspée was winding the pike's guts round his hook.

'I've not been married two years, man!' I protested.

'I was married nine months when my first child came,' said Longspée, eyebrows arched. ''Tis how it is supposed to work, you know . . .'

I wasn't about to tell him that Iselda knew all the wise-women's tricks for avoiding just such a thing, or that we had spent the first years of our love under the thick, black cloud of Montségur's destruction. We had seen little children, stiff and blue, stacked like masonry while their mothers, too starved to weep, stood and watched with empty eyes. Somehow we had never actually decided the matter, but if we were childless, it was because we had decided to be.

'I'm not saying there aren't Black Dog pups running around somewhere,' I said, to stop him looking at me like that. And for all I knew it was true – I thought about it quite often. A boy with my face in Constantinople, perhaps? Some unlucky girl with my nose in Paris? 'But I came to marriage late,' I went on. 'Sometimes it takes more than luck and God's grace, you know. I've . . . I'm not young. Nor are you, but you, sir, started out younger. I'm more of an ageing stallion – and as with old stallions, things are slowing down. They need time and patience, and though I should be in my lady's bed I find myself in Egypt. Which hasn't helped.'

'No more it would,' said Longspée hastily. Then he smiled, and reaching out, he patted my shoulder with a gut-daubed hand. 'But, Black Dog, I will see to it that you get back to your lady's bed. You will make a good father, man. A good father.'

'Do you think so?' I asked, suddenly moved almost beyond measure. He nodded.

'I do,' he said.

'I'm honoured . . .'

'Honour be damned. We are friends. Are we not?'

'We are. Indeed we are.'

The subject was dropped, to the relief of us both, and we spent the rest of our morning gossiping lazily. When we finally wandered back to the encampment, we had a good string of fish apiece, which we shared out amongst the other Englishmen. Some Frenchmen carried the body of a soldier in from a picket. Bitten by a viper, they said as they passed, sweating and sullen. The long Egyptian afternoon settled upon us, heavy as a lead coffin.

That night, as I lay keeping watch on the causeway, the trails of fire-arrows cutting lazily through the thick air, I pulled the amulet from my tunic and slipped the cord from round my neck. I dangled it over the water. I was about to let go, hoping that drowning Richard's letter would exorcise the reek of betrayal I felt was rising from me, but the pasty, choleric face of Father Matthieu came into my mind and as if a finger were tapping me on the back of the head, I had a thought. The letter was a weapon. Now that it had been rendered useless against the crusade, could it be turned against its author? If I got out of this, if I ever made my way back to what I now thought of as *life*, could my letter be a talisman to ward off Innocent? This was something I understood, at last. Why, I wondered, as the sluggish water oozed through the blackness below me, had it taken me so long to think of it?

Meanwhile, Saracen arrows were proving even more deadly than snakes. They rained down upon the causeway, and any man not sheltering in the cat-houses risked being struck by arrows that came straight down out of the sky with such speed that even helmets were not always proof against them. They did not often fall in the camp, but the hollow drumming of their iron points upon the wood and hide of the cat-house roofs became, along with the rattle of wind in the rushes and the croaks and squawkings of the marsh-beasts, a strange, disjointed music that began to prey upon our minds as we trudged towards Christmas. Saracen patrols on our side of the water had begun to test our defences, and as had happened outside Damietta, we found ourselves caught up in the draining work of keeping them at bay.

Christmas Day came with hazy sunshine, thick and muggy air and the discovery of one of the king's page-boys, dead in his blankets with a snake nestled against his breast. I took myself off fishing, to avoid the piety I knew Louis would unleash upon the camp, but an alarm sounded and I ran back to find myself in the midst of a skirmish. The Saracens had attacked and, as I found out later, had captured Pierre d'Avallon, who was having lunch with Jean de Joinville. But he was recaptured, not too badly shaken, and after the wounded were seen to and the dead – not many, thankfully – were buried, I had to find a new excuse to get away from the outpouring of grateful prayer. This was the Lord's army, and the priests and friars that Louis had brought with him strove to outdo the flies themselves in their attendance upon us. Being of no religion whatsoever, I did not mind play-acting, and as I had once been a cleric myself I could outdo many a professional God-botherer, but I found that it lowered my spirits, and so I tried to be as busy as I could to avoid too much prayer, or to slip away with my cane, line and hook whenever the incense began to smoulder. After the battle, new defences needed to be dug, and so I volunteered to lead a work party. I have always found digging ditches preferable to the drivel of priests, even at Christmas.

The causeway edged forward inch by inch, but the Saracens were getting stronger and more organised. There were more attacks by day, and I would ride out with Longspée and the English lads to see off the enemy knights, though not much harm was done by either side. Tredefeu seemed to enjoy these diversions, though I did not. Many nights I spent guarding the causeway, lying on my belly in the muggy darkness with the water rippling all around me and big bolts from a heavy crossbow whispering past like malevolent bats. But I was not on duty the night the Saracens brought Greek fire and shot it from a catapult, setting fire to the towers and almost roasting Jean de Joinville alive. We managed to save the towers, but the fire came every night, and stone shot by day, and in a few days' time the work was in smouldering ruins. We had nothing to show for our labours save a pile of charred wood and a mud bank slipping slowly but certainly into the canal. Jocelin de Cornaut began work on another covered way, but at the end of January that too was destroyed.

Two days before Shrove Tuesday I received a late invitation to dine with Joinville. I had not seen a great deal of Jean since we had left Damietta. He had been spending most of his time with Louis and the king's brothers, and I hoped he was enjoying himself: the conversation must be dull stuff, I reckoned, for what else was there to talk about but how to get the bloody army over the river and launch it at Cairo? No answers were forthcoming, and we were still here in the mud. So it was without much relish that I tramped through the complaining army to his tent. But to my surprise I found him pacing about, all bright-eyed like a man in love.

'Petrus!' He slapped me on the shoulder and, grabbing me around the neck, beckoned for wine to be brought. 'We are on our way, sir!'

'Oh, yes? Where to?'

'Cairo! I have just heard, from the king himself.'

'And how are we to get there, Jean? The last I saw, our causeway was underwater.'

'Aha.' He looked mysterious for a moment, but obviously could not contain himself. 'Someone – a Christian, a . . . what do they call themselves? A *Copt* from around here came into the camp and offered – for a price, mind you, five hundred bezants paid there and then – to show the king a ford across this bloody canal. It is upstream aways, behind Mansourah. We will go across tomorrow night, and take Mansourah in the morning. And then, my dear fellow, Cairo!'

It all sounded suspiciously easy, but I decided not to spoil the evening with gloomy prophesy, and instead sat down to a good meal of grilled bustard. We talked about the coming battle, and Jean was all on fire to crush the Saracens and take Egypt once and for all, but mostly we let ourselves slip into a pleasant nostalgia for home, which, for the sake of politeness, I took to be north-eastern France. But it was not so unpleasant to wander back to my own tent with thoughts of those gentle green hills in my head. As for the coming battle, I had heard it all before. Nothing would happen, and we would still be here in the kingdom of the eel come next Christmas.

But as it turned out, I was dead wrong. Next day, the army began to muster as the sun went down, and by nightfall we were riding south on a narrow farm track, the Ashmoun Canal somewhere to our right. Louis rode in front with his three brothers and the Grand Master of the Temple. I rode with the English contingent, just behind William Longspée, and ahead of us rode the Templars, their white surcoats glimmering, phantom-like, in the dim starlight. Beside me, I could hear Warren's teeth chattering. It was cold, but the poor lad must have been scared out of his wits. As for myself, perhaps it was the long weeks of constant but slight danger, but I was barely worried. At the back of my mind lurked the shadow of fear that had been with me since we had landed at Damietta, but I had pushed it so far into the recesses of my waking life that I paid it no heed. We had paid the helpful Copt five hundred bezants to show us the ford. He had the money already, and I would have wagered, there and then, a great deal more than those bezants that there was no ford at all, and all we would see was our Copt galloping away into the reeds. So I was less than pleased when, sometime after midnight, we came to the place and the scouts found that there was indeed a shallow place in the canal. The leaders rode up to the front to confer. Tredefeu seemed to quiver beneath me, as if he knew what was coming and could not wait to get started. I ruffled his mane and told him to calm down, but he kept on stamping and fidgeting. Word came back to us that Robert of Artois was going across first, with the Templars and the English as well as his own men, and the king would cross after us with the main body of the army and the crossbowmen. We would form up and wait for the king, and then take Mansourah.

It was very early dawn when Count Robert mounted his horse. There was an odd pinkness to the sky. It seemed somehow chalky, not luminous, and the remaining stars did not twinkle, as if they were dots of white paint spattered across the heavens. It was going to be hot, and already the midges and flies were rising up from the rushes all around us. Warren gave me a leg up into the saddle, handed me my lance, and then swung lightly onto his own mount. My helmet felt loose so I tightened the strap. Now I could not open my mouth, so I loosened it again. In front, Longspée was talking heatedly with Count Robert. Finally both men laughed and Longspée slapped the king's brother across the shoulders. Then he trotted back to the English ranks.

'We are going across now,' he announced. 'The Copt says it is deep at first, then sandy. We'll be swimming our horses, lads, but then they'll find something under them. When we're across, we are forming up on Count Robert's standard. The king has given the honour of leading the army to the Templars. Well then, may God go with you all. You are the flower of England, men – let us ride for King Henry and Jesus Christ!'

The first horses were already in the water, downstream on the right. I could see Jean de Joinville's pennant near the royal standard. Horses were slowly being engulfed in the ruffled brown water as they waded forward. But already Tredefeu's hooves were slithering as we descended the bank. Count Robert's horse was swimming, drifting slowly downstream as he tried to pull its head round to the left.

At first the Nile was warm as it seeped in through the rings of my boots and leggings. But as we went forward and sank, it became colder. Tredefeu was nervous, but I urged him forward and, rolling his eyes, he snorted and went in deeper. Up to the girth, up to the breastplate, up to my knees. Now Tredefeu was swimming, and I was sitting ballock-deep in tepid water. It seemed as if a mile of open water lay between us and the far bank, but in truth it was no more than half a bowshot. The Templars were a little upstream from us. And out ahead, in the middle of the stream, Count Robert's banner waved, rising steadily above the water, and I understood that his party had reached the sandbank that the Copt had promised us.

I must have been halfway across when I suddenly realised I was in the midst of pandemonium. Horses were braying in fear, and their riders were urging them on with shouts and curses. There was a sound like a mill wheel turning behind me, as more and more knights urged their horses into the river. And in front, Count Robert had reached the other side and was kicking his horse like a madman, forcing it to scramble up the shiny mud of the bank. His retinue was close behind him. On my right there was a crash. A horse had overbalanced on the steep bank and tumbled backwards, crushing its rider. I felt myself plunging forward as Tredefeu gained a purchase on the riverbed. Just a few yards upstream, the white surcoats of the Templars were surging ashore. I looked up, squinting into the growing light of sunrise. Against the sky, horses struggled, jerking and heaving, over the lip of the bank, the lances of their riders stabbing up into the morning sky.

By the time we reached the shore the bank in front of us had been churned into glistening black porridge. Horse rumps were struggling up, kicking up clods. A fist-sized piece hit my helmet, knocking it askew. Then Tredefeu was digging his hooves into the greasy slope. His ears were back, his eyes rolling and white. A groan, almost human in its anguish, came from between his foam-smeared teeth. The saddle heaved and bucked beneath me and I threw myself forward onto the damp hair of his mane. 'Go on, go on!' I beseeched him. The lance of the man on my right swooped down and almost took off my nose. I swatted it away with my own spear. Then Tredefeu dropped his head and heaved, and we were up.

The army was milling about, forming into loose ranks. Directly in front of us, the knights of Count Robert's retinue were bunched around the blue, red and gold of his standard. And there were the gold lions of William Longspée. Beckoning to Warren, whose cobby mare had just heaved herself up the bank, I galloped towards them. There were Guy Curtbac, John of Motcombe and William himself. Beyond, I saw that we were in cultivated land, a flat patchwork of fields dotted everywhere by the water pumps of the Egyptians, and by groves of date palms and olives. Beyond the fields, the walls of Mansourah, a mile away, bright with waving flags and pennants. And in between, a village . . . no, an encampment: pointed tents, a pavilion, a sprawl of shanties. Smoke rose from cooking fires, thin grey threads that climbed, straight as plumb-lines, into the rosy sky.

A knight in a white surcoat had galloped up to Count Robert. William Longspée noticed, looked back at his company and happened to catch my eye. He beckoned and began to trot over to the count. I followed. The Templar was the Grand Master himself, Guillaume de Sonnac, and his soaked and muddy surcoat had rendered him no less terrifying. He seemed to be arguing furiously with Count Robert, and as we drew closer I heard what they were saying.

'Your orders – and my own – could hardly be clearer, sir. We must wait for your brother to make his crossing.'

'With respect, Grand Master, the Turks are sitting there like hen pheasants on their chicks, and we are here, hungry foxes all. Look there, Guillaume! They are, what? Half a mile distant? Less! And they do not know we are here! We will have 'em – we must! What shall I tell my brother the king if your . . . your *reluctance* loses us this prize, eh?'

'The king's orders—'

'I know the king's orders, damn you! Are you with me or no? For by God I will have those Turks with you or without you!'

De Sonnac scowled and stared at the count through slitted eyes. Another man would have melted like a candle in a fireplace under such a glare, but the count raised his chin and gave it back. There was silence. Tredefeu dropped his head to the ground and began to tear at a patch of sedge. All around me I could hear the sound of horses chewing, and bridles chinking, and every so often a gasp and a curse as a latecomer came up over the river bank.

'So be it,' said the Grand Master at last. His voice was steely. 'Well, sir, if you wish to catch 'em, let us be off now.'

'Good man. Can it be contrived?' Count Robert turned in his saddle and ran his eyes over the company. We were about eight hundred knights all told: three hundred French, two hundred English and three hundred Templars, in no sort of order, everyone jostling and shuffling their horses into loose, unmannerly ranks. 'I think it can!' he answered himself. 'Guillaume, I shall lead off. You will follow close behind. Agreed? Good! Then let us earn some glory while the day is still breaking!'

Guillaume de Sonnac was plainly furious, but he had been out-glared, and now he turned and galloped back to the white ranks of his men. Count Robert turned to William.

'Shall we go, Salisbury?'

'We shall, my lord.'

'Then in Christ's name, follow me!' And with that he rammed his spurs into the flanks of his horse and took off, cantering hard across a neat field of winter wheat, kicking up black dust and vivid green shoots behind him. There was a great whoop, as hundreds of throats released the fear and anger of the river crossing to the skies in one wordless battle cry. Then we were off.

Chapter Fifteen

Everything happened very fast. We were streaking across the patchwork of farmland, bursting through stands of reeds, smashing chicken coops and ploughing up cabbages and carrots and garlic. A donkey, tied to a water-pump, shrieked with terror as we bore down on him. Bucking, he pulled down the wooden framework and was swept up in the charge, running mad-eyed alongside an English knight, still trailing the pole he was lashed to. Chickens and pigeons were exploding into the air. Ahead, the camp had burst into life and men were running to and fro, throwing themselves onto saddleless horses. Now I could hear their panicked cries, jackdaw-like, above the rumble of our hooves. A band of mounted men had formed in front of the pavilion. They milled around each other, and then they were charging towards us. I had let Tredefeu carry me right into the front rank, and I could almost make out their faces. And they were unarmoured, clad only in robes that billowed out behind them. I swallowed, although my Adam's apple felt like a thistlehead in my throat, and snugged my lance beneath my arm. Just then a cockerel shrieked and a man's face appeared before me, some farmer roused from his hut, stumbling out into the dawn. Wide eyes, grey beard, mouth in a silent black O. Then he was gone, trampled beneath the feet of a hundred Christian horses.

The Saracens were kicking their horses frenziedly, hurtling towards us as we were roaring towards them. As if in a dream they came on unnaturally fast, and then they too were gone, swallowed up in a brief welter of flailing swords. There was open ground now between us and the camp, a wide pasture of trampled brown grass. I could make out the details of the tents: the scalloped edges, the silk canopies. Steam went up as someone kicked a cauldron into a fire. '*Deus vult! Deus vult! Montjoie et Saint Denis! Saint Edward!*' I cannot remember what I shouted, though I was shouting, everyone was shouting . . .

Here are the tents. Now we are among them. A man runs towards me, bare-chested, a sword and a small round shield in his hands. Tredefeu is at full stretch. My lance catches him on the shoulder and flings him away like a rag doll. We trample a fire, and my nose fills with the stench of burned hair and wet wood, then it is gone. There are riders in front of me, Turks, no armour but wearing helmets. I get my lance up but before I can aim it Tredefeu has carried me past. All around, crusaders are weaving in and out of a maze of tents. Guy-ropes are catching in hooves and pavilions are collapsing. There are men on foot everywhere, helpless, beating on armoured legs with swords until they are spitted or hacked down. I am past the tents. I see William Longspée near me. He yells *Saint Edward!* at me and wheels his horse. I follow him back into the camp, slower now. A Saracen on horseback appears from between two burning tents. He has a lance. Tredefeu has carried me onto it before I can rein him in. It catches my shield and shatters as the man flashes past me. I turn and thrust at him with my own lance, in time to see Longspée take off his head with a backhand stroke.

Tents are burning all around us. Another rider bursts from the fire and charges at me, yelling, his eyes streaming. He sways his head out of the way of my lance, which grazes his ear, and draws back his long, curved sword. I duck under my shield and as he reaches me and I feel his blade chop into painted wood – barely an inch of wood between his steel and my arm – I punch him in the throat with the fist that still holds the lance. He goes backwards over the rump of his horse, and with one thrust I pin him to the earth before he can rise. I leave my lance – I cannot manoeuvre it in these tight quarters – and draw my sword, but as I force Tredefeu down one smoking avenue and up another, I realise it is over. The camp is ours.

I found Count Robert and Grand Master Guillaume in the wide space in front of the pavilion. Both men were grinning now, and the Templar was pointing to something that one of his knights was holding up. It was a man's head. The knight's fingers were gripping a hank of wet black curls, and from the dead man's beard dripped a dark brown liquid.

'It is their Fakr ad-Din, the Turk commander,' said Guy Curtbac, joining me. 'Seems he was in his bath, having his beard dyed – good Christ, these heathens!' He hooted with laughter. 'Came out stark ballock naked, save for his sword, and ran smack into some Templars.'

'And the rest of them? We did not kill a whole army,' I said. Warren rode up, white-faced but unhurt. I clapped him on the back and he shook his head, silently, half smiling, dazed.

'Running back to the town,' Guy was saying. 'We shall catch them up, don't worry. Did you have good sport?'

'Sport, Guy?'

'I killed three of 'em!'

'Oh. Well done.' We were talking like two lazy fellows in a tavern, yet all around us men lay dead, naked, in pieces. And Guy had a spray of blood up his left side. Before I could ask if he was hurt, he saw Longspée walking his limping horse towards Count Robert and trotted off to boast of his deeds. But Longspée just smiled and handed up the reins to him.

'Find me another mount!' he said to whoever might be listening. Then he strode up to Count Robert and leaned against the sweating neck of his horse. I walked Tredefeu over to join them, just in time to see the Grand Master's smile vanish.

'No, my lord. I have disobeyed the king's orders once, and by the grace of God we were given a victory. But I shall not do so again. We will wait for the king.'

'Guillaume, the Turk is in the open field!' cried the count. 'For Christ's sake, man, look at them!' He pointed through the sagging, smouldering tents to where a disordered host, some mounted, some on foot, were kicking up the dust as they fled towards Mansourah. It was a good two miles to the town, and they had already gone a third of that distance.

'I forbid it,' hissed de Sonnac.

'Forbid? Who are you to forbid the king's brother? You forget yourself, Grand Master. I am going on with this attack, and I order you to follow me.'

'I will not, sir! We do not have sufficient men. Our horses are tired, and . . .'

'Aha. So it is true, then? That the Templars have become soft from living in the East? That they wish to keep the Turk strong and at the throat of the Christians so that they might reap the rewards? Or is it plain cowardice, de Sonnac?'

The Templar's face went wine-red and his lips were drawing back into a snarl when, in a flurry of dust, a knight galloped up. He was gasping for breath, and he was as white as a miller from dust and the ash that was raining down from the fires, but when he dragged his sleeve across his face I saw it was Foucaud du Merle. His eyes were round with excitement, and there was blood on his sword-hand. He seized the bridle of Count Robert's horse, not noticing the argument between the two men because, of course, Foucaud was as deaf as a pillar of stone.

'After them, men! After them!' he bellowed. 'The Saracens are fleeing, my lord! After them!'

Someone had found a horse for William Longspée and after fiddling with the stirrups he was mounted again. He leaned in past Foucaud.

'My lord, the Grand Master has fought the Turk before. He is wise to say that we should wait for your brother. The king cannot be far away. And we have killed their captain, so—'

'After them, men! Let us get after them!' boomed the hollow voice of Foucaud du Merle.

'Are you a coward too, Salisbury? Are you ready to turn tail, like the English at Taillebourg? The blood of England is as thin as milk, and God knows it!'

'After them! After them!'

'This is too much, Artois,' Longspée began, but before he could say anything more, Count Robert leaned forward and cuffed Foucaud du Merle on the side of his head, hard, as one might cuff a large dog. He was grinning, and du Merle's face lit up beneath its skim of dust. The count batted du Merle's hand off his bridle and without another word, without another glance at the Templar or Longspée, he kicked at his horse so violently that a shudder went through the beast, shaking its wet and dirty hide like a ripple of wind through grass. The beast gave an indignant, pained whinny and leaped forward, almost knocking Foucaud du Merle off his own horse.

'To me, men! To me!' he yelled, the veins standing out dark in his neck. 'For France, in the name of God!'

The two horses began to dance around each other, and very quickly the dance spread to the other beasts in the company, and all the knights began to jeer at the Saracens and call on God to aid them, and still the beasts danced, until with a confused surge the company flung itself towards the Saracen line. Whether it was Count Robert who gave the command, or Foucaud, or some other man, or whether it was nothing more than the mindless urge to set forth like hounds after a fox, still in a few seconds the count and his retinue were charging over the winter wheat and the cabbages towards Mansourah, yelling to Saint Denis. Every French knight within earshot took up the cry and spurred their horses after them.

'He is a lunatic!' gasped Longspée to the Grand Master. 'We cannot—'

'Brother, we must,' said de Sonnac. 'We cannot abandon the Count of Artois! What would you tell the king, if . . .' He did not need to say more.

'Shit!' It was William Longspée. He was looking past me, back to the bank, no doubt seeing how much of the army had made it across to our side of the river. 'God, that bloody fool! What is he doing?' His eyes met mine for a moment, and I knew, clearly, that he wanted with all his heart to wait for more knights to join us. But already some of the English lads were tearing off after the Franks.

'Damn them all,' muttered Longspée. 'Damn them all!' he barked. 'Then let us go!'

And with another bitter oath William couched his lance and kicked steel into his horse's flanks. With the rest of the English, I followed. In another minute, though it seemed an eternity of confusion, of exhausted horses being coaxed and coerced, we had left the Saracen camp behind and were pounding across the flat ground after the French company. I was at Longspée's right shoulder, at the front of the pack. Beside me was John of Motcombe, holding the flag of Saint Edward, golden cross and five birds rippling against a field bluer than the burning, cloudless sky.

Tredefeu tossed his head and lunged, jumping a weedy ditch, smashing through an old stack of bean poles. A flurry of doves, freed from a toppling cage, dashed past me, so close that I smelled the sweet-sour taint of their feathers. We were forming up as we charged, swarming into a rough and ragged line. I was a little to the right of the centre, where Count Robert's flag streamed, and William Longspée was just in front of me now. I dared a look over my shoulder. Behind us was a formless shoal of knights, English and Templar riding side by side. But now Guillaume de Sonnac pulled to the side, the Templar standard blindingly white above him, and slowly the white figures of the Templars began to drift towards our flank, until we were two companies, Temple and England, crashing across the farmland of Egypt. Out in front, Count Robert and Foucaud du Merle were riding like madmen, Foucaud still bellowing like a crazed bull, the French bunched up behind their leader. Surrounded as I was by a close-packed knot of Englishmen, I was being funnelled ever closer to the front of a swarm of close on five hundred knights. The point of the funnel was Robert, Count of Artois, and it was pointed straight at the gates of Mansourah.

No one had expected to take Mansourah that day. It is a good-sized town surrounded by strong walls of apricot-coloured stone with many crenulated bastions. As I raced towards it that morning, it occurred to me that this could be any new fortress in Sicily or the Marches, some place that a strong army would expect to invest and sit in front of for months until the defenders starved or lost their nerve. And yet here we were, charging it, giving tongue as if we were romping through some nice safe deer park in the Ile de France. Date palms flashed past, an ibis burst from a ditch right under Tredefeu's hooves. The Saracen cavalry were pounding up the road in the shadow of the walls. The first man was through the gates. Count Robert's flag was almost level with the pennant flying from the last Saracen's lance.

'Follow! Follow!' cried Raoul de Coucy.

'After them! After them, you men!' roared Foucaud du Merle.

Tredefeu was galloping so fast that I could barely feel him

beneath me, so smooth was his gait. And now we were on the hard-packed mud of the main roadway that led up to the gates of the town. We must rein in now, surely? I strained to see past John's shoulder: when would Count Robert hold up his hand? But with a stab of fear I saw that he had already passed under the great stone archway, and that the hunt, the seething rabble of Christian knights, was streaming in behind him like a swarm of bees into a new skep.

This was madness. But even if any of us had lost our nerve, we were trapped. The Templars were hurtling up behind us, and 'Deus vult!' was a thunder that drowned out even the tumult of hooves. They were forcing the French and English into the gateway. I looked about wildly but there was no time. If I wheeled Tredefeu, we would tangle with the fellows next to us and go down. And if we made it through the crush, we were already at the moat.

There was a blink of shadow and I had passed through into Mansourah. I do not remember the gateway, or perhaps the memory was shocked out of me, for as soon as I was within the city my senses were attacked on all sides. Where we had been galloping across a wide, flat plain, suddenly we were hurtling down a long street, not very wide, overhung with buildings. The feeling of speed intensified – in these narrow confines it felt as if Tredefeu was carrying me along at the speed of a shooting star. I could not see up ahead, but from all sides came screeching and yelling, men's voices and women's as well, and the air was thick with the smells of a town on a hot day: cooking, smoke, rubbish, piss, shit. An arrow flashed right in front of me, angling down, disappearing under the horse next to me. I looked up and glimpsed open windows, rooftops lined with man-shaped shadows blurred against the sunlight. There was a loud bang and a flash. Tredefeu lurched to one side, just in time, for there in the middle of the street was a cart, with white-clad men trying to push it across our path. It was too high to jump, and there were four hundred howling men behind me. And then a long shadow rose up on the left, a side street. I hauled Tredefeu's head round and dived into the narrow patch of shade.

Chapter Sixteen

I was enveloped in a deep silence that became the rushing of my blood pounding through the maze of my skull, and into that loud silence came little tips and taps, like hail falling on a slate roof. Something was hurting my throat. And then all the sound came back. I was yelling, and arrows were angling down all around me, bouncing off walls and flagstones and thwacking into wood. I was hurtling down a narrow alley. Somehow I had become separated from the main force, though I could not remember how . . . And then I could: a cart in the wide street had split us like a river divides around a rocky island, and being on the left, I had almost been crushed against the walls of a grand house, only to find the alley opening up before me. There were two or three Franks ahead of me, the iron shoes on their mounts' hooves sparking against the stones of the street. A crate of oranges went flying, the bright orbs of fruit lifting for a moment through the slanting rain of arrows, then I was past them. One of the knights tumbled backwards off his horse, eyes wide and teeth bared as he went under me and Tredefeu lunged to avoid him.

There was no one on the street. Closed doors and shuttered windows were flying past, but things were falling from above. I glanced up, and there, against the vivid blue of the sky, were faces looking down at me. Men, women, young faces, old ones, all twisting, animated, mouths open as they yelled or panted, and down from this narrow strip of blue dropped bricks, clay jars, logs. A big round thing hurtled towards me and before I could twist away it struck me on the shoulder. There was a spray of bright red and as my mind told me a boulder had taken off my arm I tasted sweetness on my lips – watermelon. I began to laugh crazily as more fruit exploded around me. And then a huge melon struck the helmet of the last Frank, who had ridden quite far ahead of me, and he toppled sideways and landed with a crash on the flagstones. His shield arm came up and waved feebly. I cursed: now I'd have to stop and put him behind me on Tredefeu, and what fucking idiot would get himself knocked off his horse by fruit? But as I galloped up, a door opened in the wall next to where he lay and a woman ran out. She was dressed in the shapeless black robes of the fellahin, and something flashed in her hand. She bent over the stunned knight and as I charged up, began to hack at him. Her arm rose and fell and the man writhed for a moment and then lay still. As I came up the woman stood and I saw her face: it was pale, with great black-lined eyes. The meat cleaver in her hand was almost black with blood as she shook it at me, screaming. My lance was in my hand, but as, thoughtlessly, I shifted my grip and brought it to the left side of Tredefeu's neck, I caught what she was saying. It was a word that sailors and exiles use often, and I knew it in many tongues: *home*. *Home*, screamed that woman in the language of the Saracens, screamed it again and again at the white-skinned infidel who was about to kill her. And I raised the tip of my lance so that it passed harmlessly above her head and galloped past as she howled at my back.

I glanced over my shoulder, expecting to find more Franks behind me, but with a lurch I found I was alone. And the alley was filling up with people. They were pouring out of their houses, clutching weapons, and now arrows were beginning to whine past me horizontally. They were glancing off my back, bruising, stinging my flesh beneath the mail coat and leather hauberk. There was a blow on my helmet, forcing it down over my eyes, and I pushed it back into place, finding melon juice and blood on my hand. A brick struck Tredefeu on the neck and opened a tear in his sweaty hide, bloodless for a moment and then filling richly.

My decision to spare the fellahin woman, though it passed through my head in a flash, had somehow cleared my senses, and suddenly I was aware of chaos behind me. I turned and saw, rushing towards me like beer up the neck of a flagon, a knot of Frankish knights, forced together by the narrow walls, riding shoulder to shoulder and crashing through the tables and barrels and jars that stood outside each door. At the front I saw a shield I recognised, an English crest – and next to it the face of Longspée, daubed with white dust and scored with sweat. With a shout I reined in, wincing as an arrow hissed past my nose, and shook my lance in the air. Longspée saw me and gave an answering yell. Tredefeu was dancing as if the paving stones beneath him were the coals of hell, but in only a few of my heartbeats – and my heart was beating as fast as a sparrow's – the knights were almost upon me, and Tredefeu lunged forward, just a tail's flick ahead of the pack.

'The dirty pigs blocked the street!' shouted Longspée. Somehow he had forced his mount up next to mine.

'Yes!' I answered, turning towards him. There was an arrow sticking out of his shoulder, but the head was through, and the shaft was barely held by the ball of muscle at the top of his arm.

'It's nothing,' he shouted in answer to my silent question. 'But it's a bloody mess we're in, Petrus!'

'Where are the others?' I knew all the English knights at least by sight, and I saw hardly any of them in the press that heaved and blundered through the bloody gut of the alley.

'Some in front – I got this, and slowed up for a moment . . .'
He jerked his head towards his wounded shoulder. 'Then there
was a bloody cart in my way. Don't know who this lot are.
Templars all got through, I think.'

We were screaming at each other, spittle flying, just to make
ourselves heard above the terrible drumming of hooves in that
narrow space, the skirling of horses and of men. For we were
being slaughtered here. Already the press of knights was
thinner, and the faces that still remained, white-eyed, blood
splashed, were hollow with pain and fear. Arrows were falling
like midsummer rain. With a horrible start I saw that one man
was on fire, and that flaming brands, tumbling alongside roof
tiles, bricks, fruit, eggs, cooking pots, were being hurled down
upon us from the narrow strip of blue sky above us. Our voices,
English, French, were filling this deep ditch with a confused,
terrified roar. And then it stopped. We had come to a place
where a larger street cut across the alley, forming a sort of
square. Back in Venice there would have been a well in the
middle of it, but here there was a small domed structure of
whitewashed stucco, the tomb of a local saint. Banners of
green cloth hung about it, and dying flowers lay against its
dusty, tiled portico.

The tomb was blocking our way, and our horses, better
trained than their riders, had already made up their minds to
go right or left around the obstacle. Tredefeu's head was going
to the right, and I was looking past the curved wall of the little
building when an arrow struck my helmet hard, right between
my eyes. It did not hurt but the *tenk* of metal upon metal set
my ears ringing. As I blinked, I saw the archer, crouched behind the tomb, setting another arrow to his string. Beyond,
the street continued, wider now, and there were trees in the
distance . . .

'Trees, William! It must be the river!' I glanced across at
Longspée. He was abreast of me, and his knees were almost

touching mine as his horse slowed, turning his foam-splashed face to the left of the tomb. But the earl was leaning forward in his saddle, jerking as if an unseen hand were striking him between the shoulder blades, and from beneath the rim of his helmet jutted an arrow.

'Oh, Christ . . .' I managed to grab the reins from his hand and pulled both our horses up, almost sending us all crashing into the side of the tomb. Knights were flying past us on both sides. There was a sharp twang, sharp enough to cut through the din of hooves, and I remembered the archer. He was right in front of me, but − I have never been able to understand why − he had turned and was shooting into the stream of Franks rushing past him. With his short, curved bow he could have put an arrow right through my chain mail at such close quarters, put an arrow right through my body, or through Tredefeu's skull. Perhaps he was dazzled by the bounty of helpless targets that fate had sent him that day. I could see the sweat beading on his eyebrows. Then I put my lance through his neck.

'To me! To me!' I shrieked at the knights, almost all past us now. 'To Salisbury!' I was off Tredefeu, and William was tumbling down on top of me. I went down with him, and scrambling onto all fours, shook off my shield and hauled my friend into the doorway of the tomb. He was kicking, and there was a cracked, wet hiss rising from his throat. I held him down with a knee on his chest and bent over him, pushing off his helmet. There was blood, thick and black and welling, but it was as I feared. The arrow had lodged in his right eye. Hoping . . . hoping what? I caught hold of the shaft lightly, but it was stuck fast. Not just in the socket, then, but through to the brain.

'William!' I said. 'William! Can you hear me?' His head began to jerk from side to side, his chain-mail hood scraping the floor and sending cold echoes through the small curved space. The saint's grave was just behind us, a sober rectangle of stone draped in a threadbare green shroud embroidered with silver script. 'I'll get you to the river,' I told him. His hand flew up and cuffed my cheek, then fell back, fingers grabbing blindly. They tangled in the shroud and jerked it loose in a cloud of dust. There was some other sound coming from his mouth and I leaned closer. He had managed to find a word, somewhere in his ruined brain, and with it the strength to send it off into the darkness.

I think it was 'Mother'. But perhaps it was 'Ida'. Then he died.

I left him there, clutching the shroud of a Mussulman holy man, tomb dust already settling on his face, his feet in the Egyptian sun. How long had it taken Longspée to die? Two minutes? No more . . . but out here there was a small mound of dead men and two horses, writhing on their backs in slick puddles of blood. Jesus . . . But no, there was Tredefeu, eyes rolling wildly but still upright, waiting for me despite the hail of missiles. There was the archer I had killed, my lance in his ribcage. The last knights were clattering out of the square. I had time to pull my lance from the dead archer and jump onto Tredefeu, desperately working my arm through the straps of my shield. Behind us, out of the alley, a crowd of townsfolk was beginning to surge. Tredefeu needed no urging: as soon as my arse was in the saddle he took off after the Franks.

We charged up the wider street towards the palm trees. The arrows were even here, and crossbow bolts were slamming into the walls and the roadway. Men were tumbling from their horses, and horses were dropping and somersaulting, sending their riders flying. There was blood everywhere: on the walls, on the cobbles, the salt stink of it heavy in the air. Tredefeu jumped and jumped again over writhing men and beasts. And then the street came to an end and we emerged into a blindingly white square, white from the sun hammering from marble pavers and limed walls. There were palm trees spreading ferny shade, and beyond them, not the Nile, but a grand building topped with delicate crenulations. From between them, arrows began to hiss down. Almost at once Tredefeu was struck, the shaft appearing next to my left knee. I pulled it out as the horse plunged and shrieked. As I did so three more arrows ticked into my shield. This was not a place to stay. Behind, the alleyway was choked with enraged townsfolk. To my left, other alleyways, narrower than the one I had just ridden down. I swung Tredefeu through a storm of arrows, and there, opening between a palm tree and a fountain that looked as if it had been carved from a sugar loaf, a much wider street. There were many figures running to and fro across it and clouds of dust or smoke were thickening, but the way was not blocked. With a shout I spurred Tredefeu, who laid back his ears and bared his teeth, and lunged into an uneven canter. A Saracen on horseback, a fine-looking man in rich armour with great sprays of feathers in his silk-wrapped helmet, saw me coming and turned away from the confusion and dust. He was carrying a lance and a buckler and with a high-pitched shout he couched his lance and charged me. Although missiles were flying all around us the square was empty and, not for the first time that day, I had the feeling I was in a dream, that as I couched my own lance and hauled Tredefeu's head round I was at some imaginary tilting practice inside my own head. Tredefeu reared and threw himself forward, and my ballocks met the pommel. I roared in pain and crouched down over the horse's neck, and perhaps that saved me, for the Saracen's lance glanced off the top of my helmet and he careered past, his knee scraping mine. I pulled Tredefeu up and turned him. The Saracen knight was coming towards me again, but behind him, out of the narrow alley from which I had just escaped, people were streaming, some of them pausing to launch arrows at me, others whirling slingshots. His lance quivering, the Saracen was bounding across the flagstones. Cursing, I threw my own lance away and drew my sword, spurring Tredefeu as I did so. I was just in time to knock the tip of his lance aside with my shield, and swinging my sword I cut through the wooden shaft and let Tredefeu's speed carry the backhand stroke into the man. The sword met his silver shield with a dull clash but there was the weight of a horse and a man behind it and the Saracen went backwards over his cantle like a straw jousting target and landed heavily amongst the spent arrows. A stone from a slingshot hit the nosepiece of my helmet and another lodged in an eyeslit, jarring my head backwards. I thumbed out the stone and left the square as fast as Tredefeu could carry me.

But at once I found myself in the middle of a confused fight. Some French knights, still mounted, were hacking with their swords at a thick crowd of townsmen who were lunging at them with spears and hay forks. They saw me and gave a shout, and I swear they were smiling. I charged towards them, but even as I closed the distance, the townsmen made a rush and dragged the knights from their horses. There were other cries in French and English coming from nearby. A knot of Englishmen, all of them on foot, had their backs to the wall of a house and were trading blows with a much larger body of Saracen soldiers, while bricks and pots and firewood rained down on their heads from the upper windows. A heavy chair came crashing down, knocking three lads to the ground, and the Saracens rushed in. Tredefeu was still cantering, wild-eyed, looking for a way through, and suddenly we were surrounded by white robes: *the Templars!* I thought with a sort of mad elation. There was a great thud: a huge beam of wood, such as might serve as the roof-beam of a house, had landed just in front of us, sending up a cloud of dust. Then another, landing upright and teetering for a long moment before slamming down, then more and more, until it seemed as if a forest were planting itself around us. Out of the dust that was now as thick as smoke a face emerged: William de

Sonnac, the Grand Master, half his face a mask of blood, a broken, pulpy ball hanging from an empty eye socket.

'They are blocking all the streets!' he bellowed. Another Templar appeared at his side.

'You must leave, Grand Master!' he said. 'You!' I understood he was talking to me. 'Find some knights and take the Grand Master to safety! There is fighting by the south gate and it is still open – go!'

Two English knights rode up, dusty white and streaked with sweat, their wispy, never-shaven beards plastered to their chins. I didn't recognise them, but they knew me. They were terrified, but the rage of battle had painted the familiar, rictus smile on both faces.

'Sir Petrus, thank Christ we've found you,' croaked one.

'It is—' began the other. But whatever it was I never discovered, for an arrow, shot almost straight down from above, struck him in the neck so that the feathers quivered next to his ear, the head buried deep in his chest. Blood poured out of his mouth and he fell forward onto his horse's neck.

'Oh, Edgar, dear God . . .' moaned the other boy. 'Sir – the Earl of Salisbury, sir?'

'He's dead, too,' I snapped, and seeing the boy's face go slack, I found myself thinking, *Well, what the fuck did you expect?*

There was a swirling of the dust cloud as a tightly bunched group of knights dashed past, and for a moment the street was revealed. Where – a minute ago, no more – there had been open roadway, now lay a barricade of beams and everywhere the sprawled shapes of dead knights. I was at the centre of a tight knot of Franks, ringed by men on foot protecting the legs of the horses with their shields. Saracen fighters and armed townsmen were rushing in to hack at the shields and to try and shoot arrows at point-blank range, then darting back into the confusion. Men were going down all around us, arrows bristling from them. To my amazement I found my own shield was thick with arrows. Another three stuck out of Tredefeu's caparison at his shoulders and two at his rump. As I watched, again with that feeling that I was in a vaguely uncomfortable dream, a spear point, tangled with blood-drenched hair, slid across the underside of my shield. Reflexively I clamped down with my shield arm, trapping the shaft of the spear. A tall Saracen in robes of very dark blue embroidered with silver had fought his way through the shield wall. I saw nothing of his face save the blackness of his beard and the whites of his eyes, but the dream was gone and the din of battle swamped me again. My sword was already falling, and the edge caught the Saracen above the right ear, the heavy iron shearing through the man's thin helmet as if it were parchment and taking off his jaw, beard and all. As he fell, another man took his place, but he was set upon by the knights on foot and disappeared beneath a welter of blows.

'We have to fight our way back to the gate,' the Templar was bellowing at the Grand Master and, I supposed, me. 'Some are flying to the river, but it is too strong to cross.'

William de Sonnac turned to me, his dead eye bouncing horribly against his cheek. With a grimace of impatience he fumbled for it and pulled it free, throwing it from him as if it were no more than a burdock he had plucked from his clothing.

'What's your name?' he snapped.

'Sir Petrus Blakke Dogge,' I told him. Under the circumstances I couldn't really blame him for not recognising me.

'Petrus? English? Right, then. The bloody fools who forced our necks into this snare are all dead by now, or will be soon. We must warn the king not to come near the city. Are you with me?'

'Yes, I am,' I said. 'And you, sir, will come with us,' I added, nodding to the English lad, who was sitting rigidly upon his fidgeting horse, eyes as big as gull's eggs.

'I will find the brothers who remain and join you soon,' said the other Templar. With a cheerful nod at me, he turned his horse and vanished into the dust. I never saw him again.

'All men who can ride, to me!' called de Sonnac. There were no more than six of us now. The men on foot looked up at us balefully, but there were few of them now, and still the Saracens came on, more than before. Someone handed me a lance. I sheathed my sword and took it.

'Follow if you can,' the Grand Master told them. 'Find Artois, the damned idiot, and get yourselves out of the town.'

'He's dead in a house over yonder,' said one of the knights – a Frenchman. He was weeping through his coating of dust.

'Then save yourselves,' barked de Sonnac. 'Come on, you men! For the Temple, the Temple!'

'Wait,' I said, and grabbed the English lad's reins, for we were all trying to untangle the snarled knot of horses and men, and I saw he was about to panic. 'Where are the others? John and Guy?'

'Gone, all gone. They shot us all down as we rode back . . . The other gate was closed, and so we turned and . . .'

But we were moving now, and I let go his reins and gave my poor horse the spurs once more. Straight away we were wading through a wall of townsmen, hacking to left and right until we were through. We rode down the wide street until we came to a crossroads. Beams had been thrown across the streets but we jumped them. A thick flight of arrows came from our right, and instantly a horse stumbled and went down on its neck, throwing the rider. Another man, a Frenchman whose shield I had seen in the front of the mad chase across the fields, tried to pick up the dismounted knight but as he reached for him another three arrows caught him in the back and he went down. Now, to my dismay, we were turning towards the source of the arrows, charging, howling out battle cries we could not hear. More arrows whistled by, and then the archers were all around us and we were cutting at them. Bricks were shattering on the cobbles, and women were hooting and wailing at us from the roofs and windows.

Five of us left, and the Grand Master. I glanced at the English boy. He looked more alert now, but not much.

'Sheath your sword!' I ordered him. Startled, he obeyed. 'Shift your shield to your right arm!' He did, clumsily, but we were not moving fast, for our horses were blown and hurt. The Grand Master had lost his shield, and at a nod from me the boy moved up on his right while I urged Tredefeu along-side him on the left. Seeing what we were doing, another man dropped back until the Templar was surrounded by shields. Arrows came again, and a big spar of wood thundered onto the cobbles next to me, sending Tredefeu lurching into de Sonnac's horse. But that seemed to put a last spasm of desper-ate energy into the beasts, and we began to pick up speed until we were galloping along the cobbles, which were slippery with blood from the dead Franks and their horses, who lay every-where here. I felt hooves crunch and slither on wetly brittle things but I did not look down. I recognised the wagon and the place where I had become separated from the charge. And in the mouth of the alley, propped against a cart of burst oranges, was Guy Curtbac, half his skull gone, his severed hands in his lap.

But here, at last, was the gate. An angry crowd of Saracen soldiers and townsfolk were clustered there, and as we came closer I saw Frankish knights fighting desperately in the gate-way itself, dismounted, beating back the crowd that was fling-ing itself upon them as one enraged thing bristling with steel. They were trying to keep the way open and when one of them saw us he began to shout to his comrades, although his voice was swallowed up in the din.

'Charge them, boys!' It was the Grand Master, ordering us calmly through his hideous mask of hardened blood. The other Templars couched their lances and the English lad, mouth so tight it was little more than a white line below the nosepiece of his helmet, did the same. Oh, Christ. I followed suit. We barely had time to shake ourselves out into a line five-abreast, but there was a moment, as my head went down behind my shield and my lance steadied, when the Saracens realised they were being attacked from behind and twenty, thirty heads came round, that I felt the strength and the terrible power we possessed: so much weight, so much razor-sharp metal, hooves . . . My lance took a white-robed towns-man in the shoulder and spun him round, the blade tearing free and striking a soldier full in the chest, something – breastplate, breastbone – stopping the point. The shaft bent itself into an arc and snapped, wrenching the end from my hand. I drew my sword but we were already through, hooves echoing in the cool, arched space of the gateway and then the sun again, and all around us, the fields . . .

The Grand Master had reined in. The Templars in the gateway turned and ran towards us. There were seven of them and five of us. I pulled one up behind me and gave up a stirrup for another, who threw his arms around Tredefeu's neck and held on for dear life. When every man was mounted in some fashion we turned and stumbled down the road, for the horses, beyond the limits of their endurance, were done and could barely canter. Scattered arrows flew by. But we were moving faster than the people of Mansourah who were running after us. We had escaped.

There was the Nile, close by on our left, and further off, the Ashmoun Canal, marked with palm trees and reeds. Between us and the canal, the Saracen camp was still burning, and beyond waved the standards of the main army. Here and there across the plain, widely scattered knots of men were fleeing, some on horseback, some straggling on foot, but it was a terrifyingly small number, the tiniest fraction of the company that had charged into Mansourah. The king's army was advancing, a long line sweeping towards the burning camp. Behind us, horns were sounding, and kettledrums were beginning to thunder. Twisting in the saddle, I glanced beyond my passenger's shoulder. From the gates, and from the distance beyond the city, mounted soldiers were streaming. It was the Saracen force we had routed and chased into Mansourah, but doubled, quadrupled in size. They were not troubling to form into ranks, but were swarming into the plain, hammering towards us on horses that were fresher and faster than ours.

Tredefeu was starting to slow down, and every few steps he would falter and check his gait. The ground was uneven: we were in the gardens again, churned up from our mad charge to the city. Blood and sweat were running down Tredefeu's legs from under the chamfron, and the gash on his neck was pulsing blood with every stride he took. Arrows were sticking out from the chamfron's thick leather, and I realised with a nauseous jolt that one was jutting from my left thigh. And as soon as I saw it, my leg was convulsed in pain. I sucked the edge of my linen coif into my mouth and bit down as I snapped off the fletching. The head was not deep, the chain mail had slowed it down, but now I could feel the iron barbs gnawing at my thigh muscle.

The Grand Master's horse had a flap of meat hanging from its right haunch, and every other beast was gashed and stuck with arrows. But the king's army was rushing towards us: soon we would be swept up into its safety. The man with his foot in my stirrup was groaning softly and the hands knotted in Tredefeu's mane were almost translucent white.

'How do you fare?' I said to him. He shook his head and tried to speak, but only a thin hiss escaped his lips. I looked down: the front of his white Templar's surcoat was soaked with blood to the hem and slashed open: in the gash I saw the cut edges of his mail coat and between them, a glistening roil of innards.

'Hang on,' I said to him. 'Hang on, brother. Here's the king, look? See his flag?' But as I mumbled to him as if he were a child, Tredefeu stumbled as he leaped an irrigation ditch, jolting us. The man behind me gripped my midriff until I could not breathe, but the Templar gave a thin, agonised shriek and fainted. His hands let go of the horse's neck and before I could grab him he had dropped. His foot caught in the stirrups and he was dragged through a plot of winter cabbages, helpless, his eyes staring blankly at the sky.

'Don't stop!' yelled the man behind me into my ear. I cursed him, but then the Templar's foot slipped out of its trap and he was gone. And suddenly Tredefeu stopped running. His body began to shake beneath me and white foam bubbled from his nose and mouth, streaked with bright blood. He was still walking, head down, but as I coaxed him, and the man behind me yelled vile French curses, he sank, slowly, carefully, to his knees, and laid his great head down on the ground. We were in a shattered vegetable plot, and my good horse gasped his life out into a tangle of trampled onions as I scrambled off his back, the Frenchman clinging to me like an ape until I shook him off. He looked at me, mad with fear, and took off running. I paused and glanced down at Tredefeu. He was still alive, one liquid brown eye staring back at me. Perhaps I muttered a prayer, or thanks – I do not remember. I probably did not. The Saracen army was very close now, and the ground was shaking with the fall of their hooves. I pulled off my shield, slung the strap over my shoulder so that it hung down my back, and took off after the Frenchman. There was a small grove of fig trees up ahead, and beyond, the French army was . . . But they had stopped. The line of knights, with the white and gold of France in the centre, was standing still, just past the burning camp of the Saracens, more than a quarter-mile away.

The Grand Master, and the other riders, were swallowed up in the ranks as I reached the fig trees. I ought to be safe by now, but the Saracens were gaining. I was roughly halfway between the two armies, but the Saracens were charging at full stretch, and soon I would be ridden over. My thigh was burning with pain but I forced it to obey me. Should I stop here in the trees and make my stand? But I could not stop. I was back in the strange dream, running for the sake of movement, stumbling out into the expanse of trampled stubble beyond the gardens. I began shouting at the French, telling them to come on, to fight. I could see Louis, or a shape that must be Louis, sitting on a horse beneath the gonfalon of Saint Denis. Still I ran, jumping over a ditch, crashing through a fence of reeds, and still the hoof beats rumbled behind me.

I was done. My breath was being squeezed shallow and the pain in my thigh was much worse. I was flailing now, wading through the air, which had suddenly grown very thick. The French line was very near. In two minutes I could have strolled to where the king stood waiting. The Saracens were whooping and calling out to their god. Tripping, I stumbled forward and crawled, then forced myself upright and turned to face my end.

Five packs of horsemen were charging through the gardens, several hundred in each pack, swords and spears and polished shields flashing. Trumpets were sounding. I drew my sword and took it in both hands. What a ridiculous way to die. I closed my eyes and found Iselda's face somewhere in the turmoil inside my skull. *I'm really, really sorry*, I told her.

A sound startled me back into the world: a great mechanical clattering, a dry ripple tearing through the air behind me. Three Saracens were three spear-lengths away from me. One of them was drawing back the string on a short, curved bow, his eyes intent on me. And then he was gone. And his two mates: gone as well. A black shadow seemed to have toppled into the Saracen charge and sent horses rearing and falling. The front of each pack of horsemen dissolved into a mass of writhing limbs, horse and men thrashing together. Then another clatter and another shadow fell. Turning, I saw that crossbowmen had come through the line of French horses and were shooting over my head. Without waiting for the Saracens to recover I began to lurch across the field. Sheltered by a swooping, hissing cloud of crossbow-quarrels, I went, cursing and moaning in pain, until at last a crossbowman dropped his weapon and ran towards me. He caught me around the chest and, slinging my arm across his shoulders, half-dragged me back through the wall of horses.

'God bless you, sir,' he said, leaving me to stagger back towards the canal. I had gone only a few paces when I tripped again, and found myself surrounded by young, freshly shaven knights, who knelt and began to loosen my armour.

'Were you in the city?'

'What happened, man?' They were talking at once, eager and fearful.

'I think everyone died, my lads,' I said, sitting up and trying not to snatch at the waterskin that someone was holding out.

'The king's brother?'

'Dead. And William Longspée. All the English with him, save myself and one boy. We brought out the Grand Master of the Temple, who has lost an eye. The other Templars . . .' I took another drink.

'Dead? Every one of them?'

'I don't know. How many have come across the fields?'

'Two score, maybe? Surely that cannot be everyone?'

'The river . . . Some were trying to swim the Nile. But I don't think anybody came out after the Grand Master and the rest of us.'

'God's stones, but you are a lucky man, Sir Englishman!'

said one young fellow, clapping me on the back, looking more worried than he sounded. Beyond the horses and their riders, still fretting where they stood, the crossbowmen were sending another volley into the air. The king raised his voice and gave the order to charge. Crows were already beginning to gather, away over towards Mansourah, and around us rose the sickly vapour of crushed and spoiled vegetables.

'We'll see,' I told him. 'We'll see.'

Chapter Seventeen

Two days later the Saracens attacked us. But we were waiting for them. The king had managed to slip some spies into their ranks, and so we knew they would come at the rising of the sun. I remember standing all night in my armour, shivering in the midst of exhausted men. We had spent the day before raising embankments and spiking them with a strong palisade, and it seemed we were well defended. But at sunrise a vast army spread out over the plain around us and soon the camp was completely circled by Saracen troops: thousands of cavalry, many of them regiments of the Mamluks, the warrior lord-slaves of Egypt, and an even greater host of foot soldiers. The commander – a Mamluk, by his attire – taunted us, riding around us out of bowshot, adjusting his forces, until at noon there was a sudden thunder of kettledrums and blaring horns, and the vast noose of yelling, steel-waving men began to tighten around us.

It was my honour to be with the Templar contingent, what was left of it. Not an honour that I relished, but the brothers wanted to reward me for helping to save their Grand Master, and what greater reward than to die in their company? My spirits were quite numb by that time. I had been limping back to camp as the king made his charge against the garrison of Mansourah, and there I had lain for a day, having been stitched and dosed by various harried barber-surgeons. Apparently we had won what the chroniclers would call the Battle of Mansourah, even though the city was still in Saracen hands; and by the time the victorious army rode into the camp I, as one of only a small handful that had escaped from the town, was being called a hero. I never saw the English lad again. I supposed he must have died later that day, or fallen sick soon after. Warren died in Mansourah. Guy Curtbac, randy Simon, John de Motcombe and two hundred other men would never go back to England. But it was my own misfortune to find that I could walk and hold a sword after only a day of rest, just in time to have the honour of my presence requested by a grinning Templar brother.

I had limped across to where, by the light of torches, the retainers of the Temple were building a barricade out of captured Saracen catapults and siege engines. Someone had found me a horse, and I was led over to the Grand Master. Guillaume de Sonnac was a ghastly sight. His missing eye had been stitched shut − apparently by a butcher − over the empty socket, which was leaking a thick, dark liquor, but his good eye blazed with fevered passion. He said nothing to me, but clapped me on the shoulder and indicated that I should take my place at his side. And then there was a long, long wait. No one was in a talking mood. The Templars told their rosaries and muttered prayers and paternosters. I sank into a sort of trance as the poison from an infected wound found its way into my blood, but it was merciful, in a way, because I remember almost nothing of those twelve hours before hell slipped its bonds.

First the Saracens attacked on our left, then they threw themselves on us. A dense phalanx of infantry rushed our barricade, ignoring the crossbow bolts that were slaughtering them at close range. The Grand Master gave a shout and we charged and threw them back. But as soon as we had retreated behind our barricade they came again, and this time the cavalry pressed the foot soldiers from behind, forcing them into the deadly hail from our crossbowmen. And then the Saracen archers let loose. The air turned black – this I swear, for over the barricade dropped a belt of arrows so thick that it put a wooden ceiling between us and the sun for a brief moment – and then arrows were lancing into bodies, horse-armour, shields. Again and again the shafts poured down, until we seemed to be fighting in a field of dark corn. We charged out again, but the sheer might of their numbers threw us back.

I was using my sword to hack the arrow-shafts from my shield when the Templar next to me gave a shout.

'They are bringing Greek fire!' he yelled. I looked, and there in the ranks of Saracens, who had withdrawn a few yards, smoke was rising. Then the ranks parted and men dressed in long leather jerkins ran out, carrying earthenware pots in their thickly gloved hands. Smoke and flame poured out of the vessels' mouths. Flanking the fire-carriers, other men bore large shields. Some stumbled as arrows and quarrels found them, and one quarrel hit a pot and the man holding it vanished in a column of fire. But most got close enough to fling their firepots at the barricade, and instantly the air was full of roaring, crackling flame and tarry stink of the burning liquid.

'Damn them!' cried de Sonnac. He couched his lance and charged the fire-carriers. Skewering one, he rode over the writhing body and flung himself, full-tilt, at the wall of Saracens. Behind him, a wedge of Templars followed, and I was among them, for my horse was a Templar beast and pushed itself to the middle of the pack, while I was too weak to turn its head. But the Saracens were indeed a wall of armoured flesh, and though we hacked at them we were forced back until we were fighting in the very heart of the burning barricade. Arrows were falling all around, some of them catching fire as they fell. I saw the Templar who had come to invite me into de Sonnac's company go down with an arrow in his face. Another man's horse stumbled and flung its rider into a pyre of flaming beams. The Grand Master, blood running from his eye socket, was thrashing about him with his sword, and shouting I urged my horse through the inferno. At that moment there was a deafening bang. The Grand Master's horse reared and threw him backwards, over his cantle and onto the ground. There was another great bang, and a section of the barricade, still upright though laced with flame, vanished in a cloud of sparks and flying wood. Guillaume de Sonnac, who was struggling to his feet, clapped his hands to his face. Blood poured from between his fingers.

'Oh, Christ my saviour, I am blinded!' he cried.

Three Templars dismounted and rushed to him. There was another detonation and then another. My own horse was starting to dance and scream and so I swung out of the saddle and jumped clear of his flailing hooves. A dazzling flash, and I found myself grovelling on the burned-over ground, my ears ringing. As I picked myself up I caught sight of a tall figure pointing towards me. Next to him were two stout Saracens in the leather jerkins of fire-carriers. And they held clay pots, but these were small, and there were sparks, not flames, coming from them. As I watched, they hurled them, and a moment later two more detonations rang out among the Templars. The tall figure . . . What part of my mind was still thinking clearly in the middle of that hell I cannot imagine, but somehow I realised he was not a Saracen. And I knew him.

Ducking behind my shield, I ran at the nearest soldier, knocking him down and jumping over his body. Another man thrust his spear at me and I hacked off the point. A horse ran in front of me and I shoved my sword into the rider's leg, ducked under the hooves and came up with my eyes full of dust. Another Templar was at my side, chanting something, some song, over and over again, as he slashed away. It was the Lord's Prayer, and it broke up at the forgiving of trespasses, for an arrow had caught him in the throat and as he dropped to his knees, three Saracens rushed him and struck off his head. I swung at one of them, missed, and then an eddy opened in the seethe of men and horses and for a moment the battle shifted from where I stood, marooning me in a clearing surrounded by shrieking horror. And there at the other side of the clearing was the tall man who was not a Saracen, stooping over a large wooden basket.

Without thinking I raised my sword and sprinted, silently, though my breath rang in my ears like the bellowing of a gored bull. And as I ran I told myself that this could not be Remigius, the murderous fop, Isaac's murderer. But I had glimpsed him in Damietta, and as he looked up and saw me nearly upon him I saw I was right. With a French curse he threw one of the infernal pots at me. It struck my shield and shattered harmlessly, but I was already jumping over the basket. The top edge of my shield, caught him under the chin and he went down like a dead man.

But he was not dead. I landed on his chest with my full weight and felt ribs give way beneath me. He bleated, opened his eyes and whinnied in pain and fear. Shaking off my shield, I put the edge of my sword against his throat.

'Remigius, you fucking swine!' I hissed in his ear. 'This is well met, oh! Very well met!'

'You Ghibbeline pox-master!' he wheezed. 'I thought I saw you die in Mansourah . . .'

'Has the pope whored you to the Turk, then?' I dug my knees harder into his ribs.

'What do you know of the Holy Father? When the godly fight the godless there is no morality, you milk-fed usurer!'

'Someone was coming to learn about the Drug,' I hissed, pressing on the blade. 'It was you, of course it was you. Doing

234

Cardinal John's bidding, even if it meant treason against a Christian king?'

'Christian king! Christian king!' parroted Remigius. 'Your Christian king – I thought you were a heretic yourself, maggot – must needs be kept here so that he doesn't meddle. And your emperor, that fucking lover of Mussulmen, is missing his cousin! If Louis Capet must die here so that Frederick von Hohenstaufen dies in Italy, then that is fair exchange, and God will know His friends!'

An arrow whistled and buried itself in the ground next to Remigius's ear. He winced and turned his head, drawing his skin across the blade of my sword. A trickle of blood ran from under the steel.

'And the Drug – was it worth dying for, my friend? A bang and a flash – not enough to make the world tremble, after all.'

'The Drug . . . The *Drug*!' mocked Remigius. 'The Drug is a toy. I've been having fun. But your letter, eh, Zennorius? Do you still have it? When were you going to deliver it, lad? But no matter! I have spared you the trouble.'

Then I remembered the words of Matthieu d'Allaines in Damietta: *Are you so prideful to think that the Holy Father placed this responsibility in no other hands but yours?*

'Ah, he sees!' Remigius gasped. 'You should have given your bank over to the pope with a bow and a smile, usurer! We did *try* to warn you—'

'Warn me?' I bellowed at him, and leaned on my sword.

Remigius did not answer. He was trying to force my blade away from his flesh, but the edge was biting into his hands. 'Is that why you killed Isaac? Just to warn me?'

'Yes, to warn you. But you spat on the Church. And look! Your dear friend died in vain, didn't he? Because you are going to die here, and all your money, you heretic fuck, will be the Holy Father's—'

An arrow struck my helmet with a *tink*; another grazed

Remigius's shoulder. A spent crossbow bolt hit my leg and pierced the mail, burying itself an inch into my thigh. I looked down at the man beneath me. The suave, loose-limbed dandy from Florence was writhing, groping with one bloody hand for the basket of exploding pots. I leaned down and whispered in his ear.

'I might forgive you for being a traitorous serpent, because you were right about me: it takes one to know one. But I don't forgive you for my friend Isaac, or William Longspée.' And I put all my weight behind the blade.

The battle was flowing back, filling up the space it had made. I dodged a speeding horseman who did not notice me, and began to run back towards the pyre of the Templar barricades. My fingers were wound in Remigius's hair; his head bounced against my leg. I had no thought but that I would show it to the king, and reveal the great plot against him. I slashed and bludgeoned my way through hedges of fighting men. There was Guillaume de Sonnac's banner, just ahead . . .

There was a bang, and a horse reared up beside me and threw its rider. The man – Saracen or Christian, I did not see – landed across my back and we both crashed to the ground. I squirmed, sword trapped beneath me, and kicked at him in a frenzy, at last getting my feet between his legs and thrusting him away from me. Head singing, eyes dancing with smoke and sparks, I staggered up. I was deaf. Where was my sword? I found it and picked it up. And the head of Remigius? I cast about me like a sleepwalker but only found that I was standing amid drifts of human jetsam: limbs, bodies, half-bodies, livers, lungs and lights . . . And amid this vast butcher's stall, one man's head was lost like a snowflake in a blizzard.

We had won another great victory, or so I discovered later, and we called it the Field of Fariskur. The Saracens were beaten back. They had lost great numbers, and had fled back to

Mansourah. The camp was ringing with tales of courage and single combat, of hordes of infidels cut down by a single knight. But these tales were heard by far fewer than might have listened to them before the battle, because there had been a great slaughter among us as well. The Grand Master of the Temple was dead, blinded in his remaining eye and cut to pieces. In truth, there were almost no Templars left at all, and none who remembered that I was a hero, so that was a small mercy. The king spent the next week giving thanks to God, and as I watched the endless rituals, and saw that this was how Louis kept his courage stoked – for the King of France might have been a fool in matters of the soul, but he was as brave as any man, and suffered, without complaint, the same afflictions that tormented the lowliest of his army – I realised that I could not tell him about Remigius and Pope Innocent. I had no proof, and now that the lunacy of battle had worn off, it seemed a ludicrous story. I knew it was not, but how to make the most Christian king on God's earth see that? I would be called a traitor or a heretic, no doubt – which the letter hanging round my neck would prove I was – or simply a Ghibbeline. And if I did press home my case, what then? Louis would not retreat. Nothing was stronger than the oath he had taken, not even the truth. God, save us from those who believe in You.

Besides, I had decided that I was not going to fulfil Remigius's prophesy and die here. I wanted nothing more than to see Iselda again. What we would do, what would happen next, I put out of my mind entirely. For a week, as I tried to mend my wounds despite the best efforts of the camp surgeons, I thought of nothing more than the door of the Ca' Kanzir opening, showing me the wall, the vine, the fig tree and the old stone bench, stairs that led up to the main floor, the ancient well in the centre of the courtyard, and leaning against it, Iselda, hair like a butterfly's wing, holding out her hands to me. And again and again I threw my spirit into her arms, as the kites and the vultures feasted on the rich mulch of Mussulman and Christian flesh that ringed the camp, and the flags of the Saracen army waved, bright and confident, beyond the canal.

Chapter Eighteen

The Nile Delta, March 1250

The army was dying. The crusade was already dead. For weeks we had squatted in front of Mansourah – laying siege to it, so we told ourselves – without supplies, without news from Damietta, constantly raided and harassed by the Saracens. They knew the truth about us, of course. It was bloody obvious, as I would have told my English companions, had any of them still lived. We were, every one of us, sick with the scorbutus, or with the bloody flux. Quartan fever had struck us, and was carrying off anyone already brought low by other afflictions. Almost no one had come through the battle of Shrove Tuesday without a wound, and in the filth and heat of the delta, wounds festered, limbs blackened and men died. I could barely walk ten paces without my guts convulsing and voiding themselves, but I had managed to keep my wound clean and it was healing. Others were not so lucky: the sweet foulness of gangrene was ever present, wafting with the vapours of watery shit, unburied corpses and scorbutic breath. *No one can get out of Mansourah*, men would say to each other. *And why would they want to?* I said to myself. *To get their feet dirty in our sewage?* The Saracens were perfectly safe where they were. And if they stayed put for another month, we would all be dead where we stood. But the truth was plainer even than that. We were here on the bank of the Nile, huddled within our rough fortifications, while all around us the Saracen armies roamed at will. We were under siege ourselves, but not a man admitted it.

For a sort of madness had taken hold of the Christians. It seemed that no man opened his chapped and rotting mouth except to crow about the great victories of Shrove Tuesday and the first Friday of Lent, when it must have been plain to the dullest clodhopper that we had on both those days fought the enemy off with great loss to ourselves, and only narrowly avoided total disaster. It was as if no one had noticed that barely twenty men out of hundreds had come back from Mansourah alive. As one of those men I had tried to tell my story, but the truth had already been decided upon, and I was too weak and sickened to insist.

A few men had managed, by strength of will or character, to keep hold of their reason and humanity. The king was one of them. Louis had the scorbutus, and he was becoming as blotched and stinking as the lowest foot soldier, but he seemed not to care. In fact he told me his sickness was a blessing from the Lord, for it brought him closer to the suffering of his army. Because I had been in Mansourah when his brother was killed, Louis had made me one of his companions, so that I now belonged to the close-knit company of command, along with the king's surviving brothers, Gautier de Châtillon, Jean de Joinville and the other men of high rank who had lived through the carnage thus far. It was an honour, but it did not mean much: slightly better food and slightly more of it; wine that was less sour. It was Joinville who made me welcome at first, for I was not known to most of the nobles save as an exalted sort of merchant, a man who had earned his money, forsooth. But soon I was just one more knight, a brother amongst brothers, and while this ridiculous honour had come just when it had ceased to have much meaning, I was glad of it, for it relieved the gnawing loneliness that had dogged me since leaving Damietta.

It was nine days after the battle for the camp. The sun was blazing down. There was a crowd of men down at the water's edge, braving the badly aimed crossbow bolts that flew at them every now and again. They were fishing for eels, which along with the plump rats that infested the reed beds were the only meat any of us had eaten for a long while. The Nile was full of them, though, and eels are tasty food, so it seemed as though things could be far worse. I was cleaning my sword, greasing it with eel-fat, when there was a sudden commotion from the river. Men were crying out and cursing at the tops of their lungs. Sheathing my sword, I joined the crowd that was running down to see what the trouble was.

The men on the bank were pointing upstream. I shaded my eyes against the glare. Out in the middle of the river, in the sluggish brown wavelets, round shapes were bobbing. I saw one, then four, then nine. And then I lost count. It seemed as if great pale bubbles were coming up out of the riverbed, rising like marsh gas in a fen. They were drifting down towards the pontoon bridge that separated the two halves of the camp, and as they came nearer I saw what they were.

The men who had died in the battle for Mansourah, and those who had been killed beyond our lines in the battle for the camp, had been stripped and flung into the river by the Saracens, Christian and Mussulman alike. They had sunk in the slack water, but now, bloated with putrefaction, they were returning to the world. First one by one, then in clusters and finally in a wretched, stinking shoal, they drifted down and struck the low side of the bridge, and began to pile up, until by the afternoon a dog could have walked from bank to bank upon corpses.

But now, men were down on their knees, puking into the water, baskets of eels were tipped over, their contents squirming away between our feet. More eels were busy out in the river. Where the first corpses were catching on the bridge the water was alive, seething, and we were near enough to see what was making the ferment: a black, roiling legion of eels, some of them grotesque monsters as thick as a man's arm, fought with countless tiny fishes and swarms of water-insects as they rushed to devour this carrion feast. Flies were swarming from every corner of Egypt, so it seemed, for in a few short minutes the droning of their wings became unbearable.

'Mother of God, we've been eating those eels!' gasped a man next to me.

'Did you think they'd been eating honey cakes, down there in the mud? Don't be a fucking fool,' snapped another, but I noted that he was pea-green under his sunburn.

The dead were hauled out by a troop of ruffians, the dregs of the Christian army, and the king paid them good money to do it, though if any of them lived to spend their reward back home I did not hear about it. It took a good week. The corpses were dragged up onto the bridge with bill-hooks and examined by men with tar-soaked rags wrapped round their noses and mouths. Those that were circumcised – should the cadaver be fortunate enough to have kept its wedding tackle from the teeth of the marauding eels – were rolled across and dropped into the river on the other side, where they were free to drift away. The Christian bodies were dragged to the bank and laid out in rows, and men could be seen walking up and down, pausing to look into a face to see if it was a friend, a father or a brother. But they all looked the same: tight, bulging sacks of corruption, each face a swollen, greenish-grey mass, like old pease porridge crudely formed into a blurred mockery of ears, nose, mouth. They might never have been men at all. A vile, dark liquor seeped from them, luring insects and other creatures that might have been conjured from the fevered dreams of we who still lived. The king went down to look for his brother, but death and the river had hidden the prince and the villain behind the same appalling mask.

I wondered if Longspée was lying amongst that putrid company. For I missed my friend. I could not mourn him – it is hard to mourn when the air is almost palpable with mortality – but I found myself grieving for his children, whom I had never met. They would be at home, drinking in life as children do, quite unaware of all this. I kept thinking of them, two girls and two boys holding hands, walking up and down the rows of melting dead men, searching for their father. And then I would remember how nearly the arrow had taken me and not Longspée, and think how much better it would have been if he had lived and I had died. I would have only left Iselda behind: Longspée had been cut out of a family.

After the dead men, the sickness caught hold in earnest. We were still being supplied from Damietta, and boats would appear unpredictably but reassuringly, often bringing olives, flour and casks of salted meat. But it was Lent, and such was the piety of the king that he would not eat red meat of any kind, not the water rats or duck or bustard, but only fish. And fish meant eels. It seemed incredible to me then, and indeed it does today, but the great part of the army followed suit, even while the eel-ravaged corpses still lay along the river banks. I would not touch them. Instead I went hunting out in the reed beds, spearing frogs, catching crabs in the countless little streams and ditches, setting snares for wild birds. Every now and again I would find a turtle. The birds I would cook and eat out of sight of my fellows, for I did not wish to be seen breaking the Lenten rules, and the meat from Damietta, even if it had not been placed off limits, was usually vile, rancid stuff. But my other finds – those which were fishy enough to be eaten by the pious – I tried to share, though they were not welcomed. There were a few of us who supported ourselves thus, solitary hunters all. We would run into each other sometimes, and warily compare our catch, and slink away. So I kept the scorbutus from ravaging me, but the marks of the disease appeared anyway, slowly, growing as my strength ebbed. I knew them all too well. I had met the scorbutus before, on a long sea-journey to the shores of Greenland, and I had gaps in my teeth to remember it by. So it was with a weary resignation that I saw the purple blotches appear on my legs and arms, felt my tongue swell and my teeth loosen. By Easter I could taste gangrene in my mouth, and knew that, along with the army, I was a dead man if I did not leave soon. But then it was far too late to go anywhere.

Two weeks after the bodies appeared in the river, a little fishing boat of the sort the Saracens call *felucca* arrived in our camp. A ragged knight, whom I recognised as one of the Comte de Flandres's men, jumped out and hurried to the king's tent. It was not long before the whole camp found out what had happened.

While we had buried our dead, chewed our eels and shot useless arrows at Mansourah, the Saracens had been dragging a small fleet of galleys through the reeds out of sight and earshot of our guards. They had refloated them downstream of our camp and flung a blockade across the river. A Christian relief force had been slaughtered. The little fleet of galleys that had come upstream with the army was not strong enough to force a way through. We were as good as cut off.

The knight had brought a package of letters, and though I was wishing with every grain of my being that there could be one for me, I almost blacked out when my name was called. I saw Iselda's writing and staggered off into the reed beds to enjoy it in private.

My dearest, she wrote,
  There has been something of a calamity.

Oh, good Christ. I knew Iselda's voice; it spoke to me through the ink as though she were talking in my ear. My hands began to shake.

  But I have matters in hand. Read now, and do not worry about me. Here is the tale:
  It was in late October, about the Feast of Saint Luke. I had received the letter you sent telling me about the battle before Damietta, so I knew you were safe. And I had just written to you about the old Doge. The time had passed most tediously, my love, since you set off. I had no companions in Venice save for your hated ledgers, and God! how I have come to hate them too. The old Ca' Kanzir began to seem more and more like a cave, a cold, mossy cavern. There was no bad news from any of our agents to liven things up, and no splendid news either.
  Until, that is, the cleric paid me a visit. He brought letters of introduction from someone whose name was familiar to me: a Cardinal John of Toledo. This cleric's name is Matthieu d'Allaines, and he is a plump little fellow. If you should ever chance to meet him, and I hope you do not, you will see that while he seems to be kindly, all smiles, that is but an ill-fitting mask. There was something about him I did not like particularly, and he was quite put out that he had to deal with a woman, though he knew you were gone on crusade. He must have expected some sort of secretary, but I told him he must make do with me. The mask slipped a little bit, but I gave him to know I was head of the Banco di Corvo Marino in your absence – that, in fact, we were partners. That shocked him, I can tell you! But I think that he thought that now he had the advantage of me. He began to grow in confidence, so that, while the man who had first come to our door seemed like a fat little parish priest, I saw that he was something entirely different. I

have come on the business of the Holy Father himself, he said, and produced a letter from the good Innocent. A pious housewife might have been somewhat overawed, but I have seen many such, and told him so. The mask slipped again. So, to business. The Curia was requesting a loan. Delighted to accommodate, I said, and took the letter he was thrusting at me. Now then, do not forget that I was alone with this man on a quiet morning. Marta was in the kitchen and the servants were about the place, but there were no shipments going in and out and Paolo was visiting his mother on the Lido. So when I saw what was written there on that letter I was, to all intents and purposes, alone. And maybe — no, not maybe, my dear man, for your heart and your mind are as one with my own on many things — you can imagine what came over me when I saw the figure at the bottom of the page. It was for the precise amount — to the last denarius — held in our bank's treasure houses. You are jesting with me, I said. Oh, no, not at all, he said. You wish to serve God, do you not? The Holy Father requires this money.

It is a huge sum, I protested. I had not expected to find your loyalty in question, he said to me, oily and venomous. I denied that it was, but he began to rail about Ghibbelines and about the emperor. What have you loaned to Frederick von Hohenstaufen? he demanded, and I told him that our clients' privacy was more important to us than their gold. To cut a few unpleasant minutes short, he pressed me, and I danced around the matter, until he lost his patience entirely. If you refuse you will regret it, he said. You and your husband. I came here alone in good faith, as I did not expect to be greeted by a poisoned tongue! I protested, and tried to soothe him. It was simply a matter of the size of his request, I said, but he was not to be mollified, and then he showed his fangs, I can tell you. There is a party on its way from Rome, he fairly hissed, and with them is one Peter of Verona. The name is familiar to you . . . Oh, he was cruel, dearest one. I speak of the Inquisitor of Lombardy, he said. There are many whispers about you and your bank. If you refuse to give the Holy Father the satisfaction of this

246

loan, there is no power on this earth great enough to protect you from Brother Peter, and from the wrath of the Lord God Almighty.

There is no need to threaten, I insisted. *As you say, I cannot refuse the Holy Father. But this cannot be done in a day, or even a week. Because I love Holy Mother Church, though, in a week I shall have it done,* I assured him. *And what,* I threw in, *can the Banco di Corvo Marino expect in return? Our good opinion,* he said, and he knew what a dry old bone he had thrown me, and how well he had cowed this presumptuous bitch. But – and were I a superstitious fool like Father Matthieu I might discern the Lord's hand in this – so puffed up with his own victory was the horrible little man that he strode out wreathed in triumph, his round nose in the air, without demanding a guarantee or advance.

I told one of the serving lads, a quick little boy from Dorsoduro I hired after you left, to follow the priest. And I sent another off to fetch Piero back from the Lido. Then I went and called on Dimitri. He has grown so gouty that he finds it quite hard to walk, you know, but when I told him what I needed he seemed to shake off the years like a dog shakes off water. I told him to take command of one of our merchant galleys, the fastest, and make her ready to leave the next day. But my work was only just begun. A messenger was sent down to Florence, and I told him to kill as many horses as he needed to get there on wings. With him went a letter to Blasius, ordering him upon its receipt to suspend all business and take all the money to a place of safety away from the city and from strange eyes, ready to bring it down to the coast, to a good and secret port I recalled you talking about from the old days with my father. The business and quite possibly our lives were at risk, I let him know, and also that I was aware how much I was trusting him.

And, my dear husband, you were right about Blasius. Dimitri brought us to our meeting place in ten days. We had a brave crew, and I paid them for the journey what they might hope to make in a year, but I fear some of them will not pull an oar again, and have been well provided for. Blasius was waiting with a line of asses weighed down with bags of coin. *All was loaded safely on board, and I asked Blasius if he would come with us, but he said he would take his chances in Florence, and that now he would not have to hide his Ghibbeline colours any more. He is a brave young man, and I hope we can reward him.*

Somewhat in fear of pirates – a great irony, that, and not lost on either Dimitri or myself – we made haste down the coast, stopping only in Naples to take on some fresh souls to man the oars.

The letter broke off, and then started up again in a rushed, scratchy hand that was still Iselda's.

Forgive me – this last in haste. We are lying up in Palermo, and I have found a man leaving today for Damietta. I shall follow: it may well be folly, but my reasoning is that the bank has no better friend, or any other friend, maybe, than King Louis, and even if his friendship is only with our gold, that in itself may provide me a safe haven. And perhaps I will persuade you to come away with me . . .

I pray this reaches you in haste! The next part of my tale will follow close behind this.

With all my heart!

Your wife

Matthieu d'Allaines. I cursed him aloud, calling down the plagues of Egypt upon his pink head, and a bittern, startled by my croaking, rose booming in terror from the reeds in front of me. I looked at the letter's date again. The vile little goblin had known all this when he had come to me in Damietta. Indeed, he had come straight from Venice. So where was Iselda now? I did not like the way the letter ended, and then my thoughts shifted, quivering like a compass needle, to Remigius. The pope's reach was vast and secret but . . . No, Remigius would have boasted if something had become of Iselda. That seemed clear, but I could not trust a dead man.

I am ashamed to relate it now, but I did not worry about Iselda very much after I had tottered back to camp, for by that time I was far too weak and ill. The scorbutus had began to suck out my life in earnest, and I had been suffering from the flux for two days. I clung to the image I had formed of my wife safe with Dimitri, and in my mind I surrounded her with the protective ghosts of her father and his old crew. I tried to convince myself that she was, beyond doubt, safer than me, and the thought cheered me somewhat. As I grew weaker, I imagined that as I decayed, Iselda grew more secure, and when I started to piss blood, I almost prayed out loud with gratitude, so addled were my brains. I hardly thought of the gold. What could it buy me, here? Not even a grave: we had long since stopped burying our dead.

There were no more letters, no more supplies. Easter came and the Christians no longer had to chew carrion-gorged eels, to eat their fellow soldiers transubstantiated into the meat of fishes. But now the food that was left became more precious than gold. The few pitiful oxen who still roamed about the camp, eyed murderously by every hungry man, were now worth eighty livres. A pig – and there were some hogs that had grown as fat as German cardinals on the Saracen bodies that had washed up downstream – could be had for thirty livres, more than most men made in a year of toil. Even a plain egg was changing hands for twelve pennies. My purse, all the gold and silver I had brought from Damietta, was still untouched, and so I bought two pigs and three barrels of wine, and gave them to the men-at-arms who had come with the English knights. That cost me most of my silver, but the gold I wrapped in a silken stocking and tied round my waist. I might say I had a premonition that it would be needed soon, but in truth it would not have taken a Sybil to predict that things were coming to an end here, and not a good one at that.

Very soon, the army began to starve. The scorbutus began to ravage its victims without mercy. Men dropped dead where they stood, or walking to the privies. The weather was growing hotter, and with it came a redoubled attack by the marsh flies who brought quartan fevers with them. Not one man in the Christian army was spared. The barber-surgeons were busy from morning to nightfall, cutting dead flesh from men's mouths so that they could chew the pitiful crumbs left to us.

Jean de Joinville had been unable to leave his bed for weeks. His wounds had suppurated, he had the scorbutus and a quartan fever, and he could barely swallow water, let alone food. His mood had not been helped when his priest dropped dead while singing mass in his tent. The king was almost as ill, for the bad water had turned his guts and he was growing thinner by the day. I will admit that I spent a great deal of time in his tent, for I knew that I would be given a little wine for courtesy's sake, and wine made my rotting gums feel better, at least for a while. That, and salt, kept the black rot from my mouth, and I was lucky, for the camp was full, all day long, with the whimpers and screams of men who had opened their mouths for a surgeon's razor. As I sat with Joinville one day in the close and foul air of his tent, he sat up on his cot and clapped his hands to his ears.

'Dear Christ! It sounds like a thousand women giving birth!' he said, trying to be jovial. But then he caught my eye, and the strained smile vanished from his lips. 'But that signifies the coming of life, and this . . .'

There was no need to say more. It was soon after that, I think, when the king announced we would be moving the camp to a more defensible position across the water. There was much confusion for a brace of days, and a sharp rearguard skirmish in which we lost good men, but I was not caught up in it. I do not remember why – much of that time has gone from my memory, washed away in sweat and flux – but when the army was settled in its new position, I was called, along with the other surviving nobles, to attend the king. I had somehow come to be thought of as one of those nobles, perhaps because I was the one surviving Englishman, but when every man's clothing is stiff with his own waste, the finer points of courtly rank become somewhat meaningless. The king had propped himself up in the high-backed seat that served as a throne. He was horribly thin, and his face was all nicked and raw where the barber had tried to shave his failing skin. A knight called Geoffroy de Sargines, who was a close companion of the king's and a brave, friendly soul, was standing at his side, and the other councillors were arranged in a ragged arc, shuffling their feet and looking, to a man, like foxes who have been ravaged by the mange.

'My dear friends,' said Louis, and his voice was weak but calm, 'I will not risk the lives of you or your men any longer. It is we who are besieged. We do not have the strength any more to break through to Cairo. We are cut off from Damietta. The ships we have here cannot break through. We are starving – God love you all for your fortitude, but as a Christian king I cannot drag out your suffering for no purpose. So let it be known that my councillors' – he nodded in their direction, and they winced and shuffled as though afflicted with the stone – 'have gone to treat with the Saracen queen. I have some terms to report. The first is that we will surrender Damietta in return for Jerusalem. The second is that the queen will take care of our sick and wounded, here and in Damietta, until they can be brought to the Holy Land. And the Saracens agree to keep our stocks of salt pork for us – they will not be tempted by them, at least!'

It was the feeblest of jokes, but we managed an equally feeble titter in its honour. We were all looking at one another with narrowed eyes, trying to work things out. Had we, in fact, won? The Saracens were going to let us go, and give back Jerusalem? Perhaps they were as sick as we were. They did not seem that sick – their arrows still went straight, anyway. But the king was speaking again.

'The queen wants surety for these generous terms,' he said. 'To be plain, she wants me.'

There was a roar of outrage. 'And I say the Turks shall not have him!' cried Geoffroy de Sargines. 'I would rather they killed me . . .'

'And I!' shouted the man next to me, who could barely stand, and whom the Saracens, in a roundabout way, had already all but killed. But they took up the call, until de Sargines held up his arms.

'They shall kill us all, or take us all captive, before we give up our beloved king!' he yelled. There was a sort of enfeebled pandemonium: I saw a man, a count from Burgundy, keel over in a faint, and others sink to their knees either in prayer or because they no longer had the strength to stand. One of the king's servants was holding up a cloth of blue silk in front of the king, and because I was near I heard the sound of strangled puking from behind it.

Something had been decided, at least it appeared so, but as I wandered off in search of shade and something clean to drink, I realised that we had decided to do nothing. I picked my way through the piles of shit and thrice-chewed bones, past a bowman jibbering in his final delirium; past a priest, his face black with scorbutus, closing the eyes of a dead boy who would never have his first shave. It was the first week of April. Easter had come and gone, but there was no spring, no hope, no matter how much the priests waved their incense. The muddy Nile seeped by, and the strange, black-headed birds with their long beaks watched us from the reeds. In my fevered state I saw that they were the spirits of this place, waiting to suck out our souls. But they were patient, even kindly, and I took to muttering at them, broken prayers and incantations, as I sat doing whatever pointless tasks I thought might speed time on to its end. Today I was polishing my sword, rubbing tallow into the grained metal until it caught the pitiless Egyptian sun. My eyes could not take the glare, and so I closed them, watching the light play in shades of red through the thin flesh of my eyelids.

There was a rustle behind me. I was sitting close to a patch of dead reeds and I turned, expecting to find one of the ominous spirit-birds studying me. Instead I found myself looking into a pair of red-streaked eyes set in a hollowed-out face. No, not hollowed: deflated. For these features had once adorned a plump, well-fed man who had, through misfortune not hard to guess at, become very thin all at once. The loose skin, emptied of its fat, hung in useless wattles along his jaw and under his chin. His cheeks were scabbed with fly bites, but when he moistened his lips with his tongue I noticed that his gums were still pink. Then something in the curve of the man's diminished nose gave him away.

'Matthieu d'Allaines!' I croaked. 'What the fuck are you doing here?' The man flinched, and I saw that he was gripping the hilt of a short sword, and that the point was trembling in the air between us. I stood up and leaned the point of my own shimmering blade into the ground between us. 'I thought I had left you behind in Damietta. And am I to suppose you came here to find *me*?'

Father Matthieu opened his wasted lips but no sound came from them save a gluey smacking as he tried to force words through the dry vault of his mouth. His knuckles were white around the hilt of his sword and without thinking I looked quickly about me, seeing if, should I run this monstrous creature through and kick him into the reeds, anyone would bear witness. There were many people milling around, but all in the same fevered trance. I knew that, unless they were roused, hardly a man in the camp could think of anything but the pain in his mouth or the clawing in his guts. I had only to lift my sword . . . But at that moment a ragged black shape detached itself from a knot of pikemen and scuttled towards us, and Father Matthieu, with a throttled moan of rage, stepped back and slid his sword into its sheath. Hurrying over was a friar I recognised, a simple fellow from Rouen, and he smiled happily at me as he took Matthieu by the shoulder.

'My prodigal! Indeed, my prodigy!' he exclaimed, shaking him feebly. 'Sir knight, you have met the wonder of our army,' he said to me. 'This noble brother has come from Damietta to share the suffering of our pious king. He was caught by the blockade but threw himself into the river and hid on . . . on an eyot, is that right, brother? Hid there for weeks until he could slip past the heathen brutes. And so he has won through . . . a miracle, and miracles are sorely needed here, are they not? They are! Amen!'

'So you did not go back to Rome,' I said, eyeing the wrecked figure before me. 'Tell me, how do you fare, brother Matthieu? Have you eaten many eels? You look like a man who has feasted on our delicious Nile eels, I think.'

'Yes, I have eaten eels,' he rasped, finding his voice at last. 'And frogs, beetles, many crawling, scrabbling things.' His voice was stiff with loathing. 'No, not many – few, very few.'

'Then you must eat something more wholesome. Here.' I opened my purse with my left hand, keeping my right loose on my sword hilt, and fished out ten silver livres. These I gave to the priest from Rouen. 'Buy this brave fellow meat and wine – whatever he desires.'

Matthieu's bleared eyes widened, and the desiccated muscles of his face twitched this way and that, like lodestones in an iron mine, between the attractions of hatred and hunger.

Chapter Nineteen

5 April 1250

'I'm going,' said Jean. He was pale as dirty ivory and he could speak in nothing but a throttled hiss. 'The king has ordered us to retreat or die. I think the choice is . . .'

'There are Saracen galleys between us and Damietta,' I said. It was the second Tuesday after Easter, two days after Louis had spoken to us, and now the king, who had the flux so badly that the seat of his breeches had been cut away, had finally decided to retreat. There had been some horse-trading with the Saracen queen, but we were in no position to negotiate anything. And so we were going to try and win through to Damietta.

'Of course. Either way we die,' said Joinville. I could smell the reek of scorbutus on his breath, and his gums were mottled black. 'But I would prefer to die in action, and not have my throat slit like a sheep. Will you come with me?'

I looked around at the remains of the Christian camp. The sun was going down, and the ragged clouds were turning black against a pink sky. Acres of churned, sandy mud, trampled reeds, filthy rivulets were pocked with the figures of men, some standing in dejected groups, others crawling, still others lying motionless. Louis had ordered that great bonfires should be lit to guide the sick, those who could still move, to the galleys, that had been trapped when the Saracens blocked the river.

The smoke was beginning to rise, and already a clamour was going up from the ships. On the other side of the river, the Saracens were shooting arrows into them, idly, as if this were nothing more than a fairground. Meanwhile, men were scrambling aboard, many losing their footing or, too weak to haul themselves over the sides, dropping into the churned slurry of the Nile. The sailors were screaming at them, urging their comrades on, but they too were crippled with scorbutus and the flux. It was a terrible scene: an army utterly defeated, in arms, in body and in spirit.

'And the king?' I asked Jean, who had sunk down onto his haunches, his knees shaking with fatigue. I could barely stand upright myself. My guts were in a constant roil, and the flux had scoured and seared my body until there was little left of me but the constant urge to shit. I reeked. We all did, from the king down to the blacksmith. Living skeletons, all of us, plastered with our own dung, spitting our teeth out, dropping dead in the midst of a sentence. And always, across the river, the gaudy, shining tents of the Saracens mocked us, and the Saracens themselves, sturdy, healthy and upright, goaded us with words and picked us off with arrows.

'The king is determined to be in the rearguard,' said Jean. He coughed, and the coughing turned into a spasm of vomiting. When he looked up, there were angry tears in his eyes. 'I would stay with him, but I would like to die with my men. I owe them that much.'

'Perhaps you will get through,' I said. 'Since you mention debt, we are owed a little luck, don't you think?'

It was a feeble jest, but Jean gave a croaking laugh. 'Will you come with me?' he asked again. I shook my head.

'I will stay with the king,' I told him. 'I speak a little Saracen, and I think my sword arm still works.'

'Then God bless you!' He put out his hand and I pulled him

upright. We embraced, and I could feel the bones beneath my clothes jarring against him.

'I will see you in Damietta,' I said.

'If the Lord wills it,' he answered, and turning away he stumbled off towards a galley that had just hoisted the arms of Champagne to its masthead.

I found Louis standing with Geoffroy de Sargines in the flickering light of one of the bonfires. The sun was gone, and the galleys were going too, drifting down the river, rowed by men too feeble to walk, let alone wield an oar. There was an uproar in the Saracen camp, but over our own a thick silence hung, broken only by the groans of the dying, and the furtive chink of weapons being checked. Almost nobody was left save the knights of the rearguard, who were clustered around their horses. I recognised Philippe de Montfort, and he saluted me with a hollow smile.

'Sir Petrus!' said the king, jovially. He was leaning on the arm of a young page, and looked almost childlike himself, for sickness seemed to have burned his years from him and he seemed, in the eerie light, to be no more substantial than a starved child wearing stolen finery. I hated him then, for his jollity in the face of this great ruin his pious dreams had brought to us, but I found that I loved him too, for he suffered and tried to hide it, not from pride, I knew, but because he could not bear to distress his people. Inside its amulet, Earl Richard's letter seemed to tug at my neck. I pictured Richard, and Cardinal John, and Innocent himself, all clean and scrubbed, calmly planning the betrayal of this man, and I silently cursed them all to the slowly turning spits of eternal damnation. But the letter still hung like a brick beneath my tunic. It seemed obvious to me, plain as the agonising gaps in my teeth, that we were going to be captured – that is if we weren't butchered, which seemed far more likely. What would happen if the Saracens themselves found the letter? I would still be a traitor to Louis, but what would the Mussulmen think of an infidel carrying a letter to a dead sultan? I could think of nothing to comfort myself save the thought that, if my crime came to light, I would most probably be dead.

'Are you riding, Your Majesty?' I asked, trying to match his cheery tone and falling short.

'I am,' he said. 'We are waiting for Gautier de Châtillon and then we shall be on our way.'

'Might I join you?'

'By all means, dear man!'

'Then I shall go and find a horse.'

'Have this one.' Geoffroy de Sargines came out of the dusk leading three horses: two chargers and a small straw-coloured cob draped in a caparison of blue silk. To my slight relief he handed me the reins of one of the chargers. 'I brought this for Pierre de Baugy, but he appears to have died.'

'And I shall ride this little beast,' said the king. 'Look, when I fall off I shall not hurt myself too much, eh?' He was not joking, I saw, for when the page and I hoisted him into the saddle he could not sit upright but laid his head against the horse's pale mane. More than ever he looked like a dying child. I exchanged a glance with Geoffroy.

'Is my lord able to ride at all?' I whispered to him.

'That is as you see,' he answered. 'I believe he will not live to see the morning, but we cannot leave him.'

'No.' There was nothing more to be said. I pulled myself aboard my own horse with difficulty. I had become very weak, more than I had realised, and the effort caused my guts to let go once again. But no one noticed my soiled breeches. Every one of us was caked in his own shit, and the stench of the sorry remains of our crusade rose above us like invisible smoke, and mingled with the black fumes of our burning camp. Our gaunt, sore-pocked faces flickered in the firelight. We looked like minor demons in some corner of a painted hell.

Gautier de Châtillon came up with a pitifully small group of knights. We made off at a jog-trot along the bank. There were screams coming from behind us now. The emir's men had fallen upon the camp and were making prisoners of anyone left behind, though from the noise it was plain that they were slaughtering those too sick or hurt to walk. The night around us was full of motion: the galloping of hooves on unseen paths through the reeds; the splash of oars on the river; horrible screams, drums and jubilation from the Saracen camp; the whirr of unaimed arrows and the whirr of bats. I do not know how long we rode, save that the night became blacker. For a little time we were alone, but then the first Saracen appeared on the path ahead and charged us. Perhaps he did not realise that we were so strong a party, for he tried to rein in at the last moment, but too late: de Châtillon's sword took him in the chest and his horse fled snorting into the reeds.

But we were discovered. From the direction of the camp, a horseman came galloping up, came within a spear-thrust of the last man and turned back. In a little while we heard hooves again, and a large party of Saracens mounted on ponies came charging towards us. Some were holding torches which lit only their armour and clothes, so it seemed as if we were being attacked by faceless, yelling apparitions. De Châtillon gave a barked command and his men wheeled, put spears to shoulders and turned, spurring their horses down the path on either side of the king, who slumped, all but oblivious, in his saddle, propped up by Philippe de Montfort, who rode alongside. I drew my own sword, which I could barely lift, but by the time I had turned my horse the fight was over. The Saracens had met our charge and one was rolling limply down the river bank, but the others had drawn off and were pulling out their bows. Dropped torches had set the dried reeds alight. We set off again, faster this time. An arrow whizzed past me and struck de Montfort in the back. He cursed and scrabbled for it:

the head had not pierced the leather of his hauberk. Another arrow bounced off my shoulder, and one struck my horse in the flank. In half a minute we were out of deadly range, but one of de Châtillon's men was dying in his saddle, two others were shot through and groaning, and every one of us had arrows bristling out of hauberks and shields.

'How is the king?' called Geoffroy.

'He lives,' answered Philippe de Montfort. And that was all we learned, for at that moment fierce cries burst upon us and a large force of Saracens crashed through the reeds on our right flank.

There was pandemonium. I glimpsed de Montfort grabbing the bridle of the king's horse and spurring his own mount into an exhausted canter. Then a fluted mace struck my shield and lodged there. As its owner was tugging it free I beat him on the turban with my sword until he let go. A horse and a man shrieked together as they fell into the river. I slashed at my attacker but he was already gone. Torches had set light to more drifts of dead reeds. A hand grabbed the hood of my mail shirt, jerking the collar hard against my Adam's apple. I thrust my sword under my left arm and struck something yielding. There was a yelp and an oath and the hand let go. I raked my spurs against the bony flanks of my horse and set off after the king. I could just see the blue silk of his mount's caparison gleaming in the light from the wildfire that was flaring around us. Philippe de Montfort was with him, and Geoffroy de Sargines, and they were galloping up the path wrapped in a pall of dust.

'The king! The king!' I shouted, but my voice was almost gone, and the effort made my throat burn. How long since I had drunk anything? A Saracen came at me and I swung my sword at him. He made his horse rear and laughed at me over its neck.

'You bastard!' I croaked. He was out of reach, fitting an

arrow to the string of his short, curved bow. Kicking one more spasm of effort from my beast, I went at him and caught his arm with my shield just as he had brought his bow up to shoot. The arrow flew into the air but my shield slipped between bow and string and tangled me. I punched him in the face with the hilt of my sword and tried to free my shield arm but he would not let go of the bow and I was too close to stab him so I let go of the shield straps and let my arm slip out. Surprised in mid-pull, the Saracen jerked backwards and I stuck my sword into his shoulder, not a deep wound, but he cried out and fell under his horse, taking my shield with him.

'Damn you, damn you,' I was chanting under my breath. My head was spinning and my arms were suddenly as heavy as if they were sausage skins filled with sand. I had been cut somewhere on the head, for I could feel something warm trickling down my neck and back, but I did not remember the blow. The king and his companions were out of sight. 'Oh, God,' I moaned. I had to follow Louis. I had nowhere else to go. It was a terrible thought, but at that moment a sheet of flame sprang up in front of me as a whole thicket of reeds caught fire. The wounded Saracen screamed and his horse jumped through the fire. My own horse, terrified by the flames, gave a piercing whinny and flung herself after it. For an instant I was engulfed in searing red and orange, cupped in a fire-giant's hand, the fingers closing around me. Then I was out in the night once more, hurtling down the narrow path, the river on my left, darkness on my right. And then my horse stumbled.

I felt myself flying through the air at an unearthly speed, faster than anything I had known before. The ground suddenly appeared. I remember seeing one broken reed stalk in perfect detail. And then nothing.

I opened my eyes to find men all around me. Some on horses, for hooves were stamping close to my head. Men were barking at one another in Arabic, but my skull was empty of anything save amazed pain and I could not make out their words. Someone kicked me as he passed. Then a face appeared above me. It was the man I had wounded, who had taken my shield. He bent down and stared into my face. There was blood all over the front of his tunic, and one of his arms was thrust into a sling fashioned from a sword belt.

'Sorry,' I said in English. His eyes narrowed. Then he punched me hard in the face and I lost the world again.

When I came to, it was the thin, dishwater light of early dawn in the delta of the Nile. I was lying among other men, some sitting, others sprawled or curled up around their pain and exhaustion. Six of us in all. We were near the river, and I guessed I had been dragged a little way from where I had fallen, for the reeds were not burned here. There was a knot of Saracens nearby, leaning on long spears. Weapons bristled from their belts, and one man was seated on the ground holding a bow with an arrow knocked to the string. He was lazily drawing the arrow back and forth, aiming it at one prisoner, then another. I looked at my new companions. None of us was bound, but we had all been stripped of our weapons and armour. But the amulet still hung, with Iselda's stag, against my raw breastbone. One young man was almost naked except for a breechclout, and he sat shivering, streaked with blood and his own dung, trying to rock some warmth into his bones. I recognised one of Gautier de Châtillon's knights, but no one else. No one, save for a short, hollow-cheeked man with a dirty rag bound turban-wise round his head. He turned to watch the man with the bow and I saw the white scar on his nose. Matthieu d'Allaines. Damn him: had he followed me? And in Lucifer's name, with so many good men dead, how had he lived?

We sat there in silence, save for the moans of the wounded.

The sun began to rise, and soon afterwards a Saracen noble-man rode up on a beautifully furnished pony. He made it prance around us while he studied our faces. Some cringed, some hung their heads. I looked up at him, but the effort hurt my head. He was talking to the guards, and then he rode off down the river bank. Immediately the guards strutted over to where we sat, spears levelled. They kicked a man lying on his face: he was dead. The boy in the soiled breechcloth looked up and whimpered. Two soldiers grabbed him under the arms, pulled him roughly three or four paces from us, and set him down. The one with the bow wandered over, glanced at us, pulled back the string until the ends of the bow were almost touching his body, bent down towards the boy and released the arrow. It travelled no more than a foot before it struck him above the collarbone and buried itself vertically up to the feathers. The boy coughed once, spraying blood onto the dusty earth, and pitched forward.

Another soldier grabbed the man next to Matthieu by the hair, hauled him upright – his spindly legs could barely sup-port him, and his face and arms were daubed with the black spots of scorbutus – and dragged his pitiful frame down the river bank. He was sent sprawling at the water's edge, and as he raised himself up on his hands and knees the Saracen drew his sword and swung it at the man's neck. The blow was lazy and deflected off a neck-bone, and it took the Saracen two more hacks to take the head off, the Frank howling piteously in the meantime. The man sitting next to me turned away and vomited. But a Saracen prodded him with a spear point and forced him to his feet. Another did the same to Gautier de Châtillon's man. Without a doubt they expected to die and began to say their prayers as loudly as their strength allowed. But they were pushed and prodded onto the path down which we had ridden the night before, and made to shuffle off in the direction of our camp.

I was left in the dirt with Matthieu d'Allaines. There was little doubt what was planned for us. Summoning every dust mote of strength I still possessed, I scrambled onto my knees and pushed myself upright, wobbling like a newborn calf. As soon as my feet were planted I shook myself and raised my chin. Swallowing a draught of revulsion, I reached for Matthieu and tugged at him until he too staggered to his feet. Only then did I realise that the Saracens were laughing at us. But we were not slaughtered. Instead we were pushed, none too gently, down the path in the opposite direction from the camp, downstream.

The sun raked my exposed skin, burning into every slash and cut, drumming on my skull, sucking the last hint of moisture from my eyes and mouth. I stumbled along, seeing nothing but the man in front of me, through a dazzling nightmare-scape of reeds and crying water-birds. My legs felt numb, hollow, but with each step they filled with blazing pain. The Saracens were chattering, laughing. I caught a word here and there, but my mind could not hold on to thoughts long enough to string them together. Time stretched, then contracted, then stretched again . . .

Something hit me hard in the small of the back and I pitched sideways and slid down the bank at the side of the path. *I'm dying, I'm dying . . .* I thought, without surprise, expecting to feel a spear or an arrow. I came to rest face up, head down, cradled in a reeking mat of dead reeds. The sky glared, pure blue. Then something was hurtling towards me. I got my arms up and caught hold of cloth, and a man's face was suddenly an inch from my own, panting charnel air.

'Where is it? Where is it, you pig?' Matthieu d'Allaines was fumbling for my neck with his stubby fingers.

'What?' I croaked, trying to heave him off. There were shouts from above us.

'The letter! Give it to me! Curse you, give it to me!'

I started to laugh. Incredibly, my chest heaved and I laughed in the priest's face as I held him easily away from me. 'Help us! My friend slipped!' I shouted in Arabic to the soldier who was standing above us, and I pushed Matthieu aside and held out my hand. The soldier hesitated, and I saw his hand shift minutely on the haft of his spear. He cursed and spat wetly onto my chin and neck, but he bent down and took my hand.

I helped the priest back onto the path, though the soldier had started to beat me on the back of my thighs with his spear. But they let us start off again with only a few more kicks and oaths. Now I could feel the priest close behind me.

'If you came all this way to kill me, priest . . .' I coughed, tasting blood. 'All in vain, eh? A wasted journey. Innocent will be happy with this, though, won't he? Of course, my journey was wasted too – so Remigius told me, before I killed him.'

'If Remigius is dead . . . then he is at the Lord's side. And his blood will weigh you down even more swiftly to hell. But give me the letter. Give it to me and I will—'

'Spare my life? Not really in your remit any more, is it, Father?'

'I will absolve you!'

'The fuck you will! Remigius—'

'Remigius did his duty!'

'And here is the result. Pope Innocent has defeated a crusade. God is just!'

'God is finishing my work,' he wheezed. 'I ask only that I see you die.'

'So God in His infinite mercy sent a priest to commit murder, so that His servants . . . so that the truth would never be known, eh? The pope scheming with a Mussulman to destroy a Christian king. They should make you a saint, Father Matthieu.'

'Blaspheme some more, servant of Antichrist. Then I can be sure your torments will be the worse, when you find yourself in hell with your heretic friends. I walk in the sure knowledge of His mercy, and His justice.'

'I've seen a lot of God's mercy lately,' I muttered. 'But then I suppose I would have to be a priest to understand, eh? Too bad you didn't come earlier. You could have explained why God chose to turn His crusaders into eel-bait. Or why William Longspée's children have no father.'

'You mock what you do not understand.'

'I understand that this letter I carry will see your master the pope knocked off his throne and fighting the dogs for scraps in a Lyon gutter. If I live beyond tomorrow's sunrise, it is because I have pledged to destroy every one of you pious murderers.'

'Still very proud, my son. But your wife—'

'If you speak one more word about my wife, I will kill you.'

'The hounds are out!' He cackled, an obscene noise. 'The hounds are out!'

'What, priest? What are you talking about?' And then, in the midst of all my pain, another, worse pang struck me. 'Is she dead?'

'The heretic asks me! All your scheming, all your pride . . . Oh, you are right: God is just!' He broke off with a cry. One of the guards had lashed him on the back of his legs, and after that he could not speak, though I could hear his mouth working, trying to cough up more words.

We walked for what seemed like a week, under the savage eye of the sun, in heat that seemed to lick at us like a vast and hungry beast. Flies swarmed in my wounds. Iselda appeared in my mind, and I tried to think about what Matthieu had said, but my head could not hold anything except the will to keep my feet moving. I asked for water but whenever I opened my mouth I got a kick in the shins, and so I gave up. Matthieu walked behind me, for which I was grateful. I did not want to look at him, although it seemed I had saved his life.

But it was probably not yet noon when we reeled past the

first sagging huts of a little hamlet that squatted among the tall reeds surrounding a narrow creek that flowed sluggishly into the river a few paces away. It seemed deserted, but as soon as we reached the open space in the middle of the huts we were surrounded by a company of Saracen foot soldiers, all fresh and unbloodied. Plainly they had not been in the battle, but they made up for that. First they jeered at us as they closed in. Then one lad punched me on the shoulder, knocking me back into Matthieu. At that, they all began to rain blows on us. I tried to defend myself, clasping my arms about my head, but a kick in the ballocks put me on my knees, and then I was lost. A boot found my chin; fists were pounding on the back of my head and neck. It did not hurt any more. I felt myself buffeted, as if by a strong wind. I tasted blood, and felt a little spark of joy as some blessed wetness dribbled down my desiccated throat. Then I seemed to be floating, except that by the way the ground was moving I saw I was being dragged. A door creaked, there was a rush of air and my face was full of straw. Then darkness. Numb and beyond caring, I wriggled myself into the damp, prickly bed and fell like a lead weight into a deep, damaged sleep.

Chapter Twenty

Something was scrabbling at my chest. A rat? A fat Nile rat. I flailed at it and opened my eyes, only to find I was blind. No, not blind . . . I had expected the musty half-dark of the stable, but instead I was wrapped in white light. My thoughts swam backwards, upstream. The courtyard, the executioner, Matthieu . . . Ah. Of course: I was dead. And it was not so bad, apart from the rat. There was no pain to speak of. Something formed out of the glare, faded, established itself again. An angel – no, these must be the beings of pure light that Gilles and the Cathars believed in. So Gilles had been right after all. Was he here? I opened my mouth to call him, but nothing came out but a wasted hiss. There was the rat again. It had got underneath my tunic. I batted it again but it did not stop. I blinked, and blue, purple, green blots swirled, pulsed, and became the face of my executioner. The rat was his hand, and it was holding Iselda's golden stag.

'Rob me after I'm dead, you bastard,' I croaked in English.

The man's face came very close, very suddenly, and I flinched. He looked puzzled, even concerned.

'Are you alive, Frankish man?' he asked me, in Arabic. And to my amazement he tucked Iselda's pendant back inside my clothes.

'I think so,' I answered in his own language.

'Good.' He clapped his hands and suddenly I was being lifted. Four of the soldiers who had just been baying for my blood were hoisting me onto their shoulders. My head lolled and I saw Matthieu's body and the wide fan of his blood, already turning black. Then I was back in the realm of the beings of light, and then nothing.

When I woke up I was lying in a bed, in a whitewashed room into which a soft light was creeping through fretwork shutters. There was a strange smell in my nostrils. It troubled me, and I lay there sniffing until I understood. It was not a smell so much as the lack of one. I was clean. I was lying in clean linen. And then I saw the hands. They lay, brown, scratched, every nail black and broken, wizened as old sticks or dead blackbirds against the flawless sheets. I thought for a moment that they were some hideous talisman put there to ward off sickness, for I had seen their like before: the hand of Saint Euphemia, and a hundred others I had sold to churches and cathedrals, not holy, of course not, for they had all been hacked from ancient corpses in the deserts of Egypt, and, as I now remembered, was I not in Egypt? My scalp started to itch and I made to scratch it, and as I did so the hideous relics began to twitch and flutter and to my horror I saw they were attached to my arms.

I held them up. Old man's hands, not mine. But there were my rings. Dear God. I gingerly held them against my face. They were rough against my skin, but at the same time my fingers were not recognising the features they were exploring. Whose were these sunken cheeks, these sharp bones, the beaky nose? I sat up and looked around. On a carved and painted stand sat a wide copper dish of water and a dish of polished silver holding a little pile of figs. Swinging my stiff legs off the bed, I stood up and almost fell. My knees could barely support me and I swayed, coughing. I discovered that I was wearing a long white robe, very plain, with a slit down to my breastbone through which I could see the glint of gold. Iselda's stag was still round my neck, clicking against the old cross from Byzantium, and the silver amulet, still wrapped in its seal of rawhide. The discovery lent me a little strength, and I was able to totter over to the stand. I grasped the edges with both hands, washed my face, then picked up the dish, scattering the figs, held it up and peered into its mirror.

A stricken face looked back at me. My hair was short, though it had grown out a little since I had hacked it off before the retreat. But it was streaked with grey, and hanks of it had fallen out, revealing scabbed patches of scalp. The face beneath it was little more than sunburned skin stretched tight over the skull beneath, save for my nose, which jutted disturbingly from between my sunken eyes. A fading bruise stretched from my right eye across the temple to my ear, and there was a gash on my chin, a fat black scab surrounded by shiny, dark red skin. There was another deep cut across my brow below the hairline, and my lower lip was cracked and scabbed. Pewter stubble blotched with white encrusted my jaw. I opened my mouth in shock, and saw dark gums mottled with black. I had lost two teeth almost at the front of my lower jaw, and my tongue found another hole further back. Had I lost these before, in the camp? I could not remember.

But it was my eyes that had made me gasp. They had sunk far back into their sockets, which were themselves haloes of crinkled shadow. The whites were no longer white, but a dirty, clotted ivory. The pupils were so wide that they had all but erased the green that surrounded them, and I stared into two voids – into myself. And inside me there was nothing. I had been hollowed out. The mirror rippled again, and again. Tears were dripping down my nose and blurring my vision. I stuck my bony knuckles into the sockets of my skull and felt the wetness pooling between them. Then I was sobbing, huge, gulping sobs torn out from deep inside my ribcage.

I staggered back to bed and threw myself onto the sheets. The little golden stag was in my fist, and I gripped it as if it were the only thing keeping me alive. Hinges creaked, and there was a rustle of clothing. Cool hands stroked my brow and straightened my limbs, drawing the linen over me. I could not bear to see another face staring into the ruins of mine, so I turned over and burrowed into the pillows, biting back the sobs, willing my visitor to leave me be. But long fingers slid under my cheek and turned my face upwards. I kept my eyes screwed shut as something cold touched my lips and a thick, bitter liquid trickled through them.

'Swallow,' said a woman's voice softly. I did as I was told, and almost at once a slow warmth began to spread beneath my breastbone, numbing, soothing. The hand stroked my hair. I took a deep breath and the pain inside faded. And I slept.

When I woke again it was morning. One shutter was open, and the fierce light of Egypt was lancing through it. I sat up, realising that I felt better. My hands no longer scared me. I got up, pissed in a pot that stood in the corner, and steeled myself to peer into the dish again.

It was bad, yes. I had suffered. But now at least I recognised myself. Perhaps sleep, or the drug I had been given had relaxed my skin, for I no longer looked like a desiccated corpse. Every morsel of fat, every layer of the easy life I had lived since Montségur, had been burned away. I was starved, but I had gone hungry before. For that matter, I had lived through a siege before, though Montségur had not reduced me to quite this state. To my relief, the pupils of my eyes had shrunk back to something like their usual size, and the shadows around them had been lifted, a little. I bared my teeth and inspected my horrible gums. I had lost three teeth, and two more were loose, though they would settle in again soon enough with good food. Cupping my hand, I sniffed my breath warily. The spoiled-meat reek of scorbutus was almost gone. I had been shaved, I found – some steady hand had guided the razor around all the ruts and divots while I slept.

And someone had fed me, I guessed. My stomach growled lazily, but that was all – none of the griping, tearing panic of desperate hunger. This was good, very good. I stretched, carefully. A saltarello of pain skipped and danced up and down my limbs and through my body, but I was healing. Through the open shutter came the sound of voices. Shielding my eyes against the sun, I peered out.

I was high up, looking out through an arched, unbarred window over a courtyard surrounded on all sides by walls that rose up to delicate crenellations. In the middle of the yard was a fountain, and around its edges ran a colonnade of scalloped arches. Orange trees were growing out of brightly glazed urns, and palms cast their frondy shade on the tangled patterns of the tiled walkways. A swarm of small brown birds were busy in the branches. Figures were moving to and fro in the shadows beyond the colonnade. As they passed in and out of brief strips of sunlight I glimpsed high turbans and long robes caught at the waist with sashes of vivid colour. I looked up, past rows of windows all screened with intricately fretted stone or wood, to where the crenulations seemed to bite into the blue sky. But this did not seem like a fortress – or a prison, for that matter. And as if to prove me right, the door handle turned and the door opened. It had not been locked. I turned, guiltily, to find a slender man with very light brown eyes and a carefully trimmed beard standing in the doorway. He had his arms folded across his chest and one eyebrow was raised reproachfully.

'You should be in bed, my dear patient,' he said sternly, in perfect French.

'I am sorry. I . . . I have the feeling I have been in bed for rather a long time, and so . . .'

'You got up. And how has that turned out for you?'

'Well, I am still alive, though perhaps I've been asleep for longer than I thought. I looked into the dish over there and saw an old man looking back at me.'

The man laughed and stepped lightly across the tiled floor. He was not very old, and his face was smooth and quite unlined. He was wearing a very fine silk robe of pale green the colour of new beech leaves in springtime, and a sash of black silk shot with silver and gold was tied round his waist. His turban was white, tied in the fashion of Damascus.

'May I?' he asked with a slight bow, and without waiting for a reply he took my left hand, pinched my wrist very gently between thumb and two fingers, and cocked his head as though listening for something. The birds twittered below us in the courtyard. Finally he released me.

'Very good,' he said, approvingly. 'You are strong. And fortunate.'

'Sir, you must forgive me, but I do not know who you are.'

'I am your physician!' he said, as if that were obvious, as if I should have known from the wrist-pinching business.

'Then I thank you.' I bowed. 'I'm sure you have saved my life. My name – as you must know – is Petrus Zennorius of Venice.'

'Ah! I did know. I am delighted to meet you, Messer Petrus. And my name is Ala al-Din Abu al-Hassan Ali ibn Abi-Hazm al-Qarshi al-Dimashqi.' He grinned. 'That is rather a – what is the expression? – a *mouthful* for a Frank, so you may call me Ibn al-Nafis.'

'Nafis? My dear sir, I have heard of you!' I said, amazed.

'In Venice?' he said, sceptically. He had me by the arm again, this time guiding me back to the bed. I sat, dutifully, and he perched on the edge beside me, hands in his lap. Everything about this man was gentle but very controlled.

'A colleague, a very dear friend of mine – peace be on his soul – was a physician from al-Andalus. He wrote to you, several years ago. Something to do with blood and the brain. His name was Isaac of Toledo.'

Ibn al-Nafis made a face. Then he brightened. 'Apoplexy!' he said. 'I do remember. The matter was blood clotting within the brain. A colleague had died, and this worthy Isaac, who if I remember had studied at al-Qarawiyyin, like the great Musa ibn Maymun, peace be upon his memory . . . and this Isaac had . . .'

'Yes, he investigated,' I said. Istvan, the *Cormaran*'s sergeant-at-arms, had been carried off by a stroke while I had been besieged in Montségur, and Isaac had been so distressed – as Istvan had seemed to be in good health – that he had blamed himself and set out to find what had killed his old comrade. I was glad I had not been around for that, though I had seen worse things, and Istvan would not have cared, not being what most people generally called a Christian.

'He found something that contradicted Galen, and wrote to me about that,' the doctor went on. 'I was happy to confirm his discovery. He seemed a most meticulous person. But he is dead?'

I nodded. 'Before his time,' I murmured.

'Only God knows the time of our death,' said the doctor, gravely. 'But you are not a physician, Messer Petrus? You called him colleague.'

It was my turn to laugh. 'No, indeed I am not a physician! I am a banker, and I can barely manage that – and lately a soldier, of course.'

'Of course.' Ibn al-Nafis stood. 'Now, if you would lie down, I will examine you.' He clicked his fingers and a man who must have been standing out in the hallway came softly in carrying an ebony box inlaid with eye-befuddling mother of pearl traceries. He bowed silently and left. The doctor opened the box, revealing nestled rows of bottles and tiny drawers, from which he extracted a long silver rod with a pointed end. 'If you would just open your mouth,' he said, 'this won't hurt.'

It did hurt, of course, but not as much as the scorbutus, and after he was done he probed and palpated every inch of my body with his firm but gentle fingers, lingering particularly on my neck and belly. I understood a little of what he was about: Isaac had done similar things to the *Cormaran*'s crew when we had been ill or hurt, and I had always regarded him as being as different from those men who called themselves doctors or surgeons as a goldsmith is to a tanner. Because this man reminded me of Isaac I found myself trusting him, even when he found some slumbering cache of pain and awakened it, briefly, before moving on. He painted my nastier scabs with some dark, sharp-smelling unguent, dabbed something else on my scalp that stung wickedly, and gave me a vial full of an amber-coloured syrup to drink. It was bitter, like dandelion juice mixed with liquorice, and the taste haunted my mouth, but I swallowed it politely.

When he was done, he washed his hands carefully in the basin. 'You are recovering quickly,' he said. 'The scorbutus is fading, and the bowels have regained their function. There was some infection when you were brought to me, but it has been driven out. Having said that, you were fortunate, Messer Petrus. A man can only live so long without food and water, and the scorbutus would have killed you in another day or two.'

'What do you say about my teeth?' I asked.

'You'll keep the ones you have left. The gums are strong again.'

'That is a relief. However, sir, you must forgive my vanity, but though I am in my thirty-third year, I look like a man of eighty.'

'Do not worry. You will see the years fall away,' he said. 'Eat. Drink – especially drink. Sleep. You are in good hands.'

'It is very generous of . . . I mean, I'm waiting to be ransomed, and I doubt I am your most important prisoner.'

'My dear Messer Petrus.' Ibn al-Nafis came and sat beside me again, and patted my hand where it lay on the sheet. 'You have been ransomed already. You are not a prisoner, you are a guest. Now I recommend a little more sleep, and then luncheon.'

I began to ask for more of an explanation, but he merely smiled owlishly and padded out of the room, shutting the door carefully behind him. No key turned in the lock. I lay back and studied the coffered ceiling. Not a prisoner? How long had I been here? And who had paid my ransom? Disturbing thoughts, but the pure scent of clean linen, the lazy chatter of the birds from the courtyard and the good doctor's draught kept them from digging their claws too deeply into my mind. I let my breathing deepen. A moment later, it seemed, I opened my eyes again and there was Ibn al-Nafis's assistant with a tray of food and a slim copper jug. He pulled a small eight-sided table over, set down the tray, bowed silently and left me.

The food was excellent, though there was no wine – but why would there be wine, in a Mussulman palace? I had decided that this must be a palace, for it was not a castle and it seemed too big for a merchant's house, or even that of a nobleman. Even though I could see nothing by way of a flag or a standard, I knew I had to be in the governor's palace in Mansourah. So the walls from which I had been shot at were now sheltering me. I wondered how many other captured Franks were here. Had the prisoners all been ransomed, then? How exactly had that happened? I guessed that King Louis must be a prisoner, along with many others, but although I spent that afternoon sitting by the window, leaning on the warm stone and staring down into the courtyard, I saw no Franks, only Saracens.

Leaning out for a better view, the golden stag came free of my robe and swung, glinting, below me. As it turned slowly I remembered the hands that had found it and put it back. The man had been about to kill me, and something had stopped him. But I could bring back nothing else of that day: from the moment that Father Matthieu had been killed, everything was a vague, grey darkness. I stretched painfully and went to lie down. Soon I was asleep. Whatever the good doctor was giving me to drink, it brought deep sleep and no dreams, and that alone was a miracle.

Time went by. The brown birds sang and played about in the trees. The sun rose and set, and at every sunrise I found the fact that I was still alive a little less confusing. Then came the day that Ibn al-Nafis brought me a letter along with my morning physic. He placed it on the window sill and left the room without inspecting me with his usual thoroughness. When his footsteps had faded in the hallway I snatched it up. I recognised the seal at once, and there, in careful, clear letters, my name. It was from Iselda, and the date upon it was no more than three days old. She was alive.

Chapter Twenty-One

M y dearest,
    What joy! To hear that you lived, when all of the king's great army has come to such a sorry defeat! If I were to climb to the top of Damietta's minaret and jump off, I believe I would float down like a feather, my heart has become so light.

Yes, I am in Damietta. I got here the week after Shrove Tuesday, about the time that the Mussulmen blockaded the river. I sent letters to you, but they came back. So you never heard the end of my tale. It is a good one, and as I hear you need to rest, let this entertain you as you get strong enough to come back to me.

I thought to find you in Damietta. But the first thing I learned was that the army had left not very long after Father Matthieu had visited me, and that you were somewhere upstream. Everybody — the Franks, that is — seemed sure that Louis must have taken Cairo by then, and that it was just a matter of time before word reached us. But as you know too, too well, very soon after that the river was blockaded and the few messengers who won through told us that the king was about to surrender.

You will want to know many things, my love, but as you are safe and I do not have to worry about you — for once — let me sit here for a while and amuse myself by putting down some things that happened in Damietta. In Palermo I bought a strong French cog, for I did not like the idea of a fragile little galley loaded with gold bobbing around off the mouths of the Nile, and this ship looked the same as any other in the king's fleet. Dimitri hired the most villainous and yet trustworthy men he could find to guard it.

You had written to me of Ya'qub bin Yazdad, and when I first went ashore I sought him out. You are right: he is a fine old man, and . . . well, I shall not tell you which of his trinkets he chose to show me. He took me to the house where you lodged and made sure I was settled there.

Now, everyone left behind in Damietta is bored to the point of death, and so news of my arrival spread all over the town, and the next day I was summoned to the palace to meet Queen Marguerite. Vile man, you have never spoken of her in your letters. She is clever, witty and strong. When I first saw her she was huge with the child the king had left her to bear alone, and even so she was running the affairs of Damietta as though it were a little kingdom and she a female Charlemagne. As you must have noticed, she is also the only Frankish woman of rank in the city, and indeed, apart from her handmaidens and the small mob of camp followers outside the walls, almost the only Frankish woman of any kind. That was why my arrival had caused such a hubbub.

She received me in her inner chambers, and I was surprised to find her served by two young ladies and three very ancient knights, who plainly being too old to march off into the swamps of Egypt, had become male handmaidens. She put me to the question, very charmingly, and I expected her to be disappointed to find I was of ordinary birth. If she was, she was too nice, or too starved for the company of her own sex, to show it. And then she discovered that I was born in Toulouse. Ah, then our friendship was sealed – for so it is, even though I am sensible enough that such a friendship could not exist outside this odd and troubled circumstance – and we fell to discussing the southern lands with, dare I say it, quite some hunger. I told her that I had sung at her father's court, and then she made me sing her all the songs she loves, which are many, for she is no northern dullard with beery mud in her veins. Really, for shame,

Petroc! It is no secret that the king neglects his wife, but for him to leave that noble creature and go off fighting – and to get himself captured into the bargain! Forsooth, men are fools, and if you were here, I would tell you so to your face. For make no mistake, it was Queen Marguerite who prevented ultimate disaster falling upon the wretched army. She has kept the garrison fed as well as the townsfolk, and delivered a living son into the bargain.

Meanwhile, you are free, my love. A Saracen paid your ransom. And now I will tell you how that came to pass. You must remember how, when you won the battle on the seashore that brought you the surrender of Damietta, the Mussulmen inhabitants of the city fled along with the garrison? Well, not quite all. Ya'qub told me of at least three merchants who had remained behind to watch over their possessions. One of these, a man by the name of Abu Musa Zayd al-Ghallabi, had remained in his own home close to the bazaar. He is a member of some odd sect of the Mussulman faith that teaches the notion that the gods of all faiths are one god – I would need to sit under a palm tree for ten years listening to Abu Musa Zayd explain it before I really understood, so I won't waste ink here. Anyway, his belief means that he is friends with Christian and Jew alike, and indeed the faiths get on without very much difficulty in any case, so he was able to live unmolested when you crusaders arrived. He has a wife, two daughters and a young son, and they did not leave the house and hid themselves away in the inner rooms.

Ya'qub learned over time that I was not bound up with the strictures of any particular faith, and when I told him I was sorry I could not meet any Mussulmen, he persuaded Abu Musa Zayd to visit his house while I was there. I found him a charming, cultivated and warm-hearted man, very learned on many subjects. He is a trader and had even conducted some business with our company through a third party, his speciality being cinnamon and pepper from that very Kodungallur we talked about that day before you left for Lyon – do you remember? That long pepper in our storeroom might have come from Abu Musa Zayd. We became friends, and he was good enough to invite me to his home, where I was honoured to meet his family.

It is the custom for hosts to entertain their guests with song, and when Abu Musa Zayd's wife and his eldest daughter had sung for me, I thought it polite to return the favour, and so I gave them that song you taught me, dear one – the song you learned from the helmsman of the Cormaran. It is a little grim, about fire. Now, strange to relate, he knew the very song! Indeed he pressed me to tell him how it came to be in my possession, and I told him from you, and that you had heard it from one Nizam, who sailed with my father. He must have been from Cairo! said Abu Musa Zayd, and I said I did not know. We said no more about it, and indeed I gave it no more thought until a few days after your attack on Mansourah. We were not besieged, but we were cut off from the world outside and bad weather had kept us from being supplied by sea. There was no hunger, but sickness had taken hold; and for a time we feared for Queen Marguerite's little son, whose midwife was an ancient knight! Jean Tristram, she called him, after her sadness at being abandoned by the king. Now, as soon as her child was born and she had taken a few days' rest, the queen rose like a veritable Amazon and began to rule once more. But the soldiery was restless and dispirited by the news that trickled down the river, and trouble sometimes broke out in the town. There was not enough coin to buy food for either the soldiery or the townspeople – or rather, there was, but the queen, being in possession of a quick mind, foresaw that in the event of a defeat, the money in the royal treasure ship would be needed for ransom and defence. So I proposed a loan to her, for which she was exceedingly grateful, for it enabled her to maintain her rule, and won her the love of all, Franks and Egyptians alike.

Even so, soldiers began to terrorise the merchants in the bazaar, and there were some fights and murders. Then one day Ya'qub came looking for me. Someone had told a Frankish crossbowman *that there was a Mussulman living among them, and had named Abu Musa Zayd. A mob of soldiers, sodden with wine, had gone to his house and laid siege to it, imagining a trove of riches inside, and wanting to be revenged upon the person of a Saracen. We hurried there, and found the mob trying to batter down the door and piling dry faggots and timber around the walls, ready to set fire to the house.*

I went that instant to the queen, and told her what was happening. At first she was not greatly concerned. But I shamelessly told her that Abu Musa Zayd was a friend to Christians and an important trading partner of the Banco di Corvo Marino, and that if harm befell him it could endanger my ability to loan more money to Her Majesty.

As you have taught me, few can resist an appeal to both heart and purse; and indeed Queen Marguerite straight away ordered the royal guards to go to the merchant's house and drive away the mob. I went with them, to the queen's dismay, and after the brutes had been driven off, one with a cracked head, and the flames put out, I went inside and found my friend with his family in the little courtyard at the centre of the house, preparing for death. I told them to flee Damietta as soon as they could, and sent word to Dimitri aboard our ship, asking him to send a boat up the river with some good fighting men, who should come to the merchant's house and take him and his family out of the city. It was done, and by the day's end I was standing on the shore with Abu Musa Zayd and his family, ready to see them taken to where they could find safe passage to Cairo. After his wife and children had gone aboard, the good merchant kissed my hand. First he warned me, saying that he had heard very recently from spies beyond the walls that the Frankish army was doomed and soon that doom would fall also on Damietta. Then he implored me to tell him anything he could do to repay the debt he owed me for his family's life.

I asked him that my dearest wish was that you, my husband, should be safe. I described you, and told him that you might also be known by the little stag of gold you wore, that was unlike any other in the world. And then, which surprised me very greatly, and which is the part of this tale I have been keeping from you out of loving spite, he told me that the song I had sung had brought him many hours of wondering, for it had been written by a great man. Well, I said, a great man's songs have longer life, and travel further, than those of humble creatures like myself. But no, he said, and then he told me that the sect to which he belonged – he calls himself Sufi – has as its leader one Sheikh abd' al-Azeem al-Ansari, and the song you taught me was one of many written by him. This Sufi sheikh had many disciples among the Mamluks. If, God willing, he reached Cairo in safety, he would tell his fellow Sufis to seek you out and bring you to safety.

And so it came to pass! But first came the terrible day when the few boats full of wounded, dying and dead men drifted down the Nile, bringing word of the king's surrender. It was a horrid blow for Queen Marguerite, but she did not falter, and began to rally the city's defences. She went every day to see to the sick and wounded and I went with her, trying to find any news of you. One poor fellow, almost black with the scorbutus and with gangrene in his arm – his name was Guibert de Sougé – had seen you on the shore as he sailed away, waiting with the king's escort. He died next day. Most of those with any kind of wound or sickness died soon after they got here. And then we heard from the Saracen envoys who rode up to the walls that the king was taken, and all his knights with him, those that had not been sent to the hell reserved for infidels, and that was most of them. Then there were days of torment for me, my love, and I went aboard our ship and made ready to cast off if I heard that you had perished. But instead, one morning just at sunrise, a small fishing vessel came alongside as if to sell its catch, but instead a Saracen man asked for me by name. He brought word from Abu Musa Zayd, who had come safely to Cairo, and had discovered that you were alive. You had fallen into the hands of a band of Mamluks who followed Sheikh abd' al-Azeem, and the good merchant had caused you to be brought to the house of his cousin, who, it seems, is the governor of Mansourah. And so I am writing to you, dearest man, foolish man – lucky man! – to assure you that you are free, that your ransom was paid by the worthy Abu Musa Zayd, and that we will, very soon, be together again. The doctor whose care you are under says you are mending, and that as soon as you have the strength, you may ride to Damietta.

I will write again. Meanwhile, the sun hides behind dark and heavy clouds until you return to me.

Chapter Twenty-Two

Days passed. The thing in the mirror, the exhumed corpse that had once been Petroc of Auneford, began to resemble him again, and one morning I awoke, stretched without being racked with horrible pain, and found I was looking at myself in the silver. Scarred, of course, and my teeth would not grow back, but Ibn al-Nafis had been right: the years had fallen away. When the doctor came to make his morning inspection, I asked him if I could leave my room and take a walk. He cocked an eyebrow and told me to be patient. But not much patience was required, for an hour later he returned with his silent assistant, who carried an elegant package of clothing.

'We burned your own clothes,' said the doctor. 'I trust you will not mind looking like a Mussulman.'

'No indeed,' I said. The clothes fitted perfectly, and the long robe of silk was cool and light. When I was dressed, the doctor took me over to the window.

'You are free to walk about the courtyard,' he said, 'and below us you will find pavilions and fountains. Do not go near the women's quarters, over there. And do not go outside the palace, for a Frank would not live long beyond these gates. There. I *almost* discharge you from my care. You have healed well, my friend. But you know, there are many old scars on your body. This is worthless advice to give to a man of war, but one day soon you will not heal so readily. You are not young – not old, but believe me: you have spent much of your power recovering from these injuries. Many warriors test their bodies until they give out. If I might presume to take you for a man of some sense, I would tell you to seek a life of peace. It will reward the flesh, and also the soul.'

'If God wills it,' I said in his own language. He smiled sadly.

'But God also gave us free will,' he said. I waited for him to explain, but he did not. Instead he patted me on the shoulder. 'Do not over-exert yourself,' he said brusquely. 'An hour, no more. Longer tomorrow. I shall see you after the evening meal.'

I waited for a few minutes after they had left, and then opened the door. Beyond was a cool hallway tiled in complex patterns of stars and lines that led my eye towards the stairway. There was nobody about, though I could hear voices quite far off. The stairway was gentle but even so my legs felt like over-boiled carrots as I gingerly made my way down to the colonnade below. The fountain, which I had stared at from above, hours at a time, was chuckling to itself in the courtyard, and so, rather nervously, I padded across the tiles, under the palms and citrus trees, and dipped my hand in the water. It was cold, though the sun – the same sun that had killed crusaders by the hour just days before – was pouring its searing light almost straight down upon it. I splashed a little water onto my forehead, as I had seen men do, and sat down with my back against the low, marble side of the pool.

Little brown birds were leading busy lives in the complicated shade of the trees. From the women's quarters came the sound of laughter – not very ladylike, as if someone had just told a dirty joke. A man in a long white robe came through a door at one side of the colonnade, walked round two sides of the courtyard and went into another doorway. He did not look in my direction. It was very peaceful here, and soon I felt my eyes growing heavy. I drew one leg up and rested my chin upon my knee. The pattering water and the rustling birds were soothing, and I let myself be soothed.

People came and went under the colonnades, always men, and they never so much as glanced in my direction. I wondered what they thought of me. It was only a few weeks ago that I had been fighting for my life under the walls of this very palace. Hundreds of crusaders had died out there. For all I knew, the Saracen knight I had knocked off his horse that day was one of the silent figures gliding by in the shade. The water ran on behind me, and the little birds, growing bolder, began to swoop down and search the ground for morsels. I had the feeling I was being watched, as one does when surrounded by many shuttered or empty windows, and from the women's quarters came the faint sound of a mild argument, and then a wistful song. No doubt people were watching me. But I was too drowsy to feel much like a trespasser.

At last, the heat and the endless chiming of the water began to make me thirsty, and then the thirst overcame my lethargy and I tottered off, stiffly, to find something to drink. The brown birds took off as one creature and began to rattle the fronds of the palm leaves overhead. In the colonnade the air was cool, almost sharp. I leaned against the wall, for I found my head was spinning a little. A man, tall and bearded, walked past and I smiled and murmured a *salaamun*. He gave me a curious look but touched his forehead and returned my greeting.

I stayed there, letting the chill from the stone drive the sun from my body, until I saw a servant emerge from an archway across the courtyard. He was carrying a large pitcher with a white cloth across its mouth – water, or something drinkable. I ambled slowly to the archway and looked inside. There was a long hallway with daylight at the far end, and the unmistakeable smells and sounds of a busy kitchen.

Again I had the sensation of someone watching me. I imagined the hidden women, tittering behind their hands: 'Look, the ridiculous Frank is going to the *servants'* quarters!' A man crossed the hallway carrying a basket of vegetables. My mouth was getting unpleasantly dry, so I gave the watchers a shrug of my shoulders and went on my way. There were a number of doors on either side, storerooms and rooms where water was being boiled in great cauldrons. The kitchen must be on the other side of the small courtyard I was approaching, and which I found was a little garden planted with leafy herbs.

'What are you seeking?'

The voice came from across the herb beds. A man was standing in a doorway, smiling reassuringly. He had spoken in strangely accented Norman French, which surprised me, but I smiled back and bowed.

'*Salaamun 'Aleykum.* I am thirsty – some water? And I am sorry for intruding.'

'No matter. Here. You will come.' He beckoned and I stepped carefully through the little mazy path that led between the beds. Footsteps sounded behind me, more than one person, but I paid them no mind: more servants. The man held out his hand in greeting and I took it. He grinned: his teeth were brownish. He had deep pox-scars on his face and a freshly healed slash across the bottom of his jaw. *Looks like a soldier*, I was thinking, when his grip on my hand tightened and he pulled me towards him, taking me off balance. Then his knee came up hard between my legs. As I doubled over I heard feet trampling the garden behind me and a hand was clamped across my mouth as another arm wrapped itself around my neck. As I flailed, trying to bite, the man let go of my hand and punched me in the stomach. Someone took my ankles and pulled them out from under me as the pockmarked man caught me under the left arm. Suddenly I was being carried, fast, face-down and still gagged by someone's hand, down a narrow passage. Three men . . . They were hissing to each other urgently. The tongue was familiar but I could not understand the words. Suddenly I was dropped on my face, a knee landed with all the weight of its owner between my shoulders, and the hand left my mouth only to be replaced, in an instant, with a twist of cloth that was being knotted viciously behind my head so that I was bridled like a horse. The hand groped inside my tunic and with a horrible wrench the amulet and Iselda's stag were torn from my neck. *Of course . . .* I said to myself, groggily. Then I was gathered up again.

I was still very weak and there was no struggle in me. I was lugged like a sack up a couple of steps and through a dark, dusty space that smelled of ginger and old onions. Rusty iron scraped and screeched and we were out in the daylight. Below me, trampled earth and old rubbish. The light seemed to be coming from high above and I guessed we were in an alleyway outside the servants' quarters. Then I was dropped again, but they kept hold of my arms so that they twisted painfully behind me. A hand grabbed my hair and I was yanked onto my knees. The gag, full of my spit, was starting to swell and choke me. The man with the pockmarks bent down to look at me. He ran his eyes quickly, expertly, over my face, then nodded to his accomplices. There had been a certain interest in his eyes but no humanity. And then he glanced about quickly and drew a long knife from inside his clothes. It had a tapered, slightly curved blade and had been lovingly polished. One of the men wrenching my arms from their sockets hissed something. There was no mistaking the meaning: *get on with it.*

You get your head cut off after all, I said to myself bitterly. And then, *Thank you, Lord or life or luck, for the birds and the fountain, and for Iselda's letter . . .*

My mouth was full of dirt and ancient vegetable peelings. Somehow I was on my face again, still alive. There was sound and struggle overhead. A heel caught against my hip and a body pitched backwards across my legs. A bare foot appeared in front of me, toenails filthy and cracked. It twitched and went still. My arms were free: very carefully I got my hands underneath me and pushed myself up. Lying across the foot was an arm, and from the hand trailed four broken leather cords. I grabbed them and wrenched at the amulet and golden stag, ending up face-down again as they came free. Then I was pulled to my feet. I staggered and fell against someone. The gag was loosened, then gone.

'Are you Petros?' a man demanded. 'Petroc?'

'Petroc, yes,' I said. There was dust in my eyes and the world was wavering like the northern lights, but then a white figure came into focus. It was a man, but not the pockmarked one.

'Good. Come with us.'

I walked, supported on both sides, a few steps. As my eyes cleared I saw that I was indeed in an alley, dirty and piled, here and there, with burned stubs of wooden beams. I was being led towards a wider street, and on the corner stood four horses.

'Wait. Who are you?' I asked in Saracen, hastily knotting the cords of stag and amulet together and slipping them over my head.

'Mamluk.' The man in front spun round. He was dressed in white robes, with a white scarf wrapped round his head and draped under his chin and across his shoulders. He was young and his beard was still soft and just beginning to curl. But there was nothing soft about his manner. A *shamshir* hung from his belt and he wore soldier's boots. 'You are coming to see our master.'

'The queen?'

The man laughed, and the other two, who were dressed in the same manner, laughed as well. It was a careful laugh. I saw blood on one man's robe and I glanced behind me, to where three sprawled bodies lay in the shadow of a handcart.

'Thank you,' I said. I hoped they could tell I had rarely meant anything so sincerely.

'Why those convert pigs were going to kill you, O Frank, we do not know. Our master *does* know, so thank him.'

'I thought they were . . .'

'Moslems?' He spat. 'No, and not Egyptians either. Convert scum from Sicily – paid murderers. Fucking cowards.'

'Let us go, Aytmish!' called one of the men. He nodded. 'No more questions from you, O Frank. Now, can you ride?'

I thought I could, and when they hoisted me onto the back of a sorrel mare I found my limbs just about under my control. We took off at a trot, the young man called Aytmish – who seemed to be the leader – in front, me behind and the other two riding side by side in the rear. The street was full of people and they parted respectfully at the sight of the Mamluks. To me they threw curious, cautious glances: a battered man in dirty Saracen robes. Who knew what they thought? I hung on grimly to the reins and kept my eyes on the man in front. We were riding down the main thoroughfare of the city, but to my amazement there was little sign of the horrible battle that had happened there. The great beams of wood that had trapped the crusaders were all gone. A building was being rebuilt; I guessed one of those that had been burning as I escaped. I wondered where Robert of Artois had died, and William Longspée . . . But now we were turning right, and there were the city walls pierced by a gate, beyond which I could glimpse the dark green of the countryside. The guards saluted as we rode past, out into the chequerboard fields. The leader kicked his horse into a canter and we followed.

We were on a good, hard-packed road that ran beside a narrow canal. All around us men and women were working in the fields, pumping water and cutting reeds. Mattocks rose and fell and dust hung over everything in a haze of pale gold. The road stretched ahead over a wide, flat plain to a small, thick wood of palms, and quite soon we were riding under the outlying trees. The road divided, a narrow, unkempt path curving off to the north while the main track led straight on. We took the narrow way, and plunged immediately into green, cool silence. As I began to wonder why a company of Mamluks should have business in such a place, we came to a clearing.

It was a large, almost round space amongst the trees, through which a small stream, one of the irrigation channels that run everywhere through the delta country, flowed from a square pool with stepped sides of packed, whitewashed mud. Next to the pool stood a little building, a cube of brick topped by a low dome and pierced by small arched windows and one pointed doorway. In front of the door was an area of laid bricks, and four ancient olive trees spread their shade over it. Like the sides of the pool the little building was painted white. All around the clearing stood low tents of white cloth, some flying brightly coloured pennants, and people were sitting here and there in patches of shade. The young Mamluk reined in his horse and jumped down. He led the beast to the pool and a little boy ran out from one of the tents and, taking the reins, let it drink. I slid down gingerly and led my own horse over to the water.

'What is this place?' I asked the young man.

'The *zāwiya* of Sheikh abd' al-Azeem al-Ansari,' he said. 'The water is sweet. Drink.'

The pool was clear and still – a spring. I dipped my cupped hand and sprinkled some over my head and face, then dipped again and drank.

'It is not only the thirsty man who seeks water. The water also seeks the thirsty.' The voice was deep, and with a shock I understood that the words had been spoken in Occitan. I turned, dazed.

'Those are the words of another,' said Nizam, the helmsman. 'But in my own words I bid you welcome, brother. I was beginning to fear you had lost your way.'

Chapter Twenty-Three

Inside, the little building seemed larger than it looked. It was very plain, with white walls and a floor of fired earthen tiles. The only decoration was a thin pattern of twisting lines in gold and vivid green glaze that ran around the room just below the ceiling. Wrought-iron lanterns hung on chains, there were simple iron candle-stands, and on the floor was a thick carpet woven with an eye-aching conceit of knotted stars that seemed to become flowers and even Arabic script. There were many fat pillows and bolsters scattered about, and Nizam bade me sit.

'You should lie down, Patch. I'm afraid you do not look very well.'

'It is the joy of seeing you,' I said, but gladly pulled a collection of bolsters together and sank back into them. 'Now, it is really you, isn't it?'

'It is, my dear friend.'

'So strange . . . You vanished. I had come to think you had died, like everyone else seems to have. But you are not dead, O beloved of Mamluks. Surely you could have sent word to me!'

'I could have,' he agreed, nodding solemnly. 'But might it not seem that we were riding, very fast, in quite opposite directions? What does the man of God, sitting in the wilderness, have to say to the banker with Christendom at his feet?'

'You've heard wrong.' I laughed, but he shook his head.

'Oh, no. I have heard right. I am proud of you, brother – do not think I am not. But have you not been looking outwards, outwards all this time? I knew Michel de Montalhac very well, Patch, and I know what he taught you. I have spent the years since we last saw each other searching *inside* myself.'

'What for?' It was a foolish question, and I regretted it instantly, but Nizam grinned.

'You remembered my song all these years, brother. You know all there is to know already.'

That was too owlish for me in my present state, so I let it pass. This miraculous Nizam, this very solid ghost from my past was utterly confounding, and yet he reminded me of someone, or something. But I could not think properly just now. 'So you did become a Sufi, just as you wished,' I said, feebly.

'Ah. I was always a Sufi, Patch.'

'Always? Strange work for a holy man, steering a ship full of villains.'

'What else should a holy man do? But I am just a man, brother. Others call me holy. I am still a helmsman, only now my sea is here.' And he laid his hand flat upon his breast, above the heart.

'But you were . . . This was your life before the *Cormaran*?' I insisted. Nizam was the person with whom I had spent some of my happiest times at sea, standing beside him as he held the great beam of the tiller still and steady, yet he had never told me anything of what had brought him there, and I had not asked, for you did not do that aboard the *Cormaran*, and you learned men's tales only when they decided to honour you with them.

'A life like this,' said Nizam gently. 'I am from a country called Manden, very far away from here on the other side of the Great Desert. My father was an imam and when I was still small he sent me away to study with a holy man, because even then I was large and strong and unruly, and he did not wish me to become a warrior, but to learn the ways of God, as he had. Now this holy man was a great teacher. He lived out in the rocky waste in a place a little like this one: just himself and a few disciples. As I was bigger than any of them I had to do all the rough work, fetching water, gathering wood, digging the ditches to water our little garden. But I did not complain, for I liked the master's words. I had always felt strange and unnatural because of my size, and people would find me amusing or useful, as if I were a beast, but when the master spoke I felt different. My size melted away, and then, as time passed and I learned more, understood more, I discovered peace, and in that peace was God.

'But when I was around twenty years of age, war came down from the north, out of the desert. The army of our king came past the *zāwiya* of my master, and I was forced to go with them, so my father's fears were realised. So I left my home twice, for my master had become like a father. I did not wish to be a soldier. The master had passed his teachings on to me, and I had wanted nothing more in my life than to serve him until he died, and then carry his words to my own students, should I be worthy enough to bring any to me. But as you have guessed, there was a battle and I was captured. To tell it quickly, I was taken, with many other prisoners, across the Great Desert to the land of the al-Muwahhidun, and by the time we had got there I was almost the last man left alive. They sold me as a slave, and then I knew what it was to work as a beast works, hauling stones and building houses for others to live or worship in. All along the coast of Africa I worked, until I finished up in Alexandria, heaving timbers in a shipyard. And that was where Jean de Sol, or should I say, Michel de Montalhac found me. He needed a strong man to . . . Have you heard this tale, Patch? There was a saint's tomb in the Sinai, with a stone lid as big as a dead hippopotamus. There would not be time to set up pulleys or a block and tackle, but one strong fellow might do the trick. My master wanted to hire me out, but Jean bought me there and then and freed me in front of that dog of a man. And after I had opened the tomb and watched these strange Frankish fellows take out a wizened old corpse, which they treated as if it were a block of gold, Jean asked me if I wanted to come with them, and do you know? I thought that men who freed slaves and opened tombs might be able to teach me something I had not learned from my master, and so I said yes. And Captain Jean, who did nothing by accident, put me to work finding paths across pathless water. It was perhaps the one task in the whole world that I had been taught to do.'

Nizam had not aged, as far as I could tell. His great frame was still wound with firm muscle, and his face was unlined, though now he wore a short beard, and some grey was showing in it. He wore a tight knitted cap of white cotton and a robe of plain white linen, belted with a sash of black. His feet were bare and dusty.

'And you, Patch. A crusader? Stranger work by far than mine. What would Michel de Montalhac have said?'

'So you know he is dead.'

'I do. I have many friends amongst the merchants. News spreads as fast as money, you know.'

'The worthy Abu Musa Zayd . . . My wife wrote to me about him. It seems I owe my life twice over: to a man I have never met and to one I never thought to see again.'

'And what about God?' Nizam laughed. It was a deep and easy laugh, and it made me feel better than any medicine I had got from the good doctor back in Mansourah. 'You have side-stepped my question, though, brother.'

'Ach. As to that, I have never been a crusader. I do not want to imagine what the captain would have said if I really had taken the vow, but I was thinking of my dear master when I neglected to swear any such oath. No, I am here for quite another reason, though I still don't quite understand it.'

And I told him everything that had happened to me, starting with the death of Isaac. Words came pouring out, as if a dam had burst somewhere inside me. I had not bared my soul to anyone since I had left Iselda, and Nizam seemed to draw my story from me as the farmers out in the fields drew out the water that nourished their crops. I told him about Frederick von Hohenstaufen, Cardinal John of Toledo and of the Earl of Cornwall's impossible demand. And of course I told him of my wedding, which led me back through the thickets of time to Montségur, for I had to tell him who Iselda was, and how she came into my life after returning to the captain's. He was not much interested in the fighting for Damietta and afterwards, though he drew out of me more, perhaps, than I would have told him about the miseries that followed the battle at Mansourah.

When I was done the light was fading outside, and a veiled woman had come in and lit the lanterns and candles.

'I should send word to Ibn al-Nafis,' I said. 'Unless . . . The doctor was not part of . . .'

'Not at all,' said Nizam. 'And I have already sent word. But you haven't wondered who it was that wanted you dead?'

I realised that, very strangely, I had forgotten all about the men who had tried to kill me. Then, of course, it all came back, and my body began reminding me of what it had suffered.

'Who, then?' I asked, wincing.

'Mercenaries. Sicilian Moors – Christians, mind. You were very lucky, my brother. If they had decided to slit your throat inside the palace . . . Well, your throat would indeed have been slit.'

'So you knew it was going to happen?'

'Yes. My young friends have been watching the palace for some days now, since the last attempt.'

'But there has only been one!'

'Ah. You have been far, far luckier than you know, Patch. Your doctor is the finest in all the lands of Egypt. He found poison in your evening meal last week.'

'Why? No. It's not hard to guess. Why should I be loved? I came with a mob of thieves and villains. There must be many who would like to be revenged upon a Frank.'

'No doubt. But these men were Christians from abroad. There was a reason for that.'

'Wait. Were they sent by Cardinal John of Toledo?'

'No. The men who attacked you were killed, but Aytmish found the poisoner two days ago. That was how we knew there would be an attempt today. Now this man was made to talk – he was a mercenary, after all.'

'Was?' I asked. Nizam nodded grimly.

'His band had been hired in Sicily. They were all men who used to work at a Templar commanderie in the south-west of the island.'

'The emperor drove the Templars out of Sicily,' I said. 'They hate him with a passion . . .' I stopped. 'Sicily. I know what this is about.'

'Do you? How nice,' chuckled Nizam.

'It's my singular honour to have the pope out for my blood,' I explained. 'He thinks I lent Louis all the money for this pathetic crusade. The pope has a boiling hatred of Frederick, which no doubt you know. Louis, on the other hand, is the emperor's cousin and is so fair and honest that he has refused to back Pope Innocent against Frederick. So Innocent decided that it were best if Louis went overseas, so that he could attack the empire without any pious claptrap from Louis, who's been making sure that none of his other royal cousins give Innocent any help.'

'All well and good,' said Nizam. 'The Christians still love one another like a great big family, I see.'

'Oho, yes. Never fear. Now then, Innocent thought that, seeing I was lending money hand over fist to Louis, a most Christian king, I would have no objection to financing his war against Frederick.'

'Isn't that what the Templars are for?' Nizam put in. 'Bankers for Christ?'

'Certainly. The Templars, of course, hate the Banco di Corvo Marino, as we are almost as successful as they are. I expect someone dripped some poisoned words into Innocent's ear. After all, wouldn't it be better to have *all* the Banco's money, rather than a few little loans? So they came after Iselda.' I told Nizam what Iselda had written to me. The bank was no more, and we were wanted by the Inquisition. 'Now the Temple has some reason not to hate me any more,' I went on, and told how I had helped to bring the Grand Master out of Mansourah.

'That won't endear you to the Mamluks,' said Nizam, frowning. 'I would hide that from Aytmish, if I were you.'

'Never fear. So I doubt that the order came from any Templars in Egypt,' I finished. 'I think John of Toledo has used the Templars' greed as he's used the Inquisition. Because now that Iselda is here with the bank's money, and the king is a prisoner . . . So there is suddenly a lot of coin at the potential beck and call of Louis. There's treasure here already, of course, with the Templars. But, am I mad? Because it seems to me that if the Templars are close to the pope and loathe Frederick, when the time comes to ransom Louis and the army, and the pope wants Louis to stay safely overseas . . .'

'The Templars will have been told not to open their money chests,' said Nizam. 'No, I don't think you are mad. Caught up in a ridiculous and quite meaningless world, perhaps, but not mad. Though as you chose that world . . .' He chuckled again.

'Exactly, dear friend,' I said. 'Quite mad, in that case. So if the Templars won't pay out, we plainly will, being Louis's preferred bankers. And they tried to kill me so that no ransom would come from me. Little understanding, plainly, that Iselda has full power to do whatever she wishes. With me out of the way, Iselda *is* the Banco di Corvo Marino. But as they are blinded by the shortcomings of their pious little minds, none of them would ever believe that a woman could hold such power. Even if I'd died, they would have failed.'

'And so your death would have been unnecessary,' Nizam pointed out.

'Not very consoling,' I agreed. 'But as to my life, I don't understand how I came to be sitting here with you. How I didn't get my head cut off, and why the good doctor Ibn al-Nafis lavished all his expert care on me.'

'It is true,' Nizam agreed. 'Everything has been done for you.'

'But why? I should be a prisoner.'

'Sheikh abd' al-Azeem is not some rustic fortune-teller,' said another voice. 'He is a sayyid.' The young Mamluk was standing in the doorway. Nizam smiled indulgently at him and he bowed and sat down. 'He will not tell you this himself, but the sheikh's power is very great. I am of the Bahrid Regiment, and many of us, and our emirs, are followers of this man. The leader of our regiment is called Baybars al-Bunduqdari, and he is more powerful than the queen herself. The sheikh asked that you be treated as one of our own, and that we have done.'

'Then my thanks are doubled, for I am your enemy, and you have shown me great mercy and honour.'

'As God tells us to do,' said the young Mamluk.

'Sir Petroc – dear me, I cannot believe you are a knight, my brother – is not any Frankish barbarian, dear Aytmish,' said

Nizam, winking at me. It felt decidedly odd to be winked at by a man I had just been told was a saint, but then again, what about this day was not odd? 'I have travelled almost to the edge of the world with him and I believe, in his soul, he is as much a Sufi as you or I.'

The look on Aytmish's face told me he found that doubtful, but he saw that Nizam was serious, and gave me a cautious smile. 'Really,' he said, neutrally.

The woman returned with a tray of food, and a boy carried in a small brazier of glowing charcoals, which he set down in the centre of the floor. Nizam handed a flat bread to me, and as he leaned forward the glow from the brazier caught his face. Suddenly I was brought back to the stony ledge below the walls of Montségur and to Gilles de Peyroux after he had become a Cathar *perfecti*.

'Nizam, when you spoke of looking inside yourself . . . Gilles did the same. He told me once that it was as if someone had opened him up like a lantern and lit a fire within. "Now I'm nothing but light," he said.'

'The Good Christians believe the world is a prison made by the devil,' said Nizam, pouring water from a long-spouted pitcher. 'And that men carry an ember of God's light within them. Is that not so?' I nodded. 'Gilles found his way to God, and I rejoice. But what a shame that he saw the devil in everything!' He gave a great laugh and attacked a grilled pigeon's leg.

'He called the world a prison. God knows there was enough reason to agree with him – then and now. But I've never been able to let go of the world. Perhaps that's been my undoing.'

'Oh, no, no!' roared Nizam. 'My dear brother, do not let go of the world! We are here for such a short time! Let me tell you something. When I went out to the desert and looked within myself, what do you think I found?'

'I'm not sure. Peace?' I hazarded.

'Everything!' He slapped his knees and leaned back, gazing into the shadows between the lanterns. The young Mamluk Aytmish was gazing at him intently, adoringly. 'I found the world inside myself, the whole world, and myself in the world. No difference! The bread, the lantern, its light . . . you, Aytmish, the wind in the trees, all of it the same, all of it God Himself! You do not need to find God, Patch. Just stop trying quite so hard to ignore him!'

And so passed a strange and lovely evening that is half-dissolved in my memory but still flutters there, bidding me remember. I stayed the next day, and the next, until a week had passed, and I was feeling stronger, in body and in mind. Aytmish and other Mamluks would come every day from Mansourah, bringing news and for me, potions and enquiries from Ibn al-Nafis. That first morning I asked Nizam if we could send for Iselda, but he gave me a cryptic look and told me she was busy, and that I would learn everything when I saw her, which would be soon enough. So I spent the days with my friend, exchanging stories of the infidel world to the north for as much of his wisdom as he thought I could hold, which no doubt was not all that much. Then, one morning, Aytmish arrived in the clearing with a company of Mamluks dressed, like him, in dazzling finery. They wore armour of steel chased with silver and gold, with turbans of bright silk and robes of black and white, and they carried pennants and green flags on which were written words from their holy book.

I was sitting in my usual place, beneath an old fig tree whose knobbled trunk fitted my back nicely. It was a good place to think, and that was all I wanted to do when I was not talking with Nizam. Perhaps I was trying to find God inside myself. I did not succeed, at least I do not think so, but I did find a great stillness, and that seemed good enough to me then. Aytmish came over to where I sat. We had become friends of a sort, at least to the point where we could tell each other stories of war.

He was a serious young man and I found myself hoping, more than once, that Nizam would help him to grow a little lighter, but perhaps it was duty that laid heavily on him. Today, though, he seemed to have a new energy in him. *Something has changed*, I thought, as he bowed and held out a package to me. It was clothing folded and tied with cords, and when I had untied the knots I found I was holding a new surcoat of fine red cloth, upon which crouched the image of a black hound.

'I hope it will serve,' said Aytmish. 'Yours was burned after it was cut from you. Your armour could not be found, but I searched out a good mail suit from the spoils, and I think it will fit.'

'Thank you! But why, my friend? I have grown quite used to plain linen.'

'You are going to see your good wife. And your king,' he added as an afterthought. 'We are riding to Damietta, which is being surrendered. The master is coming too.'

There was, indeed, a suit of chain mail, little used by the feel of it, and no doubt found among the baggage of one of the Frankish nobles. Who had worn this, and had he survived? This and other misgivings ran through my head as I put it on, and drew the surcoat over it. It was strange, standing in that peaceful clearing, wearing the gear of an invader. But when Nizam came outside and saw me, he roared with laughter.

'Sir knight, sir knight! Oh, I see the Black Dog of Balecester there . . . A terrifying figure, for sure! My brother, I saw you brought aboard the *Cormaran*, no more than a boy with a knife in his shoulder. And now, a knight of England.'

'I don't think I have ever really been a knight, brother,' I told him. 'Now less than ever.'

'Still, here is a blade. It is not yours, but it is the best I could find.' Aytmish gestured, and one of his men held out an expensive-looking sword. 'This is yours, though, I believe,' he added, handing me a knife, and I saw to my amazement that it was Thorn. 'The men who captured you took it, but when they heard you sing the master's words they gave it back. The good physician has kept it for you.'

'My great thanks!' I said, taking the smooth stone handle, the colour of a winter sea.

'Yes, that was the knife,' said Nizam, peering over Aytmish's head. 'It was sticking out of you just here.' And he laid his finger gently on the place, just under my collarbone.

'Will we never be done with knives and all the rest of it?' I said, feeling grief settle over me. 'I will not go to battle again – I will take an oath on it.'

'Ah, but without knives, how will we peel our oranges?' said Nizam, holding one out to me.

We mounted beside the quiet pool and rode out of the clearing. Of all the places I have left behind, knowing I would never see them again in life, that was the most painful. Nizam must have understood, for he fell into step beside me.

'It is here,' he said, reaching over and patting my chest. 'Do not worry. Some things are not taken from us. My master's *zāwiya* has been with me every instant of my life, even when we sailed across the Sea of Darkness. Do you know, Patch, we were sitting under the date palm there, as I sang you those songs on the way to Greenland? You just did not realise it.'

Chapter Twenty-Four

I discovered the cause of the change in Aytmish the Mamluk as we came near to Damietta. We had ridden to the Ashmoun Canal, joining it near where the Frankish camp had been. Even now the stink from our ruin – shit and rubbish, corpses of men and of horses – rose up like something tangible. It seemed to flutter across my face like filthy, necrotic drapery, and until we had gone a good way downstream to where the canal flowed into the Nile I had to fight back the dismal memories that threatened to overpower me. There were many boats moving down the river, a fleet sailing from Mansourah. Some were Frankish galleys full of pale, stunned crusaders, others were Saracen vessels, this crew stern-faced, that one rejoicing.

'Is the sultan going to Damietta?' I asked Aytmish.

'There is no sultan,' he replied, flatly.

'I don't understand.'

'The sultan is dead.'

'The new sultan Turanshah? But he is a young man . . .'

''Twas not age that killed him,' called another Mamluk.

'Our commander Baybars has rid Egypt of an ungodly tyrant,' Aytmish said, and this time he did not hold back a grin. 'Our land is now under the protection of the Mamluks.'

'And is there a new sultan?' I asked, aghast. No wonder Aytmish had been so distracted of late.

'A sultana. Al-Malikah Ismat ad-Din Umm-Khalil Shajar al-Durr, may God smile upon her reign.'

'Shajar al-Durr? Sultan Ayyub's wife?'

'The same. But it is the Mamluks who have power now. Aybak, the commander of all the Mamluks, is to marry the sultana – a string of pearls to adorn a mighty warrior,' he added, evidently pleased with his wit, for *shajar al-durr* has the meaning of a necklace of pearls in the Arab tongue.

I looked at Nizam, but he just shrugged. I had learned that he was not very interested in the worldly affairs of his Mamluk followers. What would happen now, though? Louis was being taken down to Damietta to surrender the city and ransom himself and his army, but he had made a treaty with Turan-shah, and now that the Mamluks were the new rulers of Egypt – for so Aytmish had just told me, if not in so many words – would they keep to their agreement? And I did not even know what that agreement had been. Ransom, surrender and the Franks to leave this land with their tails tucked between their haunches. Well, I seemed to be under the protection of the Mamluks myself, so that must be a good thing. I rode in silence, watching the ships go by, watching for signs.

And thinking of Iselda. I had not seen my wife for a year and a half, and many times I had not expected to see her again. Yet here I was, a day away from her. Under Nizam's tree I had spent many long, slow hours trying to form her image in my mind, in the shrine behind my eyes where I had placed her that morning on the Molo in Venice. But try as I might, I could not quite see her. She formed and faded, faded and formed like a chimera. And then I found I could not even remember the smell of her hair or her skin. I began to wonder if I had faded in her mind too, and then I fell to wondering if, when she saw me for the first time in Damietta, she would even know me. She had diminished in memory, but I had done so in the flesh. I was thinking too much, I knew, but that was what one did here. Sometimes, worryingly, I found myself fading away altogether until all that was left was thought, and then even that . . . Coming to my senses, surfacing from a silent cascade of light flickering through palm leaves, I would wonder where I had been, *I*, Petroc of Sorrows, of the war, the bank. There had been a vast nothingness, silent, completely peaceful, empty – but at the same time full of some presence. I told Nizam the first time it happened, thinking I was going mad, but he had just smiled, and I knew what he was telling me: God. How strange. I had gone looking for Iselda but instead I had found God. Or was it the other way around? It was then, I think, that Nizam's *zāwiya* entered my heart.

Two days of easy riding brought us to Damietta. Early on the second day we had joined with a larger force of Mamluks from Cairo, all of them in high spirits. Many asked for Nizam's blessing, and as his companion I got numerous strange looks, not all of them friendly. By the time the gates of the city were in view, we had become an army, every warrior in his finest gear, green and white and golden banners flying overhead. We had overtaken a big Frankish galley flying the flag of Geoffroy de Sargines, and while we formed up in front of the gates the galley pulled in to the shore and Geoffroy himself, looking haggard and thin as a bulrush, came ashore. Aytmish had told me how it was Geoffroy who had saved Louis from being killed after they had been cut off from our rearguard, and how he had charged the enemy again and again until he could no longer sit upright on his horse. 'A brave fellow, certainly,' he had admitted, grudgingly. Now it seemed that Geoffroy had been entrusted with another test of courage. I was on the very far left with Nizam, but I got the gist of things: Geoffroy was surrendering Damietta to the army of the sultana.

The doors were opened, to reveal a sheepish band of Frankish merchants, and a company of men-at-arms all trying to look as harmless as possible. A Mamluk on a perfect white horse rode slowly past them, and if a horse can show disdain, this one did. The man was Baybars, the sultan's killer. Behind him, the Mamluk army filed in through the gates. I brought up the rear with Nizam, but as we were passing inside Geoffroy de Sargines noticed me and ran through the mob of unarmed crusaders and country people that had begun to grow on the banks of the Nile.

'Nizam, I will find you inside,' I said, sliding from my horse.

'Take this, my brother,' he said, and untied a green scarf embroidered with gold script from the shaft of Aytmish's spear. 'Put it round your head – it will keep you safe, God willing.' Then he was gone, swept up in the army that was pouring like water through a sluice into the city.

I knotted the scarf round my head in the manner of the fellahin when Geoffroy reached me.

'I heard they'd killed you!' he cried, and embraced me: we were two bags of bones rattling against each other.

'You look like a Turk,' he said, when we were done congratulating each other on being alive.

'And you look like a corpse,' I returned. 'Now, where is the king?'

'He is ten miles upstream or thereabouts. I have come ahead to—'

'Quite,' I said hurriedly, for the poor fellow looked as if the humiliation of surrendering the crusade's only gain was about to finish him off. 'Will you go in and see Queen Marguerite?'

'That is my next duty,' he said, sighing. 'There is much to be done before His Majesty gets here – a very great sum of money to ransom his own person and that of his brother. The city must be evacuated.'

'Where to?'

'Acre. The king wishes to go to the Holy Land immediately.'

'Christ! Why not France? Home?'

310

'Duty, dear Petrus. Duty. He feels he must wait until every Christian prisoner is set free, and besides, there is work to be done in the Holy Land.'

'What kind of work, Geoffroy?' He shook his head. The poor fellow looked as if he could sleep for a month and still look half-dead, but there was a certain fire in his eyes. I had seen it so many times during this folly: the passion of the crusader. So not even Mansourah, or the defeat, or a month in the hands of the Saracens – who evidently had not lent him the services of an Ibn al-Nafis – had been enough to quench it. I clapped him, carefully, on the shoulder. 'Enough time for that. Now, let us hurry. The queen will be wondering where you are.'

And Iselda, I was thinking. Geoffroy looked back at the galleys riding the calm waters of the Nile. 'Our fellows are going directly to sea – the Turks will not let them into the city. I suppose I must go alone.'

'Not quite alone, my friend.' I gave my horse to a Mamluk squire and arm in arm with Geoffroy de Sargines, I went back into the city. It was nearly half a year since I had gone out in the company of all those jolly young men who were going to conquer the feeble land of Egypt, and instead ended up in the bellies of crocodiles and eels.

The streets were in an uproar. All the gates had been opened and the Mussulman population, all those families that had fled when the crusader army had landed, was pouring in. Smoke was rising from beyond the walls where the Frankish camp had been torched. The new bishop and his clergy had wisely fled, and the cathedral was already a mosque once again. The Genoese and Pisan merchants had also fled, and whatever they had left behind was being shared out among noisy looters or flung onto bonfires. I hoped Ya'qub bin Yazdad and his wife were safe.

The main body of Mamluk horsemen had ridden to the

palace, and they were formed up in the paved space in front of the entrance. I found Aytmish among them by the long pheasant feathers he had stuck in his helmet, and led Geoffroy between the horses to where he stood in the second rank.

'Ah, my brother,' he said. He cast a less friendly look down onto Geoffroy, who was trying to look valiant and commanding in this forest of horses' legs. 'Our lord Baybars is treating with the emissaries of your queen. They are exceedingly old.'

'Indeed. And one of them is a midwife,' I told him. He gave me a strange look and shook his head. 'The ways of the Franks . . .' he muttered. 'Frankish knight, you are the one who surrendered the city to us, are you not?' he said to Geoffroy.

'I am,' he replied, stiffly.

'If you wish to go into the palace, go now, with my brother here. You Franks are leaving this place, and if you linger you might be taken prisoner again. Or more likely, killed.'

'My brother, may we meet again,' I told him, taking his hand.

'*Insha'Allah*,' he replied gravely. 'May we find each other again in peace.'

I left him and led Geoffroy out from the ranks. Now I could see what was going on: a stocky Mamluk in the robes of an emir, flanked by two others holding banners, was standing, fists on hips, in front of two ancient knights. One of them had a long, unkempt white beard and a small hump between his shoulders. The other wore a mail coat, and the hood hung loosely around his stubbly cheeks. We crossed the open space, footsteps echoing hollowly – it was very quiet here, despite the growing clamour from the rest of the town.

Geoffroy de Sargines had evidently remembered his station, for he drew himself up and marched across to the old men. Baybars's men grabbed their hilts, but when they saw it was

Geoffroy and that his companion wore a Sufi headscarf – and a strange sight I must have been, a Frankish knight with a dog on his surcoat and a fellahin's turban on my head – they let us pass. Geoffroy bowed to Baybars and they fell into a clipped discussion about protocols. I turned to the hump-backed knight.

'I am Petrus Blakke Dogge, and the lady Iselda de Rozers is my wife. Is she safe?'

The man's rheumy eyes, sunk into a face planed by age and worry, came to life.

'Ah! Dear God! Welcome, my dear sir!'

'A welcome indeed, good sir . . .'

'We have heard much about you. There has not been a great deal to talk about, two old men locked up with a brace of . . .' Remembering himself, he rattled his withered jowls in embarrassment. 'Let us go inside. Now that the good master of Sargines is here, I am happily made redundant in this unpleasant business. Standing around like a spare prick at a wedding while a Turk lords it over one . . .' He shook his head again and took my arm.

I had spent a good deal of time inside the palace, and when the king had been here it had thronged with people. The halls had been full of merchants arguing over tariffs and rights, and soldiers speculating when the army would leave, and whining about how bored they were and how tedious their life in camp had become. Now it was hollow, empty, and the air smelled of mildew and abandonment. A serving woman, looking terrified, scuttled across my path and disappeared through a doorway. I knew the way to the royal quarters, and though I did not mean to, the old fellow was soon limping along far behind me. I took the stairs two at a time, though my body protested vehemently, and frightened another young woman at the top.

'Iselda de Rozers!' I called to her retreating back. 'Where can I find her?'

'She is here,' came a clear voice behind me. I knew it, and yet it seemed more beautiful by far than anything I had heard before. She was standing close to the wall, a slender, dark break in the flow of twisting Saracen pattern. Her robe was dark, and her black hair was loose around her shoulders. But all I saw then was the pale heart of her face. And everything I thought I had lost, all that I had forgotten and battled to recall, came back to me in that instant. Like the first daffodil after an endless winter, the simple fact of her presence, there in that hallway, made everything else completely without meaning.

'Oh, my darling,' she said. 'You've come back.'

'I think so,' I said. 'But it's you who's come to me.'

This was a story I had told myself countless times in the stinking camp by the river, in Mansourah, and in the *zāwiya*. And now, though it wasn't a story any more, I was still telling it, watching myself, as if in a dream, walking down the hallway, reaching for my wife, both of us collapsing against the wall as we kissed lips, cheeks, eyes and twined fingers through each other's hair. It was as if my soul – if I had such a thing – could not agree that this was real, that Iselda was no longer a phantom dreamed up to comfort me through the torment of boredom and pain. It was flying away, as it had under the tree in Nizam's clearing. Then I remembered the great peace that had come over me there, and in a flash I was whole again, and Iselda was astoundingly real in my arms.

'I can't tell you how much I love you,' I whispered.

'You can. But I know anyway,' she said. And at that moment it was the crusade that became a dream, full of death and fear and stench but fading, slowly, into the waking day.

We deserved to stand there for a week, drunk on each other's touch, but though I had fought my way out of one story, there was another going on around us, and as soon as the ancient knight had tottered up the stairs and found us in the hallway, we were rudely thrust into it once more. As he stood there wheezing for breath, Geoffroy de Sargines appeared at his shoulder.

'My lady,' he said curtly, bowing to Iselda. 'I must speak to the queen.'

'Who are you?' she said, bristling. Ah, indeed this was the Iselda I loved.

'This is Geoffroy de Sargines,' I told her, trying to keep myself from laughing. 'He saved the king's life. His Majesty is coming, but he is some way behind us.'

'And things need to be made ready,' said Geoffroy. 'Petrus, who is this woman?'

'My wife,' I said, simply. Geoffroy's eyebrows went up, and he bowed a little more warmly than before.

'A great honour,' he said. 'My deepest apology. But I'm afraid we are somewhat pressed for time . . .'

'Of course, of course,' said Iselda, warmly enough to show he was forgiven. 'But the queen is not here.'

'Then where is she?' said Geoffroy, a little sharply.

'She has left for Acre. Those of us who stayed behind while you . . .' She bit her lip and cast a wry look at me. 'Those left to guard Damietta – Sir Enguerrand and Patriarch Robert, chiefly – have had to make a treaty with the sultan, and as the Saracens are about to take the city, we thought it best that the queen be taken to safety. She is still not quite recovered from her ordeal, I'm afraid, although she will regain her health. Never fear: Marguerite of Provence is as strong as any man, and stronger by far than many. The king is going to Acre as soon as the treaty is done, and she will be waiting for him. There has been a great turmoil here the past few weeks – the Pisans and Genoese tried to leave with all the food, and Her Majesty made them see reason. The garrison has tried to murder the townspeople, and then the townsfolk wished to murder the garrison, and she has kept the peace despite everything. As well as, it must be said, bearing the king a healthy baby boy, with no midwife save for the worthy Sir Enguerrand here.' The ancient knight blushed lightly and cleared his throat, but said nothing.

Geoffroy had heard Iselda out, his jaw slackening with every word. 'We thought she was here,' he stuttered. 'I saw Patriarch Robert in Fariskur, when we were negotiating the . . . the . . .'

'The surrender,' supplied Iselda. 'She left two days after the patriarch. She will be safely in Acre now. And her safety should be His Majesty's main concern, is that not so?'

'Well, yes, of course,' said Geoffroy. 'But there is, um, there are *matters* to be arranged.'

'If you are talking about His Majesty's ransom, then I'm afraid you will have to talk to me about that,' said Iselda. I looked at her, amazed. *Really?* I asked her silently.

'Really?' said Geoffroy, aloud.

'Yes. My husband, I did not put this in my letter because it happened only a few days ago, but the queen has given me the authority to treat for her until such time as the king comes to Damietta.'

'A woman? Dear God!' Geoffroy blurted.

'And so that my authority might have some weight, she also created me Comtesse de Montalhac.'

It was my turn to gape. 'You are a countess?' I squeaked.

'I am. Hereditary. Like my grandfather before me. I had no idea, but the queen knew. She can name every fief in Provence and Toulouse, even those which the French − I mean no offence, Sir Geoffroy − snatched from us.'

'This is all true and correct,' Sir Enguerrand piped up. 'The lady Iselda has been a great refuge of strength for Her Majesty. And I myself could not command the authority your wife has wielded these past months.'

'You are too modest, dear Enguerrand. I could not have delivered Jean Tristram. I would have fainted.'

'Nonsense, nonsense,' he replied. Then he turned to us. 'Sirs, it is as she has told you. The comtesse has the queen's authority in Damietta.'

Geoffroy took a deep breath, bent his knee and bowed to Iselda. 'Then I will serve you with all my strength, madam, however meagre that might be.'

'Thank you, Sir Geoffroy. Now, what do you require from me?'

Iselda led us into the royal chambers. I found I had retreated into a sort of half-trance, and when Iselda slipped her hand into mine and whispered into my ear, things seemed to be becoming even less real.

'Patch, that means you are, by the way, Comte de Montalhac. And I think you need some wine.'

She was right: I did need a drink after that, and as I had not drunk anything stronger than fruit sherbet since being taken by the Saracens, my head began to swim a little.

'The sum agreed for the ransom is four hundred thousand *livres tournois*,' Geoffroy was saying. 'Half to be paid immediately, half when the king and his brother get to Acre. That is for the king, all the surviving nobles, knights and the army, what is left of it. Do we have that to hand?'

'Something like it,' said Iselda, frowning. 'We have had to buy all the city's stocks of food, to stop the people starving to death. That has used up some coin, but I believe . . . Enguerrand, what do you think?'

'There should be sufficient,' he said, but he did not look entirely certain.

We talked for some time, Geoffroy laying out the various stipulations of the treaty and explaining what had happened to the sultan Turanshah, until we were interrupted by the palace guards, escorting a terrified boy who told us, in a thick

Genoese accent, that the king's galley had landed, that the Saracens had found the wine supplies and were getting vilely drunk, and that His Majesty and his brother and a load of other dukes and such were staying on their ship, being in fear of their lives. Would we join His Majesty, please, before the Turks made an end of us all? That seemed reasonable, and Iselda gave orders to evacuate the city. In half an hour we were marching, flanked by the whole remaining company of palace guards and a dozen Mamluks on horseback, towards the gates.

The city had changed. Saracen flags hung from every tower and a bonfire was smouldering in front of the mosque, where everything that had made it a cathedral was being put to the flames. There were groups of Mamluks everywhere, though none seemed to be drunk, unlike the Jewish and Christian Damiettans, who were noisily celebrating the humiliation of their Frankish oppressors. A few onions flew at us, but our Mamluk escort yelled at the throwers and they left off.

'All the Turks seem very impressed by your turban,' Iselda muttered to me. 'Are you going to tell me about it?'

'However strange it sounds, the Comte and Comtesse de Montalhac are under the protection of Sheikh abd' al-Azeem al-Ansari,' I whispered back. 'Which is very fitting.'

'What do you mean?'

'The Montalhac past. Your father's blessings, Iselda. When you meet the sheikh, you will see.'

Chapter Twenty-Five

I didn't tell her more, for we had passed through the gate and were walking down to the Nile, where a large galley was tied up. The banner of France was hanging from the masthead, limp in the dead, scalding air of mid-afternoon. A great gang of crossbowmen, not much less than a hundred of them, were drawn up in rough but purposeful lines on the bank in front of the ship, and small knots of Mamluks were watching them, silently, from a distance.

King Louis Capet was sitting on a pile of cushions in the shade of a tent set up in the stern. He was thin, shockingly thin, his limbs wasted, the knobs of elbows and knees painfully visible beneath his loose robes. His golden curls had thinned, and the skin on his face was yellowed and tight. Unnervingly, he still looked like a very young man, but one who had suffered horribly, and as I looked at him it was hard not to think of innocence violated. But the king was not innocent, and he knew it very well.

'Geoffroy . . . and Petrus! My dear, my very dear men!' He struggled upright, and the emaciated man at his side, whom I suddenly recognised as Philippe de Montfort, hastily bent to steady him. 'So many are dead that it is such undeserved joy to find that some friends are still with us!' He began to cough, and de Montfort held out a cup for him to spit into.

'Lord, I am weak, but there is no time for weakness. Is it done, Geoffroy?' the king asked, and when Geoffroy nodded, he let out a funereal sigh. 'Then let us settle this. I would not ask my men to suffer one more minute for my sake. They have set many of us free, but the rest must wait until the ransom is paid, and they are keeping my poor brother Alphonse as surety . . . Is the emir waiting for us?'

'He is,' said Iselda. Louis gave her a courteous, puzzled look.

'My lord, this is Iselda, Comtesse de Montalhac, whom the queen has appointed her representative,' said Geoffroy quickly.

'And my wife,' I put in. Louis looked at both of us, almost pathetically confused.

'Representative?' he said, plaintively.

'The queen has gone to Acre, Your Majesty,' said Iselda, curtseying elegantly. 'For her safety and that of your son, Jean Tristram, of whom I wish you the greatest joy.'

'The queen . . . What? Marguerite is not here?'

'No, Your Majesty. But rest assured she left only when everything possible had been done for the safety of your subjects and dependants.'

I stood, wishing I could sit in the shade next to Louis, while Iselda coolly laid out before the king exactly what had been done to protect Damietta since he had ridden off to take Cairo. *Poor Louis*, I thought. He had been waiting for his wife to come and soothe his brow, only to find she was in another country. Had Louis clung to his memories of the queen while he sickened and his men died? While he was captured and humiliated? I would never know, of course. We were almost done with Egypt now. Some money to be handed over and we would set sail. But to where? There had been no time to ask Iselda what had happened in Venice, or to tell her about Father Matthieu or Remigius. And I had failed Earl Richard. We did not have a business any longer, or a safe home. So were we to be the Count and Countess de Montalhac now? One more odd game to play, another mask to hide behind? Dear God, we couldn't hide any longer, could we? It would be mummery, play-acting the lord and lady in some French backwater, dancing the rigid steps of court life, being obliged for ever more . . .

'Petrus!' I blinked. The king was speaking to me, an indulgent smile on his withered boy's face. 'We are rowing out to the ships. Sit down, man. Share our food.'

We all sat under the tent and ate vile fritters made of hard, piss-tasting cheese – 'All the Turks had for us,' as Philippe de Montfort explained – while the galley slipped down with the current, out between the sandbanks and into open water. There was the fleet, what was left of it, for many transports, under contract from Genoa and Pisa, had abandoned the army and gone back home, and others had sailed off to Acre with the queen. But there was the royal ship, and near it the galley of the Templars, and even the vessel that had brought the English company across from Cyprus.

'That's ours,' muttered Iselda, pointing out a well-built galley anchored a little way off the port side of the Templar ship. It looked like a Venetian war galley rejigged for merchant life, and it flew no flags.

As we came alongside the king's ship, the royal standard broke out from the top of the mast. There were already some knights aboard, and they rushed to help Louis over the side. Iselda went up after him, and I followed. As I struggled up the rope ladder, marvelling at how old I felt, voices were rising on deck. Heaving myself over the rail, shamefaced but glad of a young sailor's helping hand, I saw the king and Geoffroy standing before a tall Mamluk. Baybars had got here before us. Behind him stood six armed warriors, an imam in dark robes, and a figure in simple white who towered above everyone.

'Nizam!' I shouted before I could stop myself. He grinned and raised a gigantic hand.

'Dear God's tears!' breathed Geoffroy, coming up behind me. 'Who in Beelzebub's name is that?'

'Sheikh abd' al-Azeem al-Ansari,' I said.

'No! I don't believe it!' Iselda grabbed my arm. 'Is that really the sheikh?'

'But it is,' I said. 'Let's see what's happening here, and then you shall meet him.'

The Mamluk commander had come to collect the ransom money. On the deck, the Mamluks began to set up a huge balance scale. Baybars was standing, arms folded, feet apart, listening sceptically to Louis, who was trying to explain that everything was in order.

'Then, O king, bring out your coin,' said Baybars at last. He seemed singularly without humour, except that his eyes, the only animated thing about him, were sparkling and full of life. The other Franks were bristling at the disdain being shown to their ruler, but I understood. Baybars was not being unmannerly out of spite. Louis was powerless, just another man, and not even a believer. What Baybars had come for was money, and that was what he expected: no less, and no more. Meanwhile, one of the younger knights had been sent off to the strongroom with an old man who turned out to be the Patriarch Robert. There was a long pause, in which the only sound was the grunting of the men fitting the long, heavy balance beam to the scales. The pause grew longer, and longer still. Finally the patriarch emerged, leading two red-faced seamen lugging an iron-bound chest between them. They set it down with a bang next to the scales. The Mamluks made some final adjustments, and then began unceremoniously to shovel silver coins from the chest onto the hanging pan. It took a surprisingly long time, but at last they nodded and began to pour the silver into another chest.

'Ten thousand livres,' said Baybars in good French. 'Are we agreed, gentlemen?'

'Of course,' said Louis.

'Ten thousand? We'll be here all night,' I whispered to Iselda.

We were there much longer than that, as it turned out. Two hundred thousand *livres tournois* is a great amount of coin, and it had to be dragged up from the hold, weighed, and lowered down into the Saracen felucca tied alongside us. Other galleys were bringing more nobles and knights out to the ship: the king's brother, Charles of Anjou, arrived with Philippe de Nemours, Henri du Mez, Nicole d'Acre, the Ibelin brothers, Baudouin and Guy, plus Imbert de Beaujeu, Constable of France, the Counts of Flanders and Brittany, and Jean de Soissons. And all the time we stayed standing, drawn up in our awkward rows, the balance between us like a small gallows. I kept catching Nizam's eye, and it was hard not to burst out laughing. I wanted to take him aside and have him meet Iselda, but the weighing went on and on, until, when night began to fall, Baybars called a halt.

'We will return at dawn,' he said, and without another word the Mamluk party climbed over the side and were gone. We watched their little galley, riding very low with her belly full of silver, crawl back towards Damietta.

Jean de Joinville came aboard that night, with a few others, but so many were dead, and it was a sombre reunion. Joinville was even thinner than the king.

'I had a tumour in my throat,' he told us, his voice still raspy, 'but some Mussulman knight cured me. I couldn't swallow a thing, and then this fellow, bless him, made me gargle with some vile liquid. In two days the thing began to shrink away to nothing, and lo! I am cured.'

'You need to fatten yourself up, my friend,' I told him. 'If you've had nothing to eat these past weeks save those foul cheese pies, it's not surprising the wind is whistling between your ribs.'

'And you do not look all that bad,' said Joinville. We had set up a small camp in the prow of the ship, with a pile of carpets and a brazier, and were feasting on salt pork, of which we had a vast supply, for the Saracens had insisted we remove it from Damietta. Iselda was cutting a slice for herself with Thorn. Joinville had been amazed to learn that my wife was here, and that she was a new-made countess – and I a count, of course – but far stranger things had happened to all of us, and like old soldiers do, we abandoned good manners in favour of warmth and food.

'He has been looked after by a holy man,' said Iselda. 'And he will not tell me anything about it.'

'Fate,' I said, shrugging my shoulders. '*Insha'Allah*, as they say.' I told him what had happened after we had last seen each other in the burning camp, but I knew that Joinville, being a straightforward, pious fellow and as Frankish as they came, would not understand about Nizam and his followers. So I said I had been captured by a Saracen knight I had fought at Mansourah. The holy man, I said, had lived in this knight's house. He enjoyed speaking to me of the places I had been, and in return for stories had made sure I was well cared for. Joinville was full of tales. He had passed through many dangers, nearly died a dozen times, and had won through in the end by keeping his head and his faith in the Lord. He told a good story, did Jean de Joinville. To this day I do not know how many of his tales were true, but I will warrant they have grown stranger over the years. He was weak, though, and left us before it grew too late. And so, for the first time in what seemed an entire life, Iselda and I were alone together, or as alone as one can be on the deck of a warship anchored in enemy waters.

'My darling,' I said, as soon as he was gone. I grabbed her

hands and pressed them between mine. 'Was it all true? Everything in your letter?'

'Yes. Alas, all true.'

'And is everything – the wealth of the bank, I mean, really on board that cob?'

'With Dimitri, therefore safe.'

'So . . . what now?' I wanted to ask her everything, to tell her every minute of my life since we had parted. But suddenly I had no words but these.

'My dear love, we have a ship full of silver and gold, and nothing else. The Inquisitors drove everybody out of the Ca' Kanzir and the deed now belongs to the Church. I have my spies in Venice. I'm sure the priests cannot hold on to our property – any good lawyer would see them off. But meanwhile . . .'

'And what about Florence?'

'The Banco was destroyed. Burned to the ground. They say it was the Ghibbelines – they are getting the blame for everything in Florence these days. But it's nonsense, of course.'

'Of course. What a waste. And I liked Blasius.'

'Don't worry about him. He's gone to Paris. I told him to wait things out.'

'Yes, there's Paris, and Lyon. What about all our branches?'

'Closed. There wasn't any point in keeping them open – and who wants to leave money with a bank whose heretic owners have vanished?'

'I didn't vanish! I went on crusade, for fuck's sake! How many heretics do that?'

'The confused ones, I suppose,' said Iselda, and kissed me.

'Well, Father Matthieu won't bother us any more, at least,' I said, after a while. 'You were right: he was a vile little man.'

'Was?'

'Oh, yes.' And I told her how the priest had made his way through the Saracen barricade, only to be caught up in our retreat. 'He tried to take me with him,' I muttered. Remembering the stifling hut that had been our prison, I pulled a blanket around my shoulders and hunched towards the brazier. There was the priest's face as he cursed me, and there it was, lifeless, in its own blood.

'Did he just want the money?' said Iselda, wonderingly. 'To go through all that . . .'

'And he was a priest. We have a pope who sends priests to ruin people and steal their fortune, so that he can spend it on destroying a Christian emperor. And much worse than that.'

'It could hardly be any worse!' she protested.

'No, it could. A pope who sends his creature to help a Mussulman army defeat a whole crusade.' Iselda listened, her mouth a circle of disbelief, to the tale of Mansourah and what Remigius had done there.

'So I don't know if it's really worth going home,' I finished.

'No. It's the end of the bank,' she sighed, and leaned against me. 'But I'm not sad about that. We always hated it, didn't we?'

'We did. To be driven out, though . . .'

'Do you really care about that? Bloody men!' She kissed me again, in case I didn't know she was joking. 'We've got lots of money, though.'

'But how much of it is ours?'

'Well, I've been bored enough here in Damietta to go over the books. Everything on deposit from merchants has been sent back to them. Likewise small customers. We have some big deposits from churchmen of one sort and another, and' – she lowered her voice to a whisper – 'I say fuck 'em.'

'With a mooring post, as the Greeks say,' I agreed.

'Because apart from anything else the Curia has borrowed some fat sums from us, and that's gone for ever,' she went on.

'So what's left?'

'More than . . .' She shook her head. 'A lot. And Louis

Capet owes us a great deal, don't forget. Do you think he'll ever pay it?'

'Yes. I do, actually,' I said. 'He is many things, including a God-bothering fool who's killed an entire army, but he's also the most honest man I know.'

We carved off some more salt pork. It wasn't that pleasant: very salty and as tender as damp leather, but we were sharing it, and that alone was miraculous.

'What about your title, Comtesse? Is it real?'

''Course it is,' said Iselda, digging a string of pork from between her teeth. 'Turns out that my grandfather was the Comte de Montalhac. One of the great old Languedoc families – not very rich, but cultured. The old man was a troubadour himself. Strange, isn't it. Did my father ever mention that?'

'No, he never did. But your grandfather wouldn't have been an old man, my love. He died young. I do know that story, but I won't tell it now. So Queen Marguerite knew about Montalhac? That's extraordinary.'

'The queen honestly knows the name of every fief in Provence, every troubadour who ever sang at her father's court . . . so Montalhac – of *course* she remembered Montalhac. I did not tell her that my father spent his life selling fake relics to the cream of Christendom, mind you. I said he died on crusade when I was a wee girl.'

'I expect that helped matters.'

'It did.' She chewed thoughtfully.

'So . . . can we live there?'

'Ah. Unfortunately the actual fief is held by the French wolf who stole it from . . . from Grandfather, as I've taken to calling him.'

'So we have the title only. Never mind. It's wonderful. Your – *our* father would be glad, I think. It's justice.'

'To get back the stolen title but not the stolen land? Not much justice there.'

'Oh, Christ. You really are his daughter. And you're right, it doesn't mean very much.' I shook my head. 'So we're homeless.'

'Not really, Patch! You make it sound as if we're landless villains stumbling from hayrick to chicken house. We could buy a small princedom tomorrow if we wanted to.'

'But I don't. Do you?'

'No. I like this: no bank, no ledgers. We can be out on the road again, or the water.'

I sighed. 'All those weeks by the river, when I thought I would never see you again, I thought about home. All I wanted was to sit with you under the old fig tree in the courtyard of the Ca' Kanzir, and do nothing. Listen to the boatmen, and the wasps. Just be home.'

'You're a liar, Patch,' said Iselda, gravely. 'Do you think I don't know what's really in your heart? You don't have to fear that you'll upset me. But we both know where home is for you.'

'All right. You are very wise. I did think of the Ca' Kanzir, but no, it has never been my home, and it wasn't the captain's, not really. I'll tell you, then . . . There's a brook that rises under the shoulder of Three Barrows, a short walk from the house where I was born. It isn't much, and it isn't long. It flows out of a mire, trickles across the open moor and then falls down through a small ravine into a bigger stream. Two miles at the most. Just where it leaves the High Moor there is a pool, with a thicket of rowan trees under a high bank. The brook flows down a waterfall into the pool, and there are little brown trout and frogs, and once I found a silver peel spawning there. The waterfall isn't high, perhaps the height of my shoulders, but the thing of it is, there are no rocks, just a great cushion of green moss, and the water tumbles over it and through it. On a hot day you can stand in the pool and lean against the moss, just sink into it and let the water run over you. And when the sky is as blue as a kingfisher's back and the rowan berries shine . . .'

'See? You have no secrets from me, Petroc,' said Iselda, putting her hand softly against my cheek and kissing me on the brow.

'But the Ca' Kanzir wasn't your home either,' I said, kissing her back. 'Are we going to roam for ever? I'm tired, love. I don't want to fight any more. If I go on this way, one day I'll find I've lost more of me than I ever had.'

'You have changed,' said Iselda, looking into my eyes. 'You're calmer, somehow. That didn't happen in battle.'

'No, it didn't,' I said. It was time to tell Iselda about my time with Nizam, and so I did, lying back against the cushions as the stars swayed solemnly overhead and the ship rolled softly in the quiet swell.

'So the sheikh was my father's old helmsman! I can't . . . Fate is tying itself into knots around us,' she said, wonderingly, when I was done.

'No. The world is not large – our world, I mean, of traders and merchants. Nizam had been following my life for years. He knows many Damiettan merchants. I could have found him just as easily if I had bothered. And if I had not been flinging myself headlong into the future.'

'And what did he tell you? What did you learn? Because you learned something. It has changed you.'

I did not want to talk about it. The days I had spent in Nizam's clearing in the woods were already fading, but Iselda was quite right: they had changed me. I could feel it all through me. But now she was nudging me.

'What, Patch? Unspeakable rites? Witchcraft? I need to know!'

'Stop it. Nothing like that. Just peace, and thinking.'

'About what?'

'Everything. Nothing – there. I thought about nothing. Is that unspeakable enough for you?'

But she would not be dissuaded. Her fingers were squirming into my armpits and she was looking down on me, a lovely inquisitor, her hair in my face. 'No. Tell me.'

'All right!' I sat up and took her hand. 'Nizam showed me, somehow . . . He led me to it. Something I should have known years and years ago. They should have taught it at my monastery instead of the shit they filled me up with.' I threaded my fingers through hers and winced. For some reason I was embarrassed. I had spent a lifetime scorning notions like the one that was growing inside me now. But what fools we are, when really we mean so little to the great riot of creation. 'God is everything,' I said at last, my mouth dry. 'The stars, the sea, this ship. Us. God isn't just with us, or inside us. We are God.'

I thought she would say something, but she didn't, and she did not let go of my hand. We lay back and watched the stars in silence. After a while I found she had gone to sleep, her head in the crook of my neck. But sleep was a little way off for me, and as I waited, I stared up at the scattered diamonds of the Hyades, Iselda's breath warm and regular against my skin.

Chapter Twenty-Six

'There is a difficulty,' said Jean de Joinville. We were standing around the ransom scales, and Jean had turned his head so that the Saracens would not see his lips.

'And what would that be, Jean?' I said, keeping my face blank. No one was actually looking at us, but I had noticed that Baybars seemed to see everything.

'We are running out of money,' he hissed.

'We're short? Oh, God . . . By how much?'

It was late in the afternoon. The counting had been going on since dawn with a pause for luncheon, and tempers were beginning to fray. The king had almost collapsed and was sitting in the shade under his tent. The other French noblemen were all in the hold, feverishly counting out money, and I was on deck with Jean de Joinville, overseeing the business. All of us, Franks and Mamluks, stood silent, shifting from foot to foot as coins tinkled endlessly into the copper pan of the scales. All, that is, except Iselda and Nizam, who were sitting in our nest of carpets and cushions in the bow. I had brought them together as we dined. It had been awkward, as the Mamluks were uncomfortable with a woman in their midst, but afterwards the sheikh had excused himself politely – though Baybars did not seem to be one of his followers, Nizam was the only one aboard this ship whom he treated with any warmth, and he did not refuse him now – and led her away. Now they were deep in conversation, and every now and then Nizam's deep laugh broke into our own solemn proceedings.

'About a quarter,' said Jean. 'Maybe less, but there definitely isn't enough.'

'Have you told the king?'

'Not yet.'

'Then wait.' I bowed to the Mamluks and set off up the deck, where I made a show of taking a piss over the side. Now I would be ignored, so I walked quietly over to where Iselda and Nizam sat.

'My darling,' I said, 'do you know how much money the king has in his coffers?'

'Well, I lent Marguerite a hundred and thirty thousand livres. She told me she had another hundred thousand.'

'Wait a minute – we've lent Louis Capet another hundred-odd thousand livres? That more or less makes us the owners of France, doesn't it?'

'Not quite, dearest,' said Iselda. 'What is it?'

'Nizam, what if the king cannot pay?' I asked. The French would have strung me up there and then if they had heard me, but I did not hesitate. If I could not trust Nizam, I could trust no man on earth.

'Ah. Why is this not so very surprising?' he replied, cocking an eyebrow. 'Baybars is – he is a quite extraordinary fellow, actually. But among other things he is scrupulously honourable in matters such as this. If Louis cannot pay the ransom, he will keep the rest of the Christian army prisoner – and the king's brother – until it is paid.'

'Seems pretty straightforward,' I said.

'That is what Baybars will do. But he is not the master here. This Aybak, who will be sultan very soon, mark my words, is not a man of honour. I would judge that if he feels that Louis has insulted him, he will have the prisoners killed. They are already butchering the wounded, I am afraid.'

'No! Can we stop them?'

'Oh, my dear fellow, do you think Louis does not know? He is a wise ruler, so I hear, and so he weighs such things in the balance.'

'So the ransom must be found. Can we pay it, Iselda?'

'We can, but . . .' She stood up and pointed over the rail. 'See there? The Templar treasure ship. Do you see how the Temple is keeping its distance from all this? I've been wondering about it. There are thousands upon thousands of livres aboard that ship!'

'And I know what they're doing!' I cried, and quickly lowered my voice. The Mamluks were starting to look over in our direction. No doubt they thought I was being disgracefully frivolous, consorting with my wife when there was business to be done.

'Remember what I told you about Remigius, and the men who tried to kill me in Mansourah? They don't want the king to be ransomed! They want him to stay here as a prisoner, or to trap him in some other way. You have your spies, you say – well, you know the Templars have theirs!'

'Swine,' muttered Iselda. 'I can name at least two of them.'

'I will wager that they know exactly how many livres were in the hold of this ship. And of course they do nothing.'

Iselda sighed. 'Look, why don't we just make up the difference? If you weren't here . . .' She gave me a sudden, wounded look. 'If you weren't here I would do just that.'

'No,' I said.

'Then what? We can't just leave these idiots here! God help me, and Father, forgive me! But I don't want the deaths of all these thousands of Frenchmen on my conscience. We were talking of revenge, weren't we? Would the Montalhacs be revenged if we left Louis's whole crusade here to die?'

'Yes,' I said. 'And Montségur would be avenged too. If we choose. But . . .' I glanced at Nizam. He was studying us gravely, legs crossed beneath him, fingers working at his prayer beads.

'No, we can't leave these idiots here. But we're not paying.'

'Then how—'

'The Templars. Let them pay.'

'Patch, that's what we're talking about! The fucking Templars *won't* pay!'

'But they will. It doesn't make any difference if they want to or not. They will.'

'Why?'

'I'll tell you.'

The French coffers were thirty thousand *livres tournois* short, give or take five thousand. The sun was hanging just above the western horizon when Joinville came up from the hold and went over to the king. I was on deck with the king's brother Charles, and the Master of the Trinitarian Order, usually a rather jolly fellow whose jollity had been all but wrung from him by his ordeal. As luck would have it, Baybars had just left our ship on the little Saracen galley, gone to ferry the latest load of coin across to Damietta. The two Mamluks left in charge of the scales were tired and bored and had long since ceased to pay us Franks any heed, and besides, they could not understand our language. By the look on Joinville's face I knew that the bottom of the last treasure chest had been reached. And by the look on the king's, I saw that he had not been expecting the news. His expression was that of a man who has eaten a spoiled oyster without realising it, only to have the first pangs of its poison unfold in the pit of his stomach like a cankered flower. I made an excuse to Charles and wandered nonchalantly across to the royal tent.

'Sir Petrus—' Joinville began, but the king cut him off.

'Tell him, Jean,' he said. 'Petrus, it seems that our ordeal is not quite over,' he added.

'Not quite,' said Joinville, forcing as much cheer as he could into the two words. 'But it appears we are somewhat short of the ransom amount.' He was frantically signalling to me with his eyebrows that I should be surprised.

'Oh, good heavens!' I exclaimed. 'By how much?'

'Thirty-two thousand, eight hundred and twenty-three livres,' said Joinville. 'To be precise.'

'Precision is everything,' I agreed. 'Jean, a word, if Your Majesty does not mind?' Louis waved us off, his mind far away, no doubt on his brother sitting in some Mamluk boat eating piss-tasting cheese pies. I leaned and whispered in Joinville's ear: 'Summon the Templars. They have several hundred thousand livres on their ship.'

'I know that!' he hissed. 'But they won't let a penny of it go! You know as well as I do that they are under oath not to release any money, except to the very person who left it with them, and it must be the same coin. And the king—'

'Yes, yes, I do know, thank you, Jean. The king's coin is in Acre. Nevertheless, the king needs thirty thousand livres, and the Templars have it, not a bowshot away. Is the Temple so high and mighty that it will refuse the King of France?'

'Damn them,' muttered Joinville. 'But there is no other way. Very well.' He turned to Louis. 'Your Majesty,' he said, 'the Templars have this sum of money to hand. Shall I send for the commander?'

Louis considered, a drowning man trying to work out if the long shape in the water is a sea-serpent or a mast. Then he sighed. 'Do so,' he said.

In a half-hour, Étienne d'Otricourt, Commander of the Temple, climbed over the rail, followed by another knight. Their surcoats were gleaming white. So they had had time to do their laundry, I thought bitterly. Joinville had conveyed to the Mamluks that there would be a slight delay in bringing them the last part of the ransom. They probably did not quite understand, but in any case Baybars had not yet returned, and Nizam had, thankfully, gone over to start some sort of animated debate with them, which they seemed to be enjoying. But the commander was not enjoying himself. I had spoken to him once, after Mansourah, when I had helped the Grand Master back to the Templar lines. The last time I had seen him, at Fariskur, he had been watching helplessly as the Saracens hacked the Grand Master to pieces. Now he looked as thin as the rest of us and, unmistakeably, spoiling for a fight.

'Am I to understand that Your Majesty wishes the Temple to make a loan to the Crown of France?' he said, clipped, every inch a banker, except that he wore chain mail and had a festering sword-slash across his scalp, crude stitches and stubble poking up through the yellowish scab.

'That is so,' said Joinville. Of course it was beneath Louis's dignity to haggle with anyone over money, but I was glad to see that Joinville seemed to have his hackles raised.

'And you have advised His Majesty, my lord of Joinville? I must say that you have given your sovereign some extraordinarily bad advice, young man.' The commander sniffed, and his hand wandered towards the scab on his head. 'You know very well that all our deposits are held by us under the strictest of oaths, and nothing can change that.'

'But we are discussing a temporary loan to the King of France,' said Joinville. 'King Louis has a considerable sum on deposit with the Temple, as you well know.'

'That is in Acre,' sniffed the commander.

'But we are not! Surely it does not matter – you will simply make up the deposit when we get to Acre, and we are going there as soon as—'

'You understand nothing, young man, and you are presumptuous as well as ignorant! Would you have me break my oath to God?' bristled the commander.

'Surely there are exceptions that can be made,' said Joinville, still trying to be friendly.

'How dare you, sir? Do you think I would break my oath for you, or for the king, or for any man? My authority is God Himself, young man!'

'My good brother Étienne, you are a Frenchman, are you not? Have you no loyalty?' Joinville's temper had snapped. He was trembling with rage. A fine sight we must make for the seagulls chattering up in the rigging, I thought: a mob of wasted and decrepit men barely able to raise their voices for fear their legs would give out.

'I am a Frenchman, sir! But my loyalty is to the Temple of Jerusalem, sir! And if you are impugning my honour, sir, I—'

'Excuse me,' I put in. Étienne d'Otricourt turned on me, eyes white with rage. 'Do you know me, sir?' I enquired, politely.

'If you would get me to trample on the oath I swore to my lord God, who died in agony for our sins, I know you for a rascal and a serpent!' he cried. There were a few specks of foam in his beard now. But it was plain he did not recognise me.

'I am Sir Petrus Blakke Dogge. Or as I am sometimes known, Petrus Zennorius of the Banco di Corvo Marino.'

The white-rimmed fury in his eyes went out like a pinched candle wick, and his face went slack, for a moment, with confusion. 'But I thought . . .'

'That I had died in the retreat from Fariskur? Many did, God rest their souls. And by His mercy I survived. I am flattered you remember me.' And I gave him a courtier's bow. 'Might I have a fleeting word with you in private, Commander?'

D'Otricourt looked from the king to Joinville and to me. Louis was pointedly staring out to sea, and Joinville was looking as if he might tear out the commander's throat with his teeth, and so he nodded, icily, and stepped with me to the rail.

'What is the meaning of this?' he began, but I ignored him.

'Do not spew your piety over me, sir,' I said, low enough for the others not to hear me, but loud enough for him to catch the steel in my words. 'Four men from Sicily came looking for me, and they found me too, yet here I am. And Master Remigius – a snaky fellow, quite hard to forget. I expect he had words with you, Commander. A request from Cardinal John of Toledo, perhaps, or the Holy Father himself?'

'Look, Sir Petrus – I remember you now, of course I do. The man who brought our dear Grand Master out of Mansourah. You . . . One would have taken you for a man of honour, a godly man, but instead you are insinuating . . .'

'Nothing. I am insinuating nothing at all. Shall I tell Louis Capet, the holiest prince in Christendom, that the Temple of Jerusalem has been conspiring with Pope Innocent to destroy his crusade and trap him in Egypt? Think of what would happen then. The Temple, wrecking God's work? Would you like your commanderies driven out of France, like they were thrown out of Sicily?'

'I do not know what you are talking about, sir,' said the commander. He blinked, and glanced for a split second over to where Louis stood, leaning companionably on Joinville's shoulder. And I knew I had him.

'As one banker to another, of course you don't,' I said. 'Do you think I am such a fool, Commander? You know who I am. You know my bank. Do you think I can't ruin you, whether you are guilty or not? That I care a flea's fart for your life, to say nothing of your precious honour? I do not. If this ransom is not paid, the army over there' – and I flung out my arm towards the coast, dissolving into glowing ribbons of deepening reds and browns in the half-light of evening – 'twelve thousand men, *Christian* men, and some of them Templar knights, will die. The king's brother will die. And when I tell King Louis that it was the scheming of the Temple that murdered them, for he will believe me, what will keep your order out of the midden? Out of the shit, Commander? Do you imagine there are no greedy eyes coveting the Temple's wealth? They will tear you white-draped fools to pieces and laugh when they are done.'

'Oh, so the king will believe you, commoner? Why should he – why should any man?'

'Because of a letter I was sent to deliver. You know its wording, for Remigius carried the same letter. His was delivered. Mine was not. If you would care to reacquaint yourself with its content, I can have it out in a minute or less.' I pulled the Moorish amulet from my tunic, and the last drop of blood drained from the commander's face.

'And yet if you do one small thing, I will show you mercy.' D'Otricourt's jaw clenched furiously and his eyes grew red, but I stared him down. 'Because you are in my power, Commander. The great Temple itself is in my power. But I will show you the mercy that comes from a human heart and not from your grubby dreams of honour. Lend King Louis his thirty thousand livres and your debt to me is paid off.'

He stood there, and I could feel hatred coming from him like heat from a sun-baked stone. But I could feel his fear, too, and it was stronger. He reached up and scratched the wound in his scalp and his fingernails came away bloody.

'But I cannot,' he whined. 'I am bound, no matter what . . .' The fear came into his eyes, and I knew he was trapped, though not by me now. 'If . . . *if* we were already in Acre . . .'

'God's death, man! What is that knight called?'

'Antoine de Beaubourg.'

'Brother Antoine! Would you join us, please?' I called. Joinville and the king were watching us intently. From the other side of the boat, I could see Iselda's hands clench.

'Good Brother Antoine. Please go and tell the Sieur de Joinville to fetch an axe. Then you will come back with us, and the commander here, to your ship.'

The knight could not have looked more outraged if I had pinched his buttocks, but one look at his commander's face and he went still.

'An axe?' asked Étienne d'Otricourt, faintly.

'If we take the money by force, have you broken your oath?'

'You intend to break open our coffers? Jesus—'

'—threw the moneylenders from the Temple,' I said curtly. 'I am letting you go free, Commander, and letting you save your murderous, venal face into the bargain. The greatest treason of the age, absolved for thirty thousand livres. Do not invoke Christ, sir, for it is plain you cannot recognise Christian charity when it is sitting naked in your lap.' My voice had sunk to a hiss, and the commander winced, a helpless rodent caught between the butcherbird of prudence and the thorn of outraged piety. As commanders often do, he chose prudence.

'Go, Antoine. Sir Petrus and I will be waiting in the longboat.'

As I climbed over the rail I managed to wink at Iselda, and she waved, questioningly. But Brother Antoine was crowding me, and I swung down onto the ladder. It was a short row across to the Templar ship, but we might as well have been journeying between the ice floes of the Sea of Darkness for all the good cheer aboard. We had brought two sailors with us, and Joinville had a ship's axe across his knees. The commander gazed, stone-faced, out to sea. Brother Antoine stared at Joinville and me with undisguised loathing. I grinned back.

'After you,' I said, when we were bumping against the tarry hull of the ship. The Templars bit their lips and started up the rope ladder. I let Joinville scramble up in front of me. There were a few Templar knights on deck, most of them seeing to the preparation of their dinner, and when they saw Joinville

340

and his axe a couple of them clapped hands to hilts. But the commander waved them off and stormed into the forecastle where a hatchway led down to the hold. A short, sandy-haired man with a puffy, heavy-lidded face and a huge bunch of keys jingling at his belt sat inside, poring over a ledger.

'The Marshal of the Temple, Renaud de Vichiers,' said the commander. 'Come, Brother Renaud.'

There, in the lamplit gloom, stinking of lamp-black and rat-piss, great chests were arranged carefully so that they would not unbalance the ship.

'Try that one,' I told Joinville, pointing at a huge box banded all over with curled and fretted iron.

'Jolly good,' said Joinville. He was enjoying himself. Swaggering over to the chest, he rapped on the domed lid with his knuckles, cocked his head and hefted the axe. Then he planted his feet and swung.

'Wait!' screeched Marshal Renaud. Joinville pulled his stroke and the blade hit the lid with a dull *toc*, knocking off a large flake of wood. 'Christ's bloody feet, man, I will give you the keys!'

'Did you not think we were serious?' asked Joinville, as the marshal searched for a key from the great ring at his belt.

'This is sacrilege,' he was muttering, as he found the right one and rattled it in the lock.

'Of course it is,' I said. 'Now hurry up, there's a good fellow.'

The lid swung open, to reveal a pile of leather bags. 'Fetch some scales,' I snapped. There was some scurrying about, and finally the quartermaster lowered a balance beam down through the hatch. We hooked it to a beam overhead and began to weigh out the bags.

Thirty-two thousand, eight hundred and twenty-three livres were lowered down into the longboat by torchlight. The commander had excused himself halfway through the weighing,

341

and we did not see him again, though Marshal Renaud observed us, curiously frog-like, until the last coin was fished out. He wrote us out an elaborate receipt, meticulously and with agonising slowness, and then Joinville and I bowed and left as quickly as we could. I think we were both stifling a fit of giggles as we marched past the unfriendly gaze of Templars at their dinner, and when we were safely in the boat, and crossing the open water between the Templar ship and the king's, we both burst out laughing.

'The marshal . . . The man looked like a toad with its arse down a serpent's throat!' Joinville spluttered. 'How did you do it, Petrus? How in God's creation did you pull it off?'

'My dear Jean, I simply appealed to the commander's sense of honour,' I said.

'I detest that man! Templars and their honour – they are usurers, usurers with crosses on their breasts.'

'They serve their purpose,' I said. 'But now we are done. It is over. What will you do?'

'The king wants me to go with him to Acre,' he said. 'I don't wish for much more, right this moment, than to see my own country again, but it has been my privilege to win the king's friendship while we were prisoners, and I don't want to disappoint His Majesty.'

To myself, I wondered how many lives had been spent avoiding the disappointment of kings, but I kept the thought to myself.

'And you?' Joinville was asking. 'You are coming, aren't you?'

'No. Iselda and I have some pressing affairs to put right. Things have come unravelled since I came on this . . . this adventure. And I've been to the Holy Land before, Jean. But I wish you joy.'

'And joy to you, Black Dog. They will sing songs about us, you know.'

'God, I hope not. If they ever write songs, or books, about our time in Egypt, I pray that I am left out of them.'

'The man who saved Guillaume de Sonnac? For shame, sir,' laughed Joinville.

'He died two days later,' I pointed out. 'No, let the book tell of the eels, and the scorbutus, and . . . my dear Joinville, who would read such a book anyway? We are alive, with a boat full of Templar gold. What does that feel like, man?'

'Like strong wine,' Joinville laughed. 'Like the dancing girl who catches your eye!'

'Indeed!' I cried. 'You feel it! Then, as my late master used to tell me: pay attention, Jean de Joinville.'

'I shall, Petrus Blakke Dogge. Thank you. I shall.'

Chapter Twenty-Seven

And that, more or less, was the end of the Seventh Crusade. Baybars the Mamluk received the last of the ransom, and in the small hours of the night the king's brother came aboard. I had tried to sleep, rolled up in one of the carpets next to Iselda. She had grabbed me as soon as I had appeared over the rail, and it seemed that propriety had been given a holiday, for no one cared that we stood there and kissed for an age, while the Mamluks weighed out the coins again and sent them down to their boat.

'How did you manage that?' Iselda asked me, later on, when we had given up on sleep from all the commotion going on around us as men, newly freed, began to come aboard and find their feet, and after the king had sent us a jug of almost decent wine.

'I said I would destroy him,' I replied.

'And he believed you.'

'Yes. Because I would have. And now I am finished with all of this. For good. We have risen too high, my love, if we can threaten the Commander of the Temple and he fears for his life.'

There was salt pork to eat again, and though the novelty of it was long gone, we made a feast of it. There was bustle all around us, for the king had decided to leave for Acre as soon as his brother was set free.

'I don't want to go to Acre,' I said. 'Do you?'

'I would like to see the queen again,' said Iselda. 'But what's in Acre, really?'

'More of this,' I said. 'More Franks, more crusaders. They'll try and start another war, I expect. We can sit around and watch them unlearn all the lessons this fucking disaster should have taught them. I don't think I could stand that.'

'I suppose we could do some trading,' she offered, dubiously.

'Do you want to?'

'No.'

'Then let's not, eh?'

'I love you, Patch,' she said.

'I love you too.'

'There's one thing we might do . . . But no,' she said, peering out at me from under her tresses. I knew that look.

'What might that be?' I enquired.

'I've spent a long time talking to Sheikh Nizam,' she began. 'You know, I thought you'd gone a bit mooncalf out there in the war, because you really are different. Not in a bad way. But I've never heard you talk about God – I mean, not like that. So I wanted to know what he'd done to you.'

'He didn't *do* anything to me!' I laughed.

'No, my love. He did. But then he did something to me as well. We talked about my father, and about how they sailed from place to place, for years, just sailing. And it's very strange, because as he was telling me about the ocean, how it's so vast . . . I've never seen the ocean, Patch. And he let me see it as an endless plain, always shifting, always restless, and the sailor makes paths, plots them by the stars, and Nizam said that there's a point when you don't know where the sea ends and the stars begin, that you aren't up or down, you're just *held*, somehow.'

'I remember that,' I murmured.

'And do you know what he told me? That feeling, of being cupped in the vastness, like hands – when you feel that, what you're actually feeling is your own heart.'

'And that's God,' I said.

We didn't say anything for a while. Iselda put her hand in mine. It was a little greasy from the salt pork.

'Nizam is finding us a boat,' she said softly. 'He wanted us to come and stay with him, but . . .'

'Oh. At his *zāwiya*?'

'I don't know what that is. In the desert, south of Cairo. Is that where you were?'

'No, I wasn't in the desert.' I told her about the little building in the grove.

'But then he said, "No, you need to make good." He's gone to find us a ship going to Marseille. He said if we would not come to the desert, he would make a floating desert for us. I said that sounded a little strange and he laughed. I told him I wanted to sing – they sing there in the desert, Petroc! Were there singers at your *zāwiya*?'

I thought about that. 'I didn't . . . No, there were, of course there were! I wasn't paying attention, you know – I was here.' I tapped my head.

'Oh, Patch. But you always listen!'

'No, I was, I was listening. But to something else.'

'So shall we go?'

'What about Dimitri and the money? We have a perfectly good ship . . .'

'It's all business on Dimitri's cob. I need to get away from that. As for the money, I asked Nizam. A man I'd never met, and I was happy to trust him with everything.' Iselda paused. A frown wrinkled her brow.

'So what did he tell you? Where we could hide it?'

'Oh. No, he said we would know best. It was something else. He told me that money is for nothing more than buying. Meaningless. "What do you say to a child when you've given him a penny for being good? Spend it on something you like." He said we should get rid of it. All of it.'

'You mean, give it away?'

'What would be wrong with that? But no, he said there was something we could buy. He didn't say what. We'll know, apparently.'

'I don't know anything,' I said, watching the lights flicker on the shore. 'I'm just happy to be alive.'

'Then shall we go back to our lives?'

'*Back?* Isn't everything in flames behind us?'

'Not to the bank. To what we talked about in Lyon before you went away. Those lives – the ones we haven't lived yet.'

'You remembered that?'

'Of course. And you swore me an oath.'

'So I did. Well, there's nothing else I'd rather do.'

So when the boat bringing the Comte de Poitiers came alongside, amid the blowing of trumpets and cheering from everyone on board (for no one seemed to have managed to find sleep that night) we were waiting. The king had wept when I told him we were leaving, but then he was weeping at everything. We said we were going back to Venice on our own ship. As many others had already left – the Comte de Soissons and the Comte de Flandres among them – he did not take this amiss.

'Are you certain you won't come to the Holy Land, Petrus? The *Holy* Land . . .'

'I have been there already, Your Majesty. I wish you joy of the holy places. But I must attend to my affairs, which are pressing.'

'Of course, of course. You have my great thanks and my blessings, dear man.'

'Your Majesty, please remember me to the queen,' Iselda added. Louis looked vaguely surprised, as if he had forgotten at that moment that he was married.

'Of course, of course . . .' he said, absently. And just then the trumpets skirled again and the face of Count Alphonse appeared above the railing. With a cry, Louis tottered over to him, his black, gold-spangled robes trailing. He looked like a royal phantom: the ghost of his own dead dreams, perhaps.

'Come on,' I said, taking Iselda's hand. 'Let's go.'

We clambered down into the galley, and as we stood on the deck looking around for the captain, a large form rose up from the stern.

'Nizam!' I shouted. 'What – did you find us another ship? That was a trick, in all this madness!'

He shrugged, mysteriously. 'There are secrets known only to the wise . . .' he intoned, hollowly, but when he saw us gaping, he dissolved into laughter. 'Nay,' he said, wiping his eyes. 'The good master is Genoese, and arrived here to find no one to trade with, so I suggested he take us to Marseille. I have been going backwards and forwards on this tub all night, waiting for you to make up your minds. If you had not, I would have gone up there and fetched you myself!'

With some inveigling we persuaded the captain, who felt that time was wasting, to take us across to Iselda's galley. The watch, grim-faced Venetians, were standing guard with loaded crossbows, muttering at the Genoese sailors, but when they saw Iselda they made her welcome, and someone was sent to rouse Dimitri. He emerged, bandy-legged and bleary-eyed, and when he saw us standing there he let out a bearish snarl and lurched over to embrace us. When he saw Nizam, though, he stopped dead in his tracks.

'Helmsman?' he whispered. 'Are you a ghost?'

'Not I, Dimitri, though you and I should be by now, eh?'
He bent down and hugged the old man, and I saw that both of
them had tears on their cheeks.

'Petroc! For certain, I thought you were dead!' he growled at
me at last, wiping his eyes. 'And you, my lady!' He turned a
scowl on Iselda. 'With all the smoke and the drumming, and
Turks blowing their horns, could you not have sent word?'

'I am sorry, dear Dimitri, but I did not have time.'

'Iselda has been the ruler of Damietta for a few days,' I
explained. 'She—'

'Ruler of a few scared Genoese shopkeepers,' she objected.
'But we are safe – those who deserve to be, and those who do
not.'

'Dimitri, old friend, do you have the stomach for one more
voyage? A long one?' I asked when we were seated in the tiny
cabin belowdecks. Explanations had been made, and many
years squeezed into minutes as the two old comrades pieced
together each other's lives since the *Cormaran*'s crew had last
sailed together.

'To where?' he asked gruffly.

'London. I would like you to take this ship to London, and
once you are there, place it under the protection of the Earl of
Cornwall, who is the king's brother,' I said. 'He knows me.
Iselda and I will join you there in . . .'

'We will be two months behind you,' said Iselda. 'If I
cannot go to the desert with Nizam, he will have to conjure it
for me on the deck of a Genoese galley.'

'And then?' said Dimitri. He did not look very happy with
this idea.

'Then you are free to spend one quarter of the money
aboard this ship in any way you would like,' I said.

'What did you say?' said the old warrior, cocking his good
ear in our direction. But he'd heard.

'We are dissolving the company,' I told him. 'This is the

end. The three of us are the last of Captain de Montalhac's crew – and Iselda is his daughter and heir. We were never made to be bankers, lads. The world is changing, and men, it seems, wish to be ruled by letters of credit. I say, let others rule, and let others be ruled.'

'And so do I,' said Iselda. 'My father, if he was the man I believe he was, wished us to use this wealth for our freedom, and for the confusion of those who would bind men and women to superstition and tyranny. But it has become our master. So a quarter belongs to you, Dimitri, and a quarter to Nizam.'

'I thank you, children of my old friend. But I do not wish for money,' said Nizam. 'I have no use for it.' Dimitri looked at him in amazement.

'But it is yours,' I protested. 'To do with what you will. You can throw it in the Nile for all I care, my brother.'

'And turn the crocodiles into bankers?' laughed Nizam. He rubbed his forehead with the side of his thumb. 'No, we shall not do that. Here is what shall come to pass. I give my share to Isaac, my dear friend of many voyages. And as he cannot enjoy it now, I shall give it in his name to his old school, al-Karaouine in Fes, for he often used to speak of it, and he loved learning more than any other thing.'

'So be it,' said Iselda.

'And I shall buy a fleet of galleys and live like a proper Venetian until I die,' laughed Dimitri. 'If I cannot be one of those crocodile bankers!'

So it was decided. We had kept an orderly bank, and so it would be easy to parcel out a fourth share, though it would take a while to unload it, for on board was at least five times what the King of France had just paid for his freedom and that of his army, and it was in gold: dinars and dirhams and bezants. We took what we needed from our share, kissed Dimitri on his scarred cheeks and went aboard the galley that was still waiting for us. And then, with Nizam in the stern and us in the prow, we crossed the pale sea of early morning, with our backs towards the walls of Damietta.

I will not tell of the weeks we spent at sea with Nizam. You would ask what we learned, and I might tell you *everything*, or *nothing at all*, for in truth it makes no difference. We learned peace, but what that is, you must find out for yourself. We sang, we danced under the moon, and if I tell you that we found there a small portion of what we knew to be the truth, you must be content with that. We shed our skins, and were reborn as creatures who could feel the wind on our sun-browned skin and understand that it spoke to us. Not what it said: for that we would have needed a lifetime of study. But it was enough to know that we were held by, and that we in turn held, the presence of God.

When at last we came to Marseille just after the turn of the year – it was a long crossing, because we encouraged the captain to put into as many ports as he wished to trade – we took our leave of Nizam on deck. The galley was taking him back to Egypt, for the Mamluk regiments were in need of his teaching and he planned to spend the winter at his *zāwiya*. We said no words but embraced and went ashore with light hearts, because there were no goodbyes to be said. But as we looked for an inn, we found the town all abuzz with the news that Frederick von Hohenstaufen was dead.

'It was a sickness,' I said. 'It's strange. I had a dream on the ship. Michael Scotus told me.'

In the dream, I was sitting on the river bank. A boat, one of the slender feluccas that go to and fro all along the Nile, was drifting down on the current, its white sail slack. A single figure stood in the prow, and as the boat drifted closer I saw that it was Doctor Scotus. As he passed me, the boat slowed until the water was flowing around it, but the wake did not change. Michael raised his hand to me.

351

'Doctor Scotus!' I called to him. 'Where are you going?'

'To bury the king,' he said.

'What king?'

'The king of the world.' As he said those words the river began to rise, until it flooded its banks, and the hills in the far distance were islands. But I was still dry, and Michael Scotus's boat was motionless, although the sails had filled.

'After all this, to die of the flux,' I said to Iselda. 'The Wonder of the World. Christ, how Innocent must be crowing.'

'There's nothing binding you now,' said Iselda. 'If the emperor's dead, Innocent won't care about Sicily or Earl Richard. Richard didn't really want Sicily, did he? He just didn't want to pass up a chance at making some money.'

'You're right,' I said. 'But I'm still bound. He's still my liege lord. If we are ever going to be free, we can't just ignore that.'

'So we're still fighting, then? I'd come to believe we *were* free, out there with Nizam, but nothing will ever be easy for us, will it?'

'No, it will. Richard doesn't know it, but he is going to serve freedom up to us on a silver platter. We just have to reach out our hands, and take it.'

Chapter Twenty-Eight

We sailed into the pool of London on a day in May when the sun was pawing at curtains of drizzle like a playful cat, and the trees were bright in their new robes of green. We slipped under the bridge on the flood tide and slipped into a wharf under the doleful, mossy guard of Baynard's Castle. No one noticed us as we made our way into the city. We carried all we owned. I had thrown my borrowed armour into the Nile somewhere near the pyramids and had been wearing Saracen robes ever since. Iselda wore a curious mix of Saracen and Venetian clothes. From the looks we drew from the folk teeming in the streets, I guessed we looked like what we were: a crusader and his wife, returned from the Holy Land.

Dimitri was in the buttery of the Three Coneys. This was the inn of which the Banco owned a share. The old quarter-master was suffering from a touch of gout – nothing serious, and nothing if not the due of a rich man – and he hauled himself upright and engulfed us in a bone-cracking, wine-scented embrace. He had done as we asked, and put our money under the protection of Earl Richard. It lay in the strongroom of the earl's banker, Wymer of Berwick, a man I had done business with in the past. Wymer was dull enough to put birds to sleep in mid-flight, but honest. The nagging worry that had been chewing gently on the inside of my stomach since we arrived in Marseille started to fade.

'I met your earl. Very surprised, he was, when he saw whose mitts were holding all that money!' Dimitri cackled. London had been good to him, much to his surprise. He had found a trading partner, a maker of crossbow points that he planned to sell to the Catalans. Other merchants were interested in making alliances. Now we were here, he was bound back to Venice on the first tide. 'Not that it isn't a great joy to see you both,' he assured us, 'but this city is not for the old. 'Tis damper than Venice and the sun is thinner than English wine! My joints feel like iron door hinges doused in saltwater.'

We spent that night with Dimitri, and stayed up very late, talking of our old times together. There were many tales Iselda had not heard, and I made sure she heard them. For we would not be seeing Dimitri again, not in this life. We all knew it.

'The Ca' Kanzir is yours if you want it,' I told him, as the bells of the city monasteries chimed out the Midnight Office. 'I think you'll find, by the time you get back to Venice, that Holy Mother Church has lost interest in the house of de Montalhac and its possessions.'

'So you are not coming back?' said Dimitri.

'No. Venice is our past now,' said Iselda. 'So is the bank, and the *Cormaran*.'

'Then what will you do?' Dimitri chuckled. 'Lay siege to Montalhac and drive out the Frenchman who lives there? The captain . . .' He paused. 'Ach. The captain is dead, God rest his lovely soul. And I will join him soon.' He called for more beer and the sleepy taproom boy slunk off to fetch some. 'My village was in the lands of the Emperor of Bulgaria. It is gone now. The Greeks came and burned it, many years ago. I do not believe in *home*, not any more. But I thank you, again, for I will live in the Ca' Kanzir, and when I feel like it, I will take the old *Cormaran* out and sail her down the coast, for then, you know, I will be home, for a time.'

'And I will be with you, wherever I am,' I said.

'Amen to that,' said Dimitri.

And 'Amen,' we both replied.

After we had gone with Dimitri down to the wharves and seen him aboard his ship, and after we had watched its masts slip through the bridge and become lost in the confusion of other craft, we hired a couple of horses from the innkeeper and rode out to Westminster. Iselda had never been in a city as vast as London and it was a pleasure to be her guide.

'Mercy me! How can folk bring themselves to live this way?' she marvelled, eyes wide, as we negotiated the swarms and torrents of humanity that thrummed around Saint Paul's and poured through Lud Gate. The sun was shining, and the road along the river was loud and cheerful. But when we got to the palace we soon discovered that Earl Richard was not there. He had gone to his home at Wallingford Castle. We wandered back into London and spent the rest of the day finding a boat to take us up the Thames.

So we journeyed slowly up another great river, for the Thames, to an Englishman, is every bit the Nile's equal, and though I had seen the Nile and in truth, the English river is but a reedy sluice in comparison, I let myself fall under its spell. And spell it was, for as we sailed, the light winds giving just enough breath to fill the dark red sails, I could see that Iselda was also becoming enchanted. If Earl Richard had been at Westminster, and if the English weather had been its usual sullen self, perhaps my wife would not have let Albion work itself under her skin. I have never believed in fate. If I had, I would have spent great passages of my life believing myself accursed. But that summer, through which the rain barely fell, the wheat shimmered like a cloth of gold and every growing thing seemed to give forth a clear green light, can only have been a blessing. I had not expected Iselda to like England, being a child of the south, but to my joy I watched her fall in love with the swans and the willow trees, and with the green hills that rose in the distance, dotted with sheep or fretted by the plough.

We came to Wallingford in early June, having sent word ahead that we were on the way. The earl was out hunting when we arrived at his castle, which is a strong-walled place set among green fields. His chamberlain did not quite know what to make of the two Saracen-garbed, sunburned travellers, and I had to convince him that I was indeed Petrus Zennorius.

'Then I am honoured to welcome the Black Dog Knight!' he said at last, when his doubts had been overcome. He started to beam, and to call forth the servants, until Iselda and I were convinced he had mistaken us for some other couple.

'Sir Petrus Blakke Dogge,' he said at last, when our chambers were ready, and we had been given silver goblets of excellent Rhennish wine. 'The hero of Mansourah!'

'Hero?' I said, confused. 'You are mistaken, I'm afraid . . .'

'No, no – the man who defended William Longspée's body with your own? The man who saved the Grand Master of the Temple? I am not mistaken, my very good sir, and your modesty only makes my honour the greater!'

'Who has been telling such tales?' I asked, frowning.

'Why, young FitzGilbert, of course – and you saved his life too.'

I shook my head. There was nothing I wished for less than to bring back the nightmare of Mansourah.

'The bastard son of the Earl of Hereford. The only Englishman to survive the . . . the folly, one must call it, of King Louis's crusade, or so it was thought, but since men have started to return to France there have been rumours that you also won through. All true, to my joy!'

'So the world thought you were dead,' said Iselda, wryly, when we were safely in our quarters, looking out across the moat. 'Perhaps we shouldn't have come.'

'Richard would have found out sooner or later,' I assured her. 'I have learned that it is dangerous not to give him his due. Better to come to the beast's lair, you know, than have the beast come to you.'

'And here's the beast now,' said Iselda, pointing. Horses and riders were spilling over the crest of a nearby hill and scattering the sheep. Horns blew, and dogs barked. 'We'd better get dressed,' she said.

I put on my surcoat, the one the Mamluks had made for me. Something had kept me from throwing it into the Nile along with my armour. Iselda wore a dress that Queen Marguerite had given her. We should have looked noble, but our clothes had been crammed into satchels and thrown about from Egypt to London.

'We look like play-actors,' said Iselda, grinning.

'Good,' I told her. 'We are.'

We need not have hurried ourselves. It was a while before we were summoned to the earl's presence. Richard was a clever man. I knew he toyed with people – not from cruelty or for amusement's sake, but to gain advantage – and I was perfectly aware that I should be feeling anxious. But I wasn't. I was not the same man I had been when Richard had surprised me in Lyon. Most of me had been left behind on the banks of the Ashmoun Canal, and the rest had been transmuted by the gentle magic of Nizam. So when the chamberlain finally ushered us graciously into the solar, I was feeling nothing more than happiness at having Iselda's hand in mine.

'Sir Petrus!' said Richard, imperiously. I bowed, and Iselda curtseyed gravely. 'And the lady Iselda, I take it? Charmed, of course.'

'You flatter me, my lord,' Iselda murmured, charming indeed.

'The companion of the Queen of France, one has heard,' he went on. 'And you, Petrus Blakke Dogge. A more reluctant crusader could not be imagined, and yet see how you have honoured England! They say you were with Salisbury when he died – poor Longspée! You must tell me everything.'

'I shall, my lord, I shall. But not yet,' I said. Richard frowned. 'We have some pressing matters to discuss,' I went on. 'You sent me on crusade for a purpose, and I have come to settle things.'

'Things? What things?' Richard sounded petulant, as if a favourite plaything were not working properly.

'You wanted me to discover whether you could win a monopoly on the trade routes out of Egypt,' I said. 'And if the crown of Sicily would be of profit to you. I must report that I have failed in both.' Ignoring his deepening frown, I went on. 'The Egyptian rulers have a treaty with Venice. The new sultan and his Mamluks despise the Genoese and the Pisans, who tried to force their advantage at Damietta. It will be Venice, and only Venice, who will control the pepper and the silks coming from India by sea. Venice played no part in Louis's adventure, while every other Latin and Frank has proved themselves treacherous – not to mention weak and foolish,' I added. 'Your idea is, I'm afraid, impossible. And as to Sicily itself, now that Frederick von Hohenstaufen is dead, will the pope be so desperate to install a friend in the south of Italy? He will not. I predict that Innocent will approach you again, but this time the price will be not to your liking. Pope Innocent is a man with a terrible thirst for money. He wants the Holy See to be as magnificent as any kingdom – the most magnanimous friend and the most implacable foe. Frederick was his great fear. Now that he is dead, his sons will not worry him. Now he can turn to lining his pockets.'

'His Holiness *has* approached me again,' said Richard, slowly. 'I saw him in Lyon just last year, and now he has sent me letters – but as you say, with no price mentioned this time. You are insolent as ever, Black Dog, but then I expect that, and what you say has some merit. But you sit here and tell me all the ways you have disappointed me. What am I to make of that? You know how I prize loyalty, my man, and now it seems that you have come a long way to pluck my beard. Well I remember you predicting your failure in Lyon. And I remember telling you that if you failed, you could expect nothing from me. And further, that I would tighten the knots of obligation that bind you to me. If that is why you have come, with your lovely wife, then I salute your good sense. But, sir, I do not see you bending your knee to me.'

'Because that is not why we came,' I said.

'Then why? I have heard the stories about you. You have brought honour to yourself and, yes, to me.' Richard was angry, but he was keeping it from boiling over. 'But one also hears things from the Continent. The Inquisition. The anger of the pope. You have returned a hero, but you have also failed me. If you have come to ask my protection, I do not feel inclined to give it, if this is how you choose to ask.'

'The Inquisition has already gone to work, my lord,' said Iselda gently. 'If you were simply after our money, I feel I should tell you that the Holy Father did his best to make sure he got it instead.'

'What do you mean?' Richard was struggling to remain calm.

'My lord, the Church – specifically one Cardinal John of Toledo – unleashed the hounds of the Inquisition on us after my husband had left for the crusade. Do you know, even though I pointed out that heretics aren't generally to be found on crusade, they attacked us anyway? The Banco di Corvo Marino is no more, my lord. That is all finished with now.'

'I . . .' Richard's jaw, clenched to deliver some deadly thrust, was instead hanging open. 'The bank is ruined?'

'The bank does not even exist,' I said. 'It has been dissolved. I would imagine that the Templars are delighted. Personally, I could not care less.'

'And you have come here to tell me this? I thought you were dead . . .'

'And no doubt you grieved, Earl Richard. What I came to tell you is that, although the answers are not to your liking, I did your bidding. I went to Egypt, and if circumstances have made the task you gave me pointless, that is no fault of mine. I believe I am owed what you promised me.'

'Oh, do you, sirrah? And what was that?' Richard had recovered. But he was still angry, and though he was a subtle man, I could tell that his mind had not caught up with his spleen.

'That you release me from my oath. And there is a manor house on the southern slope of Dartmoor with, if I remember, fifteen hides of ploughland and woods.'

'You were always an impudent man, Petroc of *Auneford*,' spat Richard. 'But I never took you for a fool. Do you really think your oath is so important? I have a hundred vassals more useful to me. You seem to have come back from Egypt so that I might hang you, and never fear, I will. You will wait here, and you, madam, while I call the guard.'

'But Earl Richard, that is not why we came. Didn't you wonder why we have not flung ourselves on your mercy? We are ruined and homeless. Surely a lord is obliged to comfort his loyal servants. And I have been loyal, sir. Tell me, have you spoken to Wymer of Berwick in the last month or so?'

'You are not helping yourself,' growled the earl. 'I am not a man to—'

'My lord, have you talked to your financier or not?' demanded Iselda.

'How dare you make demands, woman?' Richard's knuckles were going white.

'You have not spoken to him. Because if you had, you would know that around two months past, a sum of money was deposited with Messer Wymer in our names. He is an honest man, my husband assures me, and your patronage and protection would mean our money was safe.' Iselda folded her hands in her lap, calmly, as if she were dealing with an important though irritating client. 'And we needed it to be safe, as it is a very, very considerable sum. In gold.'

Richard looked from Iselda to me and back again. 'What has this to do with me?' he asked at last.

'My lord Richard,' I answered, 'you are right. We did not need to come here. We could have vanished. Do you know, we thought of sailing to India? Have you never wondered, my lord, in what sort of country your pepper and your ginger grow? I don't expect we would still have been your vassals in Kodungallur. Or we could have bought ourselves new names and passed our lives in some little-travelled corner of Christendom. But we did not. I have to thank you for sending me on crusade, my lord, because I learned something quite unexpected there. Men like us – and, sir, we are very alike, you and I, despite the differing qualities of our blood – spend our lives wrapping ourselves in complications. No plan is so difficult that it cannot be tangled in yet another layer of complexity. And simple ideas are for fools, are they not? I thought of two things as I rotted in the Nile mud and breathed in the stink of King Louis's dead men. One was my wife. The other was your manor in Cornwood. Now, as my teeth fell out of my mouth and my skin turned black, I would ponder how I could cheat you of that. What trick I could play that would better you. But then I was shown that those daydreams had been a folly, as much as the whole crusade was folly, and the pope's great battle with the emperor, a mere struggle of vanities . . . And what did I learn? Nothing very astounding, I'm afraid: I found simplicity. And that is what we have brought to you.'

'I fear the Egyptian sun has boiled your brains,' said Richard, a sneer tugging at one corner of his mouth.

'Of course! And I should like to enjoy it as long as I can. But here is the simple answer to our mutual difficulty, my lord. You covet my wealth, and I covet your manor at Cornwood. How much is it worth? Fifteen hides – a good price, I would estimate. Certainly a few hundred livres. We would like to make you an offer for it – the manor, *and* release from any and all obligations to your lordship.'

'And I suppose you imagine me to be some manner of dung-smeared trader at a horse-fair! I am the king's brother, sirrah! The idea that I would enter into business with . . . with . . .'

'The Comte and Comtesse of Montalhac,' Iselda broke in, politely. 'The second and hereditary creation, bestowed by Queen Marguerite of France. My father, whom you knew as Jean de Sol, was the rightful Comte of Montalhac, and his line has been restored. You are not dealing with commoners, my lord, if that soothes your feelings at all.'

'Is this true, Petroc?'

'Strange to relate, it is.'

'Well then, I congratulate you,' he said, frostily. 'But you still have the manners of a common rogue. And we are in England: you are still my vassal, sir. A vassal does not trade with his liege lord. That would be an outrage – nay, it is a blasphemy against the true ordering of the world.'

'Yes, yes, my lord,' said Iselda. Her patience was frayed

and she took no pains to hide it. 'Since we are discussing the ordering of the world, have you heard of the amount King Louis paid the Sultan of Egypt in return for his freedom?'

'Of course,' snapped Richard. 'An unearthly – an ungodly sum. Unheard of. That infidels could be allowed to humiliate a Christian monarch . . .'

'A king's ransom, in fact,' I said. 'Four hundred thousand *livres tournois*. We saw half of it being weighed out – two days in the hot sun. Silver coin, you see. Gold would have taken far less time to count.' I sighed, and leaned back in my chair.

'What would you say to a king's ransom, Earl Richard?' Iselda asked. 'Because it lies in Messer Wymer's strongroom. We will pay, for Petroc's freedom, and for your manor at Cornwood, what King Louis paid to free himself, his brothers and his army from the Turks.'

'All of it,' I added. 'Take it or leave it. You could buy Sicily, though I wouldn't advise you to. There: the wealth of the Banco di Corvo Marino, in return for a little bit of Dartmoor. It couldn't be a simpler offer, you must admit.'

Richard stood up. Anger had stiffened his joints, and he was scowling like a child whose favourite toy has just been snatched by an older sister. He turned his back on us and paced across the floor of the solar. A tapestry of roses and vines hung against the far wall and the earl made a show of contemplating its pretty curlicues. Iselda turned to me and raised an enquiring eyebrow.

'I accept.' Earl Richard was speaking to the flowers on his tapestry, and his voice was muffled and distant. Then he turned on his heels. 'I accept,' he said again. He was a subtle man, the Earl of Cornwall. And now he was granting Iselda and I the merest phantom of a smile. 'Lord and Lady de Montalhac, the manor is yours. Black Dog, I trust you will be a good neighbour – our lands butt up against each other, after all.' The smile had grown. 'But I will not be neighbours with a commoner, even one with a French title, for we are speaking of Devon and not Anjou, after all. So as I find, to my surprise, that I have sold you the Lordship of Sweetwood, you have also purchased the Barony of Slade and Sweetwood. The last baron died on the way to Jerusalem when I was a boy. My apologies, for it is a small and essentially meaningless title, but like your County of Montalhac it is hereditary, and unlike it, there is land. And, Black Dog, you understand me, I think?'

'My lord, I do,' I said. 'If I cannot be your vassal, I must needs be your brother's.'

'Should we refuse, then?' asked Iselda, quietly.

'No,' I murmured. 'Earl Richard wants to make sure I am loyal, but I am an Englishman, so I'm already the king's man. My lord,' I said to Richard, 'if you promise to leave the Barony of Slade and Sweetweed out of the affairs of England, and to leave us in peace, I accept.'

'I give my word,' said Richard, and I could see that he was already, in his mind, opening the first bag of dinars in the damp chill of a London strongroom.

'Then we are done. Let us write each other titles and receipts, and you will want to send to Messer Wymer and tell him to start counting.'

'Oh, and, Black Dog,' said Richard, lightly, as if it were nothing but an afterthought. 'Whatever became of that letter? You remember the one?'

'Oh, my apologies! I never got around to delivering it,' I said. 'I suppose it is a little late now – but it seems I never needed to.'

'Then . . .' Richard suddenly looked immensely relieved. 'Then we shall forget all about it, I think.'

'Of course,' I said, giving him my blandest smile. 'Who wishes to remember a wasted journey? If you need to refresh your memory, I have it around somewhere – somewhere safe, hopefully, but I can't imagine you would need to . . .' Absently, I touched the Moorish amulet that hung beneath my tunic. A strange talisman: it had almost killed me, but now it seemed it had become my servant at last. Ink and parchment and cheap silver: unintentioned magic. 'Though in the interests of forgetfulness,' I added, lightly, 'it might be wise to ask your dear friend Pope Innocent to lift a certain ban of excommunication.'

'Sometimes His Holiness gets a little carried away. Consider it done. Your faith is, of course, unimpeachable . . .' He trailed off.

'My *heart*, Earl Richard, is as pure as the winter's first snow. So let us all forget, eh? Memory can be such an inconvenience.'

'The king's ransom, eh?' said Richard. A lawyer had been summoned, along with the local abbot, to witness our contracts. Iselda and I both had blue fingers, for my wife had a better turn of phrase than I, and, *trobairitz* as she was, knew how words can be used to bind men tight. 'And what are you left with now that you have ransomed yourself, Petroc Blakke Dogge?' Richard went on. 'Your manor gives you a few pounds a year. Who will buy the spices and the scarlet silks?'

'I never cared for them,' I replied. There was no need to mention that Louis Capet would be repaying his very large crusading debts to us in person, as we had agreed on that last evening aboard his ship. Richard was getting the money held by Messer Wymer, and that was quite enough for him. Louis's debts were a detail, and what need did we have for details, now that we were taking the simple path? 'I have spent most of my life a monk, a vagabond or a sailor, and like my Iselda, I lost my home when I was very young,' I told him, dipping my pen for the last time. 'The money was hard-won, and there is a lot of blood upon it, some of it mine. But did we earn it? About as much, I should say, as you have. You are welcome to it, and may it bring you joy. Because we have ransomed our happiness, Lord Richard. And it was cheap at the price.'

Epilogue

The granite is rough and warm beneath my calves. Grey and yellow lichen, curls and whiskers, tiny cups for faery-folk, crackle against my fingertips as I lean back into the sunlight. There is a little breeze to rattle the sedge stalks. It hisses across the grass, and the sheep twitch their ears, thinking it is bot-flies come to pester them. A ring ouzel perches in one of the gorse bushes and calls to me. 'Come *on*, come *on*,' he says, and bobs his white neck.

The breeze dies down, flutters against my face. Down from the High Moor it has brought me the smell of peat, of sheep-shit and bilberries. I turn my head and like a weathercock I catch the moving air. It blows from the north, from Ryder's Hill, and I close my eyes and see where it has passed: Huntingdon's Hill and down into the Aune valley, then up across Zeal Plains to Old Hill, skipping across Bala Brook, Middle Brook, Red Brook and up to the stones on Hickley Plain, down through the mires that give birth to the Glazes, swooping down and up Glasscombe Ball and through the stone row set there by the old giants, like sharp black teeth on the skyline. Past Hobajon's Cross, brushing the flanks of Butterdon and Weatherdon and Burford Down, and so to me. I turn to follow it, and there are the soft rollings of the hills below me, dipping and rising, painted with copse and field and farmstead, hiding their deep lanes and winding rivers, until they surrender to the calm haze of the sea. I can see the edge of the world from here, a perfect silver line dividing the blue below from that above. All of my world, now, contained in a puff of warm and grassy air.

A thin line of white smoke rises up from the coombe. I am looking down on the tops of an oak wood. Pigeons whizz across the waves of green and bronze. Butterflies dance in little clouds above the topmost leaves, and a cuckoo calls out further down the valley. In the heart of the coombe lies the broad back of the house, and the smoke is coming from the biggest chimney. It rises, straight as a corn stalk, until it meets the breeze, which folds it over into a finger, a compass needle pointing south-south-west to the sea at Gara Rock and beyond to Finisterre, to Spain and far, far beyond the horizon's knife-edge, the land of the Berbers.

I stand up and walk through the sheep to the little brook that runs down off the moor here. The water is cold and clear, running over dappled granite between thick growths of peat moss, and I kneel and wet my face. I squint to see myself. Is that a man of thirty-five years, with a scar for every one of them? Is that the boy who once played up here? I try to see who it was that crossed the Sea of Darkness, who stole from the dead and had death steal from him; who travelled so far, so very far from home. And all I see is a wavering shape that changes as the water flows past.

There is a call from down in the coombe. I hear my name, and as I stand up there is another sound, hardly there. The breeze should catch it like the smoke and send it out to sea, but though it seems so weak, this sound is stronger than the breeze. I begin to run, scattering the sheep. Time to go down, time to go home. Forgetting what I had tried to see in the brook, forgetting my own tears, I run, and for the first time in my life I find that the cry of a newborn baby can fill the whole wide world.

Author's Note

In 1249 and 1250 Pope Innocent held long and secret negotiations with Richard Earl of Cornwall at Lyon; the chronicler Matthew Paris was convinced that Innocent was trying to persuade Richard to accept the crown of Sicily. After Emperor Frederick's death in 1250, Innocent made the offer officially, twice, but Richard declined. Matthew Paris has him telling the pope: 'You might as well say, "I make you a present of the moon – step up to the sky and take it down."'

Pope Innocent spent enormous amounts of time and energy trying to woo the kings of Christendom to his side. He did send letters to Sultan Ayub in Cairo, trying to gain an alliance against Frederick von Hohenstaufen, but I have invented the scheme he and Earl Richard cook up in my story.

King Louis's crusade to Egypt was an unmitigated disaster. This did not prevent him trying again in 1270. This time he attacked Tunis, and while laying siege to Carthage he died of a fever. In 1298 Louis Capet was declared a saint by the Church.

Michael Scotus was born in 1175. He was a great scholar who was instrumental in bringing the works of Aristotle back to light in Christian Europe, and he translated the works of Averroes and Avicenna into Latin. He was much admired by Frederick von Hohenstaufen, and was also a candidate for

Archbishop of Canterbury. He is thought to have died in 1232, but there is no proof of where it happened or where he might be buried, and the name of Michael Scotus turns up in documents as late as 1290 . . .